THE WORLD'S CLASSICS

THE CORAL ISLAND

ROBERT MICHAEL BALLANTYNE was born in Edinburgh in 1825. His family were part of the literary society of the capital, but the disastrous bankruptcy of Sir Walter Scott in 1826 ruined their printing firm, which had produced Scott's novels. When Robert was 16 he was dispatched to Canada to earn his own living as a clerk in the Hudson's Bay Company. In 1847, after many adventures, on which he was to draw for his stories and lectures for many years, he returned to Scotland. Dissatisfied with his quiet niche in the publishing business, he embarked on a full-time writing career. His first success, *Snowflakes and Sunbeams; or, The Young Fur Traders*, published in 1856, was followed, two years later, by *Ungava* and *The Coral Island*. He wrote steadily and prolifically, producing over a hundred books for boys, of which only *The Coral Island* is still read. He married in 1866, had six children, and settled to a comfortable life in Harrow. After his death in 1894, the boys of Harrow School subscribed to erect a memorial to him.

J. S. BRATTON is Reader in Theatre and Cultural Studies at Royal Holloway and Bedford New College, University of London. Her publication and research ranges over many aspects of nineteenth-century British culture, including most forms of writing and performance. She has published, amongst other things, a study of the Victorian boom in children's books.

D0995001

THE WORLD'S CLASSICS

R. M. BALLANTYNE

The Coral Island

A Tale of the Pacific Ocean

Edited with an Introduction by
J. S. BRATTON

Oxford   New York
OXFORD UNIVERSITY PRESS
1990

Oxford University Press, Walton Street, Oxford OX2 6DP

Oxford New York Toronto
Delhi Bombay Calcutta Madras Karachi
Petaling Jaya Singapore Hong Kong Tokyo
Nairobi Dar es Salaam Cape Town
Melbourne Auckland

and associated companies in
Berlin Ibadan

Oxford is a trade mark of Oxford University Press

Introduction, Note on the Text, Select Bibliography
and Explanatory Notes © J. S. Bratton 1990

First issued as a World's Classics paperback 1990

British Library Cataloguing in Publication Data

Ballantyne, R. M. (Robert Michael) 1825–1894
The coral island: a tale of the Pacific Ocean. – (The World's classics).
I. Title II. Bratton, J. S. (Jacqueline Susan) 1945– III. Series
823.8 [F]

ISBN 0–19–282644–1

Library of Congress Cataloging in Publication Data

Ballantyne, R. M. (Robert Michael), 1825–1894.
The coral island: a tale of the Pacific Ocean / R. M. Ballantyne;
edited with an introduction by J. S. Bratton.
p.   cm. — (The World's classics)
Includes bibliographical references.
[1. Shipwrecks—Fiction. 2. Survival—Fiction. 3. Adventure and
adventurers—Fiction. 4. Islands—Fiction.] I. Bratton, J. S.
(Jacqueline S.) II. Title. III. Series.
PR4057.B15C6 1990 823'.8—dc20 90–6820
ISBN 0–19–282644–1

Printed in Great Britain by
BPCC Hazell Books Ltd.
Aylesbury, Bucks

CONTENTS

INTRODUCTION

LIKE its trio of young heroes, *The Coral Island* has survived in a wreck where many others have perished. Of over a hundred books written by Robert Michael Ballantyne, only this one is still remembered, and even sometimes read by young people. Never out of print since 1858, it has an undoubted right to the status of a children's classic. There is something about this particular story, its setting or its characters, which is of abiding importance to the young reader; and at the same time, it is a potent embodiment of certain aspects of British culture in the 1850s.

Despite imperfections which betray Ballantyne's inexperience as a story-teller, there are obvious reasons for the book's success. It is one of the many tellings of a powerful mythic narrative: the story of Robinson Crusoe, the tale in which western civilization (shorn of whatever the writer regards as its blemishes) is recreated out of next to nothing by a small number of people isolated from the rest of the world by natural catastrophe. The story of 'how we live' has an inexhaustible fascination, and there is deep satisfaction in following the individual back to the basic stuff of life—a single knife, a few grains of corn—and seeing the world as we know it flower again under one pair of hands; it consoles us for our alienating and unsatisfactory experience of society by demonstrating the essential naturalness and rightness of the plant that can thus breed true from its smallest castaway seeds. Many writers, both story-tellers and critics, have taken Defoe's desert-island story and made it play a part in their own struggle to come to terms with society; and since long before Ballantyne's contribution it has seemed an ideal story with which to teach the young the nature of their social world. Rousseau set that fashion by proclaiming it the only book that a young person trained in his ideal system of self-realization should be allowed to read. A chain of desert-island books written explicitly for children followed, and it is in this tradition that Ballantyne's tale should be read; it shows vividly the version of moral and social relations which an average Briton in the stirring world of the 1850s, a man of Evangelical faith and a hearty, outdoor temperament, who was rather frightened of women, wished to pass on to the rising generation. It is not only a survival story but also an adventure, and a tale of youthful triumph; its characters are clear-cut and its situations exciting. It is by no means entirely bound to its times: for the present writer, this was the book which, when I was 7 or 8, crystallized that acute enjoyment of reading which makes an individual into a lifelong student of literature. Its vocabulary was so much beyond me at that age that I was conscious of struggling, leaping from foothold to foothold with only a few words in each long sentence on which to balance; but the narrative grip, and even more strongly the book's imaginative world, dragged me through it in a splutter of delight. As I try to recall what aspect of the book exerted this magic, it seems that the strongest memories are not of the adventures: though I long remembered the battle with the shark, I had forgotten Ralph's capture by pirates; and his protracted wanderings in the South Seas came as a complete surprise when I reread the book as a student. As a child, I had responded to something else: to the coral island itself, the perfect and paradisial place, where 'a sandy beach of dazzling whiteness lined this bright green shore, and upon it there fell a gentle ripple of the sea' (p. 21).

Half the book describes the island and the boys' perfect life there. It is vivid and eventful, but its threats and mysteries are brief, its problems satisfactorily resolved. The reader is absorbed into a world of joyous physical sensation, freed from the boring constraints of everyday life. Instead of ordinary meals, the boys pluck from the trees all the fruit they can eat, quaff lemonade from coconuts, and catch fish and hunt piglets for meat to cook on a camp fire. They get up when they like, and wash by splashing in the sea. It is a fantasy of freedom, of health, and also of beauty, feeding all the sharp perceptions and appetites of youth. The boys' playful adventures are framed by the lyrical evocation of the island. The picture of white sand and green surf, waving trees and flashing birds is completed by the underwater beauty of corals and tropical fishes. Their enjoyment of the riches of the island comes to a climax in the discovery of the Diamond Cave, which is not the hoard of treasure found by more materialistic adventurers but an underwater cavern of astonishing natural beauty, to which access is difficult (the youngest of them cannot make the dive to it unaided) and in which they take refuge when pirates threaten. It represents, perhaps, the innocence of their occupation of the island, but it is also a goal towards which they strive, and the heart of the island's beauty; from the moment its mysterious green underwater light is first seen, it has a numinous power for the reader. When Ralph foolishly emerges from it to be carried off by the pirates and leave paradise behind, he can never return except to bid it farewell. It is perhaps because paradise island is a fantasy still so prevalent in our culture that William Golding made it the starting-point for his pitiless rereading of the Crusoe myth as a parable of original sin, in *The Lord of the Flies* (1954). Ballantyne might be said to have originated the idyllic setting for the story, since the islands in *Robinson Crusoe* and its earlier rewritings for children are by no means places of unalloyed beauty, idleness, and delight.

As a twentieth-century child reader, I did not recognize as unusual the most remarkable innovation in the book and one which contributes to its sense of holiday freedom: the fact that it contains no adult mentors or guides. Jack, Ralph, and Peterkin are wrecked all alone; their world is recreated by their own unaided and unguided efforts, and adults intrude only to bring evil and scatter the perfect community. In Ballantyne's immediate source, James Bowman's *The Island Home* (1852), adults are also quickly jettisoned; but in the previously most popular versions of the tale for children, the whole family is present, and a patriarchal structure is reproduced in the microcosm of the island. In Wyss's *The Swiss Family Robinson* (1818) this is made explicit in the title, and the father is the source of all strength and knowledge; his family survives, and the reader is edified, entirely by his efforts. His wife and four sons form a gratified and deferential audience, a strictly graded hierarchy under his command. Captain Marryat, who wrote *Masterman Ready* in 1841 to fulfil a promise to his own children that he would produce a sequel to *The Swiss Family Robinson*, put down Wyss's book with scorn when he read it, contemptuous of its errors of seamanship and geography, and holding, as he says in his Preface, that 'it is necessary that the author should be particular in what may appear to be trifles, but which really are not, when it is remembered how strong the impressions are upon the juvenile mind. Fiction, when written for young people, should, at all events, be *based* upon truth.' He clearly had no objection to the social truths Wyss purveyed, and the same hidden curriculum is more than reproduced in Marryat's book, where the notion of family is extended to include the male servant, Ready—who keeps his subordinate social place even though it is his practical knowledge that enables the family to survive—and the female slave, Juno—whose physical contribution is also essential, though she is held in such low esteem that she is commonly referred to as 'poor Juno' and laughed at for her lack of knowledge. The mother is an invalid, a revered symbolic bundle to be lovingly cared for; and the children here are even less empowered than in Wyss's family. William is present chiefly to act as the butt of informative lectures, like the Swiss boys; and the only contribution of Tommy, the six-year-old, is to hinder everyone by his naughtiness and ultimately make it necessary for Ready to give his life for the family.

Ballantyne dispenses with the extended-family structure, though not with hierarchy. He distributes the necessary human attributes of his little society between his three young men: Ralph, the narrator, is a reader and recorder, providing the reflection upon events previously assigned to the father figure, but he is also the point of identification for the average reader, since he is fond of books and less than perfectly athletic and brave; Jack is the source of miscellaneous information, the father figure in the sense of seniority and leadership, and he bears responsibility for the others; Peterkin acts as baby and joker, the focus for fun and slapstick comedy, so that through him the reader is allowed to enjoy the naughtiness that in earlier works had been regarded as the aspect of childishness that existed only to be suppressed and eliminated by the process of socialization. These three characters stand in no need of such a process; the narrative suggests that they already possess between them all that makes up human happiness. They are not primarily presented as vehicles for education or admonition; the boy reader is invited to identify with their attitudes and to recognize and enjoy the characteristics Ballantyne admires in boys: not only their idealism, energy, and courage but also their facetiousness, emotional simplicity, and anti-intellectualism. Rousseau's reverence for natural innocence has become glorification of the boyish.

Ballantyne's attitude in this is an extreme instance of the state of mind of those of his contemporaries in the 1850s who were redefining virtue in terms of muscular Christianity, and asserting the value of 'simple faith' in the face of encroaching religious and scientific doubt. Charles Kingsley's *Westward Ho!*, a best-selling novel published in 1855, has a boyish hero whose conquest of the New World rests upon his childlike strength of character, his strong and simple patriotism. The mainstream of writing for children had not yet caught up with this development and was still largely prescriptive and pedagogic in intention, so that it must have been a great attraction to his first readers that Ballantyne seems to identify with the boy, and to wish to please and appeal to him, rather than aligning himself with parents and teachers. One clear token of this in *The Coral Island* is its use of the narratorial voice, which is that of the adult Ralph looking back at the adventures of his boyhood. He is rarely used to point the moral of the incidents; instead, he draws mock-serious attention to the fact that both in the present and when he was the grave 'old-fashioned' youth in the story, he did not understand ordinary boys. He admires Jack's practical knowledge and strength; Peterkin's high spirits and predilection for slang puzzle him. By identifying with Peterkin, the reader, used to being taken to task by adults for clowning about and using slang phrases like 'just the ticket', of which Ralph feigns helpless ignorance, is put in a position of superiority to the narrator. In the 1850s, adults buying books for the young were consciously seeking to supplant trashy knockabout fiction full of objectionable language; Ballantyne offered the boy reader something more like the lively slang dialogue and slapstick action of the penny blood than did most respectable writers, and implied in the ironic way he presented it that such juvenile tastes were natural and to be admired, even though adults did not understand them. The book was acceptable to the adult buyer because it veils this with the unimpeachably staid attitude of the narrator, and contains a measure of the information about geography, the mission field, and exotic flora and fauna expected from castaway stories; but its language signals a fundamental identification with what the author takes to be the attitudes of the young, and its educative project is to inform and confirm their instinctive reactions rather than to reform and lead them to maturity.

The boyish attitude of the book is, in fact, a reflection of Ballantyne's own outlook upon the world. The formative experience of his life was the six-year period spent as a clerk in the Hudson's Bay Company. From the age of 16 he served on remote Canadian trading-stations, either almost entirely alone in the Arctic wastes, keeping himself sane by learning to hunt and trek, or as part of a strongly bonded group of young men intent upon breakneck adventures and convivial nights rather than upon their slight commercial duties in the Company offices.[1] He occupied idle hours at his desk by writing accounts of his adventures. These were then sent home and on his return became the basis of his first publication, a travel memoir (1847), and later of *Snowflakes and Sunbeams; or, The Young Fur Traders* (1856), his first juvenile story. His first successes in writing offered him the glimmer of an opportunity to escape from routine daily work—he was by this time working his way up in publishing, the family profession—and he seized upon it eagerly. After escaping once more into the wilds, this time on a Norwegian fishing trip with wealthier friends, he determined to live by his talent for describing the kinds of things he and thousands of young men like him—boys unwillingly tied to school or office desks—really wanted to be doing. Consciously he proposed to himself a life of authorship and book illustration, and excused confining himself to writing for boys by the solemn observation that it was his Christian duty to work in a field where it seemed he could be of use. In fact he was establishing a style of life that would prolong indefinitely his exciting adolescence, and garner approval and admiration for it.

[1] See Eric Quayle, *Ballantyne the Brave, A Victorian Writer and His Family* (London, 1967), 29–78. All information about Ballantyne's private life is taken from this source.

Each summer he wrote one book, intended for publication on the Christmas market, and in the winters he toured the country giving lectures in which he re-enacted the picturesque and exciting elements of his youth in Canada. Wearing a trapper's costume, he sang boat songs and told tall tales, and topped off the evening by discharging his rifle at a stuffed eagle. Later he added illustrated lectures on the lifeboat service to his repertoire; like Dickens, he seems to have felt the labour of the lecture circuit a price worth paying for the excitement of these self-dramatizations before admiring throngs. In writing, however, he could not repeat the Canadian material indefinitely, and *The Coral Island* was the first book in which he turned to other people's accounts of their adventures. It draws on James Bowman's *The Island Home* (1852), the American Crusoe story for boys already mentioned, and on *Recent Exploring Expeditions to the Pacific, and the South Seas* (1853), by J. S. Jenkins.[2] The second half of the book, which tells of pirates and savages, is inspired by the numerous accounts of missionary work in the South Seas that were appearing in British books and magazines at mid-century, especially the Rt. Revd Michael Russell's *Polynesia: A History of the South Sea Islands, Including New Zealand* (1852)[3] and periodicals like *The Juvenile Missionary Magazine*. He was not content with second-hand adventures, however, and in 1864 he made an arrangement with his new publishers, Nisbet, whereby they financed expeditions to gather material for his tales. Ostensibly, his practice in choosing settings and stories resembled that of Evangelical writers like W. H. G. Kingston or educators like Henty, in that his subjects offered opportunities for him to exhort his readers to good behaviour or to instruct

[2] Eric Quayle, *The Collector's Book of Boys' Stories* (London, 1973), 52.

[3] Stuart Hannabuss, 'Ballantyne's Message of Empire', in Jeffrey Richards (ed.), *Imperialism and Juvenile Fiction* (Manchester, 1989), 53–71, 61.

them about modern institutions or inventions. He justified his research in terms of that need for accuracy in books for the young upon which Marryat had insisted. But it is difficult to avoid the conclusion that what he was actually doing when he visited lighthouses, rode on fire engines, and tried out diving-suits on the bottom of the Thames was living out his fantasies, which he then packaged and delivered for the less fortunate boys who could only read his books. The juvenile relish for excitement and fisticuffs, the sometimes tiresome bounce and banter of his style were not a matter of writing down to his boyish readership but an attempt to remain one of them. As he grew older, his loving descriptions of boyhood seem to become ever more laboured, and ultimately rather pathetic; but his readers remained loyally convinced to the end of his life that Ballantyne was one of them.

One of his young admirers was Robert Louis Stevenson, who was 15 when he met Ballantyne and informed him that he had read *The Coral Island* twice and would read it twice more.[4] *Treasure Island* (1883) is, of course, the other famous nineteenth-century Crusoe story. It focuses not upon the cast-away episode but rather upon the quest for the hoard of pirate gold. Its boy's-eye-view of the conflicts which treasure causes may be read as an ironic comment upon 'adventures', especially those conducted in distant lands by English gentlemen seeking wealth: Jim is not the powerful and self-sufficient Ballantyne boy, and he discovers the inadequacy of the simple view of right and wrong with which he sets out upon the quest. All Ballantyne's Crusoe stories—he wrote several more which draw upon the myth, including *Sunk at Sea* (1869), *Jarwin and Cuffy* (1878), *The Lonely Island* (1880), and *The Island Queen* (1885)—avoid the mercantile, treasure-seeking motifs of Defoe's story. By the

[4] Quayle, *Ballantyne the Brave*, 217.

time Stevenson was writing, the romantic adventure-story in which the bold adventurer roams the world, making discoveries, doing good, but never overtly seeking for wealth, had become one of the main genres of popular fiction; and it had become enmeshed with imperialist ideology, contributing to the national perception of the might and the right of the British Empire and suppressing awareness of its rapacious mercenary base.

The Coral Island predates the domination of the Empire and its adventures in writing for boys and men, but it is not innocent of imperialist meanings. The desert-island story occupies the first half of the book; in it the three boys experience perfect happiness, which Ballantyne compares, as he prepares to interrupt it, with the life of Adam and Eve in paradise (p. 187). He brings the Golden Age to an end with three strokes. The first is natural—a storm which maroons them temporarily on a tiny bare rock, where for a single night they experience the terror and abandonment of less fortunate castaways. They return in the morning to find their homestead on the coral island devastated—a sign that they should not rely on earthly felicity, since all the good 'that a bountiful Creator could heap on us ... might be swept away for ever'. Then their paradise is invaded by 'ferocious savages', leaving 'the white sands stained with blood' (p. 187). Like Robinson Crusoe, they at first watch from concealment as war canoes run aground on their beach; a fierce fight takes place, culminating in cannibalism. Just as Crusoe's dilemma about how to respond to the visits of cannibals resolves itself into furious and deadly intervention when he hears of a European victim in their hands, so in *The Coral Island* the sight of a light-skinned woman led out to be killed turns Jack into a berserk northern warrior, and he flings himself upon the savages, bringing the huge chief down on top of himself. Ralph and Peterkin rescue him, leading the prisoners of the defeated party whom they have set free. The encounter is laden with the central justifying symbols of colonialism. Ballantyne's racial hierarchy is more complex than Defoe's, in that the victim is Samoan not European, but her pale skin marks her out as being a step higher up the racial ladder in terms of Victorian ethnology; the chief is a monster whose hair is dyed yellow and looks like a turban, giving an unnatural impression of cultural miscegenation. Jack's behaviour, the abandonment of self-preservation and rational restraint and the release of instinctive and therefore irresistible force derived from his white ancestors, is inevitable because of his racial dominance; it is justified by invoking the chivalric code which is the basis of European civilization—the victim he defends is a weak woman.

The savages go away, but the innocent stage of the colonial encounter, in which civilized man tames the natural elements, has been terminated by the incident, and the boys' lives have been changed, in preparation for the next stage of imperialism.[5] Ralph recalls that Peterkin seemed to have 'grown two years older within a few days' (p. 188). Inevitably, the third and severing blow falls, and Ralph is captured and carried off by pirates, to prove himself a hero in confrontation with villainy. The series of adventures which follows works out on the level of narrative romance the justification of the British Empire, as it was beginning to be argued in the 1850s. One of Ballantyne's sources, Michael Russell, states the case very fully and explicitly:

There is no fanaticism, it is believed, in the persuasion, that to Britain has been intrusted by Divine Providence a greater extent of power than ever belonged to any other nation, whether in ancient or modern times, with the view that she may carry to the remotest parts of the earth the pure form of Christianity which she professes, and the equal laws whereby the happiness of her people is secured. It has been well said,

---

[5] See Peter Hulme, *Colonial Encounters: Europe and the native Caribbean, 1492–1797* (London, 1986), 186, 201.

that she is not more eminent for her prowess in arms, her success in commerce, and her rank in science, and in all the arts that minister to the embellishment of social life, than she is for her exertions in diffusing the light of knowledge and of heavenly truth over the world. Animated by motives of the highest nature, thousands have been found ready to unite their counsels and contribute their property to send to others the invaluable gift which they themselves have received from above ... Bloodshed and cruelty have given way to peace and order ... The howl of superstitious fear has been succeeded by the language of prayer, and the shouts of ferocious war by the song of Christian praise. Civilisation, too, is advancing with rapid steps in connexion with a purer faith. The hut of the Otaheitian is replaced by a comfortable house, supplied with the conveniences and even the elegances of Europe; his canoe is exchanged for ships of considerable burden; and his rude barter, or more lawless plunder, has been superseded by the intercourse of regular commerce (p. 125–6).

Ballantyne clearly accepted absolutely this view of the beneficial effects of British missionary work and the commercial, social, and cultural transformation of the life of the South Sea Islands, as did many of his compatriots: as Russell suggests, there was no shortage of enthusiastic subscribers at every level to support the missionary ventures. Charlotte Mary Yonge donated earnings from her best-selling novel *The Heir of Redclyffe* for the commissioning of a missionary ship, and the missionary magazines published subscription lists recording the hard-won pennies of Sunday School children all over the country. The cause attracted the kind of enthusiasm given to disaster funds and food-aid appeals in the 1980s. In the second half of *The Coral Island* Ballantyne seems to set out to illustrate all the good effects of British civilization Russell lists, reinforced with grisly descriptions of the evils it supplants. It is not a very coherently structured narrative, less memorable than the mythic pattern of the opening; the reader is likely to feel the earnest writing-up of the missionary cause as preaching, and the highlights of bloody incident and lurid anecdote are sometimes loosely attached to the story. The narrative has two sections. Ralph's voyage with the piratical sandalwood trader gives opportunity for him to observe the horror of an encounter between unprincipled Europeans and unconverted heathens, resulting in their mutual destruction. It establishes in the reader's mind both the absolute otherness of the natives, the raw material of the imperialist mission, and the wickedness of those born in Christian countries who have neglected or rejected their chance of salvation. Ralph himself is finally brought to feel that he is the greatest sinner of all, being almost unable to remember enough of the Bible his mother gave him to comfort and convert the dying pirate, Bloody Bill. Emblematically, he also finds that he has neglected opportunities of learning other things that belong to his superior civilization, and has to work out by trial and error enough basic mechanics to manage the pirate schooner single-handed and sail back to the coral island.

The return to paradise is short-lived; within a few days the presence of the schooner stirs the boys up to adventure. Ralph, after asserting his British boyhood sufficiently to gain the pirate captain's respect, had been horrified by the various atrocities of cannibals and pirates he was obliged to observe, but had remained largely passive; Jack, on the other hand, the epitome of young British manhood, is an active shaper of destinies, and the trio set out to rescue the Samoan woman. It is in keeping with Ballantyne's personal faith that they are not permitted to succeed: Jack takes very seriously the admonition of a native Christian teacher that they are all sinners, but he is not made a convert, and their attempt to carry off the woman by force is defeated by the greater physical strength of their enemies. It is only the intervention of a tropical hurricane that saves the boys from becoming human sacrifices. Both they and the Samoan woman are finally saved by an English missionary, who arrives

providentially to convert the islanders (his influence being auto-
matically more effective in a week than that of the native Christian in a year) and to transform them at a stroke from
bloodthirsty idolaters to a friendly and generous society intent
upon building a church and arranging their houses in neat rows.

At the end of the adventure, the boys go home empty-
handed, sorry to be leaving their island paradise. The book
closes without suggesting what their future life will be, and so
they were available for further use when Ballantyne was asked
by his publishers to produce a story quickly, for the Christmas
market in 1861, to cash in on the interest in Paul du Chaillu's
Exploration in Equatorial Africa, a travel book in which gorillas
are described as 'ferocious wild men.'[6] It is interesting to see in
The Gorilla Hunters the development of Ballantyne's imperialism, rather at the expense of his evangelical principles. By 1861
popular perceptions of Darwinian theory had created something
of a backlash against scientific progressivism, a fear that mankind might be reduced to an evolutionary stepping-stone with
no God-given superiority or right to rule the world. Ballantyne,
always a believer in progress, exploration, and science as
symbols of British superiority, found an opportunity in the new
book both to counter such fears and simultaneously to promote
the perception of the adventurous British boy as the ruling type
of humanity. In *The Gorilla Hunters*, Jack, Ralph, and Peterkin
go off to Africa like boys out for a lark, with the intention of
slaughtering as many black, bestial, humanoid monsters as possible in the name of scientific discovery. In gleefully chronicling
their violent exploits, Ballantyne not only stressed the gap
between humans and monkeys, the innate superiority of man,
who can efficiently kill and scientifically investigate beasts; he
also vested that power in the white adventurer, and translated

---

[6] Quoted in Quayle, *Ballantyne the Brave*, 146.

the feared and hated 'other' of the colonial encounter into a subhuman form: the gorilla. In this way, all the complexities of the missionary enterprise and its demands on the colonizer to exemplify the virtues it claims to embody are wiped out, and the three young men have only to enjoy roughing it in camp, while their British pluck and the ability to shoot straight conquer in the name of science. Doubts created by nightmare theories of evolution are laid to rest, and the indefatigable heroes demonstrate British superiority, returning, this time, with a hoard of exotic specimens which science may use to confirm their right to rule the world. The only overt lessons the author offers are occasional exhortations to be manly and tough—and to learn to swim.

It was probably the simplicity of Ballantyne's way of writing out his convictions that gave his books a continuing appeal to boys. Young readers became impatient with the austere and life-encompassing demands that earlier writers for children tried to make upon them. Ballantyne offered rousing adventure stories, with either exotic or thoroughly modern settings, and confined his preaching to a page or two recommending enjoyable sports, with perhaps a vehement appeal for support for some specific cause—the lifeboats or anti-slavery societies—with which the least idealistic young reader could easily engage. If it was to be achieved by enjoying oneself out of doors or through the vicarious adventures of the book, and then sending off some money for a good cause, then anyone could be a good boy—and a British patriot, a member of the race chosen to lead the world. Most of Ballantyne's books sold well, and the causes he championed had every reason to be grateful for the support he brought to them; but only *The Coral Island*, with its finger on the pulse of a more enduring myth than that of the British Empire, still survives to represent his simple, hearty, boyish view of the world.

NOTE ON THE TEXT

THE text is based on an edition printed by James Nisbet and Co., Ballantyne's publishers from 1863 onwards, checked against the first edition published by T. Nelson & Sons in 1858. Ballantyne sold his early copyrights to Nelson's outright, and he was unable to persuade them either to share their enormous profits with him or to allow his new publishers to take the early books over. He was therefore unable to make the corrections and alterations he wanted to the text of *The Coral Island*, and it was eventually reprinted by Nisbet in its original form after his death. The earliest Nelson editions were illustrated with delicate sketches by Ballantyne himself.

SELECT BIBLIOGRAPHY

(place of publication is London unless otherwise stated)

The Coral Island has been repeatedly reprinted, translated, and retold; interesting editions include one with a preface by J. M. Barrie and illustrations by Septimus E. Scott (James Nisbet & Co., 1913), and a retelling by Hadyn Parry, illustrated by C. Walter Hodges (Harrap, 1950).

Most of Ballantyne's other works are no longer reprinted, and no modern editions exist. Readers interested in exploring his other stories are quite likely to find original editions, resplendent in pictorial, gold-blocked jackets, still available in second-hand bookshops. Titles to look for include: *Snowflakes and Sunbeams; or, The Young Fur Traders* (1856); *Ungava* (1858); *Martin Rattler* (1858); *The Gorilla Hunters* (1861); *The Lifeboat* (1864); *Fighting the Flames* (1867).

AUTOBIOGRAPHY

Six Months at the Cape (1879).
Personal Reminiscences in Bookmaking (1893).

BIOGRAPHY

QUAYLE, Eric, *Ballantyne the Brave* (1967).

BIBLIOGRAPHY

QUAYLE, Eric, *R. M. Ballantyne: A bibliography of first editions* (1968).

CRITICISM AND COMMENTARY

BRATTON, J. S., *The Impact of Victorian Children's Fiction* (1981).

Fisher, Margery, *The Bright Face of Danger* (1986).

Green, Martin, *Dreams of Adventure, Deeds of Empire* (1980).

—— 'The Robinson Crusoe Story', in J. Richards (ed.), *Imperialism and Juvenile Literature* (Manchester, 1989), 34–52.

Hannabuss, Stuart, 'Islands as Metaphors', *Universities Quarterly: Culture, Education and Society*, 38, 1, Winter 1983/4, 70–82.

—— 'Ballantyne's Message of Empire', in Richards, *Imperialism and Juvenile Literature*, 53–71.

Howarth, Patrick, *Play Up and Play the Game: The Heroes of Popular Fiction* (1973).

Quayle, Eric, *The Collector's Book of Boys' Stories* (1973), 42–64.

A CHRONOLOGY OF
R. M. BALLANTYNE

1825   24 April: Robert Michael Ballantyne born in Edinburgh, ninth child of Alexander Thomson and Anne Randall Ballantyne. 'Sandie' Ballantyne was the copyist whose handwriting disguised the manuscripts of Sir Walter Scott's novels, and the younger brother of James Ballantyne, Scott's printer. They also edited the *Edinburgh Weekly Journal*. In 1826 the Ballantyne Press was overwhelmed by Scott's financial ruin, and the family was impoverished, though Robert could not remember any financial shadow on his childhood.

1835–6   Attended Edinburgh Academy for 2 years. An undistinguished scholar, chiefly interested in fishing.

1841   Apprenticed as clerk to Hudson's Bay Company. Served at various remote Canadian stations, learning to hunt and trek rather than to be a merchant. Kept notes and journals which were later used in published writings.

1847   Returns to Scotland after his father's death, to find himself head of an impoverished household—his mother and five unmarried sisters. *Hudson's Bay*, printed privately for Christmas, sold out rapidly, but published edition did not sell.

1848   Sister Madalina died in childbirth. Ballantyne deeply affected and became assiduous churchgoer and Elder of Free Church.

1849   Bought a partnership in publishing firm of Constable. Moved into house of brother John, portrait painter. Became latter's lifelong financial support. John's wife, Teenie, dominated Ballantyne's emotional and social life for many years.

1855   Gave up office job after his mother's death, and went on three-month fishing trip to Norway. Embarked on a career of writing for boys and lecturing about Hudson's Bay.

1856   *Snowflakes and Sunbeams; or, The Young Fur Traders* and *The Three Little Kittens*, both illustrated by the author, published with great success by Nelson & Sons, who paid very little for these and succeeding copyrights.

1858   *Ungava*, *The Coral Island* and *Martin Rattler* published. Ballantyne by now a literary lion and a hero to boys, but inhibited and awkward in society.

1859   Three members of Teenie's family lost in wreck off Anglesey. Ballantyne became lifelong campaigner for lifeboats.

1861   *The Gorilla Hunters* commissioned by Nelson, to take advantage of interest in recent accounts of apes, and in Darwin. Ballantyne wrote it hurriedly, using characters of *The Coral Island*.

1863   *Gascoyne and the Sandalwood Trader* published on a royalty agreement with Nisbet & Co., the beginning of a long association.

1864   Moved to London with brother's family. Arrangement began whereby Nisbet financed field trips enabling Ballantyne to experience adventures and absorb facts for writing. Trips made regularly for the next 20 years, and a story produced every Christmas, often other books as well. *The Lifeboat* published. Included a highly successful appeal for National Lifeboat Institution, which now became second topic for public lecture tours, his regular winter activity.

1866   Married Jane Dickson Grant; she was 21. They bought a house in Edinburgh with her dowry.

1867   Received a medal for rescuing people in Edinburgh fire in same week that *Fighting the Flames: A Tale of the London Fire Brigade* was published. His best seller to date.

1869   First child, Frank, born.

1870   Henty's first boys' book published.

1871   Edgar Ballantyne born.

1873   Jean Ballantyne born. *Black Ivory*, about East African slave-trading, published.

1874   Moved his family to Montreux, Switzerland, for their health.

1875   Robert James Ballantyne born.

1876   Took an extended trip to South Africa on the strength of growing prosperity from accumulating royalties.

1877   Alice Ballantyne born.

1879   Family returned to Harrow so that boys could attend public schools.

1882   Isobel, last child, born. *The Kitten Pilgrims*, a nursery version of *The Pilgrim's Progress* written for own children, published.

1883   Moved into 'Duneaves' in Harro.., built as family home. *Treasure Island* by R. L. Stevenson published.

1890   Onset of Ménière's disease, with attacks of giddiness.

1894   February: died in Rome, on the way home from attempted cure at Tivoli. Boys of Harrow School started a fund to erect a memorial to him.

THE CORAL ISLAND

PREFACE

I WAS a boy when I went through the wonderful adventures herein set down. With the memory of my boyish feelings strong upon me, I present my book specially to boys, in the earnest hope that they may derive valuable information, much pleasure, great profit, and unbounded amusement from its pages.

One word more. If there is any boy or man who loves to be melancholy and morose, and who cannot enter with kindly sympathy into the regions of fun, let me seriously advise him to shut my book and put it away. It is not meant for him.

RALPH ROVER.

CONTENTS

CHAPTER VI

CHAPTER VII

CHAPTER VIII

CHAPTER IX

CHAPTER X

CHAPTER XI

CHAPTER XII

CHAPTER XIII

CHAPTER XIV

CHAPTER XV

CHAPTER XVI

CHAPTER XVII

CHAPTER XVIII

CHAPTER XIX

CHAPTER XX

CHAPTER XXI

CHAPTER XXII

CHAPTER XXIII

CHAPTER XXIV

CHAPTER XXV

CHAPTER XXVI

CHAPTER XXVII

CHAPTER XXVIII

CHAPTER XXIX

CHAPTER XXX

CHAPTER XXXI

CHAPTER XXXII

CHAPTER XXXIII

CHAPTER XXXIV

CHAPTER XXXV

THE CORAL ISLAND

CHAPTER I

The beginning—My early life and character—I thirst for adventure
in foreign lands, and go to sea.

ROVING has always been, and still is, my ruling
passion, the joy of my heart, the very sunshine of
my existence. In childhood, in boyhood, and in man's
estate, I have been a rover; not a mere rambler among
the woody glens and upon the hilltops of my own native
land, but an enthusiastic rover throughout the length
and breadth of the wide, wide world.

It was a wild, black night of howling storm, the night
on which I was born on the foaming bosom of the broad
Atlantic Ocean. My father was a sea-captain; my grandfather was a sea-captain; my great-grandfather had been
a marine. Nobody could tell positively what occupation
his father had followed; but my dear mother used to
assert that he had been a midshipman, whose grandfather,
on the mother's side, had been an admiral in the Royal
Navy. At any rate, we knew that, as far back as our
family could be traced, it had been intimately connected
with the great watery waste. Indeed, this was the case

on both sides of the house; for my mother always went
to sea with my father on his long voyages, and so spent
the greater part of her life upon the water.

Thus it was, I suppose, that I came to inherit a roving
disposition.   Soon after I was born, my father, being old,
retired from a seafaring life, purchased a small cottage in
a fishing village on the west coast of England, and settled
down to spend the evening of his life on the shores of
that sea which had for so many years been his home.   It
was not long after this that I began to show the roving
spirit that dwelt within me.   For some time past my
infant legs had been gaining strength, so that I came to
be dissatisfied with rubbing the skin off my chubby knees
by walking on them, and made many attempts to stand
up and walk like a man, all of which attempts, however,
resulted in my sitting down violently and in sudden surprise.   One day I took advantage of my dear mother's
absence to make another effort; and, to my joy, I actually succeeded in reaching the doorstep, over which I
tumbled into a pool of muddy water that lay before my
father's cottage door.   Ah, how vividly I remember the
horror of my poor mother when she found me sweltering
in the mud amongst a group of cackling ducks, and the
tenderness with which she stripped off my dripping
clothes and washed my dirty little body!   From this
time forth my rambles became more frequent, and, as I
grew older, more distant, until at last I had wandered
far and near on the shore and in the woods around our
humble dwelling, and did not rest content until my father
bound me apprentice to a coasting vessel, and let me go
to sea.

For some years I was happy in visiting the seaports,

and in coasting along the shores of my native land. My Christian name was Ralph, and my comrades added to this the name of Rover, in consequence of the passion which I always evinced for travelling. Rover was not my real name, but as I never received any other, I came at last to answer to it as naturally as to my proper name; and as it is not a bad one, I see no good reason why I should not introduce myself to the reader as Ralph Rover. My shipmates were kind, good-natured fellows, and they and I got on very well together. They did, indeed, very frequently make game of and banter me, but not unkindly; and I overheard them sometimes saying that Ralph Rover was a "queer, old-fashioned fellow." This, I must confess, surprised me much, and I pondered the saying long, but could come at no satisfactory conclusion as to that wherein my old-fashionedness lay. It is true I was a quiet lad, and seldom spoke except when spoken to. Moreover, I never could understand the jokes of my companions, even when they were explained to me. which dulness in apprehension occasioned me much grief. However, I tried to make up for it by smiling and looking pleased when I observed that they were laughing at some witticism which I had failed to detect. I was also very fond of inquiring into the nature of things and their causes, and often fell into fits of abstraction while thus engaged in my mind. But in all this I saw nothing that did not seem to be exceedingly natural, and could by no means understand why my comrades should call me "an old-fashioned fellow."

Now, while engaged in the coasting trade, I fell in with many seamen who had travelled to almost every quarter of the globe; and I freely confess that my heart

glowed ardently within me as they recounted their wild
adventures in foreign lands—the dreadful storms they
had weathered, the appalling dangers they had escaped,
the wonderful creatures they had seen both on the land
and in the sea, and the interesting lands and strange
people they had visited. But of all the places of which
they told me, none captivated and charmed my imagina-
tion so much as the Coral Islands of the Southern Seas.
They told me of thousands of beautiful, fertile islands
that had been formed by a small creature called the coral
insect, where summer reigned nearly all the year round;
where the trees were laden with a constant harvest of
luxuriant fruit; where the climate was almost perpetually
delightful; yet where, strange to say, men were wild,
bloodthirsty savages, excepting in those favoured isles to
which the Gospel of our Saviour had been conveyed.
These exciting accounts had so great an effect upon my
mind that, when I reached the age of fifteen, I resolved to
make a voyage to the South Seas.

I had no little difficulty at first in prevailing on my
dear parents to let me go; but when I urged on my
father that he would never have become a great captain
had he remained in the coasting trade, he saw the truth
of what I said, and gave his consent. My dear mother,
seeing that my father had made up his mind, no longer
offered opposition to my wishes. "But oh, Ralph," she
said, on the day I bade her adieu, "come back soon to us,
my dear boy, for we are getting old now, Ralph, and may
not have many years to live."

I will not take up my readers' time with a minute
account of all that occurred before I took my final leave
of my dear parents. Suffice it to say that my father

placed me under the charge of an old messmate of his own, a merchant captain, who was on the point of sailing to the South Seas in his own ship, the *Arrow*. My mother gave me her blessing and a small Bible; and her last request was that I would never forget to read a chapter every day, and say my prayers; which I promised, with tears in my eyes, that I would certainly do.

Soon afterwards, I went on board the *Arrow*, which was a fine large ship, and set sail for the islands of the Pacific Ocean.

CHAPTER II

The departure—The sea—My companions—Some account of the wonderful sights we saw on the great deep—A dreadful storm and a frightful wreck.

IT was a bright, beautiful, warm day when our ship spread her canvas to the breeze, and sailed for the regions of the south. Oh, how my heart bounded with delight as I listened to the merry chorus of the sailors, while they hauled at the ropes and got in the anchor! The captain shouted; the men ran to obey; the noble ship bent over to the breeze, and the shore gradually faded from my view, while I stood looking on with a kind of feeling that the whole was a delightful dream.

The first thing that struck me as being different from anything I had yet seen during my short career on the sea, was the hoisting of the anchor on deck and lashing it firmly down with ropes, as if we had now bid adieu to the land for ever, and would require its services no more.

"There, lass," cried a broad-shouldered jack-tar, giving the fluke of the anchor a hearty slap with his hand after the housing was completed—"there, lass, take a good nap now, for we shan't ask you to kiss the mud again for many a long day to come!"

And so it was. That anchor did not "kiss the mud" for many long days afterwards; and when at last it did, it was for the last time!

There were a number of boys in the ship, but two of

them were my special favourites. Jack Martin was a tall, strapping, broad-shouldered youth of eighteen, with a handsome, good-humoured, firm face. He had had a good education, was clever and hearty and lion-like in his actions, but mild and quiet in disposition. Jack was a general favourite, and had a peculiar fondness for me. My other companion was Peterkin Gay. He was little, quick, funny, decidedly mischievous, and about fourteen years old. But Peterkin's mischief was almost always harmless, else he could not have been so much beloved as he was.

"Hallo, youngster!" cried Jack Martin, giving me a slap on the shoulder the day I joined the ship, "come below, and I'll show you your berth. You and I are to be messmates, and I think we shall be good friends, for I like the look o' you."

Jack was right. He and I, and Peterkin afterwards, became the best and staunchest friends that ever tossed together on the stormy waves.

I shall say little about the first part of our voyage. We had the usual amount of rough weather and calm; also we saw many strange fish rolling in the sea, and I was greatly delighted one day by seeing a shoal of flying-fish dart out of the water and skim through the air about a foot above the surface. They were pursued by dolphins, which feed on them, and one flying-fish in its terror flew over the ship, struck on the rigging, and fell upon the deck. Its wings were just fins elongated, and we found that they could never fly far at a time, and never mounted into the air like birds, but skimmed along the surface of the sea. Jack and I had it for dinner, and found it remarkably good.

When we approached Cape Horn, at the southern extremity of America, the weather became very cold and stormy, and the sailors began to tell stories about the furious gales and the dangers of that terrible Cape.

"Cape Horn," said one, "is the most horrible headland I ever doubled. I've sailed round it twice already, and both times the ship was a'most blow'd out o' the water."

"I've been round it once," said another, "an' that time the sails were split, and the ropes frozen in the blocks, so that they wouldn't work, and we wos all but lost."

"An' I've been round it five times," cried a third, "an' every time wos wuss than another, the gales wos so tree-mendous!"

"And I've been round it no times at all," cried Peterkin, with an impudent wink in his eye, "an' *that* time I wos blow'd inside out!"

Nevertheless, we passed the dreaded Cape without much rough weather, and, in the course of a few weeks afterwards, were sailing gently before a warm, tropical breeze over the Pacific Ocean. Thus we proceeded on our voyage, sometimes bounding merrily before a fair breeze, at other times floating calmly on the glassy wave and fishing for the curious inhabitants of the deep—all of which, although the sailors thought little of them, were strange, and interesting, and very wonderful to me.

At last we came among the Coral Islands of the Pacific, and I shall never forget the delight with which I gazed— when we chanced to pass one—at the pure, white, dazzling shores, and the verdant palm trees, which looked bright and beautiful in the sunshine. And often did we three long to be landed on one, imagining that we should certainly find perfect happiness there! Our wish was granted sooner than we expected.

One night, soon after we entered the tropics, an awful storm burst upon our ship. The first squall of wind carried away two of our masts, and left only the foremast standing. Even this, however, was more than enoug', for we did not dare to hoist a rag of sail on it. For five days the tempest raged in all its fury. Everything was swept off the decks except one small boat. The steersman was lashed to the wheel, lest he should be washed away, and we all gave ourselves up for lost. The captain said that he had no idea where we were, as we had been blown far out of our course; and we feared much that we might get among the dangerous coral reefs which are so numerous in the Pacific. At daybreak on the sixth morning of the gale we saw land ahead. It was an island encircled by a reef of coral on which the waves broke in fury. There was calm water within this reef, but we could see only one narrow opening into it. For this opening we steered, but ere we reached it a tremendous wave broke on our stern, tore the rudder completely off, and left us at the mercy of the winds and waves.

"It's all over with us now, lads!" said the captain to the men. "Get the boat ready to launch; we shall be on the rocks in less than half-an-hour."

The men obeyed in gloomy silence, for they felt that there was little hope of so small a boat living in such a sea.

"Come, boys," said Jack Martin, in a grave tone, to me and Peterkin, as we stood on the quarter-deck awaiting our fate—"come, boys; we three shall stick together. You see it is impossible that the little boat can reach the

shore, crowded with men. It will be sure to upset, so I
mean rather to trust myself to a large oar. I see through
the telescope that the ship will strike at the tail of the
reef, where the waves break into the quiet water inside;
so, if we manage to cling to the oar till it is driven over
the breakers, we may perhaps gain the shore. What say
you? will you join me?"

We gladly agreed to follow Jack, for he inspired us
with confidence, although I could perceive, by the sad
tone of his voice, that he had little hope; and, indeed,
when I looked at the white waves that lashed the reef
and boiled against the rocks as if in fury, I felt that there
was but a step between us and death. My heart sank
within me; but at that moment my thoughts turned to
my beloved mother, and I remembered those words, which
were among the last that she said to me: "Ralph, my
dearest child, always remember in the hour of danger to
look to your Lord and Saviour Jesus Christ. He alone
is both able and willing to save your body and your
soul." So I felt much comforted when I thought thereon.

The ship was now very near the rocks. The men were
ready with the boat, and the captain beside them giving
orders, when a tremendous wave came towards us. We
three ran towards the bow to lay hold of our oar, and had
barely reached it when the wave fell on the deck with a
crash like thunder. At the same moment the ship struck,
the foremast broke off close to the deck and went over
the side, carrying the boat and men along with it. Our
oar got entangled with the wreck, and Jack seized an axe
to cut it free, but, owing to the motion of the ship, he
missed the cordage and struck the axe deep into the oar.
Another wave, however, washed it clear of the wreck.

We all seized hold of it, and the next instant we were struggling in the wild sea. The last thing I saw was the boat whirling in the surf, and all the sailors tossed into the foaming waves. Then I became insensible.

On recovering from my swoon, I found myself lying on a bank of soft grass, under shelter of an overhanging rock, with Peterkin on his knees by my side, tenderly bathing my temples with water, and endeavouring to stop the blood that flowed from a wound in my forehead.

CHAPTER III

The Coral Island—Our first cogitations after landing, and the result of them—We conclude that the island is uninhabited.

THERE is a strange and peculiar sensation experienced in recovering from a state of insensibility, which is almost indescribable: a sort of dreamy, confused consciousness; a half-waking, half-sleeping condition, accompanied with a feeling of weariness, which, however, is by no means disagreeable. As I slowly recovered, and heard the voice of Peterkin inquiring whether I felt better, I thought that I must have overslept myself, and should be sent to the mast-head for being lazy; but before I could leap up in haste, the thought seemed to vanish suddenly away, and I fancied that I must have been ill. Then a balmy breeze fanned my cheek, and I thought of home, and the garden at the back of my father's cottage, with its luxuriant flowers, and the sweet-scented honey-suckle that my dear mother trained so carefully upon the trellised porch. But the roaring of the surf put these delightful thoughts to flight, and I was back again at sea, watching the dolphins and the flying-fish, and reefing topsails off the wild and stormy Cape Horn. Gradually the roar of the surf became louder and more distinct. I thought of being wrecked far, far away from my native land, and slowly opened my eyes to meet those of my companion Jack, who, with a look of intense anxiety, was gazing into my face.

"Speak to us, my dear Ralph," whispered Jack tenderly. "Are you better now?"

I smiled, and looked up, saying, "Better! why, what do you mean, Jack? I'm quite well."

"Then what are you shamming for, and frightening us in this way?" said Peterkin, smiling through his tears; for the poor boy had been really under the impression that I was dying.

I now raised myself on my elbow, and putting my hand to my forehead, found that it had been cut pretty severely, and that I had lost a good deal of blood.

"Come, come, Ralph," said Jack, pressing me gently backward, "lie down, my boy; you're not right yet. Wet your lips with this water; it's cool and clear as crystal. I got it from a spring close at hand. There now, don't say a word, hold your tongue," he said, seeing me about to speak. "I'll tell you all about it, but you must not utter a syllable till you have rested well."

"Oh! don't stop him from speaking, Jack," said Peterkin, who, now that his fears for my safety were removed, busied himself in erecting a shelter of broken branches in order to protect me from the wind, which, however, was almost unnecessary, for the rock beside which I had been laid completely broke the force of the gale. "Let him speak, Jack; it's a comfort to hear that he's alive, after lying there stiff and white and sulky for a whole hour, just like an Egyptian mummy. Never saw such a fellow as you are, Ralph, always up to mischief. You've almost knocked out all my teeth, and more than half choked me, and now you go shamming dead! It's very wicked of you, indeed it is."

While Peterkin ran on in this style, my faculties be-

came quite clear again, and I began to understand my
position. "What do you mean by saying I half choked
you, Peterkin?" said I.

"What do I mean? Is English not your mother-
tongue, or do you want me to repeat it in French, by way
of making it clearer? Don't you remember——"

"I remember nothing," said I, interrupting him, "after
we were thrown into the sea."

"Hush, Peterkin!" said Jack; "you're exciting Ralph
with your nonsense.—I'll explain it to you. You recollect that after the ship struck, we three sprang over
the bow into the sea: well, I noticed that the oar struck
your head and gave you that cut on the brow, which
nearly stunned you, so that you grasped Peterkin round
the neck without knowing apparently what you were
about. In doing so you pushed the telescope—which you
clung to as if it had been your life—against Peterkin's
mouth——"

"Pushed it against his mouth!" interrupted Peterkin;
"say, crammed it down his throat. Why, there's a distinct mark of the brass rim on the back of my gullet at
this moment!"

"Well, well, be that as it may," continued Jack, "you
clung to him, Ralph, till I feared you really would choke
him; but I saw that he had a good hold of the oar, so I
exerted myself to the utmost to push you towards the
shore, which we luckily reached without much trouble, for
the water inside the reef is quite calm."

"But the captain and crew, what of them?" I inquired
anxiously.

Jack shook his head.

"Are they lost?"

"No, they are not lost, I hope, but I fear there is not much chance of their being saved. The ship struck at the very tail of the island on which we are cast. When the boat was tossed into the sea it fortunately did not upset, although it shipped a good deal of water, and all the men managed to scramble into it; but before they could get the oars out the gale carried them past the point and away to leeward of the island. After we landed I saw them endeavouring to pull towards us; but as they had only one pair of oars out of the eight that belong to the boat, and as the wind was blowing right in their teeth, they gradually lost ground. Then I saw them put about and hoist some sort of sail—a blanket, I fancy, for it was too small for the boat—and in half-an-hour they were out of sight."

"Poor fellows!" I murmured sorrowfully.

"But the more I think about it, I've better hope of them," continued Jack, in a more cheerful tone. "You see, Ralph, I've read a great deal about these South Sea Islands, and I know that in many places they are scattered about in thousands over the sea, so they're almost sure to fall in with one of them before long."

"I'm sure I hope so," said Peterkin earnestly. "But what has become of the wreck, Jack? I saw you clambering up the rocks there while I was watching Ralph. Did you say she had gone to pieces?"

"No, she has not gone to pieces, but she has gone to the bottom," replied Jack. "As I said before, she struck on the tail of the island and stove in her bow, but the next breaker swung her clear, and she floated away to leeward. The poor fellows in the boat made a hard struggle to reach her, but long before they came near her she filled and went down. It was after she foundered that I saw them trying to pull to the island."

There was a long silence after Jack ceased speaking, and I have no doubt that each was revolving in his mind our extraordinary position. For my part, I cannot say that my reflections were very agreeable. I knew that we were on an island, for Jack had said so, but whether it was inhabited or not I did not know. If it should be inhabited, I felt certain, from all I had heard of South Sea Islanders, that we should be roasted alive and eaten. If it should turn out to be uninhabited, I fancied that we should be starved to death. " Oh," thought I, " if the ship had only struck on the rocks we might have done pretty well, for we could have obtained provisions from her, and tools to enable us to build a shelter; but now— alas! alas! we are lost!" These last words I uttered aloud in my distress.

"Lost! Ralph?" exclaimed Jack, while a smile over-spread his hearty countenance. "Saved, you should have said. Your cogitations seem to have taken a wrong road, and led you to a wrong conclusion."

"Do you know what conclusion *I* have come to?" said Peterkin. "I have made up my mind that it's capital— first-rate—the best thing that ever happened to us, and the most splendid prospect that ever lay before three jolly young tars. We've got an island all to ourselves. We'll take possession in the name of the king; we'll go and enter the service of its black inhabitants. Of course we'll rise, naturally, to the top of affairs. White men always do in savage countries. You shall be king, Jack; Ralph, prime minister; and I shall be——"

" The court-jester," interrupted Jack.

"No," retorted Peterkin; "I'll have no title at all. I shall merely accept a highly responsible situation under government; for you see, Jack, I'm fond of having an enormous salary and nothing to do."

"But suppose there are no natives?"

"Then we'll build a charming villa, and plant a lovely garden round it, stuck all full of the most splendiferous tropical flowers, and we'll farm the land, plant, sow, reap, eat, sleep, and be merry."

"But to be serious," said Jack, assuming a grave expression of countenance, which I observed always had the effect of checking Peterkin's disposition to make fun of everything, "we are really in rather an uncomfortable position. If this is a desert island, we shall have to live very much like the wild beasts, for we have not a tool of any kind, not even a knife."

"Yes, we have *that*," said Peterkin, fumbling in his trousers pocket, from which he drew forth a small penknife with only one blade, and that was broken.

"Well, that's better than nothing. But come," said Jack, rising; "we are wasting our time in *talking* instead of *doing*.—You seem well enough to walk now, Ralph. Let us see what we have got in our pockets, and then let us climb some hill and ascertain what sort of island we have been cast upon, for, whether good or bad, it seems likely to be our home for some time to come."

CHAPTER IV

We examine into our personal property, and make a happy discovery
—Our island described—Jack proves himself to be learned and
sagacious above his fellows—Curious discoveries—Natural
lemonade!

WE now seated ourselves upon a rock, and began to examine into our personal property. When we reached
the shore, after being wrecked, my companions had taken
off part of their clothes and spread them out in the sun
to dry; for although the gale was raging fiercely, there
was not a single cloud in the bright sky. They had also
stripped off most part of my wet clothes and spread them
also on the rocks. Having resumed our garments, we
now searched all our pockets with the utmost care, and
laid their contents out on a flat stone before us; and now
that our minds were fully alive to our condition, it was
with no little anxiety that we turned our several pockets
inside out, in order that nothing might escape us. When
all was collected together, we found that our worldly
goods consisted of the following articles :—

First, a small penknife with a single blade broken off
about the middle and very rusty, besides having two or
three notches on its edge. (Peterkin said of this, with
his usual pleasantry, that it would do for a saw as well
as a knife, which was a great advantage.) Second, an
old German-silver* pencil-case without any lead in it.
Third, a piece of whipcord about six yards long.

Fourth, a sailmaker's needle of a small size. Fifth, a ship's telescope, which I happened to have in my hand at the time the ship struck, and which I had clung to firmly all the time I was in the water. Indeed it was with difficulty that Jack got it out of my grasp when I was lying insensible on the shore. I cannot understand why I kept such a firm hold of this telescope. They say that a drowning man will clutch at a straw. Perhaps it may have been some such feeling in me, for I did not know that it was in my hand at the time we were wrecked. However, we felt some pleasure in having it with us now, although we did not see that it could be of much use to us, as the glass at the small end was broken to pieces. Our sixth article was a brass ring which Jack always wore on his little finger. I never understood why he wore it, for Jack was not vain of his appearance, and did not seem to care for ornaments of any kind. Peterkin said "it was in memory of the girl he left behind him!" But as he never spoke of this girl to either of us, I am inclined to think that Peterkin was either jesting or mistaken. In addition to these articles we had a little bit of tinder, and the clothes on our back. These last were as follows :—

Each of us had on a pair of stout canvas trousers, and a pair of sailors' thick shoes. Jack wore a red flannel shirt, a blue jacket, and a red Kilmarnock bonnet or nightcap, besides a pair of worsted socks, and a cotton pocket-handkerchief, with sixteen portraits of Lord Nelson printed on it, and a Union Jack in the middle. Peterkin had on a striped flannel shirt—which he wore outside his trousers, and belted round his waist, after the manner of a tunic—and a round black straw hat. He

had no jacket, having thrown it off just before we were
cast into the sea; but this was not of much consequence,
as the climate of the island proved to be extremely mild
—so much so, indeed, that Jack and I often preferred to
go about without our jackets. Peterkin had also a pair
of white cotton socks, and a blue handkerchief with white
spots all over it. My own costume consisted of a blue
flannel shirt, a blue jacket, a black cap, and a pair of
worsted socks, besides the shoes and canvas trousers
already mentioned. This was all we had, and besides
these things we had nothing else; but when we thought of
the danger from which we had escaped, and how much
worse off we might have been had the ship struck on the
reef during the night, we felt very thankful that we were
possessed of so much, although, I must confess, we
sometimes wished that we had had a little more.

While we were examining these things and talking
about them, Jack suddenly started and exclaimed—

"The oar! We have forgotten the oar."

"What good will that do us!" said Peterkin; "there's
wood enough on the island to make a thousand oars."

"Ay, lad," replied Jack; "but there's a bit of hoop-
iron at the end of it, and that may be of much use to us."

"Very true," said I, "let us go fetch it;" and with
that we all three rose and hastened down to the beach.
I still felt a little weak from loss of blood, so that my
companions soon began to leave me behind; but Jack
perceived this, and, with his usual considerate good-
nature, turned back to help me. This was now the first
time that I had looked well about me since landing, as
the spot where I had been laid was covered with thick
bushes, which almost hid the country from our view. As

we now emerged from among these and walked down the
sandy beach together, I cast my eyes about, and truly
my heart glowed within me and my spirits rose at the
beautiful prospect which I beheld on every side. The
gale had suddenly died away, just as if it had blown
furiously till it dashed our ship upon the rocks, and had
nothing more to do after accomplishing that. The island
on which we stood was hilly, and covered almost everywhere with the most beautiful and richly coloured trees,
bushes, and shrubs, none of which I knew the names of
at that time, except, indeed, the cocoa-nut palms, which
I recognised at once from the many pictures that I had
seen of them before I left home. A sandy beach of
dazzling whiteness lined this bright green shore, and
upon it there fell a gentle ripple of the sea. This last
astonished me much, for I recollected that at home the
sea used to fall in huge billows on the shore long after
a storm had subsided. But on casting my glance out to
sea, the cause became apparent. About a mile distant
from the shore, I saw the great billows of the ocean rolling like a green wall, and falling with a long, loud roar
upon a low coral reef, where they were dashed into white
foam and flung up in clouds of spray. This spray sometimes flew exceedingly high, and every here and there a
beautiful rainbow was formed for a moment among the
falling drops. We afterwards found that this coral reef
extended quite round the island, and formed a natural
breakwater to it. Beyond this the sea rose and tossed
violently from the effects of the storm; but between the
reef and the shore it was as calm and as smooth as a
pond.

My heart was filled with more delight than I can

express at sight of so many glorious objects, and my
thoughts turned suddenly to the contemplation of the
Creator of them all. I mention this the more gladly
because at that time, I am ashamed to say, I very seldom
thought of my Creator, although I was constantly surrounded by the most beautiful and wonderful of His
works. I observed, from the expression of my companion's
countenance, that he too derived much joy from the
splendid scenery, which was all the more agreeable to
us after our long voyage on the salt sea. There the
breeze was fresh and cold, but here it was delightfully
mild ; and when a puff blew off the land, it came laden
with the most exquisite perfume that can be imagined.
While we thus gazed, we were startled by a loud "Huzza!"
from Peterkin, and on looking towards the edge of the
sea, we saw him capering and jumping about like a
monkey, and ever and anon tugging with all his might
at something that lay upon the shore.

"What an odd fellow he is, to be sure!" said Jack,
taking me by the arm and hurrying forward; "come, let
us hasten to see what it is."

"Here it is, boys, hurrah! come along. Just what we
want," cried Peterkin, as we drew near, still tugging with
all his power. "First-rate; just the very ticket!"

I need scarcely say to my readers that my companion
Peterkin was in the habit of using very remarkable and
peculiar phrases. And I am free to confess that I did
not well understand the meaning of some of them—such,
for instance, as "the very ticket";* but I think it my
duty to recount everything relating to my adventures
with a strict regard to truthfulness in as far as my
memory serves me; so I write, as nearly as possible, the

exact words that my companions spoke. I often asked
Peterkin to explain what he meant by "ticket," but he
always answered me by going into fits of laughter. However, by observing the occasions on which he used it, I
came to understand that it meant to show that something
was remarkably good or fortunate.

On coming up, we found that Peterkin was vainly
endeavouring to pull the axe out of the oar, into which,
it will be remembered, Jack struck it while endeavouring
to cut away the cordage among which it had become
entangled at the bow of the ship. Fortunately for us,
the axe had remained fast in the oar, and even now all
Peterkin's strength could not draw it out of the cut.

"Ah! that is capital indeed," cried Jack, at the same
time giving the axe a wrench that plucked it out of the
tough wood. "How fortunate this is! It will be of
more value to us than a hundred knives, and the edge is
quite new and sharp."

"I'll answer for the toughness of the handle, at any
rate," cried Peterkin; "my arms are nearly pulled out of
the sockets. But see here, our luck is great. There is
iron on the blade." He pointed to a piece of hoop-iron
as he spoke, which had been nailed round the blade of the
oar to prevent it from splitting.

This also was a fortunate discovery. Jack went down
on his knees, and with the edge of the axe began carefully to force out the nails. But as they were firmly
fixed in, and the operation blunted our axe, we carried
the oar up with us to the place where we had left the rest
of our things, intending to burn the wood away from the
iron at a more convenient time.

"Now, lads." said Jack, after we had laid it on the

stone which contained our little all, "I propose that we should go to the tail of the island, where the ship struck, which is only a quarter of a mile off, and see if anything else has been thrown ashore. I don't expect anything, but it is well to see. When we get back here, it will be time to have our supper and prepare our beds."

"Agreed!" cried Peterkin and I together, as, indeed, we would have agreed to any proposal that Jack made, for, besides his being older and much stronger and taller than either of us, he was a very clever fellow, and I think would have induced people much older than himself to choose him for their leader, especially if they required to be led on a bold enterprise.

Now, as we hastened along the white beach, which shone so brightly in the rays of the setting sun that our eyes were quite dazzled by its glare, it suddenly came into Peterkin's head that we had nothing to eat except the wild berries which grew in profusion at our feet.

"What shall we do, Jack?" said he, with a rueful look; "perhaps they may be poisonous!"

"No fear," replied Jack confidently; "I have observed that a few of them are not unlike some of the berries that grow wild on our own native hills. Besides, I saw one or two strange birds eating them just a few minutes ago, and what won't kill the birds won't kill us. But look up there, Peterkin," continued Jack, pointing to the branched head of a cocoa-nut palm. "There are nuts for us in all stages."

"So there are!" cried Peterkin, who, being of a very unobservant nature, had been too much taken up with other things to notice anything so high above his head as the fruit of a palm tree. But whatever faults my young comrade had, he could not be blamed for want of activity or animal spirits. Indeed, the nuts had scarcely been pointed out to him when he bounded up the tall stem of the tree like a squirrel, and in a few minutes returned with three nuts, each as large as a man's fist.

"You had better keep them till we return," said Jack. "Let us finish our work before eating."

"So be it, captain; go ahead," cried Peterkin, thrusting the nuts into his trousers pocket. "In fact, I don't want to eat just now, but I would give a good deal for a drink. Oh that I could find a spring! but I don't see the smallest sign of one hereabouts. I say, Jack, how does it happen that you seem to be up to everything? You have told us the names of half-a-dozen trees already, and yet you say that you were never in the South Seas before."

"I'm not up to *everything*, Peterkin, as you'll find out ere long," replied Jack, with a smile; "but I have been a great reader of books of travel and adventure all my life, and that has put me up to a good many things that you are, perhaps, not acquainted with."

"O Jack, that's all humbug. If you begin to lay everything to the credit of books, I'll quite lose my opinion of you," cried Peterkin, with a look of contempt. "I've seen a lot o' fellows that were *always* poring over books, and when they came to try to *do* anything, they were no better than baboons!"

"You are quite right," retorted Jack, "and I have seen a lot of fellows who never looked into books at all, who knew nothing about anything except the things they had actually seen, and very little they knew even about these. Indeed, some were so ignorant that they did not know that cocoa-nuts grew on cocoa-nut trees!"

I could not refrain from laughing at this rebuke, for there was much truth in it as to Peterkin's ignorance.

"Humph! maybe you're right," answered Peterkin; "but I would not give *tuppence* for a man of books, if he had nothing else in him."

"Neither would I," said Jack; "but that's no reason why you should run books down, or think less of me for having read them. Suppose now, Peterkin, that you wanted to build a ship, and I were to give you a long and particular account of the way to do it, would not that be very useful?"

"No doubt of it," said Peterkin, laughing.

"And suppose I were to write the account in a letter instead of telling you in words, would that be less useful?"

"Well—no, perhaps not."

"Well, suppose I were to print it, and send it to you in the form of a book, would it not be as good and useful as ever?"

"Oh, bother! Jack, you're a philosopher, and that's worse than anything!" cried Peterkin, with a look of pretended horror.

"Very well, Peterkin, we shall see," returned Jack, halting under the shade of a cocoa-nut tree. "You said you were thirsty just a minute ago; now jump up that tree and bring down a nut—not a ripe one, bring a green, unripe one."

Peterkin looked surprised, but seeing that Jack was in earnest, he obeyed.

"Now cut a hole in it with your penknife, and clap it to your mouth, old fellow," said Jack.

Peterkin did as he was directed, and we both burst into uncontrollable laughter at the changes that instantly passed over his expressive countenance. No sooner had he put the nut to his mouth, and thrown back his head in order to catch what came out of it, than his eyes opened to twice their ordinary size with astonishment, while his throat moved vigorously in the act of swallowing. Then a smile and look of intense delight overspread his face, except, indeed, the mouth, which, being firmly fixed to the hole in the nut, could not take part in the expression; but he endeavoured to make up for this by winking at us excessively with his right eye. At length he stopped, and, drawing a long breath, exclaimed—

"Nectar! perfect nectar! I say, Jack, you're a Briton— the best fellow I ever met in my life.—Only taste that!" said he, turning to me and holding the nut to my mouth. I immediately drank, and certainly I was much surprised at the delightful liquid that flowed copiously down my throat. It was extremely cool, and had a sweet taste, mingled with acid; in fact it was the likest thing to lemonade I ever tasted, and was most grateful and refreshing. I handed the nut to Jack, who, after tasting it, said, "Now, Peterkin, you unbeliever, I never saw or tasted a cocoa-nut in my life before, except those sold in shops at home; but I once read that the green nuts contain that stuff, and you see it is true!"

"And pray," asked Peterkin, "what sort of 'stuff' does the ripe nut contain?"

"A hollow kernel," answered Jack, "with a liquid like milk in it; but it does not satisfy thirst so well as hunger. It is very wholesome food, I believe."

"Meat and drink on the same tree!" cried Peterkin; "washing in the sea, lodging on the ground—and all for nothing. My dear boys, we're set up for life; it must

be the ancient Paradise—hurrah!" and Peterkin tossed
his straw hat in the air, and ran along the beach hallooing like a madman with delight.

We afterwards found, however, that these lovely islands
were very unlike Paradise in many things. But more of
this in its proper place.

We had now come to the point of rocks on which
the ship had struck, but did not find a single article,
although we searched carefully among the coral rocks,
which at this place jutted out so far as nearly to join
the reef that encircled the island. Just as we were
about to return, however, we saw something black
floating in a little cove that had escaped our observation. Running forward, we drew it from the water, and
found it to be a long, thick, leather boot, such as fisher-
men at home wear; and a few paces farther on we picked
up its fellow. We at once recognised these as having
belonged to our captain, for he had worn them during
the whole of the storm, in order to guard his legs from
the waves and spray that constantly washed over our
decks. My first thought on seeing them was that our
dear captain had been drowned; but Jack soon put my
mind more at rest on that point, by saying that if the
captain had been drowned with the boots on, he would
certainly have been washed ashore along with them, and
that he had no doubt whatever he had kicked them off
while in the sea, that he might swim more easily.

Peterkin immediately put them on, but they were so
large that, as Jack said, they would have done for boots,
trousers, and vest too. I also tried them, but although
I was long enough in the legs for them, they were much
too large in the feet for me: so we handed them to Jack,

who was anxious to make me keep them; but as they
fitted his large limbs and feet as if they had been made
for him, I would not hear of it, so he consented at last
to use them. I may remark, however, that Jack did not
use them often, as they were extremely heavy.

It was beginning to grow dark when we returned to
our encampment; so we put off our visit to the top of
a hill till next day, and employed the light that yet
remained to us in cutting down a quantity of boughs
and the broad leaves of a tree of which none of us knew
the name. With these we erected a sort of rustic bower,
in which we meant to pass the night. There was no
absolute necessity for this, because the air of our island
was so genial and balmy that we could have slept quite
well without any shelter; but we were so little used to
sleeping in the open air that we did not quite relish
the idea of lying down without any covering over us;
besides, our bower would shelter us from the night-dews
or rain, if any should happen to fall. Having strewed
the floor with leaves and dry grass, we bethought ourselves of supper.

But it now occurred to us, for the first time, that we
had no means of making a fire.

"Now, there's a fix!" What shall we do?" said
Peterkin, while we both turned our eyes to Jack, to
whom we always looked in our difficulties. Jack seemed
not a little perplexed.

"There are flints enough, no doubt, on the beach,"
said he, "but they are of no use at all without a steel.
However, we must try." So saying, he went to the
beach, and soon returned with two flints. On one of
these he placed the tinder, and endeavoured to ignite

it; but it was with great difficulty that a very small
spark was struck out of the flints, and the tinder, being
a bad, hard piece, would not catch. He then tried the
bit of hoop-iron, which would not strike fire at all; and
after that the back of the axe, with no better success.
During all these trials Peterkin sat with his hands in
his pockets, gazing with a most melancholy visage at
our comrade, his face growing longer and more miserable
at each successive failure.

"Oh dear!" he sighed; "I would not care a button
for the cooking of our victuals—perhaps they don't need
it—but it's so dismal to eat one's supper in the dark;
and we have had such a capital day that it's a pity to
finish off in this glum style. Oh, I have it!" he cried,
starting up; "the spy-glass—the big glass at the end is
a burning-glass!"

"You forget that we have no sun," said I.

Peterkin was silent. In his sudden recollection of the
telescope he had quite overlooked the absence of the sun.

"Ah, boys, I've got it now!" exclaimed Jack, rising
and cutting a branch from a neighbouring bush, which
he stripped of its leaves. "I recollect seeing this done
once at home. Hand me the bit of whip-cord." With
the cord and branch Jack soon formed a bow. Then he
cut a piece, about three inches long, off the end of a
dead branch, which he pointed at the two ends. Round
this he passed the cord of the bow, and placed one end
against his chest, which was protected from its point by
a chip of wood; the other point he placed against the
bit of tinder, and then began to saw vigorously with the
bow, just as a blacksmith does with his drill while boring
a hole in a piece of iron. In a few seconds the tinder

began to smoke; in less than a minute it caught fire; and in less than a quarter of an hour we were drinking our lemonade and eating cocoa-nuts round a fire that would have roasted an entire sheep, while the smoke, flames, and sparks flew up among the broad leaves of the overhanging palm trees, and cast a warm glow upon our leafy bower.

That night the starry sky looked down through the gently rustling trees upon our slumbers, and the distant roaring of the surf upon the coral reef was our lullaby.

CHAPTER V

Morning, and cogitations connected therewith—We luxuriate in
the sea, try our diving powers, and make enchanting excursions among the coral groves at the bottom of the ocean—The
wonders of the deep enlarged upon.

WHAT a joyful thing it is to awaken, on a fresh
glorious morning, and find the rising sun staring
into your face with dazzling brilliancy! to see the birds
twittering in the bushes, and to hear the murmuring of a
rill, or the soft hissing ripples as they fall upon the sea-
shore! At any time and in any place such sights and
sounds are most charming, but more especially are they
so when one awakens to them, for the first time, in a
novel and romantic situation, with the soft sweet air of a
tropical climate mingling with the fresh smell of the sea,
and stirring the strange leaves that flutter overhead and
around one, or ruffling the plumage of the stranger birds
that fly inquiringly around, as if to demand what business we have to intrude uninvited on their domains.
When I awoke on the morning after the shipwreck, I
found myself in this most delightful condition; and as
I lay on my back upon my bed of leaves, gazing up
through the branches of the cocoa-nut trees into the clear
blue sky, and watched the few fleecy clouds that passed
slowly across it, my heart expanded more and more with
an exulting gladness, the like of which I had never felt
before. While I meditated, my thoughts again turned

to the great and kind Creator of this beautiful world, as
they had done on the previous day, when I first beheld
the sea and the coral reef, with the mighty waves dashing
over it into the calm waters of the lagoon.

While thus meditating, I naturally bethought me of
my Bible, for I had faithfully kept the promise, which
I gave at parting to my beloved mother, that I would
read it every morning; and it was with a feeling of
dismay that I remembered I had left it in the ship. I
was much troubled about this. However, I consoled
myself with reflecting that I could keep the second part
of my promise to her—namely, that I should never omit
to say my prayers. So I rose quietly, lest I should disturb my companions, who were still asleep, and stepped
aside into the bushes for this purpose.

On my return I found them still slumbering, so I
again lay down to think over our situation. Just at
that moment I was attracted by the sight of a very
small parrot, which Jack afterwards told me was called
a paroquet. It was seated on a twig that overhung
Peterkin's head, and I was speedily lost in admiration of
its bright green plumage, which was mingled with other
gay colours. While I looked I observed that the bird
turned its head slowly from side to side and looked downwards, first with the one eye and then with the other.
On glancing downwards I observed that Peterkin's mouth
was wide open, and that this remarkable bird was looking
into it. Peterkin used to say that I had not an atom of
fun in my composition, and that I never could understand
a joke. In regard to the latter, perhaps he was right;
yet I think that, when they were explained to me, I
understood jokes as well as most people. But in regard

to the former, he must certainly have been wrong, for
this bird seemed to me to be extremely funny; and I
could not help thinking that, if it should happen to
faint, or slip its foot, and fall off the twig into Peterkin's
mouth, he would perhaps think it funny too! Suddenly
the paroquet bent down its head and uttered a loud
scream in his face. This awoke him, and, with a cry of
surprise, he started up, while the foolish bird flew precipitately away.

"Oh, you monster!" cried Peterkin, shaking his fist at
the bird. Then he yawned, and rubbed his eyes, and
asked what o'clock it was.

I smiled at this question, and answered that, as our
watches were at the bottom of the sea, I could not tell,
but it was a little past sunrise.

Peterkin now began to remember where we were. As
he looked up into the bright sky, and snuffed the scented
air, his eyes glistened with delight, and he uttered a faint
"Hurrah!" and yawned again. Then he gazed slowly
round, till, observing the calm sea through an opening in
the bushes, he started suddenly up as if he had received
an electric shock, uttered a vehement shout, flung off his
garments, and, rushing over the white sands, plunged
into the water. The cry awoke Jack, who rose on his
elbow with a look of grave surprise; but this was followed
by a quiet smile of intelligence on seeing Peterkin in the
water. With an energy that he only gave way to in
moments of excitement, Jack bounded to his feet, threw
off his clothes, shook back his hair, and, with a lion-like
spring, dashed over the sands and plunged into the sea
with such force as quite to envelop Peterkin in a shower
of spray. Jack was a remarkably good swimmer and

diver, so that after his plunge we saw no sign of him for nearly a minute; after which he suddenly emerged, with a cry of joy, a good many yards out from the shore. My spirits were so much raised by seeing all this that I, too, hastily threw off my garments and endeavoured to imitate Jack's vigorous bound; but I was so awkward that my foot caught on a stump, and I fell to the ground; then I slipped on a stone while running over the sand, and nearly fell again, much to the amusement of Peterkin, who laughed heartily, and called me a "slow coach," while Jack cried out, "Come along, Ralph, and I'll help you." However, when I got into the water, I managed very well, for I was really a good swimmer and diver too. I could not, indeed, equal Jack, who was superior to any Englishman I ever saw; but I infinitely surpassed Peterkin, who could only swim a little, and could not dive at all.

While Peterkin enjoyed himself in the shallow water and in running along the beach, Jack and I swam out into the deep water, and occasionally dived for stones. I shall never forget my surprise and delight on first beholding the bottom of the sea. As I have before stated, the water within the reef was as calm as a pond; and, as there was no wind, it was quite clear from the surface to the bottom, so that we could see down easily even at a depth of twenty or thirty yards. When Jack and I dived into shallower water, we expected to have found sand and stones, instead of which we found ourselves in what appeared really to be an enchanted garden. The whole of the bottom of the lagoon, as we called the calm water within the reef, was covered with coral of every shape, size, and hue. Some portions were formed like large mushrooms; others appeared like the brain of a man, having stalks or necks

attached to them; but the most common kind was a
species of branching coral, and some portions were of a
lovely pale pink colour, others were pure white. Among
this there grew large quantities of seaweed of the richest
hues imaginable, and of the most graceful forms; while
innumerable fishes—blue, red, yellow, green, and striped
—sported in and out amongst the flower-beds of this
submarine garden, and did not appear to be at all afraid
of our approaching them.

On darting to the surface for breath, after our first
dive, Jack and I rose close to each other.

"Did you ever in your life, Ralph, see anything so
lovely?" said Jack, as he flung the spray from his hair.

"Never," I replied. "It appears to me like fairy
realms. I can scarcely believe that we are not dreaming."

"Dreaming!" cried Jack; "do you know, Ralph, I'm
half tempted to think that we really are dreaming. But
if so, I am resolved to make the most of it, and dream
another dive; so here goes—down again, my boy!"

We took the second dive together, and kept beside
each other while under water; and I was greatly surprised to find that we could keep down much longer than
I ever recollect having done in our own seas at home. I
believe that this was owing to the heat of the water,
which was so warm that we afterwards found we could
remain in it for two and three hours at a time without
feeling any unpleasant effects such as we used to experience in the sea at home. When Jack reached the
bottom, he grasped the coral stems, and crept along on
his hands and knees, peeping under the seaweed and
among the rocks. I observed him also pick up one or
two large oysters and retain them in his grasp, as if he

meant to take them up with him, so I also gathered a few. Suddenly he made a grasp at a fish with blue and yellow stripes on its back, and actually touched its tail, but did not catch it. At this he turned towards me and attempted to smile; but no sooner had he done so than he sprang like an arrow to the surface, where, on following him, I found him gasping and coughing, and spitting water from his mouth. In a few minutes he recovered, and we both turned to swim ashore.

"I declare, Ralph," said he, "that I actually tried to laugh under water."

"So I saw," I replied; "and I observed that you very nearly caught that fish by the tail. It would have done capitally for breakfast if you had."

"Breakfast enough here," said he, holding up the oysters, as we landed and ran up the beach. "Hallo, Peterkin! here you are, boy. Split open these fellows while Ralph and I put on our clothes. They'll agree with the cocoa-nuts excellently, I have no doubt."

Peterkin, who was already dressed, took the oysters, and opened them with the edge of our axe, exclaiming, "Now, that *is* capital. There's nothing I'm so fond of."

"Ah! that's lucky," remarked Jack. "I'll be able to keep you in good order now, Master Peterkin. You know you can't dive any better than a cat. So, sir, whenever you behave ill, you shall have no oysters for breakfast."

"I'm very glad that our prospect of breakfast is so good," said I, "for I'm very hungry."

"Here, then, stop your mouth with that, Ralph," said Peterkin, holding a large oyster to my lips. I opened my mouth and swallowed it in silence, and really it was remarkably good.

We now set ourselves earnestly about our preparations for spending the day. We had no difficulty with the fire this morning, as our burning-glass was an admirable one; and while we roasted a few oysters and ate our cocoa-nuts, we held a long, animated conversation about our plans for the future. What those plans were, and how we carried them into effect, the reader shall see hereafter.

CHAPTER VI

An excursion into the interior, in which we make many valuable and interesting discoveries—We get a dreadful fright—The bread-fruit tree—Wonderful peculiarity of some of the fruit-trees—Signs of former inhabitants.

OUR first care, after breakfast, was to place the few articles we possessed in the crevice of a rock at the farther end of a small cave which we discovered near our encampment. This cave, we hoped, might be useful to us afterwards as a storehouse. Then we cut two large clubs off a species of very hard tree which grew near at hand. One of these was given to Peterkin, the other to me, and Jack armed himself with the axe. We took these precautions because we purposed to make an excursion to the top of the mountains of the interior, in order to obtain a better view of our island. Of course we knew not what dangers might befall us by the way, so thought it best to be prepared.

Having completed our arrangements and carefully extinguished our fire, we sallied forth and walked a short distance along the sea-beach, till we came to the entrance of a valley, through which flowed the rivulet before mentioned. Here we turned our backs on the sea and struck into the interior.

The prospect that burst upon our view on entering the valley was truly splendid. On either side of us there was a gentle rise in the land, which thus formed two ridges about a mile apart on each side of the valley. These ridges—which, as well as the low grounds between them, were covered with trees and shrubs of the most luxuriant kind—continued to recede inland for about two miles, when they joined the foot of a small mountain. This hill rose rather abruptly from the head of the valley, and was likewise entirely covered even to the top with trees, except on one particular spot near the left shoulder, where was a bare and rocky place of a broken and savage character. Beyond this hill we could not see, and we therefore directed our course up the banks of the rivulet towards the foot of it, intending to climb to the top, should that be possible, as, indeed, we had no doubt it was.

Jack being the wisest and boldest among us, took the lead, carrying the axe on his shoulder. Peterkin, with his enormous club, came second, as he said he should like to be in a position to defend me if any danger should threaten. I brought up the rear, but, having been more taken up with the wonderful and curious things I saw at starting than with thoughts of possible danger, I had very foolishly left my club behind me. Although, as I have said, the trees and bushes were very luxuriant, they were not so thickly crowded together as to hinder our progress among them. We were able to wind in and out, and to follow the banks of the stream quite easily, although, it is true, the height and thickness of the foliage prevented us from seeing far ahead. But sometimes a jutting-out rock on the hillsides afforded us a position whence we could enjoy the romantic view and mark our progress towards the foot of the hill. I was particularly struck, during the walk, with the richness of the undergrowth in most places, and recognised many berries and plants that resembled those of my native land, especially a tall, elegantly formed fern, which emitted an agreeable perfume. There were several kinds of flowers, too, but I did not see so many of these as I should have expected in such a climate. We also saw a great variety of small birds of bright plumage, and many paroquets similar to the one that awoke Peterkin so rudely in the morning.

Thus we advanced to the foot of the hill without encountering anything to alarm us, except, indeed, once, when we were passing close under a part of the hill which was hidden from our view by the broad leaves of the banana trees, which grew in great luxuriance in that part. Jack was just preparing to force his way through this thicket, when we were startled and arrested by a strange pattering or rumbling sound which appeared to us quite different from any of the sounds we had heard during the previous part of our walk.

"Hallo!" cried Peterkin, stopping short and grasping his club with both hands, "what's that?"

Neither of us replied; but Jack seized his axe in his right hand, while with the other he pushed aside the broad leaves and endeavoured to peer amongst them.

"I can see nothing," he said, after a short pause. "I think it——"

Again the rumbling sound came, louder than before, and we all sprang back and stood on the defensive. For myself, having forgotten my club, and not having taken the precaution to cut another, I buttoned my jacket, doubled my fists, and threw myself into a boxing attitude. I must say, however, that I felt somewhat uneasy; and my companions afterwards confessed that their thoughts at this moment had been instantly filled with all they had ever heard or read of wild beasts and savages, torturings at the stake, roastings alive, and such like horrible things. Suddenly the pattering noise increased with tenfold violence. It was followed by a fearful crash among the bushes, which was rapidly repeated, as if some gigantic animal were bounding towards us. In another moment an enormous rock came crashing through the shrubbery, followed by a cloud of dust and small stones, and flew close past the spot where we stood, carrying bushes and young trees along with it.

"Pooh! is that all?" exclaimed Peterkin, wiping the perspiration off his forehead. "Why, I thought it was all the wild men and beasts in the South Sea Islands galloping on in one grand charge to sweep us off the face of the earth, instead of a mere stone tumbling down the mountain-side."

"Nevertheless," remarked Jack, "if that same stone had hit any of us, it would have rendered the charge you speak of quite unnecessary, Peterkin."

This was true, and I felt very thankful for our escape. On examining the spot more narrowly, we found that it lay close to the foot of a very rugged precipice, from which stones of various sizes were always tumbling at intervals. Indeed, the numerous fragments lying scattered all around might have suggested the cause of the sound, had we not been too suddenly alarmed to think of anything.

We now resumed our journey, resolving that, in our future excursions into the interior, we would be careful to avoid this dangerous precipice.

Soon afterwards we arrived at the foot of the hill and prepared to ascend it. Here Jack made a discovery which caused us all very great joy. This was a tree of a remarkably beautiful appearance, which Jack confidently declared to be the celebrated bread-fruit tree.*

"Is it celebrated?" inquired Peterkin, with a look of great simplicity.

"It is," replied Jack.

"That's odd, now," rejoined Peterkin; "I never heard of it before."

"Then it's not so celebrated as I thought it was," returned Jack, quietly squeezing Peterkin's hat over his eyes; "but listen, you ignorant booby! and hear of it now."

Peterkin readjusted his hat, and was soon listening with as much interest as myself, while Jack told us that this tree is one of the most valuable in the islands of the south; that it bears two, sometimes three, crops of fruit in the year; that the fruit is very like wheaten bread in appearance, and that it constitutes the principal food of many of the islanders.

"So," said Peterkin, "we seem to have everything ready prepared to our hands in this wonderful island—lemonade ready bottled in nuts, and loaf-bread growing on the trees!"

Peterkin, as usual, was jesting; nevertheless, it is a curious fact that he spoke almost the literal truth.

"Moreover," continued Jack, "the bread-fruit tree affords a capital gum, which serves the natives for pitching their canoes; the bark of the young branches is made by them into cloth; and of the wood, which is durable and of a good colour, they build their houses. So you see, lads, that we have no lack of material here to make us comfortable, if we are only clever enough to use it."

"But are you sure that that's it?" asked Peterkin.

"Quite sure," replied Jack; "for I was particularly interested in the account I once read of it, and I remember the description well. I am sorry, however, that I have forgotten the descriptions of many other trees which I am sure we have seen to-day, if we could but recognise them. So you see, Peterkin, I'm not up to everything yet."

"Never mind, Jack," said Peterkin, with a grave, patronising expression of countenance, patting his tall companion on the shoulder—"never mind, Jack; you know a good deal for your age. You're a clever boy, sir —a promising young man; and if you only go on as you have begun, sir, you will——"

The end of this speech was suddenly cut short by Jack tripping up Peterkin's heels and tumbling him into a mass of thick shrubs, where, finding himself comfortable, he lay still, basking in the sunshine, while Jack and I examined the bread-fruit tree.

We were much struck with the deep, rich green colour of its broad leaves, which were twelve or eighteen inches long, deeply indented, and of a glossy smoothness, like the laurel. The fruit, with which it was loaded, was nearly round, and appeared to be about six inches in diameter, with a rough rind, marked with lozenge-shaped divisions. It was of various colours, from light pea-green to brown and rich yellow. Jack said that the yellow was the ripe fruit. We afterwards found that most of the fruit-trees on the island were evergreens, and that we might, when we wished, pluck the blossom and the ripe fruit from the same tree. Such a wonderful difference from the trees of our own country surprised us not a little. The bark of the tree was rough and light-coloured; the trunk was about two feet in diameter, and it appeared to be twenty feet high, being quite destitute of branches up to that height, where it branched off into a beautiful and umbrageous head. We noticed that the fruit hung in clusters of twos and threes on the branches; but as we were anxious to get to the top of the hill, we refrained from attempting to pluck any at that time.

Our hearts were now very much cheered by our good fortune, and it was with light and active steps that we clambered up the steep sides of the hill. On reaching the summit, a new and, if possible, a grander prospect, met our gaze. We found that this was not the highest part of the island, but that another hill lay beyond, with a wide valley between it and the one on which we stood. This valley, like the first, was also full of rich trees, some dark and some light green, some heavy and thick in foliage, and others light, feathery, and graceful, while the beautiful blossoms on many of them threw a sort of rainbow tint over all, and gave to the valley the appearance of a garden of flowers. Among these we recognised many of the bread-fruit trees, laden with yellow fruit, and also a great many cocoa-nut palms. After gazing our fill, we pushed down the hillside, crossed the valley, and soon began to ascend the second mountain. It was clothed with trees nearly to the top, but the summit was bare, and in some places broken.

While on our way up we came to an object which filled us with much interest. This was the stump of a tree that had evidently been cut down with an axe!

So, then, we were not the first who had viewed this
beautiful isle. The hand of man had been at work
there before us. It now began to recur to us again that
perhaps the island was inhabited, although we had not
seen any traces of man until now; but a second glance
at the stump convinced us that we had not more reason
to think so now than formerly; for the surface of the
wood was quite decayed, and partly covered with fungus
and green matter, so that it must have been cut many
years ago.

"Perhaps," said Peterkin, "some ship or other has
touched here long ago for wood, and only taken one tree."

We did not think this likely, however, because, in such
circumstances, the crew of a ship would cut wood of small
size, and near the shore, whereas this was a large tree
and stood near the top of the mountain. In fact, it was
the highest large tree on the mountain, all above it being
wood of very recent growth.

"I can't understand it," said Jack, scratching the surface of the stump with his axe. "I can only suppose
that the savages have been here and cut it for some purpose known only to themselves. But, hallo! what have
we here?"

As he spoke, Jack began carefully to scrape away the
moss and fungus from the stump, and soon laid bare
three distinct traces of marks, as if some inscription or
initials had been cut thereon. But although the traces
were distinct, beyond all doubt, the exact form of the
letters could not be made out. Jack thought they looked
like J. S., but we could not be certain. They had apparently been carelessly cut, and long exposure to the
weather had so broken them up that we could not make

out what they were. We were exceedingly perplexed at
this discovery, and stayed a long time at the place conjecturing what these marks could have been, but without
avail; so, as the day was advancing, we left it and quickly
reached the top of the mountain.

We found this to be the highest point of the island,
and from it we saw our kingdom lying, as it were, like a
map around us. As I have always thought it impossible
to get a thing properly into one's understanding without
comprehending it, I shall beg the reader's patience for
a little while I describe our island, thus, shortly :—

It consisted of two mountains : the one we guessed
at 500 feet; the other, on which we stood, at 1000.
Between these lay a rich, beautiful valley, as already
said. This valley crossed the island from one end to
the other, being high in the middle and sloping on each
side towards the sea. The large mountain sloped, on the
side farthest from where we had been wrecked, gradually
towards the sea; but although, when viewed at a glance,
it had thus a regular sloping appearance, a more careful
observation showed that it was broken up into a multitude of very small vales, or rather dells and glens, intermingled with little rugged spots and small but abrupt
precipices here and there, with rivulets tumbling over
their edges and wandering down the slopes in little white
streams, sometimes glistening among the broad leaves
of the bread-fruit and cocoa-nut trees, or hiding altogether beneath the rich underwood. At the base of this
mountain lay a narrow bright green plain or meadow,
which terminated abruptly at the shore. On the other
side of the island, whence we had come, stood the smaller
hill, at the foot of which diverged three valleys; one

being that which we had ascended, with a smaller vale
on each side of it, and separated from it by the two
ridges before mentioned. In these smaller valleys there
were no streams, but they were clothed with the same
luxuriant vegetation.

The diameter of the island seemed to be about ten
miles, and as it was almost circular in form, its circum-
ference must have been thirty miles—perhaps a little
more, if allowance be made for the numerous bays and
indentations of the shore. The entire island was belted
by a beach of pure white sand, on which laved the gentle
ripples of the lagoon. We now also observed that the
coral reef completely encircled the island; but it varied
its distance from it here and there, in some places being
a mile from the beach, in others a few hundred yards, but
the average distance was half a mile. The reef lay very
low, and the spray of the surf broke quite over it in
many places. This surf never ceased its roar, for however calm the weather might be, there is always a gentle
swaying motion in the great Pacific, which, although
scarce noticeable out at sea, reaches the shore at last in
a huge billow. The water within the lagoon, as before
said, was perfectly still. There were three narrow openings in the reef: one opposite each end of the valley
which I have described as crossing the island; the other
opposite our own valley, which we afterwards named the
Valley of the Wreck. At each of these openings the
reef rose into two small green islets, covered with bushes
and having one or two cocoa-nut palms on each. These
islets were very singular, and appeared as if planted
expressly for the purpose of marking the channel into
the lagoon. Our captain was making for one of these

openings the day we were wrecked, and would have reached it too, I doubt not, had not the rudder been torn away. Within the lagoon were several pretty, low coral islands, just opposite our encampment; and immediately beyond these, out at sea, lay about a dozen other islands, at various distances, from half a mile to ten miles;—all of them, as far as we could discern, smaller than ours and apparently uninhabited. They seemed to be low coral islands, raised but little above the sea, yet covered with cocoa-nut trees.

All this we noted and a great deal more, while we sat on the top of the mountain. After we had satisfied ourselves we prepared to return; but here again we discovered traces of the presence of man. These were a pole or staff and one or two pieces of wood which had been squared with an axe. All of these were, however, very much decayed, and they had evidently not been touched for many years.

Full of these discoveries we returned to our encampment. On the way we fell in with the traces of some four-footed animal, but whether old or of recent date none of us were able to guess. This also tended to raise our hopes of obtaining some animal food on the island, so we reached home in good spirits, quite prepared for supper, and highly satisfied with our excursion.

After much discussion, in which Peterkin took the lead, we came to the conclusion that the island was uninhabited, and went to bed.

CHAPTER VII

Jack's ingenuity—We get into difficulties about fishing, and get out of them by a method which gives us a cold bath—Horrible encounter with a shark.

FOR several days after the excursion related in the last chapter we did not wander far from our encampment, but gave ourselves up to forming plans for the future and making our present abode comfortable.

There were various causes that induced this state of comparative inaction. In the first place, although everything around us was so delightful, and we could without difficulty obtain all that we required for our bodily comfort, we did not quite like the idea of settling down here for the rest of our lives, far away from our friends and our native land. To set energetically about preparations for a permanent residence seemed so like making up our minds to saying adieu to home and friends for ever, that we tacitly shrank from it, and put off our preparations, for one reason and another, as long as we could. Then there was a little uncertainty still as to there being natives on the island, and we entertained a kind of faint hope that a ship might come and take us off. But as day after day passed, and neither savages nor ships appeared, we gave up all hope of an early deliverance, and set diligently to work at our homestead.

During this time, however, we had not been altogether idle. We made several experiments in cooking the cocoa-nut, most of which did not improve it. Then we removed our goods, and took up our abode in the cave, but found the change so bad that we returned gladly to the bower. Besides this, we bathed very frequently, and talked a great deal: at least Jack and Peterkin did—I listened. Among other useful things, Jack, who was ever the most active and diligent, converted about three inches of the hoop-iron into an excellent knife. First he beat it quite flat with the axe. Then he made a rude handle, and tied the hoop-iron to it with our piece of whipcord, and ground it to an edge on a piece of sandstone. When it was finished, he used it to shape a better handle, to which he fixed it with a strip of his cotton handkerchief —in which operation he had, as Peterkin pointed out, torn off one of Lord Nelson's noses. However, the whipcord, thus set free, was used by Peterkin as a fishing-line. He merely tied a piece of oyster to the end of it. This the fish were allowed to swallow, and then they were pulled quickly ashore. But as the line was very short and we had no boat, the fish we caught were exceedingly small.

One day Peterkin came up from the beach, where he had been angling, and said in a very cross tone, " I'll tell you what, Jack, I'm not going to be humbugged with catching such contemptible things any longer. I want you to swim out with me on your back, and let me fish in deep water ! "

" Dear me, Peterkin ! " replied Jack, " I had no idea you were taking the thing so much to heart, else I would have got you out of that difficulty long ago. Let me see "—and Jack looked down at a piece of timber on which he had been labouring, with a peculiar gaze of abstraction, which he always assumed when trying to invent or discover anything.

"What say you to building a boat?" he inquired, looking up hastily.

"Take far too long," was the reply; "can't be bothered waiting. I want to begin at once!"

Again Jack considered. "I have it!" he cried. "We'll fell a large tree and launch the trunk of it in the water, so that when you want to fish you've nothing to do but to swim out to it."

"Would not a small raft do better?" said I.

"Much better; but we have no ropes to bind it together with. Perhaps we may find something hereafter that will do as well, but in the meantime let us try the tree."

This was agreed on, so we started off to a spot not far distant, where we knew of a tree that would suit us, which grew near the water's edge. As soon as we reached it Jack threw off his coat, and, wielding the axe with his sturdy arms, hacked and hewed at it for a quarter of an hour without stopping. Then he paused, and while he sat down to rest I continued the work. Then Peterkin made a vigorous attack on it, so that when Jack renewed his powerful blows, a few minutes' cutting brought it down with a terrible crash.

"Hurrah! now for it," cried Jack; "let us off with its head."

So saying he began to cut through the stem again, at about six yards from the thick end. This done, he cut three strong, short poles or levers from the stout branches, with which to roll the log down the beach into the sea; for, as it was nearly two feet thick at the large end, we could not move it without such helps. With the levers, however, we rolled it slowly into the sea.

Having been thus successful in launching our vessel, we next shaped the levers into rude oars or paddles, and then attempted to embark. This was easy enough to do; but after seating ourselves astride the log, it was with the utmost difficulty we kept it from rolling round and plunging us into the water. Not that we minded that much; but we preferred, if possible, to fish in dry clothes. To be sure, our trousers were necessarily wet, as our legs were dangling in the water on each side of the log; but as they could be easily dried, we did not care. After half-an-hour's practice, we became expert enough to keep our balance pretty steadily. Then Peterkin laid down his paddle, and having baited his line with a whole oyster, dropped it into deep water.

"Now then, Jack," said he, "be cautious; steer clear o' that seaweed. There! that's it; gently now, gently. I see a fellow at least a foot long down there, coming to —ha! that's it! Oh bother! he's off."

"Did he bite?" said Jack, urging the log onwards a little with his paddle.

"Bite? ay! He took it into his mouth, but the moment I began to haul he opened his jaws and let it out again."

"Let him swallow it next time," said Jack, laughing at the melancholy expression of Peterkin's visage.

"There he's again," cried Peterkin, his eyes flashing with excitement. "Look out! Now then! No! Yes! No! Why the brute *won't* swallow it!"

"Try to haul him up by the mouth, then," cried Jack. "Do it gently."

A heavy sigh and a look of blank despair showed that poor Peterkin had tried and failed again.

"Never mind, lad," said Jack, in a voice of sympathy, "we'll move on, and offer it to some other fish." So saying, Jack plied his paddle; but scarcely had he moved from the spot, when a fish with an enormous head and a little body darted from under a rock and swallowed the bait at once.

"Got him this time—that's a fact!" cried Peterkin, hauling in the line. "He's swallowed the bait right down to his tail, I declare. Oh, what a thumper!"

As the fish came struggling to the surface, we leaned forward to see it, and overbalanced the log. Peterkin threw his arms round the fish's neck, and in another instant we were all floundering in the water.

A shout of laughter burst from us as we rose to the surface like three drowned rats, and seized hold of the log. We soon recovered our position, and sat more warily, while Peterkin secured the fish, which had well-nigh escaped in the midst of our struggles. It was little worth having, however; but, as Peterkin remarked, it was better than the smouts he had been catching for the last two or three days; so we laid it on the log before us, and having re-baited the line, dropped it in again for another.

Now, while we were thus intent upon our sport, our attention was suddenly attracted by a ripple on the sea, just a few yards away from us. Peterkin shouted to us to paddle in that direction, as he thought it was a big fish, and we might have a chance of catching it. But Jack, instead of complying, said, in a deep, earnest tone of voice, which I never before heard him use—

"Haul up your line, Peterkin; seize your paddle; quick—it's a shark!"

The horror with which we heard this may well be imagined, for it must be remembered that our legs were hanging down in the water, and we could not venture to pull them up without upsetting the log. Peterkin instantly hauled up the line, and grasping his paddle, exerted himself to the utmost, while we also did our best to make for shore. But we were a good way off, and the log being, as I have before said, very heavy, moved but slowly through the water. We now saw the shark quite distinctly swimming round and round us, its sharp fin every now and then protruding above the water. From its active and unsteady motions, Jack knew it was making up its mind to attack us, so he urged us vehemently to paddle for our lives, while he himself set us the example. Suddenly he shouted, "Look out! there he comes!" and in a second we saw the monstrous fish dive close under us, and turn half over on his side. But we all made a great commotion with our paddles, which no doubt frightened it away for that time, as we saw it immediately after circling round us as before.

"Throw the fish to him," cried Jack, in a quick, suppressed voice; "we'll make the shore in time yet if we can keep him off for a few minutes."

Peterkin stopped one instant to obey the command, and then plied his paddle again with all his might. No sooner had the fish fallen on the water than we observed the shark to sink. In another second we saw its white breast rising; for sharks always turn over on their sides when about to seize their prey, their mouths being not at the point of their heads like those of other fish, but, as it

were, under their chins. In another moment his snout
rose above the water; his wide jaws, armed with a terrific
double row of teeth, appeared. The dead fish was en-
gulfed, and the shark sank out of sight. But Jack was
mistaken in supposing that it would be satisfied. In a
very few minutes it returned to us, and its quick motions
led us to fear that it would attack us at once.

Stop paddling," cried Jack suddenly. "I see it
coming up behind us. Now, obey my orders *quickly*.
Our lives may depend on it. Ralph, Peterkin, do your
best to *balance the log*. Don't look out for the shark.
Don't glance behind you. Do nothing but balance the
log."

Peterkin and I instantly did as we were ordered, being
only too glad to do anything that afforded us a chance or
a hope of escape, for we had implicit confidence in Jack's
courage and wisdom. For a few seconds, that seemed
long minutes to my mind, we sat thus silently; but I
could not resist glancing backward, despite the orders to
the contrary. On doing so, I saw Jack sitting rigid like
a statue, with his paddle raised, his lips compressed, and
his eyebrows bent over his eyes, which glared savagely
from beneath them down into the water. I also saw the
shark, to my horror, quite close under the log, in the act
of darting towards Jack's foot. I could scarce suppress
a cry on beholding this. In another moment the shark
rose. Jack drew his leg suddenly from the water, and
threw it over the log. The monster's snout rubbed
against the log as it passed, and revealed its hideous jaws,
into which Jack instantly plunged the paddle, and thrust
it down its throat. So violent was this act that Jack
rose to his feet in performing it; the log was thereby

rolled completely over, and we were once more plunged into the water. We all rose, spluttering and gasping, in a moment.

"Now, then, strike out for shore," cried Jack. "Here, Peterkin, catch hold of my collar, and kick out with a will."

Peterkin did as he was desired, and Jack struck out with such force that he cut through the water like a boat; while I, being free from all encumbrance, succeeded in keeping up with him. As we had by this time drawn pretty near to the shore, a few minutes more sufficed to carry us into shallow water; and, finally, we landed in safety, though very much exhausted, and not a little frightened by our terrible adventure.

CHAPTER VIII

The beauties of the bottom of the sea tempt Peterkin to dive—How he did it—More difficulties overcome—The Water Garden—Curious creatures of the sea—The tank—Candles missed very much, and the candle-nut tree discovered—Wonderful account of Peterkin's first voyage—Cloth found growing on a tree—A plan projected, and arms prepared for offence and defence—A dreadful cry.

OUR encounter with the shark was the first great danger that had befallen us since landing on this island, and we felt very seriously affected by it, especially when we considered that we had so often unwittingly incurred the same danger before while bathing. We were now forced to take to fishing again in the shallow water, until we should succeed in constructing a raft. What troubled us most, however, was, that we were compelled to forego our morning swimming excursions. We did, indeed, continue to enjoy our bathe in the shallow water, but Jack and I found that one great source of our enjoyment was gone, when we could no longer dive down among the beautiful coral groves at the bottom of the lagoon. We had come to be so fond of this exercise, and to take such an interest in watching the formations of coral and the gambols of the many beautiful fish amongst the forest of red and green seaweeds, that we had become quite familiar with the appearance of the fish and the localities that they chiefly haunted. We had also become expert divers. But we made it a rule never to stay long under water at a time.

Jack told me that to do so often was bad for the lungs, and, instead of affording us enjoyment, would ere long do us a serious injury. So we never stayed at the bottom as long as we might have done, but came up frequently to the top for fresh air, and dived down again immediately. Sometimes, when Jack happened to be in a humorous frame, he would seat himself at the bottom of the sea on one of the brain-corals, as if he were seated on a large paddock-stool,* and then make faces at me, in order, if possible, to make me laugh under water. At first, when he took me unawares, he nearly succeeded, and I had to shoot to the surface in order to laugh; but afterwards I became aware of his intentions, and being naturally of a grave disposition, I had no difficulty in restraining myself. I used often to wonder how poor Peterkin would have liked to be with us; and he sometimes expressed much regret at being unable to join us. I used to do my best to gratify him, poor fellow, by relating all the wonders that we saw; but this, instead of satisfying, seemed only to whet his curiosity the more, so one day we prevailed on him to try to go down with us. But although a brave boy in every other way, Peterkin was very nervous in the water, and it was with difficulty we got him to consent to be taken down, for he could never have managed to push himself down to the bottom without assistance. But no sooner had we pulled him down a yard or so into the deep clear water, than he began to struggle and kick violently; so we were forced to let him go, when he rose out of the water like a cork, gave a loud gasp and a frightful roar, and struck out for the land with the utmost possible haste.

Now all this pleasure we were to forego, and when we thought thereon, Jack and I felt very much depressed in our spirits. I could see, also, that Peterkin grieved and

sympathised with us, for when talking about this matter
he refrained from jesting and bantering us upon it.

As, however, a man's difficulties usually set him upon
devising methods to overcome them, whereby he often discovers better things than those he may have lost, so this
our difficulty induced us to think of searching for a large
pool among the rocks, where the water should be deep
enough for diving, yet so surrounded by rocks as to prevent sharks from getting at us. And such a pool we
afterwards found, which proved to be very much better
than our most sanguine hopes anticipated. It was situated not more than ten minutes' walk from our camp, and
was in the form of a small deep bay or basin, the entrance
to which, besides being narrow, was so shallow that no fish
so large as a shark could get in, at least not unless he
should be a remarkably thin one.

Inside of this basin, which we called our Water Garden, the coral formations were much more wonderful, and
the seaweed plants far more lovely and vividly coloured,
than in the lagoon itself. And the water was so clear
and still, that, although very deep, you could see the
minutest object at the bottom. Besides this, there was
a ledge of rock which overhung the basin at its deepest
part, from which we could dive pleasantly, and whereon
Peterkin could sit and see not only all the wonders I had
described to him, but also see Jack and me creeping
amongst the marine shrubbery at the bottom, like—as he
expressed it—"two great white sea-monsters." During
these excursions of ours to the bottom of the sea, we
began to get an insight into the manners and customs
of its inhabitants, and to make discoveries of wonderful
things, the like of which we never before conceived.
Among other things, we were deeply interested with

the operations of the little coral insect which, I was informed by Jack, is supposed to have entirely constructed many of the numerous islands in the Pacific Ocean. And certainly, when we considered the great reef which these insects had formed round the island on which we were cast, and observed their ceaseless activity in building their myriad cells, it did at first seem as if this might be true; but then, again, when I looked at the mountains of the island, and reflected that there were thousands of such, many of them much higher, in the South Seas, I doubted that there must be some mistake here. But more of this hereafter.

I also became much taken up with the manners and appearance of the anemones, and star-fish, and crabs, and sea-urchins, and such-like creatures; and was not content with watching those I saw during my dives in the Water Garden, but I must needs scoop out a hole in the coral rock close to it, which I filled with salt water, and stocked with sundry specimens of anemones and shell-fish, in order to watch more closely how they were in the habit of passing their time. Our burning-glass also now became a great treasure to me, as it enabled me to magnify, and so to perceive more clearly the forms and actions of these curious creatures of the deep.

Having now got ourselves into a very comfortable condition, we began to talk of a project which we had long had in contemplation—namely, to travel entirely round the island; in order, first, to ascertain whether it contained any other productions which might be useful to us; and, second, to see whether there might be any place more convenient and suitable for our permanent residence than that on which we were now encamped. Not that we were in any degree dissatisfied with it; on the contrary, we entertained quite a home-feeling to our bower and its neighbourhood; but if a better place did exist, there was no reason why we should not make use of it. At any rate, it would be well to know of its existence.

We had much earnest talk over this matter. But Jack proposed that, before undertaking such an excursion, we should supply ourselves with good defensive arms; for as we intended not only to go round all the shore, but to descend most of the valleys, before returning home, we should be likely to meet in with, he would not say *dangers*, but at least with everything that existed on the island, whatever that might be.

"Besides," said Jack, "it won't do for us to live on cocoa-nuts and oysters always. No doubt they are very excellent in their way, but I think a little animal food now and then would be agreeable as well as good for us; and as there are many small birds among the trees, some of which are probably very good to eat, I think it would be a capital plan to make bows and arrows, with which we could easily knock them over."

"First-rate!" cried Peterkin. "You will make the bows, Jack, and I'll try my hand at the arrows. The fact is, I'm quite tired of throwing stones at the birds. I began the very day we landed, I think, and have persevered up to the present time, but I've never hit anything yet."

"You forget," said I, "you hit me one day on the shin."

"Ah, true," replied Peterkin, "and a precious shindy you kicked up in consequence. But you were at least four yards away from the impudent paroquet I aimed at; so you see what a horribly bad shot I am."

"But," said I, "Jack, you cannot make three bows and

arrows before to-morrow, and would it not be a pity to waste time, now that we have made up our minds to go on this expedition? Suppose that you make one bow and arrow for yourself, and we can take our clubs?"

"That's true, Ralph. The day is pretty far advanced, and I doubt if I can make even one bow before dark. To be sure, I might work by firelight, after the sun goes down."

We had, up to this time, been in the habit of going to bed with the sun, as we had no pressing call to work o' nights; and, indeed, our work during the day was usually hard enough—what between fishing, and improving our bower, and diving in the Water Garden, and rambling in the woods; so that when night came we were usually very glad to retire to our beds. But now that we had a desire to work at night, we felt a wish for candles.

"Won't a good blazing fire give you light enough?" inquired Peterkin.

"Yes," replied Jack, "quite enough; but then it will give us a great deal more than enough of heat in this warm climate of ours."

"True," said Peterkin; "I forgot that. It would roast us."

"Well, as you're always doing that at any rate," remarked Jack, "we could scarcely call it a change. But the fact is, I've been thinking over this subject before. There is a certain nut growing in these islands which is called the candle-nut, because the natives use it instead of candles, and I know all about it, and how to prepare it for burning——"

"Then why don't you do it?" interrupted Peterkin. "Why have you kept us in the dark so long, you vile philosopher?"

"Because," said Jack, "I have not seen the tree yet, and I'm not sure that I should know either the tree or the nuts if I did see them. You see, I forget the description."

"Ah! that's just the way with me," said Peterkin, with a deep sigh. "I never could keep in my mind for half-an-hour the few descriptions I ever attempted to remember. The very first voyage I ever made was caused by my mistaking a description, or forgetting it, which is the same thing. And a horrible voyage it was. I had to fight with the captain the whole way out, and made the homeward voyage by swimming!"

"Come, Peterkin," said I, "you can't get even *me* to believe that."

"Perhaps not, but it's true notwithstanding," returned Peterkin, pretending to be hurt at my doubting his word.

"Let us hear how it happened," said Jack, while a good-natured smile overspread his face.

"Well, you must know," began Peterkin, "that the very day before I went to sea, I was greatly taken up with a game at hockey, which I was playing with my old school-fellows for the last time before leaving them—you see I was young then, Ralph." Peterkin gazed, in an abstracted and melancholy manner, out to sea. "Well, in the midst of the game, my uncle, who had taken all the bother and trouble of getting me bound 'prentice and rigged out, came and took me aside, and told me that he was called suddenly away from home, and would not be able to see me aboard, as he had intended. 'However,' said he, 'the captain knows you are coming, so that's not of much consequence; but as you'll have to find the ship yourself, you must remember her name and description. D'ye hear, boy?' I certainly did hear, but I'm afraid I did not understand, for my mind was so taken up with the game, which I saw my side was losing, that I began to grow impatient, and the moment my uncle finished his description of the ship and bade me good-bye, I bolted back to my game, with only a confused idea of three masts, and a green painted tafferel, and a gilt figure-head of Hercules with his club at the bow. Next day I was so much cast down with everybody saying good-bye, and a lot o' my female friends cryin' horribly over me, that I did not start for the harbour, where the ship was lying among a thousand others, till it was almost too late. So I had to run the whole way. When I reached the pier, there were so many masts, and so much confusion, that I felt quite humble-bumbled in my faculties. 'Now,' said I to myself, 'Peterkin, you're in a fix.' Then I fancied I saw a gilt figure-head and three masts, belonging to a ship just about to start; so I darted on board, but speedily jumped on shore again when I found that two of the masts belonged to another vessel, and the figure-head to a third! At last I caught sight of what I made sure was it—a fine large vessel just casting off her moorings. The tafferel was green. Three masts—yes, that must be it—and the gilt figure-head of Hercules. To be sure, it had a three-pronged pitchfork in its hand instead of a club; but that might be my uncle's mistake, or perhaps Hercules sometimes varied his weapons. 'Cast off!' roared a voice from the quarter-deck. 'Hold on!' cried I, rushing frantically through the crowd. 'Hold on! hold on!' repeated some of the bystanders, while the men at the ropes delayed for a minute. This threw the captain into a frightful rage; for some of his friends had come down to see him off, and having his orders contradicted so flatly was too much for him. However, the delay was sufficient. I took a race and a good leap; the ropes were cast off; the steam-tug gave a puff, and we started. Suddenly the captain walks up to me: 'Where did you come from, you scamp, and what do you want here?'

"'Please, sir,' said I, touching my cap, 'I'm your new 'prentice come aboard.'

"'New 'prentice!' said he, stamping; 'I've got no new 'prentice. My boys are all aboard already. This is a trick, you young blackguard. You've run away, you have;' and the captain stamped about the deck and swore dreadfully; for, you see, the thought of having to stop the ship and lower a boat and lose half-an-hour, all for the sake of sending a small boy ashore, seemed to make him very angry. Besides, it was blowin' fresh outside the harbour, so that to have let the steamer alongside to put me into it was no easy job. Just as we were passing the pierhead, where several boats were rowing into the harbour, the captain came up to me.

"'You've run away, you blackguard,' he said, giving me a box on the ear.

"'No, I haven't,' said I angrily; for the box was by no means a light one.

"'Hark'ee, boy, can you swim?'

"'Yes,' said I.

"'Then do it;' and seizing me by my trousers and the nape of my neck, he tossed me over the side into the sea. The fellows in the boats at the end of the pier backed their oars on seeing this; but observing that I could swim, they allowed me to make the best of my way to the pierhead. So you see, Ralph, that I really did swim my first homeward voyage."

Jack laughed, and patted Peterkin on the shoulder.

"But tell us about the candle-nut tree," said I; "you were talking about it."

"Very true," said Jack, "but I fear I can remember little about it. I believe the nut is about the size of a walnut; and I think that the leaves are white, but I am not sure."

"Eh! ha! hum!" exclaimed Peterkin, "I saw a tree answering to that description this very day."

"Did you?" cried Jack. "Is it far from this?"

"No, not half a mile."

"Then lead me to it," said Jack, seizing his axe.

In a few minutes we were all three pushing through the underwood of the forest, headed by Peterkin.

We soon came to the tree in question, which, after Jack had closely examined it, we concluded must be the candle-nut tree. Its leaves were of a beautiful silvery white, and formed a fine contrast to the dark-green foliage of the surrounding trees. We immediately filled our pockets with the nuts, after which Jack said—

"Now, Peterkin, climb that cocoa-nut tree and cut me one of the long branches."

This was soon done, but it cost some trouble, for the stem was very high, and as Peterkin usually pulled nuts from the younger trees, he was not much accustomed to climbing the high ones. The leaf or branch was a very large one, and we were surprised at its size and strength. Viewed from a little distance, the cocoa-nut tree seems to be a tall, straight stem, without a single branch except at the top, where there is a tuft of feathery-looking leaves' that seem to wave like soft plumes in the wind. But when we saw one of these leaves or branches at our feet, we found it to be a strong stalk, about fifteen feet long, with a number of narrow, pointed leaflets ranged alter-

nately on each side. But what seemed to us the most
wonderful thing about it was a curious substance resem-
bling cloth, which was wrapped round the thick end of
the stalk, where it had been cut from the tree. Peterkin
told us that he had the greatest difficulty in separating
the branch from the stem on account of this substance, as
it was wrapped quite round the tree, and, he observed,
round all the other branches, thus forming a strong support to the large leaves while exposed to high winds.
When I call this substance cloth I do not exaggerate.
Indeed, with regard to all the things I saw during my
eventful career in the South Seas, I have been exceedingly
careful not to exaggerate, or in any way to mislead or de-
ceive my readers. This cloth, I say, was remarkably like
to coarse brown cotton cloth. It had a seam or fibre
down the centre of it, from which diverged other fibres,
about the size of a bristle. There were two layers of these
fibres, very long and tough, the one layer crossing the
other obliquely, and the whole was cemented together
with a still finer fibrous and adhesive substance. When
we regarded it attentively, we could with difficulty believe
that it had not been woven by human hands. This remarkable piece of cloth we stripped carefully off, and found
it to be above two feet long by a foot broad, and we carried it home with us as a great prize.

Jack now took one of the leaflets, and, cutting out the
central spine or stalk, hurried back with it to our camp.
Having made a small fire, he baked the nuts slightly, and
then peeled off the husks. After this he wished to bore
a hole in them, which, not having anything better at
hand at the time, he did with the point of our useless
pencil-case. Then he strung them on the cocoa-nut spine,
and on putting a light to the topmost nut, we found to

our joy that it burned with a clear, beautiful flame; upon seeing which, Peterkin sprang up and danced round the fire for at least five minutes in the excess of his satisfaction.

"Now, lads," said Jack, extinguishing our candle, "the sun will set in an hour, so we have no time to lose. I shall go and cut a young tree to make my bow out of, and you had better each of you go and select good strong sticks for clubs, and we'll set to work at them after dark."

So saying he shouldered his axe and went off, followed by Peterkin, while I took up the piece of newly discovered cloth, and fell to examining its structure. So engrossed was I in this that I was still sitting in the same attitude and occupation when my companions returned.

"I told you so!" cried Peterkin, with a loud laugh. "O Ralph, you're incorrigible. See, there's a club for you. I was sure, when we left you looking at that bit of stuff, that we would find you poring over it when we came back, so I just cut a club for you as well as for myself."

"Thank you, Peterkin," said I. "It was kind of you to do that, instead of scolding me for a lazy fellow, as I confess I deserve."

"Oh, as to that," returned Peterkin, "I'll blow you up yet, if you wish it; only it would be of no use if I did, for you're a perfect mule!"

As it was now getting dark we lighted our candle, and placing it in a holder made of two crossing branches, inside of our bower, we seated ourselves on our leafy beds and began to work.

"I intend to appropriate the bow for my own use," said Jack, chipping the piece of wood he had brought with his axe. "I used to be a pretty fair shot once. But what's that you're doing?" he added, looking at Peterkin, who had drawn the end of a long pole into the tent, and was endeavouring to fit a small piece of the hoop-iron to the end of it.

"I'm going to enlist into the Lancers," answered Peterkin. "You see, Jack, I find the club rather an unwieldy instrument for my delicately formed muscles, and I flatter myself I shall do more execution with a spear."

"Well, if length constitutes power," said Jack, "you'll certainly be invincible."

The pole which Peterkin had cut was full twelve feet long, being a very strong but light and tough young tree, which merely required thinning at the butt to be a serviceable weapon.

"That's a very good idea," said I.

"Which—this?" inquired Peterkin, pointing to the spear.

"Yes," I replied.

"Humph!" said he; "you'd find it a pretty tough and matter-of-fact idea if you had it stuck through your gizzard, old boy!"

"I mean the idea of making it is a good one," said I, laughing. "And, now I think of it, I'll change my plan too. I don't think much of a club, so I'll make me a sling out of this piece of cloth. I used to be very fond of slinging, ever since I read of David slaying Goliath the Philistine, and I was once thought to be expert at it."

So I set to work to manufacture a sling. For a long time we all worked very busily without speaking. At length Peterkin looked up. "I say, Jack, I'm sorry to say I must apply to you for another strip of your handkerchief, to tie on this rascally head with. It's pretty well torn at any rate, so you won't miss it."

Jack proceeded to comply with this request, when Peterkin suddenly laid his hand on his arm and arrested him.

"Hist, man," said he, "be tender; you should never be needlessly cruel if you can help it. Do try to shave past Lord Nelson's mouth without tearing it, if possible! Thanks. There are plenty more handkerchiefs on the cocoa-nut trees."

Poor Peterkin! with what pleasant feelings I recall and record his jests and humorous sayings now!

While we were thus engaged, we were startled by a distant but most strange and horrible cry. It seemed to come from the sea, but was so far away that we could not clearly distinguish its precise direction. Rushing out of our bower, we hastened down to the beach and stayed to listen. Again it came quite loud and distinct on the night air—a prolonged, hideous cry, something like the braying of an ass. The moon had risen, and we could see the islands in and beyond the lagoon quite plainly, but there was no object visible to account for such a cry. A strong gust of wind was blowing from the point whence the sound came, but this died away while we were gazing out to sea.

"What can it be?" said Peterkin in a low whisper, while we all involuntarily crept closer to each other.

"Do you know," said Jack, "I have heard that mysterious sound twice before, but never so loud as to-night. Indeed it was so faint that I thought I must have merely fancied it, so, as I did not wish to alarm you, I said nothing about it."

We listened for a long time for the sound again, but as it did not come, we returned to the bower and resumed our work.

"Very strange," said Peterkin, quite gravely. "Do you believe in ghosts, Ralph?"

"No," I answered, "I do not. Nevertheless I must confess that strange, unaccountable sounds, such as we have just heard, make me feel a little uneasy."

"What say you to it, Jack?"

"I neither believe in ghosts nor feel uneasy," he replied. "I never saw a ghost myself, and I never met with any one who had; and I have generally found that strange and unaccountable things have almost always been accounted for, and found to be quite simple on close examination. I certainly can't imagine what *that* sound is; but I'm quite sure I shall find out before long, and if it's a ghost I'll—I'll——"

"Eat it," cried Peterkin.

"Yes, I'll eat it! Now, then, my bow and two arrows are finished; so if you are ready we had better turn in."

By this time Peterkin had thinned down his spear and tied an iron point very cleverly to the end of it; I had formed a sling, the lines of which were composed of thin strips of the cocoa-nut cloth, plaited; and Jack had made a stout bow, nearly five feet long, with two arrows, feathered with two or three large plumes which some bird had dropped. They had no barbs, but Jack said that if arrows were well feathered they did not require iron points, but would fly quite well if merely sharpened at the point; which I did not know before.

"A feathered arrow without a barb," said he, "is a good weapon, but a barbed arrow without feathers is utterly useless."

The string of the bow was formed of our piece of whipcord, part of which, as he did not like to cut it, was rolled round the bow.

Although thus prepared for a start on the morrow, we thought it wise to exercise ourselves a little in the use of our weapons before starting, so we spent the whole of the next day in practising. And it was well we did so, for we found that our arms were very imperfect, and that we were far from perfect in the use of them. First, Jack found that the bow was much too strong, and he had to thin it. Also the spear was much too heavy, and so had to be reduced in thickness, although nothing would induce Peterkin to have it shortened. My sling answered very well, but I had fallen so much out of practice that my first stone knocked off Peterkin's hat, and narrowly missed making a second Goliath of him. However, after having spent the whole day in diligent practice, we began to find some of our former expertness returning—at least Jack and I did. As for Peterkin, being naturally a neat-handed boy, he soon handled his spear well, and could run full tilt at a cocoa-nut, and hit it with great precision once out of every five times.

But I feel satisfied that we owed much of our rapid success to the unflagging energy of Jack, who insisted that since we had made him captain, we should obey him; and he kept us at work from morning till night, persever-ingly, at the same thing. Peterkin wished very much to run about and stick his spear into everything he passed; but Jack put up a cocoa-nut, and would not let him leave off running at that for a moment, except when he wanted to rest. We laughed at Jack for this, but we were both convinced that it did us much good.

That night we examined and repaired our arms ere we lay down to rest, although we were much fatigued, in order that we might be in readiness to set out on our expedition at daylight on the following morning.

CHAPTER IX

Prepare for a journey round the island—Sagacious reflections—Mysterious appearances and startling occurrences.

SCARCELY had the sun shot its first ray across the bosom of the broad Pacific, when Jack sprang to his feet, and, hallooing in Peterkin's ear to awaken him, ran down the beach to take his customary dip in the sea. We did not, as was our wont, bathe that morning in our Water Garden, but, in order to save time, refreshed ourselves in the shallow water just opposite the bower. Our breakfast was also despatched without loss of time, and in less than an hour afterwards all our preparations for the journey were completed.

In addition to his ordinary dress, Jack tied a belt of cocoa-nut cloth round his waist, into which he thrust the axe. I was also advised to put on a belt and carry a short cudgel or bludgeon in it; for, as Jack truly remarked, the sling would be of little use if we should chance to come to close quarters with any wild animal. As for Peterkin, notwithstanding that he carried such a long, and I must add, frightful-looking spear over his shoulder, we could not prevail on him to leave his club behind; "for," said he, "a spear at close quarters is not worth a button." I must say that it seemed to me that the club was, to use his own style of language, not worth a button-hole; for it was all knotted over at the head,

something like the club which I remember to have observed in picture-books of Jack the Giant Killer, besides
being so heavy that he required to grasp it with both
hands in order to wield it at all. However, he took it
with him, and in this manner we set out upon our travels.

We did not consider it necessary to carry any food
with us, as we knew that wherever we went we should be
certain to fall in with cocoa-nut trees; having which we
were amply supplied, as Peterkin said, with meat and
drink and pocket-handkerchiefs! I took the precaution,
however, to put the burning-glass into my pocket lest we
should want fire.

The morning was exceedingly lovely. It was one of
that very still and peaceful sort which made the few
noises that we heard seem to be *quiet* noises. I know no
other way of expressing this idea. Noises which, so far
from interrupting the universal tranquillity of earth, sea,
and sky, rather tended to reveal to us how quiet the
world round us really was. Such sounds as I refer to
were, the peculiar melancholy—yet, it seemed to me,
cheerful—plaint of sea-birds floating on the glassy waters
or sailing in the sky, also the subdued twittering of little
birds among the bushes, the faint ripples on the beach,
and the solemn boom of the surf upon the distant coral
reef. We felt very glad in our hearts as we walked along
the sands side by side. For my part, I felt so deeply
overjoyed that I was surprised at my own sensations, and
fell into a reverie upon the causes of happiness. I came
to the conclusion that a state of profound peace and
repose, both in regard to outward objects and within the
soul, is the happiest condition in which man can be
placed; for although I had many a time been most joyful

and happy when engaged in bustling, energetic, active pursuits or amusements, I never found that such joy or satisfaction was so deep or so pleasant to reflect upon as that which I now experienced. And I was the more confirmed in this opinion when I observed, and indeed was told by himself, that Peterkin's happiness was also very great; yet he did not express this by dancing as was his wont, nor did he give so much as a single shout, but walked quietly between us with his eye sparkling, and a joyful smile upon his countenance. My reader must not suppose that I thought all this in the clear and methodical manner in which I have set it down here. These thoughts did indeed pass through my mind, but they did so in a very confused and indefinite manner, for I was young at that time, and not much given to deep reflections. Neither did I consider that the peace whereof I write is not to be found in this world—at least in its perfection, although I have since learned that by religion a man may attain to a very great degree of it.

I have said that Peterkin walked along the sands between us. We had two ways of walking together about our island. When we travelled through the woods, we always did so in single file, as by this method we advanced with greater facility, the one treading in the other's footsteps. In such cases Jack always took the lead, Peterkin followed, and I brought up the rear. But when we travelled along the sands, which extended almost in an unbroken line of glistening white round the island, we marched abreast, as we found this method more sociable, and every way more pleasant. Jack, being the tallest, walked next the sea, and Peterkin marched between us, as by this arrangement either of us could talk to him or

he to us, while if Jack and I happened to wish to converse together, we could conveniently do so over Peterkin's head. Peterkin used to say, in reference to this
arrangement, that had he been as tall as either of us,
our order of march might have been the same; for as
Jack often used to scold him for letting everything
we said to him pass in at one ear and out at the other,
his head could of course form no interruption to our
discourse.

We were now fairly started. Half a mile's walk conveyed us round a bend in the land which shut out our
bower from view, and for some time we advanced at a
brisk pace without speaking, though our eyes were not
idle, but noted everything, in the woods, on the shore, or
in the sea, that was interesting. After passing the ridge
of land that formed one side of our valley—the Valley of
the Wreck—we beheld another small vale lying before us
in all the luxuriant loveliness of tropical vegetation. We
had, indeed, seen it before from the mountain-top, but we
had no idea that it would turn out to be so much more
lovely when we were close to it. We were about to commence the exploration of this valley, when Peterkin
stopped us, and directed our attention to a very remarkable appearance in advance along the shore.

" What's yon, think you?" said he, levelling his spear,
as if he expected an immediate attack from the object in
question, though it was full half a mile distant.

As he spoke, there appeared a white column above the
rocks, as if of steam or spray. It rose upwards to a
height of several feet, and then disappeared. Had this
been near the sea, we would not have been so greatly surprised, as it might in that case have been the surf, for at

this part of the coast the coral reef approached so near to
the island that in some parts it almost joined it. There
was therefore no lagoon between, and the heavy surf of
the ocean beat almost up to the rocks. But this white
column appeared about fifty yards inland. The rocks at
the place were rugged, and they stretched across the sandy
beach into the sea. Scarce had we ceased expressing our
surprise at this sight, when another column flew upwards
for a few seconds, not far from the spot where the first had
been seen, and disappeared; and so, at long, irregular
intervals, these strange sights recurred. We were now
quite sure that the columns were watery or composed of
spray, but what caused them we could not guess, so we
determined to go and see.

In a few minutes we gained the spot, which was very
rugged and precipitous, and, moreover, quite damp with
the falling of the spray. We had much ado to pass over
dry-shod. The ground also was full of holes here and
there. Now, while we stood anxiously waiting for the
reappearance of these water-spouts, we heard a low, rumbling sound near us, which quickly increased to a gurgling
and hissing noise, and a moment afterwards a thick spout
of water burst upwards from a hole in the rock, and
spouted into the air with much violence, and so close to
where Jack and I were standing that it nearly touched
us. We sprang aside, but not before a cloud of spray
descended, and drenched us both to the skin.

Peterkin, who was standing farther off, escaped with a
few drops, and burst into an uncontrollable fit of laughter
on beholding our miserable plight.

"Mind your eye!" he shouted eagerly, "there goes
another!" The words were scarcely out of his mouth

when there came up a spout from another hole, which served us exactly in the same manner as before.

Peterkin now shrieked with laughter; but his merriment was abruptly put a stop to by the gurgling noise occurring close to where he stood.

"Where'll it spout this time, I wonder?" he said, looking about with some anxiety, and preparing to run. Suddenly there came a loud hiss or snort; a fierce spout of water burst up between Peterkin's legs, blew him off his feet, enveloped him in its spray, and hurled him to the ground. He fell with so much violence that we feared he must have broken some of his bones, and ran anxiously to his assistance; but fortunately he had fallen on a clump of tangled herbage, in which he lay sprawling in a most deplorable condition.

It was now our turn to laugh; but as we were not yet quite sure that he was unhurt, and as we knew not when or where the next spout might arise, we assisted him hastily to jump up and hurry from the spot.

I may here add that, although I am quite certain that the spout of water was very strong, and that it blew Peterkin completely off his legs, I am not quite certain of the exact height to which it lifted him, being somewhat startled by the event, and blinded partially by the spray, so that my power of observation was somewhat impaired for the moment.

"What's to be done now?" asked Peterkin ruefully.

"Make a fire, lad, and dry ourselves," replied Jack.

"And here is material ready to our hand," said I, picking up a dried branch of a tree, as we hurried up to the woods.

In about an hour after this mishap our clothes were

again dried. While they were hanging up before the fire, we walked down to the beach, and soon observed that these curious spouts took place immediately after the fall of a huge wave, never before it; and, moreover, that the spouts did not take place excepting when the billow was an extremely large one. From this we concluded that there must be a subterraneous channel in the rock into which the water was driven by the larger waves, and finding no way of escape except through these small holes, was thus forced up violently through them. At any rate, we could not conceive any other reason for these strange water-spouts, and as this seemed a very simple and probable one, we forthwith adopted it.

"I say, Ralph, what's that in the water; is it a shark?" said Jack, just as we were about to quit the place.

I immediately ran to the overhanging ledge of rock, from which he was looking down into the sea, and bent over it. There I saw a very faint pale object of a greenish colour, which seemed to move slightly while I looked at it.

"It's like a fish of some sort," said I.

"Hallo, Peterkin!" cried Jack, "fetch your spear; here's work for it."

But when we tried to reach the object, the spear proved to be too short.

"There now," said Peterkin with a sneer, "you were always telling me it was too long."

Jack now drove the spear forcibly towards the object, and let go his hold; but although it seemed to be well aimed, he must have missed, for the handle soon rose again; and when the spear was drawn up, there was the pale green object in exactly the same spot, slowly moving its tail.

"Very odd," said Jack.

But although it was undoubtedly very odd, and although Jack and all of us plunged the spear at it repeatedly, we could neither hit it nor drive it away, so we were compelled to continue our journey without discovering what it was. I was very much perplexed at this strange appearance in the water, and could not get it out of my mind for a long time afterwards. However, I quieted myself by resolving that I would pay a visit to it again at some more convenient season.

CHAPTER X

Make discovery of many excellent roots and fruits—The resources
of the Coral Island gradually unfolded—The banyan tree—
Another tree which is supported by natural planks—Water-
fowl found—A very remarkable discovery, and a very peculiar
murder—We luxuriate on the fat of the land.

OUR examination of the little valley proved to · be
altogether most satisfactory. We found in it not
only similar trees to those we had already seen in our own
valley, but also one or two others of a different species.
We had also the satisfaction of discovering a peculiar
vegetable, which Jack concluded must certainly be that
of which he had read as being very common among the
South Sea islanders, and which was named *taro*.* Also we
found a large supply of yams, and another root like a
potato in appearance. As these were all quite new to us,
we regarded our lot as a most fortunate one, in being thus
cast on an island which was so prolific and so well stored
with all the necessaries of life. Long afterwards we found
out that this island of ours was no better in these respects
than thousands of other islands in those seas. Indeed,
many of them were much richer and more productive; but
that did not render us the less grateful for our present
good fortune. We each put one of these roots in our
pocket, intending to use them for our supper; of which
more hereafter. We also saw many beautiful birds here,
and traces of some four-footed animal again. Meanwhile

the sun began to descend, so we returned to the shore, and pushed on round the spouting rocks into the next valley. This was that valley of which I have spoken as running across the entire island. It was by far the largest and most beautiful that we had yet looked upon. Here were trees of every shape and size and hue which it is possible to conceive of, many of which we had not seen in the other valleys; for, the stream in this valley being larger, and the mould much richer than in the Valley of the Wreck, it was clothed with a more luxuriant growth of trees and plants. Some trees were dark glossy green, others of a rich and warm hue, contrasting well with those of a pale light green, which were everywhere abundant. Among these we recognised the broad dark heads of the bread-fruit, with its golden fruit; the pure, silvery foliage of the candle-nut, and several species which bore a strong resemblance to the pine; while here and there, in groups and in single trees, rose the tall forms of the cocoa-nut palms, spreading abroad, and waving their graceful plumes high above all the rest, as if they were a superior race of stately giants keeping guard over these luxuriant forests. Oh, it was a most enchanting scene, and I thanked God for having created such delightful spots for the use of man.

Now, while we were gazing around us in silent admiration, Jack uttered an exclamation of surprise, and pointing to an object a little to one side of us, said—

" That's a banyan tree."*

" And what's a banyan tree ? " inquired Peterkin, as we walked towards it.

" A very curious one, as you shall see presently," replied Jack. " It is called the *aoa* here, if I recollect rightly, and has a wonderful peculiarity about it. What an enormous one it is, to be sure!"

"*It!*" repeated Peterkin; "why, there are dozens of banyans here! What do you mean by talking bad grammar? Is your philosophy deserting you, Jack?"

"There is but one tree here of this kind," returned Jack, "as you will perceive if you will examine it." And, sure enough, we did find that what we had supposed was a forest of trees was in reality only one. Its bark was of a light colour, and had a shining appearance, the leaves being lance-shaped, small, and of a beautiful pea-green. But the wonderful thing about it was, that the branches, which grew out from the stem horizontally, sent down long shoots or fibres to the ground, which, taking root, had themselves become trees, and were covered with bark like the tree itself. Many of these fibres had descended from the branches at various distances, and thus supported them on natural pillars, some of which were so large and strong that it was not easy at first to distinguish the offspring from the parent stem. The fibres were of all sizes and in all states of advancement, from the pillars we have just mentioned to small cords which hung down and were about to take root, and thin brown threads still far from the ground, which swayed about with every motion of wind. In short, it seemed to us that, if there were only space afforded to it, this single tree would at length cover the whole island.

Shortly after this we came upon another remarkable tree, which, as its peculiar formation afterwards proved extremely useful to us, merits description. It was a splendid chestnut,* but its proper name Jack did not know. However, there were quantities of fine nuts upon it, some of which we put in our pockets. But its stem was the most wonderful part of it. It rose to about twelve feet without a branch, and was not of great thickness : on the contrary, it was remarkably slender for the size of the tree; but, to make up for this, there were four or five wonderful projections in this stem, which I cannot better describe than by asking the reader to suppose that five planks of two inches thick and three feet broad had been placed round the trunk of the tree, with their *edges* closely fixed to it, from the ground up to the branches, and that these planks had been covered over with the bark of the tree and incorporated with it. In short, they were just natural buttresses, without which the stem could not have supported its heavy and umbrageous top. We found these chestnuts to be very numerous. They grew chiefly on the banks of the stream, and were of all sizes.

While we were examining a small tree of this kind, Jack chipped a piece off a buttress with his axe, and found the wood to be firm and easily cut. He then struck the axe into it with all his force, and very soon split it off close to the tree, first, however, having cut it across transversely above and below. By this means he satisfied himself that we could now obtain short planks, as it were all ready sawn, of any size and thickness that we desired; which was a very great discovery indeed, perhaps the most important we had yet made.

We now wended our way back to the coast, intending to encamp near the beach, as we found that the mosquitoes were troublesome in the forest. On our way we could not help admiring the birds which flew and chirped around us. Among them we observed a pretty kind of

paroquet, with a green body, a blue head, and a red
breast; also a few beautiful turtle-doves, and several flocks
of wood-pigeons. The hues of many of these birds were
extremely vivid—bright green, blue, and scarlet being the
prevailing tints. We made several attempts throughout
the day to bring down one of these, both with the bow
and the sling—not for mere sport, but to ascertain whether
they were good for food. But we invariably missed,
although once or twice we were very near hitting. As
evening drew on, however, a flock of pigeons flew past. I
slung a stone into the midst of them at a venture, and
had the good fortune to kill one. We were startled, soon
after, by a loud whistling noise above our heads; and on
looking up, saw a flock of wild-ducks making for the coast.
We watched these, and observing where they alighted,
followed them up until we came upon a most lovely blue
lake, not more than two hundred yards long, embosomed
in verdant trees. Its placid surface, which reflected
every leaf and stem as if in a mirror, was covered with
various species of wild ducks, feeding among the sedges
and broad-leaved water-plants which floated on it, while
numerous birds like water-hens ran to and fro most
busily on its margin. These all with one accord flew
tumultuously away the instant we made our appearance.
While walking along the margin we observed fish in the
water, but of what sort we could not tell.

Now, as we neared the shore, Jack and I said we would
go a little out of our way to see if we could procure one
of those ducks; so, directing Peterkin to go straight to the
shore and kindle a fire, we separated, promising to rejoin
him speedily. But we did not find the ducks, although
we made a diligent search for half-an-hour. We were

about to retrace our steps, when we were arrested by one of the strangest sights that we had yet beheld.

Just in front of us, at the distance of about ten yards, grew a superb tree, which certainly was the largest we had yet seen on the island. Its trunk was at least five feet in diameter, with a smooth grey bark; above this the spreading branches were clothed with light green leaves, amid which were clusters of bright yellow fruit, so numerous as to weigh down the boughs with their great weight. This fruit seemed to be of the plum species, of an oblong form, and a good deal larger than the magnum-bonum plum. The ground at the foot of this tree was thickly strewn with the fallen fruit, in the midst of which lay sleeping, in every possible attitude, at least twenty hogs of all ages and sizes, apparently quite surfeited with a recent banquet.

Jack and I could scarce restrain our laughter as we gazed at these coarse, fat, ill-looking animals while they lay groaning and snoring heavily amid the remains of their supper.

"Now, Ralph," said Jack, in a low whisper, "put a stone in your sling—a good big one—and let fly at that fat fellow with his back toward you. I'll try to put an arrow into yon little pig."

"Don't you think we had better put them up first?" I whispered; "it seems cruel to kill them while asleep."

"If I wanted *sport*, Ralph, I would certainly set them up; but as we only want *pork*, we'll let them lie. Besides, we're not sure of killing them; so, fire away."

Thus admonished, I slung my stone with so good aim that it went bang against the hog's flank as if against the head of a drum; but it had no other effect than that of causing the animal to start to its feet, with a frightful yell of surprise, and scamper away. At the same instant Jack's bow twanged, and the arrow pinned the little pig to the ground by the ear.

"I've missed, after all," cried Jack, darting forward with uplifted axe, while the little pig uttered a loud squeal, tore the arrow from the ground, and ran away with it, along with the whole drove, into the bushes and disappeared, though we heard them screaming long afterwards in the distance.

"That's very provoking, now," said Jack, rubbing the point of his nose.

"Very," I replied, stroking my chin.

"Well, we must make haste and rejoin Peterkin," said Jack. "It's getting late." And without further remark we threaded our way quickly through the woods towards the shore.

When we reached it, we found wood laid out, the fire lighted and beginning to kindle up, with other signs of preparation for our encampment, but Peterkin was nowhere to be found. We wondered very much at this; but Jack suggested that he might have gone to fetch water; so he gave a shout to let him know that we had arrived, and sat down upon a rock, while I threw off my jacket, and seized the axe, intending to split up one or two billets of wood. But I had scarce moved from the spot when, in the distance, we heard a most appalling shriek, which was followed up by a chorus of yells from the hogs, and a loud hurrah.

"I do believe," said I, "that Peterkin has met with the hogs."

"When Greek meets Greek," said Jack, soliloquising, "then comes the tug of——""

"Hurrah!" shouted Peterkin in the distance.

We turned hastily towards the direction whence the sound came, and soon descried Peterkin walking along the beach towards us with a little pig transfixed on the end of his long spear!

"Well done, my boy!" exclaimed Jack, slapping him on the shoulder when he came up; "you're the best shot amongst us."

"Look here, Jack!" cried Peterkin, as he disengaged the animal from his spear. "Do you recognise that hole?" said he, pointing to the pig's ear; "and are you familiar with this arrow, eh?"

"Well, I declare!" said Jack.

"Of course you do," interrupted Peterkin; "but, pray, restrain your declarations at this time, and let's have supper, for I'm uncommonly hungry, I can tell you; and it's no joke to charge a whole herd of swine with their great-grandmother bristling like a giant porcupine at the head of them!"

We now set about preparing supper; and, truly a good display of viands we made, when all was laid out on a flat rock in the light of the blazing fire. There was, first of all, the little pig; then there were the taro-root, and the yam, and the potato, and six plums; and, lastly, the wood-pigeon. To these Peterkin added a bit of sugar-cane, which he had cut from a little patch of that plant which he had found not long after separating from us; "and," said he, "the patch was somewhat in a square form, which convinces me it must have been planted by man."

"Very likely," replied Jack. "From all we have seen, I'm inclined to think that some of the savages must have dwelt here long ago."

We found no small difficulty in making up our minds how we were to cook the pig. None of us had ever cut up

one before, and we did not know exactly how to begin;
besides, we had nothing but the axe to do it with, our knife
having been forgotten. At last Jack started up and said—

"Don't let us waste more time talking about it, boys.—
Hold it up, Peterkin. There, lay the hind-leg on this block
of wood—so;" and he cut it off, with a large portion of the
haunch, at a single blow of the axe. "Now the other—
that's it." And having thus cut off the two hind-legs, he
made several deep gashes in them, thrust a sharp-pointed
stick through each, and stuck them up before the blaze to
roast. The wood-pigeon was then split open, quite flat,
washed clean in salt water, and treated in a similar manner.
While these were cooking, we scraped a hole in the sand
and ashes under the fire, into which we put our vegetables,
and covered them up.

The taro-root was of an oval shape, about ten inches
long and four or five thick. It was of a mottled-grey
colour, and had a thick rind. We found it somewhat like
an Irish potato, and exceedingly good. The yam was
roundish, and had a rough brown skin. It was very sweet
and well flavoured. The potato, we were surprised to find,
was quite sweet and exceedingly palatable, as also were the
plums; and, indeed, the pork and pigeon too, when we
came to taste them. Altogether this was decidedly the
most luxurious supper we had enjoyed for many a day;
and Jack said it was out-of-sight better than we ever got
on board ship; and Peterkin said he feared that if we
should remain long on the island he would infallibly become a glutton or an epicure: whereat Jack remarked that
he need not fear that, for he was *both* already! And so,
having eaten our fill, not forgetting to finish off with a plum,
we laid ourselves comfortably down to sleep upon a couch
of branches, under the overhanging ledge of a coral rock.

CHAPTER XI

Effects of over-eating, and reflections thereon—Humble advice
regarding cold water—The "horrible cry" accounted for—
The curious birds called penguins—Peculiarity of the cocoa-
nut palm—Questions on the formation of coral islands—
Mysterious footsteps—Strange discoveries and sad sights.

WHEN we awoke on the following morning, we found
that the sun was already a good way above the
horizon, so I came to the conclusion that a heavy supper
is not conducive to early rising. Nevertheless we felt
remarkably strong and well, and much disposed to have
our breakfast. First, however, we had our customary
morning bathe, which refreshed us greatly.

I have often wondered very much in after years that the
inhabitants of my own dear land did not make more frequent use of this most charming element, water. I mean
in the way of cold bathing. Of course, I have perceived
that it is not convenient for them to go into the sea or
the rivers in winter, as we used to do on the Coral Island;
but then I knew from experience that a large washing-tub
and a sponge do form a most pleasant substitute. The
feelings of freshness, of cleanliness, of vigour, and extreme
hilarity, that always followed my bathes in the sea, and
even, when in England, my ablutions in the wash-tub, were
so delightful, that I would sooner have gone without my
breakfast than without my bathe in cold water. My readers
will forgive me for asking whether they are in the habit of

bathing thus every morning; and if they answer " No," they will pardon me for recommending them to begin at once. Of late years, since retiring from the stirring life of adventure which I have led so long in foreign climes, I have heard of a system called the cold-water cure. Now, I do not know much about that system, so I do not mean to uphold it, neither do I intend to run it down. Perhaps, in reference to it, I may just hint that there may be too much of a good thing. I know not, but of this I am quite certain, that there may also be too little of a good thing; and the great delight I have had in cold bathing during the course of my adventurous career inclines me to think that it is better to risk taking too much than to content one's self with too little. Such is my opinion, derived from much experience; but I put it before my readers with the utmost diffidence and with profound modesty, knowing that it may possibly jar with their feelings of confidence in their own ability to know and judge as to what is best and fittest in reference to their own affairs. But, to return from this digression, for which I humbly crave forgiveness.

We had not advanced on our journey much above a mile or so, and were just beginning to feel the pleasant glow that usually accompanies vigorous exercise, when, on turning a point that revealed to us a new and beautiful cluster of islands, we were suddenly arrested by the appalling cry which had so alarmed us a few nights before. But this time we were by no means so much alarmed us on the previous occasion, because, whereas at that time it was night, now it was day; and I have always found, though I am unable to account for it, that daylight banishes many of the fears that are apt to assail us in the dark.

On hearing the sound, Peterkin instantly threw forward his spear.

"Now, what can it be?" said he, looking round at Jack. "I tell you what it is: if we are to go on being pulled up in a constant state of horror and astonishment, as we have been for the last week, the sooner we're out o' this island the better, notwithstanding the yams and lemonade, and pork and plums!"

Peterkin's remark was followed by a repetition of the cry, louder than before.

"It comes from one of these islands," said Jack.

"It must be the ghost of a jackass, then," said Peterkin, "for I never heard anything so like."

We all turned our eyes towards the cluster of islands, where, on the largest, we observed curious objects moving on the shore.

"Soldiers they are—that's flat!" cried Peterkin, gazing at them in the utmost amazement.

And, in truth, Peterkin's remark seemed to me to be correct; for, at the distance from which we saw them, they appeared to be an army of soldiers. There they stood, rank and file, in lines and in squares, marching and countermarching, with blue coats and white trousers. While we were looking at them, the dreadful cry came again over the water, and Peterkin suggested that it must be a regiment sent out to massacre the natives in cold blood. At this remark Jack laughed and said—

"Why, Peterkin, they are penguins!"

"Penguins?" repeated Peterkin.

"Ay, penguins, Peterkin, penguins—nothing more or less than big sea-birds, as you shall see one of these days, when we pay them a visit in our boat, which

I mean to set about building the moment we return to our bower."

"So, then, our dreadful yelling ghosts and our murdering army of soldiers," remarked Peterkin, "have dwindled down to penguins—big sea-birds! Very good. Then I propose that we continue our journey as fast as possible, lest our island should be converted into a dream before we get completely round it."

Now, as we continued on our way, I pondered much over this new discovery, and the singular appearance of these birds, of which Jack could only give us a very slight and vague account; and I began to long to commence our boat, in order that we might go and inspect them more narrowly. But by degrees these thoughts left me, and I began to be much taken up again with the interesting peculiarities of the country which we were passing through.

The second night we passed in a manner somewhat similar to the first, at about two-thirds of the way round the island, as we calculated, and we hoped to sleep on the night following at our bower. I will not here note so particularly all that we said and saw during the course of this second day, as we did not make any further discoveries of great importance. The shore along which we travelled, and the various parts of the woods through which we passed, were similar to those which have been already treated of. There were one or two observations that we made, however, and these were as follows:—

We saw that, while many of the large fruit-bearing trees grew only in the valleys, and some of them only near the banks of the streams, where the soil was peculiarly rich, the cocoa-nut palm grew in every place whatsoever;

not only on the hillsides, but also on the seashore, and even, as has been already stated, on the coral reef itself, where the soil, if we may use the name, was nothing better than loose sand mingled with broken shells and coral rock. So near to the sea, too, did this useful tree grow, that in many places its roots were washed by the spray from the breakers. Yet we found the trees growing thus on the sands to be quite as luxuriant as those growing in the valleys, and the fruit as good and refreshing also. Besides this, I noticed that on the summit of the high mountain, which we once more ascended at a different point from our first ascent, were found abundance of shells and broken coral formations; which Jack and I agreed proved either that this island must have once been under the sea, or that the sea must once have been above the island. In other words, that as shells and coral could not possibly climb to the mountain-top, they must have been washed upon it while the mountain-top was on a level with the sea. We pondered this very much; and we put to ourselves the question, "What raised the island to its present height above the sea?" But to this we could by no means give to ourselves a satisfactory reply. Jack thought it might have been blown up by a volcano; and Peterkin said he thought it must have jumped up of its own accord! We also noticed, what had escaped us before, that the solid rocks of which the island was formed were quite different from the live coral rocks on the shore, where the wonderful little insects were continually working. They seemed, indeed, to be of the same material— a substance like limestone; but while the coral rocks were quite full of minute cells in which the insects lived, the other rocks inland were hard and solid, without the appearance of cells at all. Our thoughts and conversations on this subject were sometimes so profound that Peterkin said we should certainly get drowned in them at last, even although we were such good divers! Nevertheless we did not allow his pleasantry on this and similar points to deter us from making our notes and observations as we went along.

We found several more droves of hogs in the woods, but abstained from killing any of them, having more than sufficient for our present necessities. We saw also many of their footprints in this neighbourhood. Among these we also observed the footprints of a smaller animal, which we examined with much care, but could form no certain opinion as to them. Peterkin thought they were those of a little dog, but Jack and I thought differently. We became very curious on this matter, the more so that we observed these footprints to lie scattered about in one locality, as if the animal which had made them was wandering round about in a very irregular manner, and without any object in view. Early in the forenoon of our third day we observed these footprints to be much more numerous than ever, and in one particular spot they diverged off into the woods in a regular beaten track, which was, however, so closely beset with bushes that we pushed through it with difficulty. We had now become so anxious to find out what animal this was and where it went to, that we determined to follow the track, and, if possible, clear up the mystery. Peterkin said, in a bantering tone, that he was sure it would be cleared up, as usual, in some frightfully simple way, and prove to be no mystery at all!

The beaten track seemed much too large to have been

formed by the animal itself, and we concluded that some larger animal had made it, and that the smaller one made use of it. But everywhere the creeping plants and tangled bushes crossed our path, so that we forced our way along with some difficulty. Suddenly, as we came upon an open space, we heard a faint cry, and observed a black animal standing in the track before us.

"A wild-cat!" cried Jack, fitting an arrow to his bow, and discharging it so hastily that he missed the animal, and hit the earth about half a foot to one side of it. To our surprise the wild-cat did not fly, but walked slowly towards the arrow, and snuffed at it.

"That's the most comical wild-cat I ever saw!" cried Jack.

"It's a tame wild-cat, I think," said Peterkin, levelling his spear to make a charge.

"Stop!" cried I, laying my hand on his shoulder; "I do believe the poor beast is blind. See, it strikes against the branches as it walks along. It must be a very old one;" and I hastened towards it.

"Only think," said Peterkin, with a suppressed laugh, "of a superannuated wild-cat!"

We now found that the poor cat was not only blind, or nearly so, but extremely deaf, as it did not hear our footsteps until we were quite close behind it. Then it sprang round, and putting up its back and tail, while the black hair stood all on end, uttered a hoarse mew and a fuff.

"Poor thing," said Peterkin, gently extending his hand, and endeavouring to pat the cat's head. "Poor pussy; chee, chee, chee; puss, puss, puss; cheetie pussy!"

No sooner did the cat hear these sounds than all signs

of anger fled, and advancing eagerly to Peterkin, it allowed itself to be stroked, and rubbed itself against his legs, purring loudly all the time, and showing every symptom of the most extreme delight.

"It's no more a wild-cat than I am!" cried Peterkin, taking it in his arms; "it's quite tame.—Poor pussy, cheetie pussy!"

We now crowded around Peterkin, and were not a little surprised, and, to say truth, a good deal affected, by the sight of the poor animal's excessive joy. It rubbed its head against Peterkin's cheek, licked his chin, and thrust its head almost violently into his neck, while it purred more loudly than I ever heard a cat purr before, and appeared to be so much overpowered by its feelings, that it occasionally mewed and purred almost in the same breath. Such demonstrations of joy and affection led us at once to conclude that this poor cat must have known man before, and we conjectured that it had been left either accidentally or by design on the island many years ago, and was now evincing its extreme joy at meeting once more with human beings. While we were fondling the cat and talking about it, Jack glanced round the open space in the midst of which we stood.

"Hallo!" exclaimed he, "this looks something like a clearing. The axe has been at work here. Just look at these tree-stumps."

We now turned to examine these, and without doubt we found trees that had been cut down here and there, also stumps and broken branches; all of which, however, were completely covered over with moss, and bore evidence of having been in this condition for some years. No human footprints were to be seen either on the track or among the bushes, but those of the cat were found everywhere. We now determined to follow up the track as far as it went, and Peterkin put the cat down; but it seemed to be so weak, and mewed so very pitifully, that he took it up again and carried it in his arms, where in a few minutes it fell sound asleep.

About ten yards farther on, the felled trees became more numerous, and the track, diverging to the right, followed for a short space the banks of a stream. Suddenly we came to a spot where once must have been a rude bridge, the stones of which were scattered in the stream, and those on each bank entirely covered over with moss. In silent surprise and expectancy we continued to advance, and, a few yards farther on, beheld, under the shelter of some bread-fruit trees, a small hut or cottage. I cannot hope to convey to my readers a very correct idea of the feelings that affected us on witnessing this unexpected sight. We stood for a long time in silent wonder, for there was a deep and most melancholy stillness about the place that quite overpowered us; and when we did at length speak, it was in subdued whispers, as if we were surrounded by some awful or supernatural influence. Even Peterkin's voice, usually so quick and lively on all occasions, was hushed now; for there was a dreariness about this silent, lonely, uninhabited cottage—so strange in its appearance, so far away from the usual dwellings of man, so old, decayed, and deserted in its aspect—that fell upon our spirits like a thick cloud, and blotted out as with a pall the cheerful sunshine that had filled us since the commencement of our tour round the island.

The hut or cottage was rude and simple in its construction. It was not more than twelve feet long by ten feet broad, and about seven or eight feet high. It had one window, or rather a small frame in which a window might perhaps once have been, but which was now empty. The door was exceedingly low, and formed of rough boards, and the roof was covered with broad cocoa-nut and plantain leaves. But every part of it was in a state of the utmost decay. Moss and green matter grew in spots all over it. The woodwork was quite perforated with holes; the roof had nearly fallen in, and appeared to be prevented from doing so altogether by the thick matting of creeping-plants and the interlaced branches which years of neglect had allowed to cover it almost entirely; while the thick, luxuriant branches of the bread-fruit and other trees spread above it, and flung a deep, sombre shadow over the spot, as if to guard it from the heat and the light of day. We conversed long and in whispers about this strange habitation ere we ventured to approach it; and when at length we did so, it was, at least on my part, with feelings of awe.

At first Jack endeavoured to peep in at the window, but from the deep shadow of the trees already mentioned, and the gloom within, he could not clearly discern objects; so we lifted the latch and pushed open the door. We observed that the latch was made of iron, and almost eaten away with rust. In the like condition were also the hinges, which creaked as the door swung back. On entering, we stood still and gazed around us, while we were much impressed with the dreary stillness of the room. But what we saw there surprised and shocked us not a little. There was no furniture in the apartment save a little wooden stool and an iron pot, the latter almost eaten through with rust. In the corner farthest from the door was a low bedstead, on which lay two skeletons, embedded in a little heap of dry dust. With beating hearts we went forward to examine them. One was the skeleton of a man, the other that of a dog, which was extended close beside that of the man, with its head resting on his bosom.

Now we were very much concerned about this discovery, and could scarce refrain from tears on beholding these sad remains. After some time we began to talk about what we had seen, and to examine in and around the hut, in order to discover some clue to the name or history of this poor man, who had thus died in solitude, with none to mourn his loss save his cat and his faithful dog. But we found nothing—neither a book nor a scrap of paper. We found, however, the decayed remnants of what appeared to have been clothing, and an old axe. But none of these things bore marks of any kind; and, indeed, they were so much decayed as to convince us that they had lain in the condition in which we found them for many years.

This discovery now accounted to us for the tree-stump at the top of the mountain with the initials cut on it; also for the patch of sugar-cane and other traces of man which we had met with in the course of our rambles over the island. And we were much saddened by the reflection that the lot of this poor wanderer might possibly be our own, after many years' residence on the island, unless we should be rescued by the visit of some vessel or the arrival of natives. Having no clue whatever to account for the presence of this poor human being in such a lonely spot, we fell to conjecturing what could have brought him there. I was inclined to think that he must have been a shipwrecked sailor, whose vessel had been lost here, and all the crew been drowned except himself and his dog and cat. But Jack thought it more likely that he had run away from his vessel, and had taken the dog and cat to keep him company. We were also much occupied in our minds with the wonderful difference between the cat and the dog. For here we saw that while the one perished like a loving friend by its master's side, with its head resting on his bosom, the other had sought to sustain itself by prowling abroad in the forest, and had lived in solitude to a good old age. However, we did not conclude from this that the cat was destitute of affection, for we could not forget its emotions on first meeting with us; but we saw from this that the dog had a great deal more of generous love in its nature than the cat, because it not only found it impossible to live after the death of its master, but it must needs, when it came to die, crawl to his side and rest its head upon his lifeless breast.

While we were thinking on these things, and examining into everything about the room, we were attracted by an exclamation from Peterkin.

"I say, Jack," said he, "here is something that will be of use to us."

"What is it?" said Jack, hastening across the room.

"An old pistol," replied Peterkin, holding up the weapon, which he had just pulled from under a heap of broken wood and rubbish that lay in a corner.

"That, indeed, might have been useful," said Jack, examining it, "if we had any powder; but I suspect the bow and the sling will prove more serviceable."

"True, I forgot that," said Peterkin; "but we may as

well take it with us, for the flint will serve to strike fire with when the sun does not shine."

After having spent more than an hour at this place without discovering anything of further interest, Peterkin took up the old cat, which had lain very contentedly asleep on the stool whereon he had placed it, and we prepared to take our departure. In leaving the hut, Jack stumbled heavily against the doorpost, which was so much decayed as to break across, and the whole fabric of the hut seemed ready to tumble about our ears. This put into our heads that we might as well pull it down, and so form a mound over the skeleton. Jack, therefore, with his axe, cut down the other doorpost, which, when it was done, brought the whole hut in ruins to the ground, and thus formed a grave to the bones of the poor recluse and his dog. Then we left the spot, having brought away the iron pot, the pistol, and the old axe, as they might be of much use to us hereafter.

During the rest of this day we pursued our journey, and examined the other end of the large valley, which we found to be so much alike to the parts already described, that I shall not recount the particulars of what we saw in this place. I may, however, remark that we did not quite recover our former cheerful spirits until we arrived at our bower, which we did late in the evening, and found everything just in the same condition as we had left it three days before.

CHAPTER XII

Something wrong with the tank—Jack's wisdom and Peterkin's impertinence—Wonderful behaviour of a crab—Good wishes for those who dwell far from the sea—Jack commences to build a little boat.

REST is sweet as well for the body as for the mind. During my long experience, amid the vicissitudes of a chequered life, I have found that periods of profound rest at certain intervals, in addition to the ordinary hours of repose, are necessary to the well-being of man. And the nature as well as the period of this rest varies, according to the different temperaments of individuals, and the peculiar circumstances in which they may chance to be placed. To those who work with their minds, bodily labour is rest. To those who labour with the body, deep sleep is rest. To the downcast, the weary, and the sorrowful, joy and peace are rest. Nay, further, I think that to the gay, the frivolous, the reckless, when sated with pleasures that cannot last, even sorrow proves to be rest of a kind, although, perchance, it were better that I should call it relief than rest. There is, indeed, but one class of men to whom rest is denied—there is no rest to the wicked. At this I do but hint, however, as I treat not of that rest which is spiritual, but more particularly of that which applies to the mind and to the body.

Of this rest we stood much in need on our return home, and we found it exceedingly sweet when we indulged in it after completing the journey just related. It had not, indeed, been a very long journey, nevertheless we had pursued it so diligently that our frames were not a little prostrated. Our minds were also very much exhausted in consequence of the many surprises, frequent alarms, and much profound thought to which they had been subjected; so that when we lay down on the night of our return under the shelter of the bower, we fell immediately into very deep repose. I can state this with much certainty, for Jack afterwards admitted the fact, and Peterkin, although he stoutly denied it, I heard snoring loudly at least two minutes after lying down. In this condition we remained all night and the whole of the following day without awaking once, or so much as moving our positions. When we did awake it was near sunset, and we were all in such a state of lassitude that we merely rose to swallow a mouthful of food. As Peterkin remarked, in the midst of a yawn, we took breakfast at tea-time, and then went to bed again, where we lay to the following forenoon.

After this we arose very greatly refreshed, but much alarmed lest we had lost count of a day. I say we were much alarmed on this head, for we had carefully kept count of the days since we were cast upon our island, in order that we might remember the Sabbath-day, which day we had hitherto with one accord kept as a day of rest, and refrained from all work whatsoever. However, on considering the subject, we all three entertained the same opinion as to how long we had slept, and so our minds were put at ease.

We now hastened to our Water Garden to enjoy a bathe, and to see how did the animals which I had placed in the tank. We found the garden more charming, pellucid, and inviting than ever, and Jack and I plunged into its depth and gambolled among its radiant coral groves, while Peterkin wallowed at the surface, and tried occasionally to kick us as we passed below. Having dressed, I then hastened to the tank; but what was my surprise and grief to find nearly all the animals dead, and the water in a putrid condition! I was greatly distressed at this, and wondered what could be the cause of it.

"Why, you precious humbug," said Peterkin, coming up to me, "how could you expect it to be otherwise? When fishes are accustomed to live in the Pacific Ocean, how can you expect them to exist in a hole like that?"

"Indeed, Peterkin," I replied, "there seems to be truth in what you say. Nevertheless, now I think of it, there must be some error in your reasoning; for if I put in but a few very small animals, they will bear the same proportion to this pond that the millions of fish bear to the ocean."

"I say, Jack," cried Peterkin, waving his hand, "come here, like a good fellow. Ralph is actually talking philosophy. Do come to our assistance, for he's out o' sight beyond me already!"

"What's the matter?" inquired Jack, coming up, while he endeavoured to scrub his long hair dry with a towel of cocoa-nut cloth.

I repeated my thoughts to Jack, who, I was happy to find, quite agreed with me. "The best plan," he said, "will be to put very few animals at first into your tank, and add more as you find it will bear them. And look here," he added, pointing to the sides of the tank, which, for the space of two inches above the water-level, were encrusted with salt, "you must carry your philosophy a little further, Ralph. That water has evaporated so much that it is too salt for anything to live in. You will require to add *fresh* water now and then, in order to keep it at the same degree of saltness as the sea."

"Very true, Jack; that never struck me before," said I.

"And, now I think of it," continued Jack, "it seems to me that the surest way of arranging your tank so as to get it to keep pure and in good condition, will be to *imitate* the ocean in it. In fact, make it a miniature Pacific. I don't see how you can hope to succeed unless you do that."

"Most true," said I, pondering what my companion said. "But I fear that that will be very difficult."

"Not at all," cried Jack, rolling his towel up into a ball and throwing it into the face of Peterkin, who had been grinning and winking at him during the last five minutes —"not at all. Look here. There is water of a certain saltness in the sea; well, fill your tank with sea-water, and keep it at that saltness by marking the height at which the water stands on the sides. When it evaporates a little, pour in *fresh* water from the brook till it comes up to the mark, and then it will be right, for the salt does not evaporate with the water. Then there's lots of seaweed in the sea; well, go and get one or two bits of seaweed and put them into your tank. Of course the weed must be alive, and growing to little stones; or you can chip a bit off the rocks with the weed sticking to it. Then, if you like, you can throw a little sand and gravel into your tank and the thing's complete."

"Nay, not quite," said Peterkin, who had been gravely attentive to this off-hand advice—"not quite; you must first make three little men to dive in it before it can be said to be perfect; and that would be rather difficult, I fear, for two of them would require to be philosophers. But hallo! what's this? I say, Ralph, look here. There's one o' your crabs up to something uncommon. It's performing the most remarkable operation for a crab I ever saw—taking off its coat, I do believe, before going to bed!"

We hastily stooped over the tank, and certainly were not a little amused at the conduct of one of the crabs which still survived its companions. It was one of the common small crabs, like to those that are found running about everywhere on the coasts of England. While we gazed at it, we observed its back to split away from the lower part of its body, and out of the gap thus formed came a soft lump which moved and writhed unceasingly. This lump continued to increase in size until it appeared like a bunch of crab's legs; and, indeed, such it proved in a very few minutes to be, for the points of the toes were at length extricated from the hole in its back, the legs spread out, the body followed, and the crab walked away quite entire, even to the points of its nipper-claws, leaving a perfectly entire shell behind it, so that, when we looked, it seemed as though there were two complete crabs instead of one.

"Well!" exclaimed Peterkin, drawing a long breath, "I've *heard* of a man jumping out of his skin and sitting down in his skeleton in order to cool himself, but I never expected to *see* a crab do it!"

We were, in truth, much amazed at this spectacle, and the more so when we observed that the new crab was larger than the crab that it came out of. It was also quite soft, but by next morning its skin had hardened into a good shell. We came thus to know that crabs grow in this way, and not by the growing of their shells, as we had always thought before we saw this wonderful operation.

Now I considered well the advice which Jack had given me about preparing my tank, and the more I thought of it the more I came to regard it as very sound and worthy of being acted on. So I forthwith put his plan in execution, and found it to answer excellently well, indeed, much beyond my expectation; for I found that, after a little experience had taught me the proper proportion of sea-weed and animals to put into a certain amount of water, the tank needed no further attendance; and, moreover, I did not require ever afterwards to renew or change the sea-water, but only to add a very little fresh water from the brook, now and then, as the other evaporated. I therefore concluded that if I had been suddenly conveyed, along with my tank, into some region where there was no salt sea at all, my little sea and my sea-fish would have continued to thrive and to prosper notwithstanding. This made me greatly to desire that those people in the world who live far inland might know of my wonderful tank, and, by having materials like to those of which it was made conveyed to them, thus be enabled to watch the habits of those most mysterious animals that reside in the sea, and examine with their own eyes the wonders of the great deep.

For many days after this, while Peterkin and Jack were busily employed in building a little boat out of the curious natural planks of the chestnut tree, I spent much of my time in examining with the burning-glass the marvellous operations that were constantly going on in my tank. Here I saw those anemones which cling, like little red,

yellow, and green blobs of jelly, to the rocks, put forth, as
it were, a multitude of arms and wait till little fish or
other small animalcules unwarily touched them, when they
would instantly seize them, fold arm after arm around their
victims, and so engulf them in their stomachs.   Here I
saw the ceaseless working of those little coral insects whose
efforts have encrusted the islands of the Pacific with vast
rocks and surrounded them with enormous reefs.   And I
observed that many of these insects, though extremely
minute, were very beautiful, coming out of their holes in a
circle of fine threads, and having the form of a shuttle-
cock.   Here I saw curious little barnacles opening a hole
in their backs and constantly putting out a thin, feathery
hand, with which, I doubt not, they dragged their food
into their mouths.   Here, also, I saw those crabs which
have shells only on the front of their bodies, but no shell
whatever on their remarkably tender tails, so that, in order
to find a protection to them, they thrust them into the
empty shells of whelks, or some such fish, and when they
grow too big for one, change into another.   But, most
curious of all, I saw an animal which had the wonderful
power, when it became ill, of casting its stomach and its
teeth away from it, and getting an entirely new set in the
course of a few months !   All this I saw, and a great deal
more, by means of my tank and my burning-glass ; but I
refrain from setting down more particulars here, as I have
still much to tell of the adventures that befell us while we
remained on this island.

CHAPTER XIII

Notable discovery at the spouting cliffs—The mysterious green monster explained—We are thrown into unutterable terror by the idea that Jack is drowned—The Diamond Cave.

"COME, Jack," cried Peterkin, one morning about three weeks after our return from our long excursion, "let's be jolly to-day, and do something vigorous. I'm quite tired of hammering and bammering, hewing and screwing, cutting and butting, at that little boat of ours, that seems as hard to build as Noah's ark. Let us go on an excursion to the mountain-top, or have a hunt after the wild-ducks, or make a dash at the pigs. I'm quite flat—flat as bad ginger-beer—flat as a pancake; in fact, I want something to rouse me, to toss me up, as it were. Eh! what do you say to it?"

"Well," answered Jack, throwing down the axe with which he was just about to proceed towards the boat, "if that's what you want, I would recommend you to make an excursion to the water-spouts. The last one we had to do with tossed you up a considerable height; perhaps the next will send you higher—who knows?—if you're at all reasonable or moderate in your expectations!"

"Jack, my dear boy," said Peterkin gravely, "you are really becoming too fond of jesting. It's a thing I don't at all approve of, and if you don't give it up, I fear that, for our mutual good, we shall have to part."

"Well then, Peterkin," replied Jack with a smile, "what would you have?"

"Have?" said Peterkin; "I would *have* nothing. I didn't say I wanted to *have*; I said that I wanted to *do*."

"By-the-bye," said I, interrupting their conversation, "I am reminded by this that we have not yet discovered the nature of yon curious appearance that we saw near the water-spouts, on our journey round the island. Perhaps it would be well to go for that purpose."

"Humph!" ejaculated Peterkin, "I know the nature of it well enough."

"What was it?" said I.

"It was of a *mysterious* nature to be sure!" said he, with a wave of his hand, while he rose from the log on which he had been sitting and buckled on his belt, into which he thrust his enormous club.

"Well, then, let us away to the water-spouts," cried Jack, going up to the bower for his bow and arrows; "and bring your spear, Peterkin. It may be useful."

We now, having made up our minds to examine into this matter, sallied forth eagerly in the direction of the water-spout rocks, which, as I have before mentioned, were not far from our present place of abode. On arriving there we hastened down to the edge of the rocks and gazed over into the sea, where we observed the pale-green object still distinctly visible, moving its tail slowly to and fro in the water.

"Most remarkable!" said Jack.

"Exceedingly curious!" said I.

"Beats everything!" said Peterkin.

"Now, Jack," he added, "you made such a poor figure in your last attempt to stick that object, that I would advise you to let me try it. If it has got a heart at all, I'll engage to send my spear right through the core of it; if it hasn't got a heart, I'll send it through the spot where its heart ought to be."

" Fire away then, my boy," replied Jack with a laugh.

Peterkin immediately took the spear, poised it for a second or two above his head, then darted it like an arrow into the sea. Down it went straight into the centre of the green object, passed quite through it, and came up immediately afterwards, pure and unsullied, while the mysterious tail moved quietly as before!

" Now," said Peterkin gravely, "that brute is a heartless monster; I'll have nothing more to do with it."

" I'm pretty sure now," said Jack, " that it is merely a phosphoric light; but I must say, I'm puzzled at its staying always in that exact spot."

I also was much puzzled, and inclined to think with Jack that it must be phosphoric light, of which luminous appearance we had seen much while on our voyage to these seas. " But," said I, " there is nothing to hinder us from diving down to it, now that we are sure it is not a shark."

" True," returned Jack, stripping off his clothes; " I'll go down, Ralph, as I'm better at diving than you are.— Now then, Peterkin, out o' the road!" Jack stepped forward, joined his hands above his head, bent over the rocks, and plunged into the sea. For a second or two the spray caused by his dive hid him from view; then the water became still, and we saw him swimming far down in the midst of the green object. Suddenly he sank below it, and vanished altogether from our sight! We gazed anxiously down at the spot where he had disappeared for nearly a minute, expecting every moment to see him rise

again for breath; but fully a minute appeared, and still
he did not reappear. Two minutes passed! and then a
flood of alarm rushed in upon my soul, when I considered
that, during all my acquaintance with him, Jack had never
stayed under water more than a minute at a time; indeed,
seldom so long.

"O Peterkin!" I said, in a voice that trembled with
increasing anxiety, "something has happened. It is more
than three minutes now." But Peterkin did not answer, and
I observed that he was gazing down into the water with a
look of intense fear mingled with anxiety, while his face
was overspread with a deadly paleness. Suddenly he
sprang to his feet and rushed about in a frantic state,
wringing his hands, and exclaiming, "O Jack, Jack! he
is gone! It must have been a shark, and he is gone for
ever!"

For the next five minutes I know not what I did; the
intensity of my feelings almost bereft me of my senses.
But I was recalled to myself by Peterkin seizing me by
the shoulders and staring wildly into my face, while he
exclaimed, "Ralph! Ralph! perhaps he has only fainted.
Dive for him, Ralph!"

It seemed strange that this did not occur to me sooner.
In a moment I rushed to the edge of the rocks, and without waiting to throw off my garments, was on the point to
spring into the waves, when I observed something black
rising up through the green object. In another moment
Jack's head rose to the surface, and he gave a wild shout,
flinging back the spray from his locks, as was his wont
after a dive. Now we were almost as much amazed at
seeing him reappear, well and strong, as we had been at
first at his non-appearance; for, to the best of our judg-

ment, he had been nearly ten minutes under water, perhaps longer, and it required no exertion of our reason to convince us that this was utterly impossible for mortal man to do and retain his strength and faculties. It was therefore with a feeling akin to superstitious awe that I held down my hand and assisted him to clamber up the steep rocks. But no such feeling affected Peterkin. No sooner did Jack gain the rocks and seat himself on one, panting for breath, than he threw his arms round his neck and burst into a flood of tears. " O Jack, Jack ! " said he, " where were you ? What kept you so long ? "

After a few moments Peterkin became composed enough to sit still and listen to Jack's explanation, although he could not restrain himself from attempting to wink every two minutes at me, in order to express his joy at Jack's safety. I say he attempted to wink, but I am bound to add that he did not succeed, for his eyes were so much swollen with weeping, that his frequent attempts only resulted in a series of violent and altogether idiotical contortions of the face, that were very far from expressing what he intended. However, I knew what the poor fellow meant by it, so I smiled to him in return, and endeavoured to make believe that he was winking.

" Now, lads," said Jack, when we were composed enough to listen to him, " yon green object is not a shark ; it is a stream of light issuing from a cave in the rocks. Just after I made my dive, I observed that this light came from the side of the rock above which we are now sitting ; so I struck out for it, and saw an opening into some place or other that appeared to be luminous within. For one instant I paused to think whether I ought to venture. Then

I made up my mind, and dashed into it. For you see,
Peterkin, although I take some time to tell this, it happened
in the space of a few seconds, so that I knew I had wind
enough in me to serve to bring me out o' the hole and
up to the surface again. Well, I was just on the point of
turning—for I began to feel a little uncomfortable in such
a place—when it seemed to me as if there was a faint light
right above me. I darted upwards, and found my head out
of water. This relieved me greatly, for I now felt that I
could take in air enough to enable me to return the way I
came. Then it all at once occurred to me that I might
not be able to find the way out again; but, on glancing
downwards, my mind was put quite at rest by seeing the
green light below me streaming into the cave, just like the
light that we had seen streaming out of it, only what I now
saw was much brighter.

" At first I could scarcely see anything as I gazed around
me, it was so dark ; but gradually my eyes became accustomed to it, and I found that I was in a huge cave,
part of the walls of which I observed on each side of me.
The ceiling just above me was also visible, and I fancied
that I could perceive beautiful glittering objects there ;
but the farther end of the cave was shrouded in darkness.
While I was looking around me in great wonder, it came
into my head that you two would think I was drowned ; so
I plunged down through the passage again in a great hurry,
rose to the surface, and—here I am ! "

When Jack concluded his recital of what he had seen
in this remarkable cave, I could not rest satisfied till I
had dived down to see it : which I did, but found it so
dark, as Jack had said, that I could scarcely see anything.
When I returned, we had a long conversation about it,

during which I observed that Peterkin had a most lugu-
brious expression on his countenance.

"What's the matter, Peterkin?" said I.

"The matter?" he replied. "It's all very well for you
two to be talking away like mermaids about the wonders
of this cave, but you know I must be content to hear about
it, while you are enjoying yourselves down there like mad
dolphins. It's really too bad."

"I'm very sorry for you, Peterkin, indeed I am," said
Jack, "but we cannot help you. If you would only learn
to dive——"

"Learn to fly, you might as well say!" retorted Peterkin
in a very sulky tone.

"If you would only consent to keep still," said I, "we
would take you down with us in ten seconds."

"Hum!" returned Peterkin; "suppose a salamander
was to propose to you 'only to keep still,' and he would
carry you through a blazing fire in a few seconds, what
would you say?"

We both laughed and shook our heads, for it was
evident that nothing was to be made of Peterkin in the
water. But we could not rest satisfied till we had seen
more of this cave; so, after further consultation, Jack
and I determined to try if we could take down a torch
with us, and set fire to it in the cavern. This we found
to be an undertaking of no small difficulty, but we accomplished it at last by the following means: First, we made
a torch of a very inflammable nature out of the bark of a
certain tree, which we cut into strips, and, after twisting,
cemented together with a kind of resin or gum, which we
also obtained from another tree; neither of which trees, however, was known by name to Jack. This, when prepared,

we wrapped up in a great number of plies of cocoa-nut cloth, so that we were confident it could not get wet during the short time it should be under water. Then we took a small piece of the tinder, which we had carefully treasured up lest we should require it, as before said, when the sun should fail us; also, we rolled up some dry grass and a few chips, which, with a little bow and drill, like those described before, we made into another bundle, and wrapped it up in cocoa-nut cloth. When all was ready, we laid aside our garments, with the exception of our trousers, which, as we did not know what rough scraping against the rocks we might be subjected to, we kept on.

Then we advanced to the edge of the rocks, Jack carrying one bundle, with the torch, I the other, with the things for producing fire.

"Now don't weary for us, Peterkin, should we be gone some time," said Jack; "we'll be sure to return in half-an-hour at the very latest, however interesting the cave should be, that we may relieve your mind."

"Farewell!" said Peterkin, coming up to us with a look of deep but pretended solemnity, while he shook hands and kissed each of us on the cheek. "Farewell! and while you are gone I shall repose my weary limbs under the shelter of this bush, and meditate on the changefulness of all things earthly, with special reference to the forsaken condition of a poor shipwrecked sailor boy!" So saying, Peterkin waved his hand, turned from us, and cast himself upon the ground with a look of melancholy resignation, which was so well feigned that I would have thought it genuine had he not accompanied it with a gentle wink. We both laughed, and springing from the rocks together, plunged head first into the sea.

We gained the interior of the submarine cave without difficulty, and, on emerging from the waves, supported ourselves for some time by treading water, while we held the two bundles above our heads. This we did in order to let our eyes become accustomed to the obscurity. Then, when we could see sufficiently, we swam to a shelving rock, and landed in safety. Having wrung the water from our trousers, and dried ourselves as well as we could under the circumstances, we proceeded to ignite the torch. This we accomplished without difficulty in a few minutes; and no sooner did it flare up than we were struck dumb with the wonderful objects that were revealed to our gaze. The roof of the cabin just above us seemed to be about ten feet high, but grew higher as it receded into the distance, until it was lost in darkness. It seemed to be made of coral, and was supported by massive columns of the same material. Immense icicles (as they appeared to us) hung from it in various places. These, however, were formed not of ice, but of a species of limestone, which seemed to flow in a liquid form towards the point of each, where it became solid. A good many drops fell, however, to the rock below, and these formed little cones, which rose to meet the points above. Some of them had already met, and thus we saw how the pillars were formed, which at first seemed to us as if they had been placed there by some human architect to support the roof. As we advanced farther in, we saw that the floor was composed of the same material as the pillars; and it presented the curious appearance of ripples such as are formed on water when gently ruffled by the wind. There were several openings on either hand in the walls that seemed to lead into other caverns; but, these we did not explore at this time. We also observed that the ceiling was curiously marked in many places, as if it were the fretwork of a noble cathedral; and the walls, as well as the roof, sparkled in the light of our torch, and threw back gleams and flashes as if they were covered with precious stones. Although we proceeded far into this cavern, we did not come to the end of it; and we were obliged to return more speedily than we would otherwise have done, as our torch was nearly expended. We did not observe any openings in the roof, or any indications of places whereby light might enter; but near the entrance to the cavern stood an immense mass of pure white coral rock, which caught and threw back the little light that found an entrance through the cave's mouth, and thus produced, we conjectured, the pale-green object which had first attracted our attention. We concluded, also, that the reflecting power of this rock was that which gave forth the dim light that faintly illumined the first part of the cave.

Before diving through the passage again we extinguished the small piece of our torch that remained, and left it in a dry spot; conceiving that we might possibly stand in need of it, if at any future time we should chance to wet our torch while diving into the cavern. As we stood for a few minutes after it was out, waiting till our eyes became accustomed to the gloom, we could not help remarking the deep, intense stillness and the unutterable gloom of all around us; and, as I thought of the stupendous dome above, and the countless gems that had sparkled in the torchlight a few minutes before, it came into my mind to consider how strange it is that God should make such wonderful and exquisitely beautiful works never to

be seen at all, except, indeed, by chance visitors such as
ourselves.

I afterwards found that there were many such caverns
among the islands of the South Seas, some of them larger
and more beautiful than the one I have just described.

"Now, Ralph, are you ready?" said Jack, in a low
voice, that seemed to echo up into the dome above.

"Quite ready."

"Come along, then," said he; and plunging off the
ledge of the rock into the water, we dived through the
narrow entrance. In a few seconds we were panting on
the rocks above, and receiving the congratulations of our
friend Peterkin.

CHAPTER XIV

Strange peculiarity of the tides—Also of the twilight—Peterkin's remarkable conduct in embracing a little pig and killing a big sow—Sage remarks on jesting—Also on love.

IT was quite a relief to us to breathe the pure air and to enjoy the glad sunshine after our long ramble in the Diamond Cave, as we named it; for although we did not stay more than half-an-hour away, it seemed to us much longer. While we were dressing, and during our walk home, we did our best to satisfy the curiosity of poor Peterkin, who seemed to regret, with lively sincerity, his inability to dive.

There was no help for it, however, so we condoled with him as we best could. Had there been any great rise or fall in the tide of these seas, we might perhaps have found it possible to take him down with us at low water; but as the tide never rose or fell more than eighteen inches or two feet, this was impossible.

This peculiarity of the tide—its slight rise and fall— had not attracted our observation till some time after our residence on the island. Neither had we observed another curious circumstance until we had been some time there. This was the fact that the tide rose and fell with constant regularity, instead of being affected by the changes of the moon as in our own country, and as it is in most other parts of the world—at least in all those parts with which I am acquainted. Every day and every night, at twelve o'clock precisely, the tide is at the full; and at six o'clock every morning and evening it is ebb. I can speak with much confidence on this singular circumstance, as we took particular note of it, and never found it to alter. Of course, I must admit, we had to guess the hour of twelve midnight, and I think we could do this pretty correctly; but in regard to twelve noon we are quite positive, because we easily found the highest point that the sun reached in the sky by placing ourselves at a certain spot whence we observed the sharp summit of a cliff resting against the sky, just where the sun passed.

Jack and I were surprised that we had not noticed this the first few days of our residence here, and could only account for it by our being so much taken up with the more obvious wonders of our novel situation. I have since learned, however, that this want of observation is a sad and very common infirmity of human nature, there being hundreds of persons before whose eyes the most wonderful things are passing every day, who nevertheless are totally ignorant of them. I therefore have to record my sympathy with such persons, and to recommend to them a course of conduct which I have now for a long time myself adopted—namely, the habit of forcing my attention upon *all* things that go on around me, and of taking some degree of interest in them, whether I feel it naturally or not. I suggest this the more earnestly, though humbly, because I have very frequently come to know that my indifference to a thing has generally been caused by my ignorance in regard to it.

We had much serious conversation on this subject of

the tides; and Jack told us, in his own quiet, philo-
sophical way, that these tides did great good to the world
in many ways, particularly in the way of cleansing the
shores of the land, and carrying off the filth that was
constantly poured into the sea therefrom; which, Peterkin
suggested, was remarkably *tidy* of it to do.   Poor Peterkin
could never let slip an opportunity to joke, however in-
opportune it might be: which at first we found rather a
disagreeable propensity, as it often interrupted the flow
of very agreeable conversation—and, indeed, I cannot too
strongly record my disapprobation of this tendency in
general—but we became so used to it at last that we
found it no interruption whatever; indeed, strange to say,
we came to feel that it was a necessary part of our enjoyment (such is the force of habit), and found the sudden
outbursts of mirth, resulting from his humorous disposition, quite natural and refreshing to us in the midst of
our more serious conversations.   But I must not mis-
represent Peterkin.   We often found, to our surprise,
that he knew many things which we did not; and I also
observed that those things which he learned from experience were never forgotten.   From all these things I came
at length to understand that things very opposite and
dissimilar in themselves, when united, do make an agreeable whole; as, for example, we three on this our island,
although most unlike in many things, when united, made
a trio so harmonious that I question if there ever met
before such an agreeable triumvirate.   There was, indeed,
no note of discord whatever in the symphony we played
together on that sweet Coral Island; and I am now persuaded that this was owing to our having been all tuned
to the same key, namely, that of *love!*   Yes, we loved one

another with much fervency while we lived on that island; and, for the matter of that, we love each other still.

And while I am on this subject, or rather the subject that just preceded it—namely, the tides—I may here remark on another curious natural phenomenon. We found that there was little or no twilight in this island. We had a distinct remembrance of the charming long twilight at home, which some people think the most delightful part of the day, though for my part I have always preferred sunrise; and when we first landed, we used to sit down on some rocky point or eminence, at the close of our day's work, to enjoy the evening breeze; but no sooner had the sun sunk below the horizon than all became suddenly dark. This rendered it necessary that we should watch the sun when we happened to be out hunting; for to be suddenly left in the dark while in the woods was very perplexing, as, although the stars shone with great beauty and brilliancy, they could not pierce through the thick umbrageous boughs that interlaced above our heads.

But to return: after having told all we could to Peterkin about the Diamond Cave under Spouting Cliff, as we named the locality, we were wending our way rapidly homewards, when a grunt and a squeal were borne down by the land breeze to our ears.

" That's the ticket!" was Peterkin's remarkable exclamation, as he started convulsively and levelled his spear.

" Hist!" cried Jack; " these are your friends, Peterkin. They must have come over expressly to pay you a friendly visit, for it is the first time we have seen them on this side the island."

" Come along!" cried Peterkin, hurrying towards the

wood, while Jack and I followed, smiling at his impatience.

Another grunt and half-a-dozen squeals, much louder than before, came down the valley. At this time we were just opposite the small vale which lay between the Valley of the Wreck and Spouting Cliff.

"I say, Peterkin," cried Jack in a hoarse whisper.

"Well, what is't?"

"Stay a bit, man. These grunters are just up there on the hillside. If you go and stand with Ralph in the lee of yon cliff, I'll cut round behind and drive them through the gorge, so that you'll have a better chance of picking out a good one. Now, mind you pitch into a fat young pig, Peterkin," added Jack, as he sprang into the bushes.

"Won't I, just!" said Peterkin, licking his lips, as we took our station beside the cliff. "I feel quite a tender affection for young pigs in my heart. Perhaps it would be more correct to say in my s——"

"There they come!" cried I, as a terrific yell from Jack sent the whole herd screaming down the hill. Now Peterkin, being unable to hold back, crept a short way up a very steep, grassy mound, in order to get a better view of the hogs before they came up; and just as he raised his head above its summit, two little pigs, which had outrun their companions, rushed over the top with the utmost precipitation. One of these brushed close past Peterkin's ear; the other, unable to arrest its headlong flight, went, as Peterkin himself afterwards expressed it, "bash" into his arms with a sudden squeal, which was caused more by the force of the blow than the will of the animal, and both of them rolled violently down to the foot of the mound. No sooner was this reached than the little pig recovered its feet, tossed up its tail, and fled shrieking from the spot. But I slung a large stone after it, which, being fortunately well aimed, hit it behind the ear, and felled it to the earth.

"Capital, Ralph! that's your sort!" cried Peterkin, who, to my surprise, and great relief, had risen to his feet apparently unhurt, though much dishevelled. He rushed franticly towards the gorge, which the yells of the hogs told us they were now approaching. I had made up my mind that I would abstain from killing another, as, if Peterkin should be successful, two were more than sufficient for our wants at the present time. Suddenly they all burst forth—two or three little round ones in advance, and an enormous old sow with a drove of hogs at her heels.

"Now, Peterkin," said I, "there's a nice little fat one; just spear it."

But Peterkin did not move; he allowed it to pass unharmed. I looked at him in surprise, and saw that his lips were compressed and his eyebrows knitted, as if he were about to fight with some awful enemy.

"What is it?" I inquired, with some trepidation.

Suddenly he levelled his spear, darted forward, and, with a yell that nearly froze the blood in my veins, stabbed the old sow to the heart. Nay, so vigorously was it done that the spear went in at one side and came out at the other!

"O Peterkin," said I, going up to him, "what have you done?"

"Done? I've killed their great-great-grandmother, that's all," said he, looking with a somewhat awe-struck expression at the transfixed animal.

"Hallo! what's this?" said Jack, as he came up. "Why, Peterkin, you must be fond of a tough chop. If you mean to eat this old hog, she'll try your jaws, I warrant. What possessed you to stick *her*, Peterkin?"

"Why, the fact is, I want a pair of shoes."

"What have your shoes to do with the old hog?" said I, smiling.

"My present shoes have certainly nothing to do with her," replied Peterkin; "nevertheless, she will have a good deal to do with my future shoes. The fact is, when I saw you floor that pig so neatly, Ralph, it struck me that there was little use in killing another. Then I remembered all at once that I had long wanted some leather or tough substance to make shoes of, and this old grandmother seemed so tough that I just made up my mind to stick her, and you see I've done it!"

"That you certainly have, Peterkin," said Jack, as he was examining the transfixed animal.

We now considered how we were to carry our game home, for, although the distance was short, the hog was very heavy. At length we hit on the plan of tying its four feet together, and passing the spear handle between them. Jack took one end on his shoulder, I took the other on mine, and Peterkin carried the small pig.

Thus we returned in triumph to our bower, laden, as Peterkin remarked, with the glorious spoils of a noble hunt. As he afterwards spoke in similarly glowing terms in reference to the supper that followed, there is every reason to believe that we retired that night to our leafy beds in a high state of satisfaction.

CHAPTER XV

Boat-building extraordinary—Peterkin tries his hand at cookery, and fails most signally—The boat finished—Curious conversation with the cat and other matters.

FOR many days after this Jack applied himself with unremitting assiduity to the construction of our boat, which at length began to look something like one. But those only who have had the thing to do can entertain a right idea of the difficulty involved in such an undertaking, with no other implements than an axe, a bit of hoop-iron, a sail-needle, and a broken penknife. But Jack did it. He was of that disposition which *will* not be conquered. When he believed himself to be acting rightly, he overcame all obstacles. I have seen Jack, when doubtful whether what he was about to do were right or wrong, as timid and vacillating as a little girl; and I honour him for it!

As this boat was a curiosity in its way, a few words here relative to the manner of its construction may not be amiss.

I have already mentioned the chestnut tree with its wonderful buttresses or planks. This tree, then, furnished us with the chief part of our material. First of all, Jack sought out a limb of a tree of such a form and size as, while it should form the keel, a bend at either end should form the stem and stern-posts. Such a piece, however, was not easy to obtain; but at last he procured it by

rooting up a small tree which had a branch growing at
the proper angle about ten feet up its stem, with two
strong roots growing in such a form as enabled him to
make a flat-sterned boat. This placed, he procured three
branching roots of suitable size, which he fitted to the
keel at equal distances, thus forming three strong ribs.
Now the squaring and shaping of these, and the cutting
of the grooves in the keel, was an easy enough matter, as
it was all work for the axe, in the use of which Jack was
become wonderfully expert; but it was quite a different
affair when he came to nailing the ribs to the keel, for we
had no instrument capable of boring a large hole, and no
nails to fasten them with. We were, indeed, much perplexed here; but Jack at length devised an instrument
that served very well. He took the remainder of our
hoop-iron and beat it into the form of a pipe or cylinder,
about as thick as a man's finger. This he did by means
of our axe and the old rusty axe we had found at the
house of the poor man at the other side of the island.
This, when made red hot, bored slowly through the
timbers; and, the better to retain the heat, Jack shut
up one end of it and filled it with sand. True, the work
was very slowly done, but it mattered not, we had little
else to do. Two holes were bored in each timber, about
an inch and a half apart, and also down into the keel, but
not quite through. Into these were placed stout pegs
made of a tree called iron-wood; and, when they were
hammered well home, the timbers were as firmly fixed
as if they had been nailed with iron. The gunwales,
which were very stout, were fixed in a similar manner.
But, besides the wooden nails, they were firmly lashed to
the stem and stern-posts and ribs by means of a species of

cordage which we had contrived to make out of the fibrous husk of the cocoa-nut. This husk was very tough, and when a number of the threads were joined together they formed excellent cordage. At first we tied the different lengths together; but this was such a clumsy and awkward complication of knots that we contrived, by careful interlacing of the ends together before twisting, to make good cordage of any size or length we chose. Of course it cost us much time and infinite labour, but Jack kept up our spirits when we grew weary, and so all that we required was at last constructed.

Planks were now cut off the chestnut trees of about an inch thick. These were dressed with the axe—but clumsily, for an axe is ill adapted for such work. Five of these planks on each side were sufficient; and we formed the boat in a very rounded, barrel-like shape, in order to have as little twisting of the planks as possible, for although we could easily bend them, we could not easily twist them. Having no nails to rivet the planks with, we threw aside the ordinary fashion of boat-building and adopted one of our own. The planks were therefore placed on each other's edges, and sewed together with the tough cordage already mentioned. They were also thus sewed to the stem, the stern, and the keel. Each stitch or tie was six inches apart, and was formed thus: Three holes were bored in the upper plank and three in the lower—the holes being above each other, that is, in a vertical line. Through these holes the cord was passed, and, when tied, formed a powerful stitch of three-ply. Besides this, we placed between the edges of the planks layers of cocoa-nut fibre, which, as it swelled when wetted, would, we hoped, make our little vessel water-tight. But in order further to secure this end, we collected a large quantity of pitch from the bread-fruit tree, with which, when boiled in our old iron pot, we paid the whole of the inside of the boat, and, while it was yet hot, placed large pieces of cocoa-nut cloth on it, and then gave it another coat above that. Thus the interior was covered with a tough, water-tight material; while the exterior, being uncovered, and so exposed to the swelling action of the water, was, we hoped, likely to keep the boat quite dry. I may add that our hopes were not disappointed.

While Jack was thus engaged, Peterkin and I sometimes assisted him; but as our assistance was not much required, we more frequently went a-hunting on the extensive mud-flats at the entrance of the long valley which lay nearest to our bower. Here we found large flocks of ducks of various kinds, some of them bearing so much resemblance to the wild ducks of our own country that I think they must have been the same. On these occasions we took the bow and the sling, with both of which we were often successful, though I must confess that I was the least so. Our suppers were thus pleasantly varied, and sometimes we had such a profusion spread out before us that we frequently knew not with which of the dainties to begin.

I must also add that the poor old cat which we had brought home had always a liberal share of our good things, and so well was it looked after, especially by Peterkin, that it recovered much of its former strength, and seemed to improve in sight as well as hearing.

The large flat stone, or rock of coral, which stood just in front of the entrance to our bower, was our table. On this rock we had spread out the few articles we possessed the day we were shipwrecked; and on the same rock, during many a day afterwards, we spread out the bountiful supply with which we had been blessed on our Coral Island. Sometimes we sat down at this table to a feast consisting of hot rolls—as Peterkin called the newly baked bread-fruit—a roast pig, roast duck, boiled and roasted yams, cocoa-nuts, taro, and sweet potatoes; which we followed up with a dessert of plums, apples, and plantains—the last being a large-sized and delightful fruit, which grew on a large shrub or tree not more than twelve feet high, with light-green leaves of enormous length and breadth. These luxurious feasts were usually washed down with cocoa-nut lemonade.

Occasionally Peterkin tried to devise some new dish —"a conglomerate," as he used to say; but these generally turned out such atrocious compounds that he was ultimately induced to give up his attempts in extreme disgust—not forgetting, however, to point out to Jack that his failure was a direct contradiction to the proverb which he (Jack) was constantly thrusting down his throat —namely, that "where there's a will there's a way." For he had a great will to become a cook, but could by no means find a way to accomplish that end.

One day, while Peterkin and I were seated beside our table, on which dinner was spread, Jack came up from the beach, and, flinging down his axe, exclaimed—

"There, lads, the boat's finished at last! So we've nothing to do now but shape two pair of oars, and then we may put to sea as soon as we like."

This piece of news threw us into a state of great joy; for, although we were aware that the boat had been gradually getting near its completion, it had taken so long that we did not expect it to be quite ready for at least two or three weeks. But Jack had wrought hard and said nothing, in order to surprise us.

"My dear fellow," cried Peterkin, "you're a perfect trump. But why did you not tell us it was so nearly ready? Won't we have a jolly sail to-morrow, eh?"

"Don't talk so much, Peterkin," said Jack; "and, pray, hand me a bit of that pig."

"Certainly, my dear," cried Peterkin, seizing the axe. "What part will you have? A leg, or a wing, or a piece of the breast—which?"

"A hind leg, if you please," answered Jack; "and, pray, be so good as to include the tail."

"With all my heart," said Peterkin, exchanging the axe for his hoop-iron knife, with which he cut off the desired portion. "I'm only too glad, my dear boy, to see that your appetite is so wholesale, and there's no chance whatever of its dwindling down into re-tail again, at least, in so far as this pig is concerned.—Ralph, lad, why don't you laugh, eh?" he added, turning suddenly to me with a severe look of inquiry.

"Laugh!" said I; "what at, Peterkin? Why should I laugh?"

Both Jack and Peterkin answered this inquiry by themselves laughing so immoderately that I was induced to believe I had missed noticing some good joke, so I begged that it might be explained to me; but as this only produced repeated roars of laughter, I smiled and helped myself to another slice of plantain.

"Well, but," continued Peterkin, "I was talking of a sail to-morrow. Can't we have one, Jack?"

"No," replied Jack, "we can't have a sail, but I hope

we shall have a row, as I intend to work hard at the oars this afternoon, and, if we can't get them finished by sunset, we'll light our candle-nuts, and turn them out of hands before we turn into bed."

"Very good," said Peterkin, tossing a lump of pork to the cat, who received it with a mew of satisfaction. "I'll help you, if I can."

"Afterwards," continued Jack, "we will make a sail out of the cocoa-nut cloth, and rig up a mast, and then we shall be able to sail to some of the other islands, and visit our old friends the penguins."

The prospect of being so soon in a position to extend our observations to the other islands and enjoy a sail over the beautiful sea afforded us much delight, and after dinner we set about making the oars in good earnest. Jack went into the woods and blocked them roughly out with the axe, and I smoothed them down with the knife, while Peterkin remained in the bower spinning, or rather twisting, some strong, thick cordage with which to fasten them to the boat.

We worked hard and rapidly, so that when the sun went down, Jack and I returned to the bower with four stout oars, which required little to be done to them save a slight degree of polishing with the knife. As we drew near, we were suddenly arrested by the sound of a voice. We were not a little surprised at this—indeed, I may almost say alarmed; for, although Peterkin was undoubtedly fond of talking, we had never up to this time found him talking to himself. We listened intently, and still heard the sound of a voice, as if in conversation. Jack motioned me to be silent, and, advancing to the bower on tip-toe, we peeped in.

The sight that met our gaze was certainly not a little amusing. On the top of a log which we sometimes used as a table sat the black cat, with a very demure expression on its countenance, and in front of it, sitting on the ground with his legs extended on either side of the log, was Peterkin. At the moment we saw him, he was gazing intently into the cat's face, with his nose about four inches from it, his hands being thrust into his breeches pockets.

"Cat," said Peterkin, turning his head a little on one side, "I love you!"

There was a pause, as if Peterkin awaited a reply to this affectionate declaration. But the cat said nothing.

"Do you hear me?" cried Peterkin sharply. "I love you—I do! Don't you love me?"

To this touching appeal the cat said "Mew" faintly.

"Ah! that's right. You're a jolly old rascal. Why did you not speak at once, eh?" and Peterkin put forward his mouth and kissed the cat on the nose!

"Yes," continued Peterkin, after a pause, "I love you. D'you think I'd say so if I didn't, you black villain? I love you because I've got to take care of you, and to look after you, and to think about you, and to see that you don't die——"

"Mew, me-a-w!" said the cat.

"Very good," continued Peterkin; "quite true, I have no doubt. But you've no right to interrupt me, sir. Hold your tongue till I have done speaking. Moreover, cat, I love you because you came to me the first time you ever saw me, and didn't seem to be afraid, and appeared to be fond of me, though you didn't know that I wasn't going to kill you. Now that was brave, that was bold, and very jolly, old boy, and I love you for it—I do!"

Again there was a pause of a few minutes, during which the cat looked placid, and Peterkin dropped his eyes upon its toes, as if in contemplation. Suddenly he looked up.

"Well, cat, what are you thinking about now? Won't speak, eh? Now tell me, don't you think it's a monstrous shame that those two scoundrels, Jack and Ralph, should keep us waiting for our supper so long?"

Here the cat arose, put up its back and stretched itself, yawned slightly, and licked the point of Peterkin's nose!

"Just so, old boy; you're a clever fellow. I really do believe the brute understands me!" said Peterkin, while a broad grin overspread his face as he drew back and surveyed the cat.

At this point Jack burst into a loud fit of laughter. The cat uttered an angry fuff and fled, while Peterkin sprang up and exclaimed—

"Bad luck to you, Jack! you've nearly made the heart jump out of my body, you have."

"Perhaps I have," replied Jack, laughing, as we entered the bower, "but as I don't intend to keep you or the cat any longer from your supper, I hope that you'll both forgive me."

Peterkin endeavoured to turn this affair off with a laugh, but I observed that he blushed very deeply at the time we discovered ourselves, and he did not seem to relish any allusion to the subject afterwards; so we refrained from remarking on it ever after, though it tickled us not a little at the time.

After supper we retired to rest and to dream of wonderful adventures in our little boat and distant voyages upon the sea.

CHAPTER XVI

The boat launched—We visit the coral reef—The great breaker
that never goes down—Coral insects—The way in which coral
islands are made—The boat's sail—We tax our ingenuity to
form fish-hooks—Some of the fish we saw—And a monstrous
whale—Wonderful shower of little fish—Water-spouts.

IT was a bright, clear, beautiful morning when we first
launched our little boat, and rowed out upon the placid
waters of the lagoon. Not a breath of wind ruffled the
surface of the deep. Not a cloud spotted the deep blue
sky. Not a sound that was discordant broke the stillness
of the morning, although there were many sounds, sweet,
tiny, and melodious, that mingled in the universal harmony
of nature. The sun was just rising from the Pacific's ample
bosom and tipping the mountain-tops with a red glow.
The sea was shining like a sheet of glass, yet heaving with
the long deep swell that, all the world round, indicates the
life of ocean; and the bright seaweeds and the brilliant
corals shone in the depths of that pellucid water, as we
rowed over it, like rare and precious gems. Oh! it was
a sight fitted to stir the soul of man to its profoundest
depths, and, if he owned a heart at all, to lift that heart
in adoration and gratitude to the great Creator of this
magnificent and glorious universe.

At first, in the strength of our delight, we rowed
hither and thither without aim or object. But after the

effervescence of our spirits was abated, we began to look about us and to consider what we should do.

"I vote that we row to the reef," cried Peterkin.

"And I vote that we visit the islands within the lagoon," said I.

"And I vote we do both," cried Jack; "so pull away, boys."

As I have already said, we had made four oars, but our boat was so small that only two were necessary. The extra pair were reserved in case any accident should happen to the others. It was therefore only needful that two of us should row, while the third steered, by means of an oar, and relieved the rowers occasionally.

First we landed on one of the small islands and ran all over it, but saw nothing worthy of particular notice. Then we landed on a larger island, on which were growing a few cocoa-nut trees. Not having eaten anything that morning, we gathered a few of the nuts and breakfasted. After this we pulled straight out to sea and landed on the coral reef.

This was indeed a novel and interesting sight to us. We had now been so long on shore that we had almost forgotten the appearance of breakers, for there were none within the lagoon; but now, as we stood beside the foam-crested billow of the open sea, all the enthusiasm of the sailor was awakened in our breasts, and as we gazed on the widespread ruin of that single magnificent breaker that burst in thunder at our feet, we forgot the Coral Island behind us; we forgot our bower and the calm repose of the scented woods; we forgot all that had passed during the last few months, and remembered nothing but the storms, the calms, the fresh breezes and the surging billows of the open sea.

This huge, ceaseless breaker, to which I have so often alluded, was a much larger and more sublime object than we had at all imagined it to be. It rose many yards above the level of the sea, and could be seen approaching at some distance from the reef. Slowly and majestically it came on, acquiring greater volume and velocity as it advanced, until it assumed the form of a clear watery arch, which sparkled in the bright sun. On it came with resistless and solemn majesty — the upper edge lipped gently over, and it fell with a roar that seemed as though the heart of Ocean were broken in the crash of tumultuous water, while the foam-clad coral reef appeared to tremble beneath the mighty shock !

We gazed long and wonderingly at this great sight, and it was with difficulty we could tear ourselves away from it. As I have once before mentioned, this wave broke in many places over the reef and scattered some of its spray into the lagoon, but in most places the reef was sufficiently broad and elevated to receive and check its entire force. In many places the coral rocks were covered with vegetation—the beginning, as it appeared to us, of future islands. Thus, on this reef, we came to perceive how most of the small islands of those seas are formed. On one part we saw the spray of the breaker washing over the rocks, and millions of little, active, busy creatures continuing the work of building up this living rampart. At another place, which was just a little too high for the waves to wash over it, the coral insects were all dead; for we found that they never did their work above water. They had faithfully completed the mighty work which their Creator had given them to do, and they were now all dead. Again, in other spots the ceaseless lashing of the sea had broken the dead coral in pieces, and cast it up in the form of sand. Here sea-birds had alighted, little pieces of seaweed and stray bits of wood had been washed up, seeds of plants had been carried by the wind, and a few lovely blades of bright green had already sprung up, which, when they died, would increase the size and fertility of these emeralds of Ocean. At other places these islets had grown apace, and were shaded by one or two cocoa-nut trees, which grew, literally, in the sand, and were constantly washed by the ocean spray; yet, as I have before remarked, their fruit was most refreshing and sweet to our taste.

Again at this time Jack and I pondered the formation of the large coral islands. We could now understand how the low ones were formed; but the larger islands cost us much consideration, yet we could arrive at no certain conclusion on the subject.

Having satisfied our curiosity and enjoyed ourselves during the whole day in our little boat, we returned somewhat wearied, and withal rather hungry, to our bower.

"Now," said Jack, "as our boat answers so well, we will get a mast and sail made immediately."

"So we will," cried Peterkin, as we all assisted to drag the boat above high-water mark. "We'll light our candle and set about it this very night. Hurrah, my boys, pull away!"

As we dragged our boat, we observed that she grated heavily on her keel, and as the sands were in this place mingled with broken coral rocks, we saw portions of the wood being scraped off.

"Hallo!" cried Jack on seeing this, "that won't do. Our keel will be worn off in no time at this rate."

"So it will," said I, pondering deeply as to how this might be prevented. But I am not of a mechanical turn naturally, so I could conceive no remedy save that of putting a plate of iron on the keel; but as we had no iron, I knew not what was to be done. "It seems to me, Jack," I added, "that it is impossible to prevent the keel being worn off thus."

"Impossible!" cried Peterkin. "My dear Ralph, you are mistaken; there is nothing so easy."

"How?" I inquired, in some surprise.

"Why, by not using the boat at all!" replied Peterkin.

"Hold your impudent tongue, Peterkin," said Jack, as he shouldered the oars; "come along with me, and I'll give you work to do. In the first place, you will go and collect cocoa-nut fibre, and set to work to make sewing twine with it——"

"Please, captain," interrupted Peterkin, "I've got lots of it made already—more than enough, as a little friend of mine used to be in the habit of saying every day after dinner."

"Very well," continued Jack; "then you'll help Ralph to collect cocoa-nut cloth, and cut it into shape, after which we'll make a sail of it. I'll see to getting the mast and the gearing; so let's to work."

And to work we went right busily, so that in three days from that time we had set up a mast and sail, with the necessary rigging, in our little boat. The sail was not, indeed, very handsome to look at, as it was formed of a number of oblong patches of cloth; but we had sewed it well by means of our sail-needle, so that it was strong, which was the chief point. Jack had also overcome the difficulty about the keel, by pinning to it a *false* keel. This was a piece of tough wood, of the same length and width as the real keel, and about five inches deep. He made it of this depth because the boat would be thereby rendered not only much more safe, but more able to beat against the wind; which, in a sea where the trade-winds blow so long and so steadily in one direction, was a matter of great importance. This piece of wood was pegged very firmly to the keel; and we now launched our boat with the satisfaction of knowing that when the false keel should be scraped off, we could easily put on another; whereas, should the real keel have been scraped away, we could not have renewed it without taking our boat to pieces, which Peterkin said made his "marrow quake to think upon."

The mast and sail answered excellently, and we now sailed about in the lagoon with great delight, and examined with much interest the appearance of our island from a distance. Also, we gazed into the depths of the water, and watched for hours the gambols of the curious and bright-coloured fish among the corals and seaweed. Peterkin also made a fishing-line, and Jack constructed a number of hooks, some of which were very good, others remarkably bad. Some of these hooks were made of iron-wood, which did pretty well, the wood being extremely hard, and Jack made them very thick and large. Fish there are not particular. Some of the crooked bones in fish-heads also answered for this purpose pretty well. But that which formed our best and most serviceable hook was the brass finger-ring belonging to Jack. It gave him not a little trouble to manufacture it. First he cut it with the axe, then twisted it into the form of a hook. The barb took him several hours to cut. He did it by means of constant sawing with the broken penknife. As for the point, an hour's rubbing on a piece of sandstone made an excellent one.

It would be a matter of much time and labour to describe the appearance of the multitudes of fish that were day after day drawn into our boat by means of the brass hook. Peterkin always caught them—for we observed that he derived much pleasure from fishing—while Jack and I found ample amusement in looking on, also in gazing down at the coral groves, and in baiting the hook. Among the fish that we saw, but did not catch, were porpoises and sword-fish, whales and sharks. The porpoises came frequently into our lagoon in shoals, and amused us not a little by their bold leaps into the air and their playful gambols in the sea. The sword-fish were wonderful creatures; some of them apparently ten feet in length, with an ivory spear six or eight feet long projecting from their noses. We often saw them darting after other fish, and no doubt they sometimes killed them with their ivory swords. Jack remembered having heard once of a sword-fish attacking a ship—which seemed strange indeed; but as they are often in the habit of attacking whales, perhaps it mistook the ship for one. This sword-fish ran against the vessel with such force that it drove its sword quite through the thick planks, and when the ship arrived in harbour, long afterwards, the sword was found still sticking in it!

Sharks did not often appear, but we took care never again to bathe in deep water without leaving one of our number in the boat to give us warning, if he should see a shark approaching. As for the whales, they never came into our lagoon, but we frequently saw them spouting in the deep water beyond the reef. I shall never forget my surprise the first day I saw one of these huge monsters close to me. We had been rambling about on the reef during the morning, and were about to re-embark in our little boat to return home, when a loud blowing sound caused us to wheel rapidly round. We were just in time to see a shower of spray falling, and the flukes or tail of some monstrous fish disappear in the sea a few hundred yards off. We waited some time to see if he would rise again. As we stood, the sea seemed to open up at our very feet; an immense spout of water was sent with a snort high into the air, and the huge, blunt head of a sperm whale rose before us. It was so large that it could easily have taken our little boat, along with ourselves, into its mouth! It plunged slowly back into the sea, like a large ship foundering, and struck the water with its tail so forcibly as to cause a sound like a cannon shot.

We also saw a great number of flying-fish, although we caught none; and we noticed that they never flew out of the water except when followed by their bitter foe the dolphin, from whom they thus endeavoured to escape. But of all the fish that we saw, none surprised us so much as those that we used to find in shallow pools after a shower of rain; and this not on account of their appearance, for they were ordinary-looking and very small, but on account of their having descended in a shower of rain! We could account for them in no other way, because the pools in which we found these fish were quite dry before the shower, and at some distance above high-water mark. Jack, however, suggested a cause which seemed to me very probable. We used often to see water-spouts in the sea. A water-spout is a whirling body of water, which rises from the sea like a sharp-pointed pillar. After rising a good way, it is met by a long tongue, which comes down from the clouds; and when the two have joined, they look something like an hour-glass. The water-spout is then carried by the wind, sometimes gently, sometimes with violence, over the sea, sometimes up into the clouds, and then, bursting asunder, it descends in a deluge. This often happens over the land as well as over the sea; and it sometimes does much damage, but frequently it passes gently away. Now, Jack thought that the little fish might perhaps have been carried up in a water-spout, and so sent down again in a shower of rain. But we could not be certain as to this point, yet we thought it likely.

During these delightful fishing and boating excursions we caught a good many eels, which we found to be very good to eat. We also found turtles among the coral rocks, and made excellent soup in our iron kettle. Moreover, we discovered many shrimps and prawns, so that we had no lack of variety in our food; and, indeed, we never passed a week without making some new and interesting discovery of some sort or other, either on the land or in the sea.

CHAPTER XVII

A monster wave and its consequences—The boat lost and found—
Peterkin's terrible accident—Supplies of food for a voyage in
the boat—We visit Penguin Island, and are amazed beyond
measure—Account of the penguins.

ONE day, not long after our little boat was finished, we
were sitting on the rocks at Spouting Cliff, and talking of an excursion which we intended to make to Penguin
Island the next day.

"You see," said Peterkin, "it might be all very well
for a stupid fellow like me to remain here and leave the
penguins alone, but it would be quite inconsistent with
your characters as philosophers to remain any longer in
ignorance of the habits and customs of these birds; so
the sooner we go the better."

"Very true," said I; "there is nothing I desire so much
as to have a closer inspection of them."

"And I think," said Jack, "that you had better
remain at home, Peterkin, to take care of the cat;
for I'm sure the hogs will be at it in your absence, out
of revenge for your killing their great-grandmother so
recklessly."

"Stay at home!" cried Peterkin. "My dear fellow,
you would certainly lose your way, or get upset, if I were
not there to take care of you."

"Ah, true," said Jack gravely; "that did not occur to
me; no doubt you must go. Our boat does require a

good deal of ballast; and all that you say, Peterkin, carries so much weight with it, that we won't need stones if you go."

Now, while my companions were talking, a notable event occurred, which, as it is not generally known, I shall be particular in recording here.

While we were talking, as I have said, we noticed a dark line, like a low cloud or fog-bank, on the seaward horizon. The day was a fine one, though cloudy, and a gentle breeze was blowing, but the sea was not rougher or the breaker on the reef higher than usual. At first we thought that this looked like a thunder-cloud, and as we had had a good deal of broken weather of late, accompanied by occasional peals of thunder, we supposed that a storm must be approaching. Gradually, however, this line seemed to draw nearer without spreading up over the sky, as would certainly have been the case if it had been a storm-cloud. Still nearer it came, and soon we saw that it was moving swiftly towards the island; but there was no sound till it reached the islands out at sea. As it passed these islands, we observed, with no little anxiety, that a cloud of white foam encircled them, and burst in spray into the air; it was accompanied by a loud roar. This led us to conjecture that the approaching object was an enormous wave of the sea; but we had no idea how large it was till it came near to ourselves. When it approached the outer reef, however, we were awe-struck with its unusual magnitude; and we sprang to our feet, and clambered hastily up to the highest point of the precipice, under an indefinable feeling of fear.

I have said before that the reef opposite Spouting Cliff was very near to the shore, while just in front of the bower, it was at a considerable distance out to sea. Owing to this formation, the wave reached the reef at the latter point before it struck at the foot of Spouting Cliff. The instant it touched the reef we became aware, for the first time, of its awful magnitude. It burst completely over the reef at all points, with a roar that seemed louder to me than thunder; and this roar continued for some seconds, while the wave rolled gradually along towards the cliff on which we stood. As its crest reared before us, we felt that we were in great danger, and turned to flee; but we were too late. With a crash that seemed to shake the solid rock the gigantic billow fell, and instantly the spouting-holes sent up a gush of water-spouts with such force that they shrieked on issuing from their narrow vents. It seemed to us as if the earth had been blown up with water. We were stunned and confused by the shock, and so drenched and blinded with spray, that we knew not for a few moments whither to flee for shelter. At length we all three gained an eminence beyond the reach of the water; but what a scene of devastation met our gaze as we looked along the shore! This enormous wave not only burst over the reef, but continued its way across the lagoon, and fell on the sandy beach of the island with such force that it passed completely over it and dashed into the woods, levelling the smaller trees and bushes in its headlong course.

On seeing this, Jack said he feared our bower must have been swept away, and that the boat, which was on the beach, must have been utterly destroyed. Our hearts sank within us as we thought of this, and we hastened round through the woods towards our home. On reaching it we found, to our great relief of mind, that the force of the

wave had been expended just before reaching the bower;
but the entrance to it was almost blocked up by the torn-
up bushes and tangled heaps of seaweed. Having satisfied ourselves as to the bower, we hurried to the spot
where the boat had been left; but no boat was there.
The spot on which it had stood was vacant, and no sign
of it could we see on looking around us.

"It may have been washed up into the woods," said
Jack, hurrying up the beach as he spoke. Still no boat
was to be seen, and we were about to give ourselves over
to despair, when Peterkin called to Jack and said—

"Jack, my friend, you were once so exceedingly
sagacious and wise as to make me acquainted with the
fact that cocoa-nuts grow upon trees; will you now be so
good as to inform me what sort of fruit that is growing
on the top of yonder bush? for I confess to being ignorant,
or, at least, doubtful on the point."

We looked towards the bush indicated, and there, to
our surprise, beheld our little boat snugly nestled among
the leaves. We were very much overjoyed at this, for we
would have suffered any loss rather than the loss of our
boat. We found that the wave had actually borne the
boat on its crest from the beach into the woods, and there
launched it into the heart of this bush; which was extremely fortunate, for had it been tossed against a rock or
a tree, it would have been dashed to pieces, whereas it had
not received the smallest injury. It was no easy matter,
however, to get it out of the bush and down to the sea
again. This cost us two days of hard labour to
accomplish.

We had also much ado to clear away the rubbish from
before the bower, and spent nearly a week in constant

labour ere we got the neighbourhood to look as clean and orderly as before; for the uprooted bushes and seaweed that lay on the beach formed a more dreadfully confused-looking mass than one who had not seen the place after the inundation could conceive.

Before leaving the subject, I may mention, for the sake of those who interest themselves in the curious natural phenomena of our world, that this gigantic wave occurs regularly on some of the islands of the Pacific once, and sometimes twice, in the year. I heard this stated by the missionaries during my career in those seas. They could not tell me whether it visited all of the islands, but I was certainly assured that it occurred periodically in some of them.

After we had got our home put to rights, and cleared of the débris of the inundation, we again turned our thoughts to paying the penguins a visit. The boat was therefore overhauled and a few repairs done. Then we prepared a supply of provisions, for we intended to be absent at least a night or two, perhaps longer. This took us some time to do, for while Jack was busy with the boat, Peterkin was sent into the woods to spear a hog or two, and had to search long, sometimes, ere he found them. Peterkin was usually sent on this errand when we wanted a pork chop (which was not seldom), because he was so active and could run so wonderfully fast that he found no difficulty in overtaking the hogs; but, being dreadfully reckless, he almost invariably tumbled over stumps and stones in the course of his wild chase, and seldom returned home without having knocked the skin off his shins. Once, indeed, a more serious accident happened to him. He had been out all the morning alone, and did not return

at the usual time to dinner. We wondered at this, for
Peterkin was always very punctual at the dinner-hour.
As supper-time drew near, we began to be anxious about
him, and at length sallied forth to search the woods.   For
a long time we sought in vain, but a little before dark we
came upon the tracks of the hogs, which we followed up
until we came to the brow of a rather steep bank or
precipice. Looking over this, we beheld Peterkin lying
in a state of insensibility at the foot, with his cheek
resting on the snout of a little pig, which was pinned to
the earth by the spear. We were dreadfully alarmed, but
hastened to bathe his forehead with water, and had soon
the satisfaction of seeing him revive. After we had
carried him home, he related to us how the thing had
happened.

"You must know," said he, "I walked about all the
forenoon, till I was as tired as an old donkey, without
seeing a single grunter—not so much as a track of one;
but as I was determined not to return empty-handed, I
resolved to go without my dinner, and——"

"What!" exclaimed Jack, "did you *really* resolve to
do that?"

"Now, Jack, hold your tongue," returned Peterkin.
"I say that I resolved to forego my dinner and to push to
the head of the small valley, where I felt pretty sure of
discovering the hogs. I soon found that I was on the
right scent, for I had scarcely walked half a mile in the
direction of the small plum tree we found there the other
day, when a squeak fell on my ear. 'Ho, ho,' said I,
'there you go, my boys;' and I hurried up the glen. I
soon started them, and, singling out a fat pig, ran tilt at
him. In a few seconds I was up with him, and stuck my

spear right through his dumpy body. Just as I did so, I saw that we were on the edge of a precipice, whether high or low I knew not; but I had been running at such a pace that I could not stop, so the pig and I gave a howl in concert and went plunging over together. I remembered nothing more after that, till I came to my senses and found you bathing my temples, and Ralph wringing his hands over me."

But although Peterkin was often unfortunate in the way of getting tumbles, he was successful on the present occasion in hunting, and returned before evening with three very nice little hogs. I also was successful in my visit to the mud-flats, where I killed several ducks. So that, when we launched and loaded our boat at sunrise the following morning, we found our store of provisions to be more than sufficient. Part had been cooked the night before, and on taking note of the different items, we found the account to stand thus:—

10 Bread-fruits (two baked, eight unbaked).
20 Yams (six roasted, the rest raw).
6 Taro roots.
50 Fine large plums.
6 Cocoa-nuts, ripe.
6 Ditto, green (for drinking).
4 Large ducks and two small ones (raw).
3 Cold roast pigs, with stuffing.

I may here remark that the stuffing had been devised by Peterkin specially for the occasion. He kept the manner of its compounding a profound secret, so I cannot tell what it was; but I can say, with much confidence, that we found it to be atrociously bad, and, after the first tasting, scraped it carefully out and threw it overboard. We calculated that this supply would last us for several days; but we afterwards found that it was much more than we required, especially in regard to the cocoa-nuts, of which we found large supplies wherever we went. However, as Peterkin remarked, it was better to have too much than too little, as we knew not to what straits we might be put during our voyage.

It was a very calm, sunny morning when we launched forth and rowed over the lagoon towards the outlet in the reef, and passed between the two green islets that guarded the entrance. We experienced some difficulty and no little danger in passing the surf of the breaker, and shipped a good deal of water in the attempt; but, once past the billow, we found ourselves floating placidly on the long oily swell that rose and fell slowly as it rolled over the wide ocean.

Penguin Island lay on the other side of our own island at about a mile beyond the outer reef, and we calculated that it must be at least twenty miles distant by the way we should have to go. We might, indeed, have shortened the way by coasting round our island inside of the lagoon, and going out at the passage in the reef nearly opposite to Penguin Island; but we preferred to go by the open sea—first, because it was more adventurous, and, secondly, because we should have the pleasure of again feeling the motion of the deep, which we all loved very much, not being liable to sea-sickness.

" I wish we had a breeze," said Jack.

"So do I," cried Peterkin, resting on his oar and wiping his heated brow; "pulling is hard work. Oh dear, if we could only catch a hundred or two of these gulls, tie them to the boat with long strings, and make them fly as we want them, how capital it would be!"

"Or bore a hole through a shark's tail, and reeve a rope through it, eh?" remarked Jack. "But I say, it seems that my wish is going to be granted, for here comes a breeze. Ship your oar, Peterkin. Up with the mast, Ralph; I'll see to the sail. Mind your helm; look out for squalls!"

This last speech was caused by the sudden appearance of a dark-blue line on the horizon, which, in an incredibly short space of time, swept down on us, lashing up the sea in white foam as it went. We presented the stern of the boat to its first violence, and in a few seconds it moderated into a steady breeze, to which we spread our sail and flew merrily over the waves. Although the breeze died away soon afterwards, it had been so stiff while it lasted that we were carried over the greater part of our way before it fell calm again; so that, when the flapping of the sail against the mast told us that it was time to resume the oars, we were not much more than a mile from Penguin Island.

"There go the soldiers!" cried Peterkin, as we came in sight of it; "how spruce their white trousers look this morning! I wonder if they will receive us kindly. D'you think they are hospitable, Jack?"

"Don't talk, Peterkin, but pull away, and you shall see shortly."

As we drew near to the island we were much amused by the manœuvres and appearance of these strange birds. They seemed to be of different species, for some had crests on their heads while others had none, and while some were about the size of a goose, others appeared nearly as large

as a swan. We also saw a huge albatross soaring above
the heads of the penguins. It was followed and surrounded
by numerous flocks of sea-gulls. Having approached to
within a few yards of the island, which was a low rock,
with no other vegetation on it than a few bushes, we lay on
our oars and gazed at the birds with surprise and pleasure,
they returning our gaze with interest. We now saw that
their soldier-like appearance was owing to the stiff, erect
manner in which they sat on their short legs—" bolt-
upright," as Peterkin expressed it. They had black heads,
long sharp beaks, white breasts, and bluish backs. Their
wings were so short that they looked more like the fins of
a fish, and, indeed, we soon saw that they used them for
the purpose of swimming under water. There were no
quills on these wings, but a sort of scaly feathers, which
also thickly covered their bodies. Their legs were short,
and placed so far back that the birds, while on land, were
obliged to stand quite upright in order to keep their
balance; but in the water they floated like other water-
fowl. At first we were so stunned with the clamour which
they and other sea-birds kept up around us, that we knew
not which way to look—for they covered the rocks in
thousands; but, as we continued to gaze, we observed
several quadrupeds (as we thought) walking in the midst
of the penguins.

" Pull in a bit," cried Peterkin, " and let's see what
these are. They must be fond of noisy company, to con-
sort with such creatures."

To our surprise, we found that these were no other than
penguins which had gone down on all fours, and were
crawling among the bushes on their feet and wings, just
like quadrupeds. Suddenly one big old bird, that had

been sitting on a point very near to us, gazing in mute astonishment, became alarmed, and, scuttling down the rocks, plumped or fell, rather than ran, into the sea. It dived in a moment, and, a few seconds afterwards, came out of the water far ahead, with such a spring, and such a dive back into the sea again, that we could scarcely believe it was not a fish that had leaped in sport.

"That beats everything," said Peterkin, rubbing his nose, and screwing up his face with an expression of exasperated amazement. "I've heard of a thing being neither fish, flesh, nor fowl, but I never did expect to live to see a brute that was all three together—at once —in one! But look there!" he continued — pointing with a look of resignation to the shore—"look there! there's no end to it. What *has* that brute got under its tail?"

We turned to look in the direction pointed out, and there saw a penguin walking slowly and very sedately along the shore with an egg under its tail. There were several others, we observed, burdened in the same way; and we found afterwards that these were a species of penguin that always carried their eggs so. Indeed, they had a most convenient cavity for the purpose, just between the tail and the legs. We were very much impressed with the regularity and order of this colony. The island seemed to be apportioned out into squares, of which each penguin possessed one, and sat in stiff solemnity in the middle of it, or took a slow march up and down the spaces between. Some were hatching their eggs, but others were feeding their young ones in a manner that caused us to laugh not a little. The mother stood on a mound or raised rock, while the young one stood patiently

below her on the ground.   Suddenly the mother raised her
head and uttered a series of the most discordant cackling
sounds.

"She's going to choke," cried Peterkin.

But this was not the case, although, I confess, she looked
like it.   In a few seconds she put down her head and
opened her mouth, into which the young one thrust its beak
and seemed to suck something from her throat.   Then the
cackling was renewed, the sucking continued, and so the
operation of feeding was carried on till the young one was
satisfied; but what she fed her little one with we could
not tell.

"Now, just look yonder!" said Peterkin in an excited
tone; "if that isn't the most abominable piece of maternal
deception I ever saw!   That rascally old lady penguin has
just pitched her young one into the sea, and there's another
about to follow her example."

This indeed seemed to be the case, for on the top of a
steep rock close to the edge of the sea we observed an old
penguin endeavouring to entice her young one into the
water; but the young one seemed very unwilling to go,
and, notwithstanding the enticements of its mother, moved
very slowly towards her.   At last she went gently behind
the young bird and pushed it a little towards the water,
but with great tenderness, as much as to say, "Don't be
afraid, darling; I won't hurt you, my pet!" but no sooner
did she get it to the edge of the rock, where it stood
looking pensively down at the sea, than she gave it a
sudden and violent push, sending it headlong down the
slope into the water, where its mother left it to scramble
ashore as it best could.   We observed many of them employed in doing this, and we came to the conclusion that

this is the way in which old penguins teach their children to swim.

Scarcely had we finished making our remarks on this, when we were startled by about a dozen of the old birds hopping in the most clumsy and ludicrous manner towards the sea. The beach here was a sloping rock, and when they came to it some of them succeeded in hopping down in safety, but others lost their balance, and rolled and scrambled down the slope in the most helpless manner. The instant they reached the water, however, they seemed to be in their proper element. They dived and bounded out of it and into it again with the utmost agility; and so, diving and bounding and sputtering—for they could not fly—they went rapidly out to sea.

On seeing this, Peterkin turned with a grave face to us and said: "It's my opinion that these birds are all stark, staring mad, and that this is an enchanted island. I therefore propose that we should either put about ship and fly in terror from the spot, or land valorously on the island, and sell our lives as dearly as we can."

"I vote for landing; so pull in, lads," said Jack, giving a stroke with his oar that made the boat spin. In a few seconds we ran the boat into a little creek, where we made her fast to a projecting piece of coral, and running up the beach, entered the ranks of the penguins armed with our cudgels and our spear. We were greatly surprised to find that, instead of attacking us or showing signs of fear at our approach, these curious birds did not move from their places until we laid hands on them, and merely turned their eyes on us in solemn, stupid wonder as we passed. There was one old penguin, however, that began to walk slowly towards the sea, and Peterkin took it into his head that he would try to interrupt its progress, so he ran between it and the sea and brandished his cudgel in its face. But this proved to be a resolute old bird. It would not retreat; nay, more, it would not cease to advance, but battled with Peterkin bravely and drove him before it until it reached the sea. Had Peterkin used his club he could easily have felled it, no doubt; but as he had no wish to do so cruel an act merely out of sport, he let the bird escape.

We spent fully three hours on this island in watching the habit of these curious birds, but when we finally left them, we all three concluded, after much consultation, that they were the most wonderful creatures we had ever seen; and further, we thought it probable that they were the most wonderful creatures in the world!

CHAPTER XVIII

An awful storm and its consequences—Narrow escape—A rock
    proves a sure foundation—A fearful night and a bright morn-
    ing—Deliverance from danger.

IT was evening before we left the island of the penguins.
    As we had made up our minds to encamp for the
night on a small island, whereon grew a few cocoa-nut
trees. which was about two miles off, we lay to our oars
with some energy. But a danger was in store for us
which we had not anticipated. The wind which had
carried us so quickly to Penguin Island freshened as
evening drew on to a stiff breeze, and before we had
made half the distance to the small island, it became a
regular gale. Although it was not so directly against us
as to prevent our rowing in the course we wished to go,
yet it checked us very much; and although the force of
the sea was somewhat broken by the island, the waves
soon began to rise, and to roll their broken crests against
our small craft, so that she began to take in water, and
we had much ado to keep ourselves afloat. At last the
wind and sea together became so violent that we found it
impossible to make the island, so Jack suddenly put the
head of the boat round and ordered Peterkin and me to
hoist a corner of the sail, intending to run back to Penguin
Island.

"We shall at least have the shelter of the bushes," he

said, as the boat flew before the wind, "and the penguins will keep us company."

As Jack spoke, the wind suddenly shifted, and blew so much against us that we were forced to hoist more of the sail in order to beat up for the island, being by this change thrown much to leeward of it. What made matters worse was that the gale came in squalls, so that we were more than once nearly upset.

"Stand by, both of you," cried Jack in a quick, earnest tone; "be ready to douse the sail. I very much fear we won't make the island after all."

Peterkin and I were so much in the habit of trusting everything to Jack that we had fallen into the way of not considering things, especially such things as were under Jack's care. We had, therefore, never doubted for a moment that all was going well, so that it was with no little anxiety that we heard him make the above remark. However, we had no time for question or surmise, for at the moment he spoke a heavy squall was bearing down upon us; and as we were then flying with our lee gunwale dipping occasionally under the waves, it was evident that we should have to lower our sail altogether. In a few seconds the squall struck the boat, but Peterkin and I had the sail down in a moment, so that it did not upset us; but when it was past we were more than half full of water. This I soon baled out, while Peterkin again hoisted a corner of the sail; but the evil which Jack had feared came upon us. We found it quite impossible to make Penguin Island. The gale carried us quickly past it towards the open sea, and the terrible truth flashed upon us that we should be swept out and left to perish miserably in a small boat in the midst of the wide ocean

This idea was forced very strongly upon us because we saw nothing in the direction whither the wind was blowing us save the raging billows of the sea; and, indeed, we trembled as we gazed around us, for we were now beyond the shelter of the islands, and it seemed as though any of the huge billows, which curled over in masses of foam, might swallow us up in a moment. The water, also, began to wash in over our sides, and I had to keep constantly baling, for Jack could not quit the helm nor Peterkin the sail for an instant without endangering our lives. In the midst of this distress Jack uttered an exclamation of hope, and pointed towards a low island or rock which lay directly ahead. It had been hitherto unobserved, owing to the dark clouds that obscured the sky and the blinding spray that seemed to fill the whole atmosphere.

As we neared this rock, we observed that it was quite destitute of trees and verdure, and so low that the sea broke completely over it. In fact, it was nothing more than the summit of one of the coral formations, which rose only a few feet above the level of the water, and was, in stormy weather, all but invisible. Over this island the waves were breaking in the utmost fury, and our hearts sank within us as we saw that there was not a spot where we could thrust our little boat without its being dashed to pieces.

"Show a little bit more sail," cried Jack, as we swept past the weather side of the rock with fearful speed.

"Ay, ay," answered Peterkin, hoisting about a foot more of our sail.

Little though the addition was, it caused the boat to lie over and creak so loudly as we cleft the foaming waves,

that I expected to be upset every instant; and I blamed
Jack in my heart for his rashness. But I did him injus-
tice, for although during two seconds the water rushed inboard in a torrent, he succeeded in steering us sharply
round to the leeward side of the rock, where the water was
comparatively calm and the force of the breeze broken.

"Out your oars now, lads! that's well done. Give
way!" We obeyed instantly. The oars splashed into
the waves together. One good, hearty pull, and we were
floating in a comparatively calm creek that was so narrow
as to be barely able to admit our boat. Here we were in
perfect safety, and as we leaped on shore and fastened our
cable to the rocks, I thanked God in my heart for our
deliverance from so great danger. But although I have
said we were now in safety, I suspect that few of my
readers would have envied our position. It is true we
had no lack of food, but we were drenched to the skin;
the sea was foaming round us and the spray flying over
our heads, so that we were completely enveloped, as it
were, in water; the spot on which we had landed was not
more than twelve yards in diameter, and from this spot we
could not move without the risk of being swept away by
the storm. At the upper end of the creek was a small
hollow or cave in the rock, which sheltered us from the
fury of the winds and waves; and as the rock extended in
a sort of ledge over our heads, it prevented the spray from
falling upon us.

"Why," said Peterkin, beginning to feel cheery again,
"it seems to me that we have got into a mermaid's cave;
for there is nothing but water all round us, and as for
earth and sky, they are things of the past."

Peterkin's idea was not inappropriate, for what with the

sea roaring in white foam up to our very feet, and the
spray flying in white sheets continually over our heads,
and the water dripping heavily from the ledge above like
a curtain in front of our cave, it did seem to us very much
more like being below than above water.

"Now, boys," cried Jack, "bestir yourselves, and let's
make ourselves comfortable.—Toss out our provisions,
Peterkin: and here, Ralph, lend a hand to haul up the
boat. Look sharp."

"Ay, ay, captain," we cried, as we hastened to obey,
much cheered by the hearty manner of our comrade.

Fortunately the cave, although not very deep, was quite
dry, so that we succeeded in making ourselves much more
comfortable than could have been expected. We landed
our provisions, wrung the water out of our garments,
spread our sail below us for a carpet, and, after having
eaten a hearty meal, began to feel quite cheerful. But as
night drew on our spirits sank again, for with the daylight
all evidence of our security vanished away. We could no
longer see the firm rock on which we lay, while we were
stunned with the violence of the tempest that raged
around us. The night grew pitchy dark as it advanced,
so that we could not see our hands when we held them up
before our eyes, and were obliged to feel each other occasionally to make sure that we were safe, for the storm at
last became so terrible that it was difficult to make our
voices audible. A slight variation of the wind, as we
supposed, caused a few drops of spray ever and anon to
blow into our faces; and the eddy of the sea, in its mad
boiling, washed up into our little creek until it reached our
feet and threatened to tear away our boat. In order to
prevent this latter calamity, we hauled the boat farther

up and held the cable in our hands.   Occasional flashes of
lightning shone with a ghastly glare through the watery
curtains around us, and lent additional horror to the scene.
Yet we longed for those dismal flashes, for they were less
appalling than the thick blackness that succeeded them.
Crashing peals of thunder seemed to tear the skies in twain,
and fell upon our ears through the wild yelling of the hurricane as if it had been but a gentle summer breeze; while
the billows burst upon the weather side of the island until
we fancied that the solid rock was giving way, and in our
agony we clung to the bare ground, expecting every
moment to be whirled away and whelmed in the black
howling sea.   Oh, it was a night of terrible anxiety! and
no one can conceive the feelings of intense gratitude and
relief with which we at last saw the dawn of day break
through the vapoury mists around us.

For three days and three nights we remained on this
rock, while the storm continued to rage with unabated
fury.   On the morning of the fourth day it suddenly
ceased, and the wind fell altogether; but the waves still
ran so high that we did not dare to put off in our boat.
During the greater part of this period we scarcely slept
above a few minutes at a time, but on the third night we
slept soundly, and awoke early on the fourth morning to
find the sea very much down, and the sun shining brightly
again in the clear blue sky.

It was with light hearts that we launched forth once
more in our little boat and steered away for our island
home, which, we were overjoyed to find, was quite visible
on the horizon, for we had feared that we had been blown
out of sight of it altogether.   As it was a dead calm, we
had to row during the greater part of the day; but towards

the afternoon a fair breeze sprang up, which enabled us to hoist our sail. We soon passed Penguin Island and the other island which we had failed to reach on the day the storm commenced; but as we had still enough of provisions, and were anxious to get home, we did not land, to the great disappointment of Peterkin, who seemed to entertain quite an affection for the penguins.

Although the breeze was pretty fresh for several hours, we did not reach the outer reef of our island till nightfall, and before we had sailed more than a hundred yards into the lagoon, the wind died away altogether, so that we had to take to our oars again. It was late, and the moon and stars were shining brightly, when we arrived opposite the bower and leaped upon the strand. So glad were we to be safe back again on our beloved island, that we scarcely took time to drag the boat a short way up the beach, and then ran up to see that all was right at the bower. I must confess, however, that my joy was mingled with a vague sort of fear lest our home had been visited and destroyed during our absence; but on reaching it we found everything just as it had been left, and the poor black cat curled up, sound asleep, on the coral table in front of our humble dwelling.

CHAPTER XIX

Shoemaking—The even tenor of our way suddenly interrupted—An unexpected visit and an appalling battle—We all become warriors, and Jack proves himself to be a hero.

FOR many months after this we continued to live on our island in uninterrupted harmony and happiness. Sometimes we went out a-fishing in the lagoon, and sometimes went a-hunting in the woods, or ascended to the mountain-top, by way of variety, although Peterkin always asserted that we went for the purpose of hailing any ship that might chance to heave in sight. But I am certain that none of us wished to be delivered from our captivity, for we were extremely happy; and Peterkin used to say that, as we were very young, we should not feel the loss of a year or two. Peterkin, as I have said before, was thirteen years of age, Jack eighteen, and I fifteen. But Jack was very tall, strong, and manly for his age, and might easily have been mistaken for twenty.

The climate was so beautiful that it seemed to be a perpetual summer, and as many of the fruit-trees continued to bear fruit and blossom all the year round, we never wanted for a plentiful supply of food. The hogs, too, seemed rather to increase than diminish, although Peterkin was very frequent in his attacks on them with his spear. If at any time we failed in finding a drove, we had only to pay a visit to the plum tree before mentioned, where we always found a large family of them asleep under its branches.

We employed ourselves very busily during this time in making various garments of cocoa-nut cloth, as those with which we had landed were beginning to be very ragged. Peterkin also succeeded in making excellent shoes out of the skin of the old hog, in the following manner. He first cut a piece of the hide, of an oblong form, a few inches longer than his foot. This he soaked in water, and while it was wet he sewed up one end of it, so as to form a rough imitation of that part of the heel of a shoe where the seam is. This done, he bored a row of holes all round the edge of the piece of skin, through which a tough line was passed. Into the sewed-up part of this shoe he thrust his heel; then, drawing the string tight, the edges rose up and overlapped his foot all round. It is true there were a great many ill-looking puckers in these shoes; but we found them very serviceable notwithstanding, and Jack came at last to prefer them to his long boots. We also made various other useful articles, which added to our comfort, and once or twice spoke of building us a house; but we had so great an affection for the bower, and withal found it so serviceable, that we determined not to leave it, nor to attempt the building of a house, which in such a climate might turn out to be rather disagreeable than useful.

We often examined the pistol that we had found in the house on the other side of the island, and Peterkin wished much that we had powder and shot, as it would render pig-killing much easier; but, after all, we had become so expert in the use of our sling and bow and spear, that we were independent of more deadly weapons

Diving in the Water Garden also continued to afford us as much pleasure as ever; and Peterkin began to be a little more expert in the water from constant practice. As for Jack and me, we began to feel as if water were our native element, and revelled in it with so much confidence and comfort that Peterkin said he feared we would turn into fish some day and swim off and leave him, adding that he had been for a long time observing that Jack was becoming more and more like a shark every day. Whereupon Jack remarked that if he, Peterkin, were changed into a fish, he would certainly turn into nothing better or bigger than a shrimp. Poor Peterkin did not envy us our delightful excursions under water, except, indeed, when Jack would dive down to the bottom of the Water Garden, sit down on a rock, and look up and make faces at him. Peterkin did feel envious then, and often said he would give anything to be able to do that. I was much amused when Peterkin said this; for if he could only have seen his own face when he happened to take a short dive, he would have seen that Jack's was far surpassed by it: the great difference being, however, that Jack made faces on purpose—Peterkin couldn't help it!

Now, while we were engaged with these occupations and amusements, an event occurred one day which was as unexpected as it was exceedingly alarming and very horrible.

Jack and I were sitting, as we were often wont to do, on the rocks at Spouting Cliff, and Peterkin was wringing the water from his garments, having recently fallen by accident into the sea—a thing he was constantly doing—when our attention was suddenly arrested by two objects which appeared on the horizon.

"What are yon, think you?" I said, addressing Jack.

"I can't imagine," answered he. "I've noticed them for some time, and fancied they were black sea-gulls, but the more I look at them the more I feel convinced they are much larger than gulls."

"They seem to be coming towards us," said I.

"Hallo! what's wrong?" inquired Peterkin, coming up.

"Look there," said Jack.

"Whales!" cried Peterkin, shading his eyes with his hand. "No—eh—*can* they be boats, Jack?"

Our hearts beat with excitement at the very thought of seeing human faces again.

"I think you are about right, Peterkin. But they seem to me to move strangely for boats," said Jack in a low tone, as if he were talking to himself.

I noticed that a shade of anxiety crossed Jack's countenance as he gazed long and intently at the two objects, which were now nearing us fast. At last he sprang to his feet. "They are canoes, Ralph! Whether war-canoes or not I cannot tell; but this I know, that all the natives of the South Sea Islands are fierce cannibals, and they have little respect for strangers. We must hide if they land here, which I earnestly hope they will not do."

I was greatly alarmed at Jack's speech, but I confess I thought less of what he said than of the earnest, anxious manner in which he said it; and it was with very uncomfortable feelings that Peterkin and I followed him quickly into the woods.

"How unfortunate," said I, as we gained the shelter of the bushes, "that we have forgotten our arms!"

"It matters not," said Jack; "here are clubs enough and to spare." As he spoke, he laid his hand on a bundle of stout poles of various sizes, which Peterkin's ever-busy hands had formed during our frequent visits to the cliff, for no other purpose, apparently, than that of having something to do.

We each selected a stout club according to our several tastes, and lay down behind a rock, whence we could see the canoes approach, without ourselves being seen. At first we made an occasional remark on their appearance, but after they entered the lagoon, and drew near the beach, we ceased to speak, and gazed with intense interest at the scene before us.

We now observed that the foremost canoe was being chased by the other, and that it contained a few women and children, as well as men—perhaps forty souls altogether; while the canoe which pursued it contained only men. They seemed to be about the same in number, but were better armed, and had the appearance of being a war-party. Both crews were paddling with all their might, and it seemed as if the pursuers exerted themselves to overtake the fugitives ere they could land. In this, however, they failed. The foremost canoe made for the beach close beneath the rocks behind which we were concealed. Their short paddles flashed like meteors in the water, and sent up a constant shower of spray. The foam curled from the prow, and the eyes of the rowers glistened in their black faces, as they strained every muscle of their naked bodies; nor did they relax their efforts till the canoe struck the beach with a violent shock, then with a shout of defiance the whole party sprang, as if by magic, from the canoe to the shore. Three women, two of whom carried infants in their arms, rushed into the woods; and the men crowded to the water's edge, with stones in their hands, spears levelled, and clubs brandished, to resist the landing of their enemies.

The distance between the two canoes had been about half a mile, and, at the great speed they were going, this was soon passed. As the pursuers neared the shore, no sign of fear or hesitation was noticeable. On they came like a wild charger—received but recked not of a shower of stones. The canoe struck, and with a yell that seemed to issue from the throats of incarnate fiends, they leaped into the water, and drove their enemies up the beach.

The battle that immediately ensued was frightful to behold. Most of the men wielded clubs of enormous size and curious shapes, with which they dashed out each other's brains. As they were almost entirely naked, and had to bound, stoop, leap, and run in their terrible hand-to-hand encounters, they looked more like demons than human beings. I felt my heart grow sick at the sight of this bloody battle, and would fain have turned away, but a species of fascination seemed to hold me down and glue my eyes upon the combatants. I observed that the attacking party was led by a most extraordinary being, who, from his size and peculiarity, I concluded was a chief. His hair was frizzed out to an enormous extent, so that it resembled a large turban. It was of a light-yellow hue, which surprised me much, for the man's body was as black as coal, and I felt convinced that the hair must have been dyed. He was tattooed from head to foot, and his face, besides being tattooed, was besmeared with red paint, and streaked with white. Altogether, with his yellow, turban-like hair, his Herculean black frame, his glittering eyes and white teeth, he seemed the most terrible monster I ever beheld. He was very active in the fight, and had already killed four men.

Suddenly the yellow-haired chief was attacked by a man quite as strong and large as himself. He flourished a heavy club something like an eagle's beak at the point. For a second or two these giants eyed each other warily, moving round and round, as if to catch each other at a disadvantage; but seeing that nothing was to be gained by this caution, and that the loss of time might effectually turn the tide of battle either way, they apparently made up their minds to attack at the same instant, for, with a wild shout and simultaneous spring, they swung their heavy clubs, which met with a loud report. Suddenly the yellow-haired savage tripped, his enemy sprang forward, the ponderous club was swung, but it did not descend, for at that moment the savage was felled to the ground by a stone from the hand of one who had witnessed his chief's danger. This was the turning-point in the battle. The savages who landed first turned and fled towards the bush, on seeing the fall of their chief. But not one escaped. They were all overtaken and felled to the earth. I saw, however, that they were not all killed. Indeed, their enemies, now that they were conquered, seemed anxious to take them alive; and they succeeded in securing fifteen, whom they bound hand and foot with cords, and carrying them up into the woods, laid them down among the bushes. Here they left them, for what purpose I knew not, and returned to the scene of the late battle, where the remnant of the party were bathing their wounds.

Out of the forty blacks that composed the attacking party, only twenty-eight remained alive, two of whom were sent into the bush to hunt for the women and children. Of the other party, as I have said, only fifteen survived, and these were lying bound and helpless on the grass.

Jack and Peterkin and I now looked at each other, and whispered our fears that the savages might clamber up the rocks to search for fresh water, and so discover our place of concealment; but we were so much interested in watching their movements that we agreed to remain where we were—and, indeed, we could not easily have risen without exposing ourselves to detection. One of the savages now went up to the wood, and soon returned with a bundle of firewood, and we were not a little surprised to see him set fire to it by the very same means used by Jack the time we made our first fire—namely, with the bow and drill. When the fire was kindled, two of the party went again to the woods and returned with one of the bound men. A dreadful feeling of horror crept over my heart as the thought flashed upon me that they were going to burn their enemies. As they bore him to the fire my feelings almost overpowered me. I gasped for breath, and seizing my club, endeavoured to spring to my feet; but Jack's powerful arm pinned me to the earth. Next moment one of the savages raised his club, and fractured the wretched creature's skull. He must have died instantly; and, strange though it may seem, I confess to a feeling of relief when the deed was done, because I now knew that the poor savage could not be burned alive. Scarcely had his limbs ceased to quiver when the monsters cut slices of flesh from his body, and, after roasting them slightly over the fire, devoured them.

Suddenly there arose a cry from the woods, and in a few seconds the two savages hastened towards the fire dragging the three women and their two infants along with them. One of those women was much younger than her companions, and we were struck with the modesty of her demeanour and the gentle expression of her face, which, although she had the flattish nose and thick lips of the others, was of a light-brown colour, and we conjectured that she must be of a different race. She and her companions wore short petticoats and a kind of tippet on their shoulders. Their hair was jet black, but instead of being long, was short and curly—though not woolly—somewhat like the hair of a young boy. While we gazed with interest and some anxiety at these poor creatures, the big chief advanced to one of the elder females and laid his hand upon the child. But the mother shrank from him, and clasping the little one to her bosom, uttered a wail of fear. With a savage laugh, the chief tore the child from her arms and tossed it into the sea. A low groan burst from Jack's lips as he witnessed this atrocious act and heard the mother's shriek, as she fell insensible on the sand. The rippling waves rolled the child on the beach, as if they refused to be a party in such a foul murder, and we could observe that the little one still lived.

The young girl was now brought forward, and the chief addressed her; but although we heard his voice and even the words distinctly, of course we could not understand what he said. The girl made no answer to his fierce questions, and we saw by the way in which he pointed to the fire that he threatened her life.

"Peterkin," said Jack in a hoarse whisper, "have you got your knife?"

"Yes," replied Peterkin, whose face was pale as death.

"That will do. Listen to me, and do my bidding quick.—Here is the small knife, Ralph.—Fly both of you through the bush, cut the cords that bind the prisoners, and set them free. There! quick, ere it be too late." Jack sprang up, and seized a heavy but short bludgeon, while his strong frame trembled with emotion, and large drops rolled down his forehead.

At this moment the man who had butchered the savage a few minutes before advanced towards the girl with his heavy club. Jack uttered a yell that rang like a death-shriek among the rocks. With one bound he leaped over a precipice full fifteen feet high, and before the savages had recovered from their surprise, was in the midst of them; while Peterkin and I dashed through the bushes towards the prisoners. With one blow of his staff Jack felled the man with the club; then, turning round with a look of fury, he rushed upon the big chief with the yellow hair. Had the blow which Jack aimed at his head taken effect, the huge savage would have needed no second stroke; but he was agile as a cat, and avoided it by springing to one side, while at the same time he swung his ponderous club at the head of his foe. It was now Jack's turn to leap aside, and well was it for him that the first outburst of his blind fury was over, else he had become an easy prey to his gigantic antagonist; but Jack was cool now. He darted his blows rapidly and well, and the superiority of his light weapon was strikingly proved in this combat; for while he could easily evade the blows of the chief's heavy club, the chief could not so easily evade those of his light one. Nevertheless, so quick was he, and so frightfully did he fling about the mighty weapon, that although Jack struck him almost every blow, the strokes had to be delivered so quickly that they wanted force to be very effectual.

It was lucky for Jack that the other savages considered the success of their chief in this encounter to be so certain that they refrained from interfering. Had they doubted it, they would have probably ended the matter at once by felling him. But they contented themselves with awaiting the issue.

The force which the chief expended in wielding his club now began to be apparent. His movements became slower, his breath hissed through his clinched teeth, and the surprised savages drew nearer in order to render assistance. Jack observed this movement. He felt that his fate was sealed, and resolved to cast his life upon the next blow. The chief's club was again about to descend on his head. He might have evaded it easily, but instead of doing so, he suddenly shortened his grasp of his own club, rushed in under the blow, struck his adversary right between the eyes with all his force, and fell to the earth, crushed beneath the senseless body of the chief. A dozen clubs flew high in air, ready to descend on the head of Jack; but they hesitated a moment, for the massive body of the chief completely covered him. That moment saved his life. Ere the savages could tear the chief's body away, seven of their number fell prostrate beneath the clubs of the prisoners whom Peterkin and I had set free, and two others fell under our own hand. We could never have accomplished this had not our enemies been so engrossed with the fight between Jack and their chief that they had failed to observe us until we were upon them. They still outnumbered our party by three; but we were flushed with victory, while they were taken by surprise and dispirited by the fall of their chief. Moreover, they were awe-struck by the sweeping fury of Jack, who seemed to have lost his senses altogether, and had no sooner shaken himself free of the chief's body than he rushed into the midst of them, and in three blows equalised our numbers. Peterkin and I flew to the rescue, the savages followed us, and in less than ten minutes the whole of our opponents were knocked down or made prisoners, bound hand and foot, and extended side by side upon the sea-shore.

CHAPTER XX

AFTER the battle was over, the savages crowded round
us and gazed at us in surprise, while they continued
to pour upon us a flood of questions, which, being wholly
unintelligible, of course we could not answer. However,
by way of putting an end to it, Jack took the chief (who
had recovered from the effects of his wound) by the hand
and shook it warmly. No sooner did the blacks see that
this was meant to express good-will than they shook hands
with us all round. After this ceremony was gone through,
Jack went up to the girl, who had never once moved from
the rock where she had been left, but had continued an
eager spectator of all that had passed. He made signs to
her to follow him, and then, taking the chief by the hand,
was about to conduct him to the bower, when his eye fell on
the poor infant which had been thrown into the sea and
was still lying on the shore. Dropping the chief's hand, he
hastened towards it, and, to his great joy, found it to be
still alive. We also found that the mother was beginning
to recover slowly.

"Here, get out o' the way," said Jack, pushing us
aside, as we stooped over the poor woman and endeavoured
to restore her; "I'll soon bring her round." So saying,
he placed the infant on her bosom and laid its warm

cheek on hers. The effect was wonderful. The woman opened her eyes, felt the child, looked at it, and with a cry of joy clasped it in her arms, at the same time endeavouring to rise, for the purpose, apparently, of rushing into the woods.

"There, that's all right," said Jack, once more taking the chief by the hand. "Now, Ralph and Peterkin, make the women and these fellows follow me to the bower. We'll entertain them as hospitably as we can."

In a few minutes the savages were all seated on the ground in front of the bower making a hearty meal off a cold roast pig, several ducks, and a variety of cold fish, together with an unlimited supply of cocoa-nuts, bread-fruits, yams, taro, and plums; with all of which they seemed to be quite familiar and perfectly satisfied.

Meanwhile, we three, being thoroughly knocked up with our day's work, took a good draught of cocoa-nut lemonade, and, throwing ourselves on our beds, fell fast asleep. The savages, it seems, followed our example, and in half-an-hour the whole camp was buried in repose.

How long we slept I cannot tell, but this I know, that when we lay down the sun was setting, and when we awoke it was high in the heavens. I awoke Jack, who started up in surprise, being unable at first to comprehend our situation. "Now then," said he, springing up, "let's see after breakfast. Hallo, Peterkin, lazy fellow! how long do you mean to lie there?"

Peterkin yawned heavily. "Well," said he, opening his eyes and looking up after some trouble, "if it isn't to-morrow morning, and me thinking it was to-day all this time? Hallo, Venus, where did you come from? You seem tolerably at home, anyhow! Bah! might as well speak to the cat as to you—better, in fact, for it understands me, and you don't."

This remark was called forth by the sight of one of the elderly females, who had seated herself on the rock in front of the bower, and having placed her child at her feet, was busily engaged in devouring the remains of a roast pig.

By this time the natives outside were all astir, and breakfast in an advanced state of preparation. During the course of it we made sundry attempts to converse with the natives by signs, but without effect. At last we hit upon a plan of discovering their names. Jack pointed to his breast and said "Jack" very distinctly; then he pointed to Peterkin and to me, repeating our names at the same time. Then he pointed to himself again and said "Jack," and laying his finger on the breast of the chief, looked inquiringly into his face. The chief instantly understood him, and said "Tararo" twice distinctly. Jack repeated it after him, and the chief, nodding his head approvingly, said "Chuck," on hearing which Peterkin exploded with laughter; but Jack turned, and with a frown rebuked him, saying: "I must look even more indignantly at you than I feel, Peterkin, you rascal, for these fellows don't like to be laughed at." Then turning towards the youngest of the women, who was seated at the door of the bower, he pointed to her; whereupon the chief said "Avatea," and pointing towards the sun, raised his finger slowly towards the zenith, where it remained steadily for a minute or two.

"What can that mean, I wonder?" said Jack, looking puzzled.

"Perhaps," said Peterkin, "the chief means she is an

angel come down to stay here for a while. If so, she's an uncommonly black one!"

We did not feel quite satisfied with this explanation, so Jack went up to her and said "Avatea." The woman smiled sadly, and nodded her head, at the same time pointing to her breast and then to the sun, in the same manner as the chief had done. We were much puzzled to know what this could signify, but as there was no way of solving our difficulty we were obliged to rest content.

Jack now made signs to the natives to follow him, and taking up his axe, he led them to a place where the battle had been fought. Here we found the prisoners, who had passed the night on the beach, having been totally forgotten by us, as our minds had been full of our guests, and were ultimately overcome by sleep. They did not seem the worse for their exposure, however, as we judged by the hearty appetite with which they devoured the breakfast that was soon after given to them. Jack then began to dig a hole in the sand, and after working a few seconds, he pointed to it and to the dead bodies that lay exposed on the beach. The natives immediately perceived what he wanted, and running for their paddles, dug a hole in the course of half-an-hour that was quite large enough to contain all the bodies of the slain. When it was finished they tossed their dead enemies into it with so much indifference that we felt assured they would not have put themselves to this trouble had we not asked them to do so. The body of the yellow-haired chief was the last thrown in. This wretched man would have recovered from the blow with which Jack felled him, and, indeed, he did endeavour to rise during the *mêlée* that followed his fall; but one of his enemies, happening to notice the action, dealt him a blow with his club that killed him on the spot.

While they were about to throw the sand over this chief, one of the savages stooped over him, and with a knife, made apparently of stone, cut a large slice of flesh from his thigh. We knew at once that he intended to make use of this for food, and could not repress a cry of horror and disgust.

"Come, come, you blackguard!" cried Jack, starting up and seizing the man by the arm, "pitch that into the hole. Do you hear?"

The savage, of course, did not understand the command, but he perfectly understood the look of disgust with which Jack regarded the flesh, and his fierce gaze as he pointed towards the hole. Nevertheless, he did not obey. Jack instantly turned to Tararo and made signs to him to enforce obedience. The chief seemed to understand the appeal, for he stepped forward, raised his club, and was on the point of dashing out the brains of his offending subject, when Jack sprang forward and caught his uplifted arm.

"Stop," he shouted, "you blockhead! I don't want you to kill the man." He then pointed again to the flesh and to the hole. The chief uttered a few words, which had the desired effect; for the man threw the flesh into the hole, which was immediately filled up. This man was of a morose, sulky disposition, and during all the time he remained on the island, regarded us, especially Jack, with a scowling visage. His name, we found, was Mahine.

The next three or four days were spent by the savages

in mending their canoe, which had been damaged by the violent shock it had sustained on striking the shore. This canoe was a very curious structure. It was about thirty feet long, and had a high, towering stern. The timbers of which it was partly composed, were fastened much in the same way as those of our little boat were put together; but the part that seemed most curious to us was a sort of outrigger, or long plank, which was attached to the body of the canoe by means of two stout cross-beams. These beams kept the plank parallel with the canoe, but not in contact with it, for it floated in the water with an open space between; thus forming a sort of double canoe. This we found was intended to prevent the upsetting of the canoe, which was so narrow that it could not have maintained an upright position without the outrigger. We could not help wondering both at the ingenuity and the clumsiness of this contrivance.

When the canoe was ready, we assisted the natives to carry the prisoners into it, and helped them to load it with provisions and fruit. Peterkin also went to the plum tree for the purpose of making a special onslaught upon the hogs, and killed no less than six of them. These we baked and presented to our friends on the day of their departure. On that day Tararo made a great many energetic signs to us, which, after much consideration, we came to understand were proposals that we should go away with him to his island; but having no desire to do so, we shook our heads very decidedly. However, we consoled him by presenting him with our rusty axe, which we thought we could spare, having the excellent one which had been so providentially washed ashore to us the day we were wrecked. We also gave him a piece of wood with our names carved on it, and a piece of string to hang it round his neck as an ornament.

In a few minutes more we were all assembled on the beach. Being unable to speak to the savages, we went through the ceremony of shaking hands, and expected they would depart; but before doing so, Tararo went up to Jack and rubbed noses with him, after which he did the same with Peterkin and me! Seeing that this was their mode of salutation, we determined to conform to their custom, so we rubbed noses heartily with the whole party, women and all! The only disagreeable part of the process was when we came to rub noses with Mahine, and Peterkin afterwards said that when he saw his wolfish eyes glaring so close to his face, he felt much more inclined to *bang* than to *rub* his nose. Avatea was the last to take leave of us, and we experienced a feeling of real sorrow when she approached to bid us farewell. Besides her modest air and gentle manners, she was the only one of the party who exhibited the smallest sign of regret at parting from us. Going up to Jack, she put out her flat little nose to be rubbed, and thereafter paid the same compliment to Peterkin and me.

An hour later the canoe was out of sight, and we, with an indefinable feeling of sadness creeping round our hearts, were seated in silence beneath the shadow of our bower, meditating on the wonderful events of the last few days.

CHAPTER XXI

Sagacious and moral remarks in regard to life—A sail!—An unexpected salute—The end of the black cat—A terrible dive—
An incautious proceeding and a frightful catastrophe.

LIFE is a strange compound Peterkin used to say of
it that it beat a druggist's shop all to sticks; for
whereas the first is a compound of good and bad, the
other is a horrible compound of all that is utterly detest-
able. And indeed the more I consider it the more I am
struck with the strange mixture of good and evil that
exists not only in the material earth but in our own
natures. In our own Coral Island we had experienced
every variety of good that a bountiful Creator could heap
on us. Yet on the night of the storm we had seen how
almost, in our case—and altogether, no doubt, in the case
of others less fortunate—all this good might be swept
away for ever We had seen the rich fruit-trees waving
in the soft air, the tender herbs shooting upwards under
the benign influence of the bright sun; and the next day
we had seen these good and beautiful trees and plants
uprooted by the hurricane, crushed and hurled to the
ground in destructive devastation. We had lived for
many months in a clime for the most part so beautiful
that we had often wondered whether Adam and Eve had
found Eden more sweet; and we had seen the quiet soli-
tudes of our paradise suddenly broken in upon by ferocious
savages, and the white sands stained with blood and

strewed with lifeless forms; yet among these cannibals we had seen many symptoms of a kindly nature. I pondered these things much, and while I considered them there recurred to my memory those words which I had read in my Bible—"The works of God are wonderful, and His ways past finding out."

After these poor savages had left us we used to hold long and frequent conversations about them, and I noticed that Peterkin's manner was now much altered. He did not, indeed, jest less heartily than before, but he did so less frequently, and often there was a tone of deep seriousness in his manner, if not in his words, which made him seem to Jack and me as if he had grown two years older within a few days. But indeed I was not surprised at this, when I reflected on the awful realities which we had witnessed so lately. We could by no means shake off a tendency to gloom for several weeks afterwards; but as time wore away our usual good spirits returned somewhat, and we began to think of the visit of the savages with feelings akin to those with which we recall a terrible dream.

One day we were all enjoying ourselves in the Water Garden, preparatory to going on a fishing excursion; for Peterkin had kept us in such constant supply of hogs that we had become quite tired of pork, and desired a change. Peterkin was sunning himself on the ledge of rock, while we were creeping among the rocks below. Happening to look up, I observed Peterkin cutting the most extraordinary capers and making violent gesticulations for us to come up; so I gave Jack a push and rose immediately.

"A sail! a sail!—Ralph, look; Jack, away on the

horizon there, just over the entrance to the lagoon!"
cried Peterkin, as we scrambled up the rocks.

"So it is, and a schooner, too!" said Jack, as he proceeded hastily to dress.

Our hearts were thrown into a terrible flutter by this
discovery, for if it should touch at our island we had no
doubt the captain would be happy to give us a passage to
some of the civilised islands, where we could find a ship sailing for England, or some other part of Europe. Home,
with all its associations, rushed in upon my heart like a
flood; and much though I loved the Coral Island and
the bower, which had now been our home so long, I felt
that I could have quitted all at that moment without a
sigh. With joyful anticipations we hastened to the
highest point of rock near our dwelling, and awaited
the arrival of the vessel; for we now perceived that
she was making straight for the island, under a steady
breeze.

In less than an hour she was close to the reef, where
she rounded to and backed her topsails, in order to survey
the coast. Seeing this, and fearing that they might not
perceive us, we all three waved pieces of cocoa-nut cloth
in the air, and soon had the satisfaction of seeing them
beginning to lower a boat and bustle about the decks as
if they meant to land. Suddenly a flag was run up to
the peak, a little cloud of white smoke rose from the
schooner's side, and before we could guess their intentions,
a cannon-shot came crashing through the bushes, carried
away several cocoa-nut trees in its passage, and burst in
atoms against the cliff a few yards below the spot on
which we stood.

With feelings of terror we now observed that the

flag at the schooner's peak was black, with a Death's-head and cross-bones upon it. As we gazed at each other in blank amazement, the word "pirate" escaped our lips simultaneously.

"What is to be done?" cried Peterkin, as we observed a boat shoot from the vessel's side and make for the entrance of the reef. "If they take us off the island, it will either be to throw us overboard for sport, or to make pirates of us."

I did not reply, but looked at Jack, as being our only resource in this emergency. He stood with folded arms, and his eyes fixed with a grave, anxious expression on the ground. "There is but one hope," said he, turning with a sad expression of countenance to Peterkin; "perhaps, after all, we may not have to resort to it. If these villains are anxious to take us, they will soon overrun the whole island. But come, follow me."

Stopping abruptly in his speech, Jack bounded into the woods, and led us by a circuitous route to Spouting Cliff. Here he halted, and, advancing cautiously to the rocks, glanced over their edge. We were soon by his side, and saw the boat, which was crowded with armed men, just touching the shore. In an instant the crew landed, formed line, and rushed up to our bower.

In a few seconds we saw them hurrying back to the boat, one of them swinging the poor cat round his head by the tail. On reaching the water's edge, he tossed it far into the sea, and joined his companions, who appeared to be holding a hasty council.

"You see what we may expect," said Jack bitterly. "The man who will wantonly kill a poor brute for sport will think little of murdering a fellow-creature.

Now, boys, we have but one chance left—the Diamond Cave."

"The Diamond Cave!" cried Peterkin; "then my chance is a poor one, for I could not dive into it if all the pirates on the Pacific were at my heels."

"Nay, but," said I, " we will take you down, Peterkin, if you will only trust us."

As I spoke, we observed the pirates scatter over the beach, and radiate, as if from a centre, towards the woods and along shore.

"Now, Peterkin," said Jack in a solemn tone, " you must make up your mind to do it, or we must make up our minds to die in your company."

"O Jack, my dear friend," cried Peterkin, turning pale, "leave me; I don't believe they'll think it worth while to kill me. Go, you and Ralph, and dive into the cave."

"That will not I," answered Jack quietly, while he picked up a stout cudgel from the ground.—"So now, Ralph, we must prepare to meet these fellows. Their motto is, 'No quarter.' If we can manage to floor those coming in this direction, we may escape into the woods for a while."

"There are five of them," said I; " we have no chance."

"Come, then," cried Peterkin, starting up, and grasping Jack convulsively by the arm, "let us dive; I will go."

Those who are not naturally expert in the water know well the feelings of horror that overwhelm them, when in it, at the bare idea of being held down even for a few seconds—that spasmodic, involuntary recoil from compulsory immersion which has no connection whatever with cowardice; and they will understand the amount of resolution that it required in Peterkin to allow himself to be dragged down to a depth of ten feet, and then, through a narrow tunnel, into an almost pitch-dark cavern. But there was no alternative. The pirates had already caught sight of us, and were now within a short distance of the rocks.

Jack and I seized Peterkin by the arms.

"Now, keep quite still; no struggling," said Jack, " or we are lost."

Peterkin made no reply, but the stern gravity of his marble features, and the tension of his muscles, satisfied us that he had fully made up his mind to go through with it. Just as the pirates gained the foot of the rocks, which hid us for a moment from their view, we bent over the sea, and plunged down together head foremost. Peterkin behaved like a hero. He floated passively between us like a log of wood, and we passed the tunnel and rose into the cave in a shorter space of time than I had ever done it before.

Peterkin drew a long, deep breath on reaching the surface, and in a few seconds we were all standing on the ledge of rock in safety. Jack now searched for the tinder and torch which always lay in the cave. He soon found them, and, lighting the torch, revealed to Peterkin's wondering gaze the marvels of the place. But we were too wet to waste much time in looking about us. Our first care was to take off our clothes and wring them as dry as we could. This done, we proceeded to examine into the state of our larder, for, as Jack truly remarked, there was no knowing how long the pirates might remain on the island.

"Perhaps," said Peterkin, " they may take it into their

heads to stop here altogether, and so we shall be buried alive in this place."

"Don't you think, Peterkin, that it's the nearest thing to being drowned alive that you ever felt?" said Jack with a smile. "But I have no fear of that. These villains never stay long on shore. The sea is their home, so you may depend upon it that they won't stay more than a day or two at the furthest."

We now began to make arrangements for spending the night in the cavern. At various periods Jack and I had conveyed cocoa-nuts and other fruits, besides rolls of cocoa-nut cloth, to this submarine cave, partly for amusement, and partly from a feeling that we might possibly be driven one day to take shelter here from the savages. Little did we imagine that the first savages who would drive us into it would be white savages, perhaps our own countrymen. We found the cocoa-nuts in good condition, and the cooked yams, but the bread-fruits were spoiled. We also found the cloth where we had left it, and on opening it out there proved to be sufficient to make a bed; which was important, as the rock was damp. Having collected it all together, we spread out our bed, placed our torch in the midst of us, and ate our supper. It was indeed a strange chamber to feast in; and we could not help remarking on the cold, ghastly appearance of the walls, and the black water at our side, with the thick darkness beyond, and the sullen sound of the drops that fell at long intervals from the roof of the cavern into the still water, and the strong contrast between all this and our bed and supper, which, with our faces, were lit up with the deep red flame of the torch.

We sat long over our meal, talking together in sub-

dued voices, for we did not like the dismal echoes that
rang through the vault above when we happened to raise
them. At last the faint light that came through the
opening died away, warning us that it was night and
time for rest. We therefore put out our torch and lay
down to sleep.

On awaking, it was some time ere we could collect our
faculties so as to remember where we were, and we were
in much uncertainty as to whether it was early or late.
We saw by the faint light that it was day, but could not
guess at the hour; so Jack proposed that he should dive
out and reconnoitre.

"No, Jack," said I; "do you rest here. You've had
enough to do during the last few days. Rest yourself
now, and take care of Peterkin, while I go out to see
what the pirates are about. I'll be very careful not
to expose myself, and I'll bring you word again in a
short time."

"Very well, Ralph," answered Jack, "please yourself,
but don't be long; and if you'll take my advice you'll go
in your clothes, for I would like to have some fresh cocoa-
nuts, and climbing trees without clothes is uncomfortable,
to say the least of it."

"The pirates will be sure to keep a sharp look-out,"
said Peterkin, "so, pray, be careful."

"No fear," said I; "good-bye."

"Good-bye," answered my comrades.

And while the words were yet sounding in my ears, I
plunged into the water, and in a few seconds found myself
in the open air. On rising, I was careful to come up
gently and to breathe softly, while I kept close in beside
the rocks; but as I observed no one near me, I crept

slowly out, and ascended the cliff a step at a time, till I
obtained a full view of the shore. No pirates were to be
seen—even their boat was gone; but as it was possible
they might have hidden themselves, I did not venture too
boldly forward. Then it occurred to me to look out to
sea, when, to my surprise, I saw the pirate schooner sailing
away almost hull down on the horizon! On seeing this I
uttered a shout of joy. Then my first impulse was to
dive back to tell my companions the good news; but I
checked myself, and ran to the top of the cliff, in order to
make sure that the vessel I saw was indeed the pirate
schooner. I looked long and anxiously at her, and giving
vent to a deep sigh of relief, said aloud, "Yes, there she
goes; the villains have been balked of their prey this
time at least."

"Not so sure of that!" said a deep voice at my side,
while at the same moment a heavy hand grasped my
shoulder, and held it as if in a vice.

CHAPTER XXII

I fall into the hands of pirates—How they treated me, and what I said to them—The result of the whole ending in a melancholy separation and in a most unexpected gift.

MY heart seemed to leap into my throat at the words; and turning round, I beheld a man of immense stature and fierce aspect regarding me with a smile of contempt. He was a white man—that is to say, he was a man of European blood, though his face, from long exposure to the weather, was deeply bronzed. His dress was that of a common seaman, except that he had on a Greek skull-cap, and wore a broad shawl of the richest silk round his waist. In this shawl were placed two pairs of pistols and a heavy cutlass. He wore a beard and moustache, which, like the locks on his head, were short, curly, and sprinkled with grey hairs.

"So, youngster," he said with a sardonic smile, while I felt his grasp tighten on my shoulder, "the villains have been balked of their prey, have they? We shall see, we shall see. Now, you whelp, look yonder." As he spoke, the pirate uttered a shrill whistle. In a second or two it was answered, and the pirate boat rowed round the point at the Water Garden, and came rapidly towards us. "Now, go, make a fire on that point; and hark'ee, youngster, if you try to run away, I'll send a quick and sure messenger after you," and he pointed significantly at his pistols.

I obeyed in silence, and as I happened to have the burning-glass in my pocket, a fire was speedily kindled, and a thick smoke ascended into the air. It had scarcely appeared for two minutes when the boom of a gun rolled over the sea, and looking up, I saw that the schooner was making for the island again. It now flashed across me that this was a ruse on the part of the pirates, and that they had sent their vessel away, knowing that it would lead us to suppose that they had left altogether. But there was no use of regret now. I was completely in their power, so I stood helplessly beside the pirate watching the crew of the boat as they landed on the beach. For an instant I contemplated rushing over the cliff into the sea; but this I saw I could not now accomplish, as some of the men were already between me and the water.

There was a good deal of jesting at the success of their scheme, as the crew ascended the rocks and addressed the man who had captured me by the title of captain. They were a ferocious set of men, with shaggy beards and scowling brows. All of them were armed with cutlasses and pistols, and their costumes were, with trifling variations, similar to that of the captain. As I looked from one to the other, and observed the low, scowling brows that never unbent, even when the men laughed, and the mean, rascally expression that sat on each face, I felt that my life hung by a hair.

"But where are the other cubs?" cried one of the men, with an oath that made me shudder. "I'll swear to it there were three, at least, if not more."

"You hear what he says, whelp: where are the other dogs?" said the captain.

"If you mean my companions," said I in a low voice, "I won't tell you."

A loud laugh burst from the crew at this answer.

The pirate captain looked at me in surprise. Then drawing a pistol from his belt, he cocked it and said, "Now, youngster, listen to me. I've no time to waste here. If you don't tell me all you know, I'll blow your brains out! Where are your comrades?"

For an instant I hesitated, not knowing what to do in this extremity. Suddenly a thought occurred to me.

"Villain," said I, shaking my clenched fist in his face, "to blow my brains out would make short work of me, and be soon over; death by drowning is as sure, and the agony prolonged: yet I tell you to your face, if you were to toss me over yonder cliff into the sea, I would not tell you where my companions are, and I dare you to try me!"

The pirate captain grew white with rage as I spoke. "Say you so?" cried he, uttering a fierce oath.—"Here, lads, take him by the legs and heave him in—quick!"

The men, who were utterly silenced with surprise at my audacity, advanced and seized me, and as they carried me towards the cliff I congratulated myself not a little on the success of my scheme; for I knew that once in the water I should be safe, and could rejoin Jack and Peterkin in the cave. But my hopes were suddenly blasted by the captain crying out, "Hold on, lads, hold on! We'll give him a taste of the thumb-screws before throwing him to the sharks. Away with him into the boat. Look alive! the breeze is freshening."

The men instantly raised me shoulder high, and hurrying down the rocks, tossed me into the bottom of the boat, where I lay for some time stunned with the violence of my fall.

On recovering sufficiently to raise myself on my elbow, I perceived that we were already outside the coral reef, and close alongside the schooner, which was of small size and clipper built. I had only time to observe this much, when I received a severe kick on the side from one of the men, who ordered me, in a rough voice, to jump aboard. Rising hastily, I clambered up the side. In a few minutes the boat was hoisted on deck, the vessel's head put close to the wind, and the Coral Island dropped slowly astern as we beat up against a head sea.

Immediately after coming aboard, the crew were too busily engaged in working the ship and getting in the boat to attend to me, so I remained leaning against the bulwarks close to the gangway, watching their operations. I was surprised to find that there were no guns or carronades of any kind in the vessel, which had more the appearance of a fast-sailing trader than a pirate. But I was struck with the neatness of everything. The brass work of the binnacle and about the tiller, as well as the copper belaying-pins, were as brightly polished as if they had just come from the foundry. The decks were pure white, and smooth. The masts were clean-scraped and varnished except at the cross-trees and truck, which were painted black. The standing and running rigging was in the most perfect order, and the sails white as snow. In short, everything, from the single narrow red stripe on her low, black hull to the trucks on her tapering masts, evinced an amount of care and strict discipline that would have done credit to a ship of the Royal Navy. There was nothing lumbering or unseemly about the vessel, excepting, perhaps, a boat, which lay on the deck with its keel up between the fore and main masts. It seemed disproportionately large for the schooner; but when I saw that the crew amounted to between thirty and forty men, I concluded that this boat was held in reserve in case of any accident compelling the crew to desert the vessel.

As I have before said, the costumes of the men were similar to that of the captain. But in head-gear they differed not only from him but from each other, some wearing the ordinary straw hat of the merchant service, while others wore cloth caps and red worsted night-caps. I observed that all their arms were sent below, the captain only retaining his cutlass and a single pistol in the folds of his shawl. Although the captain was the tallest and most powerful man in the ship, he did not strikingly excel many of his men in this respect; and the only difference that an ordinary observer would have noticed was a certain degree of open candour, straightforward daring, in the bold, ferocious expression of his face, which rendered him less repulsive than his low-browed associates, but did not by any means induce the belief that he was a hero. This look was, however, the indication of that spirit which gave him the pre-eminence among the crew of desperadoes who called him captain. He was a lion-like villain, totally devoid of personal fear, and utterly reckless of consequences, and therefore a terror to his men, who individually hated him, but unitedly felt it to be to their advantage to have him at their head.

But my thoughts soon reverted to the dear companions whom I had left on shore, and as I turned towards the Coral Island, which was now far away to leeward, I sighed deeply, and the tears rolled slowly down my cheeks as I thought that I might never see them more.

"So you're blubbering, are you, you obstinate whelp?" said the deep voice of the captain, as he came up and gave me a box on the ear that nearly felled me to the deck. "I don't allow any such weakness aboard o' this ship. So clap a stopper on your eyes, or I'll give you something to cry for."

I flushed with indignation at this rough and cruel treatment, but felt that giving way to anger would only make matters worse, so I made no reply, but took out my handkerchief and dried my eyes.

"I thought you were made of better stuff," continued the captain angrily. "I'd rather have a mad bulldog aboard than a water-eyed puppy. But I'll cure you, lad, or introduce you to the sharks before long. Now go below, and stay there till I call you."

As I walked forward to obey, my eye fell on a small keg standing by the side of the main-mast, on which the word *gunpowder* was written in pencil. It immediately flashed across me that, as we were beating up against the wind, anything floating in the sea would be driven on the reef encircling the Coral Island. I also recollected—for thought is more rapid than the lightning—that my old companions had a pistol. Without a moment's hesitation, therefore, I lifted the keg from the deck and tossed it into the sea! An exclamation of surprise burst from the captain and some of the men who witnessed this act of mine.

Striding up to me, and uttering fearful imprecations, the captain raised his hand to strike me, while he shouted, "Boy! whelp! what mean you by that?"

"If you lower your hand," said I in a loud voice, while I felt the blood rush to my temples, "I'll tell you. Until you do so I'm dumb."

The captain stepped back and regarded me with a look of amazement.

"Now," continued I, "I threw that keg into the sea because the wind and waves will carry it to my friends on the Coral Island, who happen to have a pistol, but no powder. I hope that it will reach them soon; and my only regret is that the keg was not a bigger one. Moreover, pirate, you said just now that you thought I was made of better stuff. I don't know what stuff I am made of—I never thought much about that subject—but I'm quite certain of this, that I am made of such stuff as the like of you shall never tame, though you should do your worst."

To my surprise the captain, instead of flying into a rage, smiled, and thrusting his hand into the voluminous shawl that encircled his waist, turned on his heel and walked aft, while I went below.

Here, instead of being rudely handled, as I had expected, the men received me with a shout of laughter, and one of them, patting me on the back, said, "Well done, lad! you're a brick, and I have no doubt will turn out a rare cove. Bloody Bill there was just such a fellow as you are, and he's now the biggest cut-throat of us all."

"Take a can of beer, lad," cried another, "and wet your whistle after that speech o' your'n to the captain. If any one o' us had made it, youngster, he would have had no whistle to wet by this time."

"Stop your clapper, Jack," vociferated a third. "Give

the boy a junk o' meat. Don't you see he's a'most going
to kick the bucket?"

"And no wonder," said the first speaker with an oath,
"after the tumble you gave him into the boat. I guess
it would have broke *your* neck if you had got it."

I did indeed feel somewhat faint, which was owing,
doubtless, to the combined effects of ill-usage and hunger;
for it will be recollected that I had dived out of the cave
that morning before breakfast, and it was now near mid-
day. I therefore gladly accepted a plate of boiled pork
and a yam, which were handed to me by one of the men
from the locker on which some of the crew were seated
eating their dinner. But I must add that the zest with
which I ate my meal was much abated in consequence of
the frightful oaths and the terrible language that flowed
from the lips of these godless men, even in the midst of
their hilarity and good-humour. The man who had been
alluded to as Bloody Bill was seated near me, and I could
not help wondering at the moody silence he maintained
among his comrades. He did indeed reply to their
questions in a careless off-hand tone, but he never
volunteered a remark. The only difference between him
and the others was his taciturnity and his size, for he was
nearly, if not quite, as large a man as the captain.

During the remainder of the afternoon I was left to my
own reflections, which were anything but agreeable; for
I could not banish from my mind the threat about the
thumb-screws, of the nature and use of which I had a
vague but terrible conception. I was still meditating on
my unhappy fate, when, just after nightfall, one of the
watch on deck called down the hatchway—

"Hallo there! one o' you tumble up and light the

cabin lamp, and send that boy aft to the captain—sharp!"

"Now then, do you hear, youngster? the captain wants you. Look alive," said Bloody Bill, raising his huge frame from the locker on which he had been asleep for the last two hours. He sprang up the ladder, and I instantly followed him, and going aft was shown into the cabin by one of the men, who closed the door after me.

A small silver lamp which hung from a beam threw a dim, soft light over the cabin, which was a small apartment, and comfortably but plainly furnished. Seated on a camp-stool at the table, and busily engaged in examining a chart of the Pacific, was the captain, who looked up as I entered, and in a quiet voice bade me be seated, while he threw down his pencil, and rising from the table, stretched himself on a sofa at the upper end of the cabin.

"Boy," said he, looking me full in the face, "what is your name?"

"Ralph Rover," I replied.

"Where did you come from, and how came you to be on that island? How many companions had you on it? Answer me, now, and mind you tell no lies."

"I never tell lies," said I firmly.

The captain received this reply with a cold, sarcastic smile, and bade me answer his questions.

I then told him the history of myself and my companions from the time we sailed till the day of his visit to the island, taking care, however, to make no mention of the Diamond Cave. After I had concluded, he was silent for a few minutes; then looking up, he said, "Boy, I believe you."

I was surprised at this remark, for I could not imagine

why he should not believe me. However, I made no reply.

"And what," continued the captain, "makes you think that this schooner is a pirate?"

"The black flag," said I, "showed me what you are; and if any further proof were wanting, I have had it in the brutal treatment I have received at your hands."

The captain frowned as I spoke, but subduing his anger he continued, "Boy, you are too bold. I admit that we treated you roughly, but that was because you made us lose time and gave us a good deal of trouble. As to the black flag, that is merely a joke that my fellows play off upon people sometimes in order to frighten them. It is their humour, and does no harm. I am no pirate, boy, but a lawful trader—a rough one, I grant you, but one can't help that in these seas, where there are so many pirates on the water and such murderous blackguards on the land. I carry on a trade in sandal-wood with the Feejee Islands; and if you choose, Ralph, to behave yourself and be a good boy, I'll take you along with me and give you a good share of the profits. You see I'm in want of an honest boy like you to look after the cabin and keep the log and superintend the traffic on shore sometimes. What say you, Ralph: would you like to become a sandal-wood trader?"

I was much surprised by this explanation, and a good deal relieved to find that the vessel, after all, was not a pirate; but, instead of replying, I said, "If it be as you state, then why did you take me from my island, and why do you not now take me back?"

The captain smiled as he replied, "I took you off in anger, boy, and I'm sorry for it. I would even now take you back, but we are too far away from it. See, there it is," he added, laying his finger on the chart, "and we are now here—fifty miles at least. It would not be fair to my men to put about now, for they have all an interest in the trade."

I could make no reply to this; so, after a little more conversation, I agreed to become one of the crew—at least, until we could reach some civilised island where I might be put ashore. The captain assented to this proposition, and after thanking him for the promise, I left the cabin and went on deck with feelings that ought to have been lighter, but which were, I could not tell why, marvellously heavy and uncomfortable still.

CHAPTER XXIII

Bloody Bill—Dark surmises—A strange sail, and a strange crew, and a still stranger cargo—New reasons for favouring mission-aries—A murderous massacre, and thoughts thereon.

THREE weeks after the conversation narrated in the last chapter, I was standing on the quarter-deck of the schooner, watching the gambols of a shoal of por-poises that swam round us. It was a dead calm—one of those still, hot, sweltering days so common in the Pacific, when nature seems to have gone to sleep, and the only thing in water or in air that proves her still alive is her long, deep breathing in the swell of the mighty sea. No cloud floated in the deep blue above; no ripple broke the reflected blue below. The sun shone fiercely in the sky, and a ball of fire blazed with almost equal power from out the bosom of the water. So intensely still was it, and so perfectly transparent was the surface of the deep, that had it not been for the long swell already alluded to, we might have believed the surrounding universe to be a huge, blue, liquid ball, and our little ship the one solitary material speck in all creation, floating in the midst of it.

No sound broke on our ears save the soft puff now and then of a porpoise, the slow creak of the masts as we swayed gently on the swell, the patter of the reef-points, and the occasional flap of the hanging sails. An awning covered the fore and after parts of the schooner, under which the men composing the watch on deck lolled in

sleepy indolence, overcome with excessive heat. Bloody
Bill, as the men invariably called him, was standing at
the tiller; but his post for the present was a sinecure, and
he whiled away the time by alternately gazing in dreamy
abstraction at the compass in the binnacle, and by walking
to the taffrail in order to spit into the sea. In one of
these turns he came near to where I was standing, and,
leaning over the side, looked long and earnestly down into
the blue wave.

This man, although he was always taciturn and often
surly, was the only human being on board with whom I
had the slightest desire to become better acquainted. The
other men, seeing that I did not relish their company, and
knowing that I was a protégé of the captain, treated me
with total indifference. Bloody Bill, it is true, did the
same; but as this was his conduct to every one else, it
was not peculiar in reference to me. Once or twice I tried
to draw him into conversation, but he always turned away
after a few cold monosyllables. As he now leaned over
the taffrail close beside me, I said to him—

" Bill, why is it that you are so gloomy? Why do you
never speak to any one? "

Bill smiled slightly as he replied, " Why, I s'pose it's
because I hain't got nothin' to say ! "

"That's strange," said I musingly; " you look like a
man that could think, and such men can usually speak."

" So they can, youngster," rejoined Bill somewhat
sternly; " and I could speak, too, if I had a mind to, but
what's the use o' speakin' here? The men only open their
mouths to curse and swear, an' they seem to find it enter-
tainin'; but I don't, so I hold my tongue."

" Well, Bill, that's true, and I would rather not hear

you speak at all than hear you speak like the other men; but *I* don't swear, Bill, so you might talk to me sometimes, I think. Besides, I'm weary of spending day after day in this way, without a single soul to say a pleasant word to. I've been used to friendly conversation, Bill, and I really would take it kind if you would talk with me a little now and then."

Bill looked at me in surprise, and I thought I observed a sad expression pass across his sunburned face.

"An' where have you been used to friendly conversation?" said Bill, looking down again into the sea; "not on that Coral Island, I take it."

"Yes, indeed," said I energetically; "I have spent many of the happiest months in my life on that Coral Island." And without waiting to be further questioned, I launched out into a glowing account of the happy life that Jack and Peterkin and I had spent together, and related minutely every circumstance that befell us while on the island.

"Boy, boy," said Bill, in a voice so deep that it startled me, "this is no place for you."

"That's true," said I. "I am of little use on board, and I don't like my comrades; but I can't help it, and at any rate I hope to be free again soon."

"Free?" said Bill, looking at me in surprise.

"Yes, free," returned I; "the captain said he would put me ashore after this trip was over."

"*This trip!* Hark'ee, boy," said Bill, lowering his voice, "what said the captain to you the day you came aboard?"

"He said that he was a trader in sandal-wood, and no pirate, and told me that if I would join him for this trip he would give me a good share of the profits, or put me on shore in some civilised island if I chose."

Bill's brows lowered savagely as he muttered, "Ay, he said truth when he told you he was a sandal-wood trader, but he lied when——"

"Sail ho!" shouted the look-out at the masthead.

"Where away?" cried Bill, springing to the tiller; while the men, startled by the sudden cry, jumped up and gazed round the horizon.

"On the starboard quarter, hull down, sir," answered the look-out.

At this moment the captain came on deck, and mounting into the rigging, surveyed the sail through the glass. Then sweeping his eye round the horizon, he gazed steadily at a particular point.

"Take in top-sails," shouted the captain, swinging himself down on the deck by the main-back stay.

"Take in top-sails," roared the first mate.

"Ay, ay, sir-r-r," answered the men, as they sprang into the rigging and went aloft like cats.

Instantly all was bustle on board the hitherto quiet schooner. The top-sails were taken in and stowed, the men stood by the sheets and halyards, and the captain gazed anxiously at the breeze which was now rushing towards us like a sheet of dark blue. In a few seconds it struck us. The schooner trembled as if in surprise at the sudden onset, while she fell away, then bending gracefully to the wind, as though in acknowledgment of her subjection, she cut through the waves with her sharp prow like a dolphin, while Bill directed her course towards the strange sail.

In half-an-hour we neared her sufficiently to make out that she was a schooner, and from the clumsy appearance of her masts and sails we judged her to be a trader. She evidently did not like our appearance, for the instant the breeze reached her she crowded all sail and showed us her stern. As the breeze had moderated a little, our top-sails were again shaken out, and it soon became evident—despite the proverb, " A stern chase is a long one "—that we doubled her speed and would overhaul her speedily. When within a mile we hoisted British colours, but receiving no acknowledgment, the captain ordered a shot to be fired across her bows. In a moment, to my surprise, a large portion of the bottom of the boat amidships was removed, and in the hole thus exposed appeared an immense brass gun. It worked on a swivel, and was elevated by means of machinery. It was quickly loaded and fired. The heavy ball struck the water a few yards ahead of the chase, and ricochetting into the air, plunged into the sea a mile beyond it.

This produced the desired effect. The strange vessel backed her top-sails and hove-to, while we ranged up and lay-to about a hundred yards off.

" Lower the boat," cried the captain.

In a second the boat was lowered and manned by a part of the crew, who were all armed with cutlasses and pistols. As the captain passed me to get into it, he said, " Jump into the stern-sheets, Ralph; I may want you." I obeyed, and in ten minutes more we were standing on the stranger's deck. We were all much surprised at the sight that met our eyes. Instead of a crew of such sailors as we were accustomed to see, there were only fifteen blacks, standing on the quarter-deck and regarding us with looks of undisguised alarm. They were totally unarmed, and most of them unclothed; one or two, however,

wore portions of European attire. One had on a pair of
duck trousers which were much too large for him, and
stuck out in a most ungainly manner. Another wore
nothing but the common scanty native garment round
the loins, and a black beaver hat.* But the most ludicrous personage of all, and one who seemed to be chief,
was a tall, middle-aged man, of a mild, simple expression
of countenance, who wore a white cotton shirt, a swallow-
tailed coat, and a straw hat, while his black, brawny legs
were totally uncovered below the knees.

"Where's the commander of this ship?" inquired our
captain, stepping up to this individual.

"I is capin," he answered, taking off his straw hat and
making a low bow.

"You!" said our captain in surprise. "Where do
you come from, and where are you bound? What cargo
have you aboard?"

"We is come," answered the man with the swallow-
tail, "from Aitutaki; we was go for Rarotonga.* We is
native miss'nary ship; our name is de *Olive Branch;* an'
our cargo is two tons cocoa-nuts, seventy pigs, twenty
cats, and de Gosp'l."

This announcement was received by the crew of our
vessel with a shout of laughter, which, however, was
peremptorily checked by the captain, whose expression
instantly changed from one of severity to that of frank
urbanity as he advanced towards the missionary and
shook him warmly by the hand.

"I am very glad to have fallen in with you," said he,
"and I wish you much success in your missionary labours.
Pray take me to your cabin, as I wish to converse with
you privately."

The missionary immediately took him by the hand, and as he led him away I heard him saying, "Me most glad to find you trader; we t'ought you be pirate. You very like one 'bout the masts."

What conversation the captain had with this man I never heard, but he came on deck again in a quarter of an hour, and shaking hands cordially with the missionary, ordered us into our boat and returned to the schooner, which was immediately put before the wind. In a few minutes the *Olive Branch* was left far behind us.

That afternoon, as I was down below at dinner, I heard the men talking about this curious ship.

"I wonder," said one, "why our captain looked so sweet on yon swallow-tailed supercargo o' pigs and Gospels. If it had been an ordinary trader, now, he would have taken as many o' the pigs as he required and sent the ship with all on board to the bottom."

"Why, Dick, you must be new to these seas if you don't know that," cried another. "The captain cares as much for the Gospel as you do (an' that's precious little), but he knows, and everybody knows, that the only place among the southern islands where a ship can put in and get what she wants in comfort is where the Gospel has been sent to. There are hundreds o' islands, at this blessed moment, where you might as well jump straight into a shark's maw as land without a band o' thirty comrades armed to the teeth to back you."

"Ay," said a man with a deep scar over his right eye, "Dick's new to the work. But if the captain takes us for a cargo o' sandal-wood to the Feejees, he'll get a taste o' these black gentry in their native condition. For my part, I don't know and I don't care what the Gospel does to them, but I know that when any o' the islands chance to get it, trade goes all smooth and easy; but where they ha'nt got it, Beelzebub himself could hardly desire better company."

"Well, you ought to be a good judge," cried another, laughing, "for you've never kept any company but the worst all your life!"

"Ralph Rover!" shouted a voice down the hatchway, "captain wants you, aft."

Springing up the ladder, I hastened to the cabin, pondering as I went the strange testimony borne by these men to the effect of the Gospel on savage natures —testimony which, as it was perfectly disinterested, I had no doubt whatever was strictly true.

On coming again on deck, I found Bloody Bill at the helm, and as we were alone together, I tried to draw him into conversation. After repeating to him the conversation in the forecastle about the missionaries, I said—

"Tell me, Bill, is this schooner really a trader in sandal-wood?"

"Yes, Ralph, she is; but she's just as really a pirate. The black flag you saw flying at the peak was no deception."

"Then how can you say she's a trader?" asked I.

"Why, as to that, she trades when she can't take by force; but she takes by force when she can, in preference. Ralph," he added, lowering his voice, "if you had seen the bloody deeds that I have witnessed done on these decks, you would not need to ask if we were pirates. But you'll find it out soon enough. As for the missionaries, the captain favours them because they are useful to him. The South Sea Islanders are such incarnate fiends that they are the better of being tamed, and the missionaries are the only men who can do it."

Our track after this lay through several clusters of small islets, among which we were becalmed more than once. During this part of our voyage the watch on deck and the look-out at the masthead were more than usually vigilant, as we were not only in danger of being attacked by the natives (who, I learned from the captain's remarks, were a bloody and deceitful tribe at this group), but we were also exposed to much risk from the multitudes of coral reefs that rose up in the channels between the islands, some of them just above the surface, others a few feet below it. Our precautions against the savages, I found, were indeed necessary.

One day we were becalmed among a group of small islands, most of which appeared to be uninhabited. As we were in want of fresh water, the captain sent the boat ashore to bring off a cask or two. But we were mistaken in thinking there were no natives; for scarcely had we drawn near to the shore when a band of naked blacks rushed out of the bush and assembled on the beach, brandishing their clubs and spears in a threatening manner. Our men were well armed, but refrained from showing any signs of hostility, and rowed nearer in order to converse with the natives; and I now found that more than one of the crew could imperfectly speak dialects of the language peculiar to the South Sea Islanders. When within forty yards of the shore, we ceased rowing, and the first mate stood up to address the multitude; but instead of answering us, they replied with a shower of stones, some of which cut the men severely. Instantly our muskets were levelled, and a volley was about to be

fired, when the captain hailed us in a loud voice from
the schooner, which lay not more than five or six hundred yards off the shore.

"Don't fire!" he shouted angrily. "Pull off to the
point ahead of you."

The men looked surprised at this order, and uttered
deep curses as they prepared to obey, for their wrath was
roused and they burned for revenge. Three or four of
them hesitated, and seemed disposed to mutiny.

"Don't distress yourselves, lads," said the mate, while
a bitter smile curled his lip. "Obey orders. The captain's not the man to take an insult tamely. If Long
Tom does not speak presently I'll give myself to the
sharks."

The men smiled significantly as they pulled from the
shore, which was now crowded with a dense mass of
savages, amounting probably to five or six hundred. We
had not rowed off above a couple of hundred yards when
a loud roar thundered over the sea, and the big brass gun
sent a withering shower of grape point-blank into the
midst of the living mass, through which a wide lane was
cut, while a yell, the like of which I could not have
imagined, burst from the miserable survivors as they fled
to the woods. Amongst the heaps of dead that lay on
the sand just where they had fallen, I could distinguish
mutilated forms writhing in agony, while ever and anon
one and another rose convulsively from out the mass,
endeavoured to stagger towards the wood, and ere they
had taken a few steps, fell and wallowed on the bloody
sand. My blood curdled within me as I witnessed this
frightful and wanton slaughter; but I had little time to
think, for the captain's deep voice came again over the

water towards us : "Pull ashore, lads, and fill your water-casks." The men obeyed in silence, and it seemed to me as if even their hard hearts were shocked by the ruthless deed. On gaining the mouth of the rivulet at which we intended to take in water, we found it flowing with blood, for the greater part of those who were slain had been standing on the banks of the stream, a short way above its mouth. Many of the wretched creatures had fallen into it, and we found one body, which had been carried down, jammed between two rocks, with the staring eye-balls turned towards us, and his black hair waving in the ripples of the blood-red stream. No one dared to oppose our landing now, so we carried our casks to a pool above the murdered group, and having filled them, returned on board. Fortunately, a breeze sprang up soon afterwards, and carried us away from the dreadful spot; but it could not waft me away from the memory of what I had seen.

"And this," thought I, gazing in horror at the captain, who, with a quiet look of indifference, leaned upon the taffrail smoking a cigar and contemplating the fertile green islets as they passed like a lovely picture before our eyes—"this is the man who favours the missionaries because they are useful to him and can tame the savages better than any one else can do it!" Then I wondered in my mind whether it were possible for any missionary to tame *him!*

CHAPTER XXIV

Bloody Bill is communicative and sagacious—Unpleasant prospects
—Retrospective meditations interrupted by volcanic agency—
The pirates negotiate with a Feejee chief—Various etceteras
that are calculated to surprise and horrify.

IT was many days after the events just narrated ere I
recovered a little of my wonted spirits. I could not
shake off the feeling for a long time that I was in a
frightful dream, and the sight of our captain filled me
with so much horror that I kept out of his way as much
as my duties about the cabin would permit. Fortunately
he took so little notice of me that he did not observe my
changed feelings towards him, otherwise it might have
been worse for me.

But I was now resolved that I would run away the
very first island we should land at, and commit myself to
the hospitality of the natives rather than remain an hour
longer than I could help in the pirate schooner. I
pondered this subject a good deal, and at last made up
my mind to communicate my intention to Bloody Bill;
for during several talks I had had with him of late, I felt
assured that he too would willingly escape if possible.
When I told him of my design he shook his head. "No,
no, Ralph," said he, "you must not think of running away
here. Among some of the groups of islands you might do
so with safety, but if you tried it here you would find
that you had jumped out of the fryin'-pan into the fire."

"How so, Bill?" said I; "would the natives not receive me?"

"That they would, lad; but they would eat you too."

"Eat me!" said I in surprise; "I thought the South Sea Islanders never ate anybody except their enemies."

"Humph!" ejaculated Bill. "I s'pose 'twas yer tender-hearted friends in England that put that notion into your head. There's a set o' soft-hearted folk at home that I knows on who don't like to have their feelin's ruffled, and when you tell them anything they don't like —that shocks them, as they call it—no matter how true it be, they stop their ears and cry out, 'Oh, that is *too* horrible! We can't believe that!' An' they say truth. They can't believe it 'cause they won't believe it. Now, I believe there's thousands o' the people in England who are sich born drivellin' *won't-believers* that they think the black fellows hereaways at the worst eat an enemy only now an' then, out o' spite; whereas I know for certain, and many captains of the British and American navies know as well as me, that the Feejee Islanders eat not only their enemies but one another; and they do it not for spite, but for pleasure. It's a *fact* that they prefer human flesh to any other. But they don't like white men's flesh so well as black; they say it makes them sick."

"Why, Bill," said I, "you told me just now that they would eat *me* if they caught me."

"So I did, and so I think they would. I've only heard some o' them say they don't like white men *so well* as black; but if they was hungry they wouldn't be particular. Anyhow, I'm sure they would kill you. You see, Ralph, I've been a good while in them parts, and I've visited the different groups of islands oftentimes as a

trader. And thorough-goin' blackguards some o' them
traders are; no better than pirates, I can tell you. One
captain that I sailed with was not a chip better than the
one we're with now. He was trading with a friendly chief
one day, aboard his vessel. The chief had swum off to us
with the thing for trade tied atop of his head, for them
chaps are like otters in the water. Well, the chief was
hard on the captain, and would not part with some o' his
things. When their bargainin' was over they shook
hands, and the chief jumped overboard to swim ashore;
but before he got forty yards from the ship the captain
seized a musket and shot him dead. He then hove up
anchor and put to sea, and as we sailed along the shore,
he dropped six black fellows with his rifle, remarkin' that
'that would spoil the trade for the next comers.' But, as
I was sayin', I'm up to the ways o' these fellows. One o'
the laws o' the country is, that every shipwrecked person
who happens to be cast ashore, be he dead or alive, is
doomed to be roasted and eaten. There was a small
tradin' schooner wrecked off one of these islands when we
were lyin' there in harbour during a storm. The crew
was lost, all but three men, who swam ashore. The
moment they landed they were seized by the natives and
carried up into the woods. We knew pretty well what
their fate would be, but we could not help them, for our
crew was small, and if we had gone ashore they would
likely have killed us all. We never saw the three men
again; but we heard frightful yelling and dancing and
merrymaking that night; and one of the natives, who
came aboard to trade with us next day, told us that the
long pigs, as he called the men, had been roasted and
eaten, and their bones were to be converted into sail-

needles. He also said that white men were bad to eat, and that most o' the people on shore were sick."

I was very much shocked and cast down in my mind at this terrible account of the natives, and asked Bill what he would advise me to do. Looking round the deck to make sure that we were not overheard, he lowered his voice and said, "There are two or three ways that we might escape, Ralph, but none o' them's easy. If the captain would only sail for some o' the islands near Tahiti, we might run away there well enough, because the natives are all Christians; an' we find that wherever the savages take up with Christianity they always give over their bloody ways, and are safe to be trusted. I never cared for Christianity myself," he continued in a soliloquising voice, "and I don't well know what it means; but a man with half an eye can see what it does for these black critters. However, the captain always keeps a sharp look-out after us when we get to these islands, for he half suspects that one or two o' us are tired of his company. Then we might manage to cut the boat adrift some fine night when it's our watch on deck, and clear off before they discovered that we were gone. But we would run the risk o' bein' caught by the blacks. I wouldn't like to try that plan. But you and I will think over it, Ralph, and see what's to be done. In the meantime it's our watch below, so I'll go and turn in."

Bill then bade me good-night, and went below, while a comrade took his place at the helm; but feeling no desire to enter into conversation with him, I walked aft, and leaning over the stern, looked down into the phosphorescent waves that gurgled around the rudder, and streamed out like a flame of blue light in the vessel's wake. My thoughts were very sad, and I could scarce refrain from tears as I contrasted my present wretched position with the happy, peaceful time I had spent on the Coral Island with my dear companions. As I thought upon Jack and Peterkin, anxious forebodings crossed my mind, and I pictured to myself the grief and dismay with which they would search every nook and corner of the island, in a vain attempt to discover my dead body; for I felt assured that if they did not see any sign of the pirate schooner or boat when they came out of the cave to look for me, they would never imagine that I had been carried away. I wondered, too, how Jack would succeed in getting Peterkin out of the cave without my assistance; and I trembled when I thought that he might lose presence of mind, and begin to kick when he was in the tunnel! These thoughts were suddenly interrupted and put to flight by a bright red blaze which lighted up the horizon to the southward and cast a crimson glow far over the sea. This appearance was accompanied by a low growling sound, as of distant thunder, and at the same time the sky above us became black, while a hot, stifling wind blew around us in fitful gusts.

The crew assembled hastily on deck, and most of them were under the belief that a frightful hurricane was pending; but the captain, coming on deck, soon explained the phenomena.

"It's only a volcano," said he. "I knew there was one hereabouts, but thought it was extinct. Up there and furl top-gallant sails; we'll likely have a breeze, and it's well to be ready."

As he spoke a shower began to fall, which we quickly observed was not rain but fine ashes. As we were many miles distant from the volcano, these must have been carried to us from it by the wind. As the captain had predicted, a stiff breeze soon afterwards sprang up, under the influence of which we speedily left the volcano far behind us; but during the greater part of the night we could see its lurid glare and hear its distant thunder. The shower did not cease to fall for several hours, and we must have sailed under it for nearly forty miles, perhaps farther. When we emerged from the cloud, our decks and every part of the rigging were completely covered with a thick coat of ashes. I was much interested in this, and recollected that Jack had often spoken of many of the islands of the Pacific as being volcanoes, either active or extinct, and had said that the whole region was more or less volcanic, and that some scientific men were of opinion that the islands of the Pacific were nothing more or less than the mountain tops of a huge continent which had sunk under the influence of volcanic agency.

Three days after passing the volcano, we found ourselves a few miles to windward of an island of considerable size and luxuriant aspect. It consisted of two mountains, which seemed to be nearly four thousand feet high. They were separated from each other by a broad valley, whose thick-growing trees ascended a considerable distance up the mountain sides; and rich, level plains, or meadowland, spread round the base of the mountains, except at the point immediately opposite the large valley, where a river seemed to carry the trees, as it were, along with it down to the white, sandy shore. The mountain tops, unlike those of our Coral Island, were sharp, needle-shaped, and bare, while their sides were more rugged and grand in outline than anything I had yet seen in those seas. Bloody Bill was beside me when the island first hove in sight.

"Ha!" he exclaimed, "I know that island well. They call it Emo."*

"Have you been there before, then?" I inquired.

"Ay, that I have, often, and so has this schooner. 'Tis a famous island for sandal-wood. We have taken many cargoes of it already, and have paid for them, too; for the savages are so numerous that we dared not try to take it by force. But our captain has tried to cheat them so often, that they're beginnin' not to like us overmuch now. Besides, the men behaved ill the last time we were here, and I wonder the captain is not afraid to venture. But he's afraid o' nothing earthly, I believe."

We soon ran inside the barrier coral-reef, and let go our anchor in six fathoms water, just opposite the mouth of a small creek, whose shores were densely covered with mangroves and tall umbrageous trees. The principal village of the natives lay about half a mile from this point. Ordering the boat out, the captain jumped into it, and ordered me to follow him. The men, fifteen in number, were well armed, and the mate was directed to have Long Tom ready for emergencies.

"Give way, lads," cried the captain.

The oars fell into the water at the word, the boat shot from the schooner's side, and in a few minutes reached the shore. Here, contrary to our expectation, we were met with the utmost cordiality by Romata, the principal chief of the island, who conducted us to his house and gave us mats to sit upon. I observed in passing that the natives, of whom there were two or three thousand, were totally unarmed.

After a short preliminary palaver, a feast of baked pigs and various roots was spread before us; of which we partook sparingly, and then proceeded to business. The captain stated his object in visiting the island, regretted that there had been a slight misunderstanding during the last visit, and hoped that no ill-will was borne by either party, and that a satisfactory trade would be accomplished.

Romata answered that he had forgotten there had been any differences between them, protested that he was delighted to see his friends again, and assured them they should have every assistance in cutting and embarking the wood. The terms were afterwards agreed on, and we rose to depart. All this conversation was afterwards explained to me by Bill, who understood the language pretty well.

Romata accompanied us on board, and explained that a great chief from another island was then on a visit to him, and that he was to be ceremoniously entertained on the following day. After begging to be allowed to introduce him to us, and receiving permission, he sent his canoe ashore to bring him off. At the same time, he gave orders to bring on board his two favourites, a cock and a paroquet. While the canoe was gone on this errand, I had time to regard the savage chief attentively. He was a man of immense size, with massive but beautifully moulded limbs and figure, only parts of which, the broad chest and muscular arms, were uncovered; for although the lower orders generally wore no other clothing than a strip of cloth called *maro**round their loins, the chief, on particular occasions, wrapped his person in voluminous folds of a species of native cloth, made from the bark of the Chinese paper-mulberry.* Romata wore a magnificent black beard and moustache, and his hair was frizzed out to such an extent that it resembled a large turban, in which was stuck a long wooden pin! I afterwards found that this pin served for scratching the head, for which purpose the fingers were too short without disarranging the hair. But Romata put himself to much greater inconvenience on account of his hair, for we found that he slept with his head resting on a wooden pillow, in which was cut a hollow for the neck, so that the hair of the sleeper might not be disarranged.

In ten minutes the canoe returned, bringing the other chief, who certainly presented a most extraordinary appearance, having painted one half of his face red and the other half yellow, besides ornamenting it with various designs in black! Otherwise he was much the same in appearance as Romata, though not so powerfully built. As this chief had never seen a ship before, except, perchance, some of the petty traders that at long intervals visit these remote islands, he was much taken up with the neatness and beauty of all the fittings of the schooner. He was particularly struck with a musket which was shown to him, and asked where the white men got hatchets hard enough to cut the tree of which the barrel was made! While he was thus engaged, his brother chief stood aloof, talking with the captain, and fondling a superb cock and a little blue-headed paroquet, the favourites of which I have before spoken. I observed that all the other natives walked in a crouching posture while in the presence of Romata. Before our guests left us, the captain ordered the brass gun to be uncovered and fired for their gratification; and I have every reason to believe he did so for the purpose of showing our superior power, in case the natives

should harbour any evil designs against us. Romata had
never seen this gun before, as it had not been uncovered
on previous visits, and the astonishment with which he
viewed it was very amusing. Being desirous of knowing
its power, he begged that the captain would fire it; so a
shot was put into it. The chiefs were then directed to
look at a rock about two miles out at sea, and the gun
was fired. In a second the top of the rock was seen to
burst asunder, and to fall in fragments into the sea.

Romata was so delighted with the success of this shot
that he pointed to a man who was walking on the shore
and begged the captain to fire at him, evidently supposing that his permission was quite sufficient to justify the
captain in such an act. He was therefore surprised, and
not a little annoyed, when the captain refused to fire at
the native, and ordered the gun to be housed.

Of all the things, however, that afforded matter of
amusement to these savages, that which pleased Romata's
visitor most was the ship's pump. He never tired of examining it and pumping up the water. Indeed, so much
was he taken up with this pump, that he could not be
prevailed on to return on shore, but sent a canoe to fetch
his favourite stool, on which he seated himself, and spent
the remainder of the day in pumping the bilge-water out
of the ship!

Next day the crew went ashore to cut sandal-wood,
while the captain, with one or two men, remained on
board, in order to be ready, if need be, with the brass gun,
which was unhoused and conspicuously elevated, with its
capacious muzzle directed point-blank at the chief's house.
The men were fully armed, as usual; and the captain
ordered me to go with them, to assist in the work. I was

much pleased with this order, for it freed me from the
captain's company, which I could not now endure, and it
gave me an opportunity of seeing the natives.

As we wound along in single file through the rich,
fragrant groves of banana, cocoa-nut, bread-fruit, and
other trees, I observed that there were many of the plum
and banian trees, with which I had become familiar on
the Coral Island. I noticed also large quantities of taro-
roots, yams, and sweet potatoes growing in enclosures.
On turning into an open glade of the woods, we came
abruptly upon a cluster of native houses. They were
built chiefly of bamboos, and were thatched with the
large, thick leaves of the pandanus;* but many of them
had little more than a sloping roof and three sides with
an open front, being the most simple shelter from the
weather that could well be imagined. Within these and
around them were groups of natives—men, women, and
children—who all stood up to gaze at us as we marched
along, followed by the party of men whom the chief had
sent to escort us. About half a mile inland we arrived at
the spot where the sandal-wood grew, and while the men
set to work I clambered up an adjoining hill to observe
the country.

About mid-day the chief arrived with several followers,
one of whom carried a baked pig on a wooden platter, with
yams and potatoes on several plantain leaves, which he
presented to the men, who sat down under the shade of a
tree to dine. The chief sat down to dine also; but, to
my surprise, instead of feeding himself, one of his wives
performed that office for him! I was seated beside Bill,
and asked him the reason of this.

" It is beneath his dignity, I believe, to feed himself,"

answered Bill; "but I daresay he's not particular, except on great occasions. They've a strange custom among them, Ralph, which is called *tabu*, and they carry it to great lengths. If a man chooses a particular tree for his god, the fruit o' that tree is tabued to him; and if he eats it, he is sure to be killed by his people, and eaten, of course, for killing means eating hereaway. Then, you see that great mop o' hair on the chief's head? Well, he has a lot o' barbers to keep it in order; and it's a law that whoever touches the head of a living chief or the body of a dead one, his hands are tabued; so in that way the barbers' hands are always tabued, and they daren't use them for their lives, but have to be fed like big babies, as they are, sure enough!"

"That's odd, Bill. But look there," said I, pointing to a man whose skin was of a much lighter colour than the generality of the natives. "I've seen a few of these light-skinned fellows among the Feejeeans. They seem to me to be of quite a different race."

"So they are," answered Bill. "These fellows come from the Tongan Islands, which lie a long way to the eastward. They come here to build their big war-canoes; and, as these take two and sometimes four years to build, there's always some o' the brown-skins among the black sarpents o' these islands."

"By the way, Bill," said I, "your mentioning serpents reminds me that I have not seen a reptile of any kind since I came to this part of the world."

"No more there are any," said Bill, "if ye except the niggers themselves; there's none on the islands but a lizard or two, and some sich harmless things. But I never seed any myself. If there's none on the land, however, there's

more than enough in the water, and that reminds me of a
wonderful brute they have here. But come, I'll show it to
you." So saying, Bill arose, and, leaving the men still
busy with the baked pig, led me into the forest. After
proceeding a short distance, we came upon a small pond
of stagnant water. A native lad had followed us, to whom
we called and beckoned him to come to us. On Bill saying
a few words to him which I did not understand, the boy
advanced to the edge of the pond and gave a low, peculiar
whistle. Immediately the water became agitated, and an
enormous eel thrust its head above the surface and allowed
the youth to touch it. It was about twelve feet long, and
as thick round the body as a man's thigh.

"There!" said Bill, his lip curling with contempt;
"what do you think of that for a god, Ralph? This is
one o' their gods, and it has been fed with dozens o' livin'
babies already. How many more it'll get afore it dies is
hard to say."

"Babies!" said I, with an incredulous look.

"Ay, babies," returned Bill. "Your soft-hearted folk
at home would say, 'Oh, horrible! impossible!' to that,
and then go away as comfortable and unconcerned as if
their sayin' 'Horrible! impossible!' had made it a lie.
But I tell you, Ralph, it's a *fact*. I've seed it with my
own eyes the last time I was here, an' mayhap if you stop
a while at this accursed place, and keep a sharp look-out,
you'll see it too. They don't feed it regularly with livin'
babies, but they give it one now and then as a treat.
Bah, you brute!" cried Bill in disgust, giving the reptile
a kick on the snout with his heavy boot that sent it
sweltering back in agony into its loathsome pool. I
thought it lucky for Bill, indeed for all of us, that the

native youth's back happened to be turned at the time; for I am certain that if the poor savages had come to know that we had so rudely handled their god, we should have had to fight our way back to the ship. As we retraced our steps I questioned my companion further on this subject.

"How comes it, Bill, that the mothers allow such a dreadful thing to be done?"

"Allow it? the mothers *do* it! It seems to me that there's nothing too fiendish or diabolical for these people to do. Why, in some of the islands they have an institution called the *Aréoi*,* and the persons connected with that body are ready for any wickedness that mortal man can devise. In fact they stick at nothing; and one o' their customs is to murder their infants the moment they are born. The mothers agree to it, and the fathers do it. And the mildest ways they have of murdering them is by sticking them through the body with sharp splinters of bamboo, strangling them with their thumbs, or burying them alive and stamping them to death while under the sod."

I felt sick at heart while my companion recited these horrors.

"But it's a curious fact," he continued after a pause, during which we walked in silence towards the spot where we had left our comrades—"it's a curious fact, that wherever the missionaries get a footin' all these things come to an end at once, an' the savages take to doin' each other good and singin' psalms, just like Methodists."

"God bless the missionaries!" said I, while a feeling of enthusiasm filled my heart, so that I could speak with difficulty. "God bless and prosper the missionaries till they get a footing in every island of the sea!"

"I would say Amen to that prayer, Ralph, if I could," said Bill, in a deep, sad voice ; "but it would be a mere mockery for a man to ask a blessing for others who dare not ask one for himself.   But, Ralph," he continued, "I've not told you half o' the abominations I have seen durin' my life in these seas. If we pull long together, lad, I'll tell you more; and if times have not changed very much since I was here last, it's like that you'll have a chance o' seeing a little for yourself before long."

CHAPTER XXV

The sandal-wood party—Native children's games somewhat sur-
   prising—Desperate amusements suddenly and fatally brought
   to a close—An old friend recognised—News—Romata's mad
   conduct.

NEXT day the wood-cutting party went ashore again,
   and I accompanied them as before. During the
dinner-hour I wandered into the woods alone, being dis-
inclined for food that day. I had not rambled far when
I found myself unexpectedly on the sea-shore, having
crossed a narrow neck of land which separated the native
village from a large bay. Here I found a party of the
islanders busy with one of their war-canoes, which was
almost ready for launching. I stood for a long time
watching this party with great interest, and observed that
they fastened the timbers and planks to each other very
much in the same way in which I had seen Jack fasten
those of our little boat. But what surprised me most
was its immense length, which I measured carefully, and
found to be a hundred feet long; and it was so capacious
that it could have held three hundred men. It had the
unwieldy outrigger and enormously high stern-posts which
I had remarked on the canoe that came to us while I was
on the Coral Island. Observing some boys playing at
games a short way along the beach, I resolved to go and
watch them; but as I turned from the natives who were
engaged so busily and cheerfully at their work, I little

thought of the terrible event that hung on the completion of that war-canoe.

Advancing towards the children, who were so numerous that I began to think this must be the general playground of the village, I sat down on a grassy bank under the shade of a plantain tree to watch them. And a happier or more noisy crew I have never seen. There were at least two hundred of them, both boys and girls, all of whom were clad in no other garments than their own glossy little black skins, except the maro, or strip of cloth round the loins of the boys, and a very short petticoat or kilt on the girls. They did not all play at the same game, but amused themselves in different groups.

One band was busily engaged in a game exactly similar to our blind man's buff. Another set were walking on stilts, which raised the children three feet from the ground. They were very expert at this amusement, and seldom tumbled. In another place I observed a group of girls standing together, and apparently enjoying themselves very much; so I went up to see what they were doing, and found that they were opening their eyelids with their fingers till their eyes appeared of an enormous size, and then thrusting pieces of straw between the upper and lower lids, across the eyeball, to keep them in that position! This seemed to me, I must confess, a very foolish as well as dangerous amusement. Nevertheless the children seemed to be greatly delighted with the hideous faces they made. I pondered this subject a good deal, and thought that if little children knew how silly they seemed to grown-up people when they make faces, they would not be so fond of doing it. In another place were a number of boys engaged in flying kites, and I could not help wondering that some of the games of those little savages should be so like to our own, although they had never seen us at play. But the kites were different from ours in many respects, being of every variety of shape. They were made of very thin cloth, and the boys raised them to a wonderful height in the air by means of twine made from the cocoa-nut husk. Other games there were, some of which showed the natural depravity of the hearts of these poor savages, and made me wish fervently that missionaries might be sent out to them. But the amusement which the greatest number of the children of both sexes seemed to take chief delight in was swimming and diving in the sea, and the expertness which they exhibited was truly amazing. They seemed to have two principal games in the water, one of which was to dive off a sort of stage which had been erected near a deep part of the sea, and chase each other in the water. Some of them went down to an extraordinary depth; others skimmed along the surface, or rolled over and over like porpoises, or diving under each other, came up unexpectedly and pulled each other down by a leg or an arm. They never seemed to tire of this sport, and from the great heat of the water in the South Seas, they could remain in it nearly all day without feeling chilled. Many of these children were almost infants, scarce able to walk; yet they staggered down the beach, flung their round, fat little black bodies fearlessly into deep water, and struck out to sea with as much confidence as ducklings.

The other game to which I have referred was swimming in the surf. But as this is an amusement in which all engage, from children of ten to grey-headed men of sixty, and as I had an opportunity of witnessing it in perfection the day following, I shall describe it more minutely.

I suppose it was in honour of their guest that this grand swimming-match was got up, for Romata came and told the captain that they were going to engage in it, and begged him to " come and see."

" What sort of amusement is this surf-swimming?" I inquired of Bill, as we walked together to a part of the shore on which several thousands of the natives were assembled.

" It's a very favourite lark with these 'xtr'or'nary critters," replied Bill, giving a turn to the quid of tobacco that invariably bulged out of his left cheek. " Ye see, Ralph, them fellows take to the water as soon a'most as they can walk, an' long before they can do that anything respectably, so that they are as much at home in the sea as on the land. Well, ye see, I s'pose they found swimmin' for miles out to sea, and divin' fathoms deep, wasn't excit-ing enough, so they invented this game o' swimmin' on the surf. Each man and boy, as you see, has got a short board or plank, with which he swims out for a mile or more to sea, and then, gettin' on the top o' yon thunderin' breaker, they come to shore on the top of it, yellin' and screechin' like fiends. It's a marvel to me that they're not dashed to shivers on the coral reef, for sure an' sartin' am I that if any o' us tried it, we wouldn't be worth the fluke of a broken anchor after the wave fell. But there they go ! "

As he spoke, several hundreds of the natives, amongst whom we were now standing, uttered a loud yell, rushed down the beach, plunged into the surf, and were carried off by the seething foam of the retreating wave.

At the point where we stood, the encircling coral reef joined the shore, so that the magnificent breakers, which a recent stiff breeze had rendered larger than usual, fell in thunder at the feet of the multitudes who lined the beach. For some time the swimmers continued to strike out to sea, breasting over the swell like hundreds of black seals. Then they all turned, and watching an approaching billow, mounted its white crest, and each laying his breast on the short, flat board, came rolling towards the shore, careering on the summit of the mighty wave, while they and the on-lookers shouted and yelled with excitement. Just as the monster wave curled in solemn majesty to fling its bulky length upon the beach, most of the swimmers slid back into the trough behind; others, slipping off their boards, seized them in their hands, and plunging through the watery waste, swam out to repeat the amusement; but a few, who seemed to me the most reckless, continued their career until they were launched upon the beach, and en-veloped in the churning foam and spray. One of these last came in on the crest of the wave most manfully, and landed with a violent bound almost on the spot where Bill and I stood. I saw by his peculiar head-dress that he was the chief whom the tribe entertained as their guest. The sea-water had removed nearly all the paint with which his face had been covered, and as he rose panting to his feet, I recognised, to my surprise, the features of Tararo, my old friend of the Coral Island!

Tararo at the same moment recognised me, and advanc-ing quickly, took me round the neck and rubbed noses; which had the effect of transferring a good deal of the moist paint from his nose to mine. Then, recollecting that this was not the white man's mode of salutation, he grasped me by the hand and shook it violently.

"Hallo, Ralph!" cried Bill in surprise, "that chap

seems to have taken a sudden fancy to you, or he must be an old acquaintance."

"Right, Bill," I replied; "he is indeed an old acquaintance;" and I explained in a few words that he was the chief whose party Jack and Peterkin and I had helped to save.

Tararo having thrown away his surf-board, entered into an animated conversation with Bill, pointing frequently during the course of it to me; whereby I concluded he must be telling him about the memorable battle and the part we had taken in it. When he paused, I begged of Bill to ask him about the woman Avatea, for I had some hope that she might have come with Tararo on this visit. "And ask him," said I, "who she is, for I am persuaded she is of a different race from the Feejeeans." On the mention of her name the chief frowned darkly, and seemed to speak with much anger.

"You're right, Ralph," said Bill, when the chief had ceased to talk; "she's not a Feejee girl, but a Samoan. How she ever came to this place the chief does not very clearly explain, but he says she was taken in war, and that he got her three years ago, an' kept her as his daughter ever since. Lucky for her, poor girl, else she'd have been roasted and eaten like the rest."

"But why does Tararo frown and look so angry?" said I.

"Because the girl's somewhat obstinate, like most o' the sex, an' won't marry the man he wants her to. It seems that a chief of some other island came on a visit to Tararo and took a fancy to her, but she wouldn't have him on no account, bein' already in love, and engaged to a young chief whom Tararo hates, and she kicked up a desperate shindy; so, as he was going on a war-expedition in his

canoe, he left her to think about it, sayin' he'd be back
in six months or so, when he hoped she wouldn't be so
obstropolous. This happened just a week ago; an' Tararo
says that if she's not ready to go when the chief returns,
as his bride, she'll be sent to him as a *long pig*."

"As a long pig!" I exclaimed in surprise; "why, what
does he mean by that?"

"He means somethin' very unpleasant," answered Bill
with a frown. "You see these blackguards eat men an'
women just as readily as they eat pigs; and as baked pigs
and baked men are very like each other in appearance,
they call men *long* pigs. If Avatea goes to this fellow
as a long pig, it's all up with her, poor thing."

"Is she on the island now?" I asked eagerly.

"No; she's at Tararo's island."

"And where does it lie?"

"About fifty or sixty miles to the south'ard o' this,'
returned Bill; "but I——"

At this moment we were startled by the cry of "Mao!
mao!—a shark! a shark!" which was immediately followed by a shriek that rang clear and fearfully loud above
the tumult of cries that arose from the savages in the
water and on the land. We turned hastily towards the
direction whence the cry came, and had just time to observe
the glaring eyeballs of one of the swimmers as he tossed
his arms in the air. Next instant he was pulled under
the waves. A canoe was instantly launched, and the hand
of the drowning man was caught, but only half of his
body was dragged from the maw of the monster, which
followed the canoe until the water became so shallow that
it could scarcely swim. The crest of the next billow was
tinged with red as it rolled towards the shore.

In most countries of the world this would have made a deep impression on the spectators, but the only effect it had upon these islanders was to make them hurry with all speed out of the sea, lest a similar fate should befall some of the others; but so utterly reckless were they of human life, that it did not for a moment suspend the progress of their amusements. It is true the surf-swimming ended for that time somewhat abruptly, but they immediately proceeded with other games. Bill told me that sharks do not often attack the surf-swimmers, being frightened away by the immense numbers of men and boys in the water, and by the shouting and splashing that they make. "But," said he, "such a thing as you have seen just now don't frighten them much. They'll be at it again to-morrow or next day, just as if there wasn't a single shark between Feejee and Nova Zembla."

After this the natives had a series of wrestling and box-ing matches; and being men of immense size and muscle, they did a good deal of injury to each other, especially in boxing, in which not only the lower orders but several of the chiefs and priests engaged. Each bout was very quickly terminated, for they did not pretend to a scientific knowledge of the art, and wasted no time in sparring, but hit straight out at each other's heads, and their blows were delivered with great force. Frequently one of the com-batants was knocked down with a single blow; and one gigantic fellow hit his adversary so severely that he drove the skin entirely off his forehead. This feat was hailed with immense applause by the spectators.

During these exhibitions, which were very painful to me, though I confess I could not refrain from beholding them, I was struck with the beauty of many of the figures and designs that were tattooed on the persons of the chiefs and principal men. One figure, that seemed to me very elegant, was that of a palm tree tattooed on the back of a man's leg, the roots rising, as it were, from under his heel, the stem ascending the tendon of the ankle, and the graceful head branching out upon the calf. I afterwards learned that this process of tattooing is very painful, and takes long to do, commencing at the age of ten, and being continued at intervals up to the age of thirty. It is done by means of an instrument made of bone, with a number of sharp teeth with which the skin is punctured. Into these punctures a preparation made from the kernel of the candle-nut, mixed with cocoa-nut oil, is rubbed, and the mark thus made is indelible. The operation is performed by a class of men whose profession it is, and they tattoo as much at a time as the person on whom they are operating can bear; which is not much, the pain and inflammation caused by tattooing being very great, sometimes causing death. Some of the chiefs were tattooed with an ornamental stripe down the legs, which gave them the appearance of being clad in tights; others had marks round the ankles and insteps which looked like tight-fitting and elegant boots. Their faces were also tattooed, and their breasts were very profusely marked with every imaginable species of device—muskets, dogs, birds, pigs clubs, and canoes, intermingled with lozenges, squares circles, and other arbitrary figures.

The women were not tattooed so much as the men, having only a few marks on their feet and arms. But I must say, however objectionable this strange practice may be, it nevertheless had this good effect, that it took away very much from their appearance of nakedness.

Next day, while we were returning from the woods to our schooner, we observed Romata rushing about in the neighbourhood of his house, apparently mad with passion.

"Ah!" said Bill to me, "there he's at his old tricks again. That's his way when he gets drink. The natives make a sort of drink o' their own, and it makes him bad enough; but when he gets brandy he's like a wild tiger. The captain, I suppose, has given him a bottle, as usual, to keep him in good humour. After drinkin' he usually goes to sleep, and the people know it well, and keep out of his way, for fear they should waken him. Even the babies are taken out of ear-shot; for when he's waked up he rushes out just as you see him now, and spears or clubs the first person he meets."

It seemed at the present time, however, that no deadly weapon had been in his way, for the infuriated chief was raging about without one. Suddenly he caught sight of an unfortunate man who was trying to conceal himself behind a tree. Rushing towards him, Romata struck him a terrible blow on the head, which knocked out the poor man's eye and also dislocated the chief's finger. The wretched creature offered no resistance; he did not even attempt to parry the blow. Indeed, from what Bill said, I found that he might consider himself lucky in having escaped with his life, which would certainly have been forfeited had the chief been possessed of a club at the time.

"Have these wretched creatures no law among themselves," said I, "which can restrain such wickedness?"

"None," replied Bill. "The chief's word is law. He might kill and eat a dozen of his own subjects any day for nothing more than his own pleasure, and nobody would take the least notice of it."

This ferocious deed took place within sight of our party as we wended our way to the beach, but I could not observe any other expression on the faces of the men than that of total indifference or contempt. It seemed to me a very awful thing that it should be possible for men to come to such hardness of heart and callousness to the sight of bloodshed and violence; but, indeed, I began to find that such constant exposure to scenes of blood was having a slight effect upon myself, and I shuddered when I came to think that I too was becoming callous.

I thought upon this subject much that night while I walked up and down the deck during my hours of watch, and I came to the conclusion that if I, who hated, abhorred, and detested such bloody deeds as I had witnessed within the last few weeks, could so soon come to be less sensitive about them, how little wonder that these poor ignorant savages, who were born and bred in familiarity therewith, should think nothing of them at all, and should hold human life in so very slight esteem!

CHAPTER XXVI

Mischief brewing—My blood is made to run cold—Evil consultations and wicked resolves—Bloody Bill attempts to do good, and fails—The attack—Wholesale murder—The flight—The escape.

NEXT morning I awoke with a feverish brow and a feeling of deep depression at my heart, and the more I thought on my unhappy fate, the more wretched and miserable did I feel.

I was surrounded on all sides by human beings of the most dreadful character, to whom the shedding of blood was mere pastime. On shore were the natives, whose practices were so horrible that I could not think of them without shuddering. On board were none but pirates of the blackest dye, who, although not cannibals, were foul murderers, and more blameworthy even than the savages, inasmuch as they knew better. Even Bill, with whom I had, under the strange circumstances of my lot, formed a kind of intimacy, was so fierce in his nature as to have acquired the title of "Bloody" from his vile companions. I felt very much cast down the more I considered the subject and the impossibility of delivery, as it seemed to me—at least, for a long time to come. At last, in my feeling of utter helplessness, I prayed fervently to the Almighty that He would deliver me out of my miserable condition; and when I had done so I felt some degree of comfort.

When the captain came on deck, before the hour at which the men usually started for the woods, I begged of him to permit me to remain aboard that day, as I did not feel well; but he looked at me angrily, and ordered me, in a surly tone, to get ready to go on shore as usual. The fact was that the captain had been out of humour for some time past. Romata and he had had some differences, and high words had passed between them, during which the chief had threatened to send a fleet of his war-canoes, with a thousand men, to break up and burn the schooner; whereupon the captain smiled sarcastically, and, going up to the chief, gazed sternly in his face, while he said, "I have only to raise my little finger just now, and my big gun will blow your whole village to atoms in five minutes!" Although the chief was a bold man, he quailed before the pirate's glance and threat, and made no reply; but a bad feeling had been raised, and old sores had been opened.

I had, therefore, to go with the wood-cutters that day. Before starting, however, the captain called me into the cabin, and said—

"Here, Ralph; I've got a mission for you, lad. That blackguard Romata is in the dumps, and nothing will mollify him but a gift; so do you go up to his house and give him these whale's teeth, with my compliments. Take with you one of the men who can speak the language."

I looked at the gift in some surprise, for it consisted of six white whale's teeth, and two of the same dyed bright red, which seemed to me very paltry things. However, I did not dare to hesitate or ask any questions; so, gathering them up, I left the cabin, and was soon on my way to the chief's house, accompanied by Bill. On expressing my surprise at the gift, he said—

"They're paltry enough to you or me, Ralph, but they're considered of great value by them chaps. They're a sort o' cash among them. The red ones are the most prized, one of them bein' equal to twenty o' the white ones. I suppose the only reason for their bein' valuable is that there ain't many of them, and they're hard to be got."

On arriving at the house, we found Romata sitting on a mat, in the midst of a number of large bales of native cloth and other articles, which had been brought to him as presents from time to time by inferior chiefs. He received us rather haughtily; but on Bill explaining the nature of our errand, he became very condescending, and his eyes glistened with satisfaction when he received the whale's teeth, although he laid them aside with an assumption of kingly indifference.

"Go," said he, with a wave of the hand—"go tell your captain that he may cut wood to-day, but not to-morrow. He must come ashore; I want to have a palaver with him."

As we left the house to return to the woods, Bill shook his head.

"There's mischief brewin' in that black rascal's head. I know him of old. But what comes here?"

As he spoke, we heard the sound of laughter and shouting in the wood, and presently there issued from it a band of savages, in the midst of whom were a number of men bearing burdens on their shoulders. At first I thought that these burdens were poles with something rolled round them, the end of each pole resting on a man's shoulder; but on a nearer approach I saw that they were human beings, tied hand and foot, and so lashed to the poles that they could not move. I counted twenty of them as they passed.

"More murder!" said Bill, in a voice that sounded between a hoarse laugh and a groan.

"Surely they are not going to murder them?" said I, looking anxiously into Bill's face.

"I don't know, Ralph," replied Bill, "what they're goin' to do with them; but I fear they mean no good when they tie fellows up in that way."

As we continued our way towards the wood-cutters, I observed that Bill looked anxiously over his shoulder in the direction where the procession had disappeared. At last he stopped, and turning abruptly on his heel, said—

"I tell ye what it is, Ralph: I must be at the bottom o' that affair. Let us follow these black scoundrels and see what they're goin' to do."

I must say I had no wish to pry further into their bloody practices; but Bill seemed bent on it, so I turned and went. We passed rapidly through the bush, being guided in the right direction by the shouts of the savages. Suddenly there was a dead silence, which continued for some time, while Bill and I involuntarily quickened our pace until we were running at the top of our speed across the narrow neck of land previously mentioned. As we reached the verge of the wood, we discovered the savages surrounding the large war-canoe, which they were apparently on the point of launching. Suddenly the multitude put their united strength to the canoe; but scarcely had the huge machine begun to move, when a yell, the most appalling that ever fell upon my ear, rose high above the shouting of the savages. It had not died away when another and another smote upon my throbbing ear; and then I saw that these inhuman monsters were actually launching their canoe over the living bodies of their victims. But there was no pity in the breasts of these men. Forward they went in ruthless indifference, shouting as they went, while high above their voices rang the dying shrieks of those wretched creatures, as, one after another, the ponderous canoe passed over them, burst the eyeballs from their sockets, and sent the life-blood gushing from their mouths. O reader, this is no fiction. I would not, for the sake of thrilling you with horror, invent so terrible a scene. It was witnessed. It is true—true as that accursed sin which has rendered the human heart capable of such diabolical enormities!

When it was over, I turned round and fell upon the grass with a deep groan; but Bill seized me by the arm, and lifting me up as if I had been a child, cried—

"Come along, lad; let's away!"—and so, staggering and stumbling over the tangled underwood, we fled from the fatal spot.

During the remainder of that day, I felt as if I were in a horrible dream. I scarce knew what was said to me, and was more than once blamed by the men for idling my time. At last the hour to return aboard came. We marched down to the beach, and I felt relief for the first time when my feet rested on the schooner's deck.

In the course of the evening I overheard part of a conversation between the captain and the first mate, which startled me not a little. They were down in the cabin, and conversed in an undertone; but the skylight being off, I overheard every word that was said.

"I don't half like it," said the mate. "It seems to me that we'll only have hard fightin' and no pay."

"No pay!" repeated the captain, in a voice of sup-

pressed anger. "Do you call a good cargo all for nothing
no pay?"

"Very true," returned the mate; "but we've got the
cargo aboard. Why not cut your cable and take French
leave o' them? What's the use o' tryin' to kill the blackguards when it'll do us no manner o' good?"

"Mate," said the captain in a low voice, "you talk like
a fresh-water sailor. I can only attribute this shyness
to some strange delusion; for surely" (his voice assumed
a slightly sneering tone as he said this), "surely I am not
to suppose that *you* have become soft-hearted! Besides,
you are wrong in regard to the cargo being aboard; there's
a good quarter of it lying in the woods, and that blackguard chief knows it and won't let me take it off. He
defied us to do our worst yesterday."

"Defied us! did he?" cried the mate with a bitter
laugh. "Poor, contemptible thing!"

"And yet he seems not so contemptible but that you
are afraid to attack him."

"Who said I was afraid?" growled the mate sulkily.
"I'm as ready as any man in the ship. But, captain,
what is it that you intend to do?"

"I intend to muffle the sweeps and row the schooner up
to the head of the creek there, from which point we can
command the pile of sandal-wood with our gun. Then I
shall land with all the men except two, who shall take care
of the schooner and be ready with the boat to take us
off. We can creep through the woods to the head of the
village, where these cannibals are always dancing round
their suppers of human flesh, and if the carbines of the
men are loaded with a heavy charge of buck-shot we can
drop forty or fifty at the first volley. After that the

thing will be easy enough. The savages will take to the
mountains in a body, and we shall take what we require,
up anchor, and away."

To this plan the mate at length agreed. As he left
the cabin I heard the captain say—

"Give the men an extra glass of grog, and don't forget
the buck-shot."

The reader may conceive the horror with which I heard
this murderous conversation. I immediately repeated it
to Bill, who seemed much perplexed about it. At length
he said—

"I'll tell you what I'll do, Ralph. I'll swim ashore
after dark and fix a musket to a tree not far from the
place where we'll have to land, and I'll tie a long string to
the trigger, so that when our fellows cross it they'll let it
off, and so alarm the village in time to prevent an attack,
but not in time to prevent us gettin' back to the boat.
So, Master Captain," added Bill, with a smile that for the
first time seemed to me to be mingled with good-natured
cheerfulness, "you'll be balked at least for once in your
life by Bloody Bill."

After it grew dark, Bill put this resolve in practice.
He slipped over the side with a musket in his left hand,
while with his right he swam ashore and entered the
woods. He soon returned, having accomplished his purpose, and got on board without being seen, I being the
only one on deck.

When the hour of midnight approached the men were
mustered on deck, the cable was cut, and the muffled
sweeps got out. These sweeps were immensely large oars,
each requiring a couple of men to work it. In a few
minutes we entered the mouth of the creek, which was

indeed the mouth of a small river, and took about half-an-hour to ascend it, although the spot where we intended to land was not more than six hundred yards from the mouth, because there was a slight current against us, and the mangroves which narrowed the creek impeded the rowers in some places. Having reached the spot, which was so darkened by overhanging trees that we could see with difficulty, a small kedge anchor attached to a thin line was let softly down over the stern.

"Now, lads," whispered the captain, as he walked along the line of men, who were all armed to the teeth, "don't be in a hurry, aim low, and don't waste your first shots."

He then pointed to the boat, into which the men crowded in silence. There was no room to row; but oars were not needed, as a slight push against the side of the schooner sent the boat gliding to the shore.

"There's no need of leaving two in the boat," whispered the mate, as the men stepped out; "we shall want all our hands. Let Ralph stay."

The captain assented, and ordered me to stand in readiness with the boat-hook, to shove ashore at a moment's notice if they should return, or to shove off if any of the savages should happen to approach. He then threw his carbine into the hollow of his arm and glided through the bushes, followed by his men. With a throbbing heart I awaited the result of our plan. I knew the exact locality where the musket was placed, for Bill had described it to me, and I kept my straining eyes fixed upon the spot. But no sound came, and I began to fear that either they had gone in another direction or that Bill had not fixed the string properly. Suddenly I heard a faint click, and observed one or two bright sparks among the bushes. My

heart immediately sank within me, for I knew at once that
the trigger had indeed been pulled, but that the priming
had not caught. The plan, therefore, had utterly failed.
A feeling of dread now began to creep over me as I stood
in the boat, in that dark, silent spot, awaiting the issue of
this murderous expedition. I shuddered as I glanced at
the water that glided past like a dark reptile. I looked
back at the schooner, but her hull was just barely visible,
while her tapering masts were lost among the trees which
overshadowed her. Her lower sails were set, but so thick
was the gloom that they were quite invisible.

Suddenly I heard a shot. In a moment a thousand
voices raised a yell in the village; again the cry rose on
the night air, and was followed by broken shouts as of
scattered parties of men bounding into the woods. Then
I heard another shout loud and close at hand. It was the
voice of the captain cursing the man who had fired the
premature shot. Then came the order, "Forward!" followed by a wild hurrah of our men as they charged the
savages. Shots now rang in quick succession, and at last
a loud volley startled the echoes of the woods. It was
followed by a multitude of wild shrieks, which were immediately drowned in another hurrah from the men; the
distance of the sound proving that they were driving their
enemies before them towards the sea.

While I was listening intently to these sounds, which
were now mingled in confusion, I was startled by the rustling of the leaves not far from me. At first I thought it
was a party of savages who had observed the schooner,
but I was speedily undeceived by observing a body of
natives—apparently several hundreds, as far as I could
guess in the uncertain light—bounding through the woods
towards the scene of battle. I saw at once that this was

a party who had outflanked our men, and would speedily attack them in the rear. And so it turned out; for in a short time the shouts increased tenfold, and among them I thought I heard a death-cry uttered by voices familiar to my ear.

At length the tumult of battle ceased, and from the cries of exultation that now arose from the savages, I felt assured that our men had been conquered. I was immediately thrown into dreadful consternation. What was I now to do? To be taken by the savages was too horrible to be thought of; to flee to the mountains was hopeless, as I should soon be discovered; and to take the schooner out of the creek without assistance was impossible. I resolved, however, to make the attempt, as being my only hope, and was on the point of pushing off, when my hand was stayed, and my blood chilled by an appalling shriek, in which I recognised the voice of one of the crew. It was succeeded by a shout from the savages. Then came another and another shriek of agony, making my ears to tingle, as I felt convinced they were murdering the pirate crew in cold blood. With a bursting heart and my brain whirling as if on fire, I seized the boat-hook to push from shore, when a man sprang from the bushes.

"Stop! Ralph, stop!—there now, push off," he cried, and bounded into the boat so violently as nearly to upset her. It was Bill's voice! In another moment we were on board—the boat made fast, the line of the anchor cut, and the sweeps run out. At the first stroke of Bill's giant arm the schooner was nearly pulled ashore, for in his haste he forgot that I could scarcely move the unwieldy oar. Springing to the stern, he lashed the rudder in such a position as that, while it aided me, it acted against him, and so rendered the force of our strokes nearly equal. The schooner now began to glide quickly down the creek; but before we reached its mouth, a yell from a thousand voices on the bank told that we were discovered. Instantly a number of the savages plunged into the water and swam towards us; but we were making so much way that they could not overtake us. One, however, an immensely powerful man, succeeded in laying hold of the cut rope that hung from the stern, and clambered quickly upon deck. Bill caught sight of him the instant his head appeared above the taffrail; but he did not cease to row, and did not appear even to notice the savage until he was within a yard of him. Then, dropping the sweep, he struck him a blow on the forehead with his clenched fist that felled him to the deck. Lifting him up, he hurled him overboard, and resumed the oar. But now a greater danger awaited us, for the savages had outrun us on the bank, and were about to plunge into the water ahead of the schooner. If they succeeded in doing so, our fate was sealed. For one moment Bill stood irresolute. Then, drawing a pistol from his belt, he sprang to the brass gun, held the pan of his pistol over the touch-hole, and fired. The shot was succeeded by the hiss of the cannon's priming; then the blaze and the crushing thunder of the monstrous gun burst upon the savages with such deafening roar that it seemed as if their very mountains had been rent asunder.

This was enough. The moment of surprise and hesitation caused by the unwonted sound gave us time to pass the point; a gentle breeze, which the dense foliage had hitherto prevented us from feeling, bulged out our sails; the schooner bent before it, and the shouts of the disappointed savages grew fainter and fainter in the distance as we were slowly wafted out to sea.

CHAPTER XXVII

Reflections—The wounded man—The squall—True consolation—
Death.

THERE is a power of endurance in human beings, both
in their bodies and in their minds, which, I have
often thought, seems to be wonderfully adapted and
exactly proportioned to the circumstances in which individuals may happen to be placed—a power which, in
most cases, is sufficient to carry a man through and over
every obstacle that may happen to be thrown in his path
through life, no matter how high or how steep the mountain may be, but which often forsakes him the moment
the summit is gained, the point of difficulty passed, and
leaves him prostrated, with energies gone, nerves unstrung,
and a feeling of incapacity pervading the entire frame
that renders the most trifling effort almost impossible.

During the greater part of that day I had been subjected to severe mental and much physical excitement,
which had almost crushed me down by the time I was
relieved from duty in the course of the evening. But
when the expedition whose failure has just been narrated
was planned, my anxieties and energies had been so
powerfully aroused that I went through the protracted
scenes of that terrible night without a feeling of the
slightest fatigue. My mind and body were alike active
and full of energy. No sooner was the last thrilling fear
of danger past, however, than my faculties were utterly

relaxed; and when I felt the cool breezes of the Pacific
playing around my fevered brow, and heard the free
waves rippling at the schooner's prow, as we left the
hated island behind us, my senses forsook me, and I fell
in a swoon upon the deck.

From this state I was quickly aroused by Bill, who
shook me by the arm, saying—

"Hallo, Ralph boy! rouse up, lad; we're safe now.
Poor thing! I believe he's fainted." And, raising me in
his arms, he laid me on the folds of the gaff top-sail, which
lay upon the deck near the tiller. "Here, take a drop o'
this; it'll do you good, my boy," he added, in a voice of
tenderness which I had never heard him use before, while
he held a brandy-flask to my lips.

I raised my eyes gratefully as I swallowed a mouthful;
next moment my head sank heavily upon my arm, and I
fell fast asleep. I slept long, for when I awoke the sun
was a good way above the horizon. I did not move on
first opening my eyes, as I felt a delightful sensation of
rest pervading me, and my eyes were riveted on and
charmed with the gorgeous splendour of the mighty ocean
that burst upon my sight. It was a dead calm; the sea
seemed a sheet of undulating crystal, tipped and streaked
with the saffron hues of sunrise, which had not yet merged
into the glowing heat of noon; and there was a deep calm
in the blue dome above that was not broken even by the
usual flutter of the sea-fowl. How long I would have
lain in contemplation of this peaceful scene I know not,
but my mind was recalled suddenly and painfully to the
past and the present by the sight of Bill, who was seated
on the deck at my feet, with his head reclining, as if in
sleep, on his right arm, which rested on the tiller. As he

seemed to rest peacefully, I did not mean to disturb him, but the slight noise I made in raising myself on my elbow caused him to start and look round.

"Well, Ralph, awake at last, my boy? You have slept long and soundly," he said, turning towards me.

On beholding his countenance I sprang up in anxiety. He was deadly pale, and his hair, which hung in dishevelled locks over his face, was clotted with blood. Blood also stained his hollow cheeks and covered the front of his shirt, which, with the greater part of his dress, was torn and soiled with mud.

"O Bill!" said I with deep anxiety, "what is the matter with you? You are ill. You must have been wounded."

"Even so, lad," said Bill in a deep, soft voice, while he extended his huge frame on the couch from which I had just risen. "I've got an ugly wound, I fear, and I've been waiting for you to waken, to ask you to get me a drop o' brandy and a mouthful o' bread from the cabin lockers. You seemed to sleep so sweetly, Ralph, that I didn't like to disturb you. But I don't feel up to much just now."

I did not wait till he had done talking, but ran below immediately, and returned in a few seconds with a bottle of brandy and some broken biscuit. He seemed much refreshed after eating a few morsels and drinking a long draught of water mingled with a little of the spirits. Immediately afterwards he fell asleep, and I watched him anxiously until he awoke, being desirous of knowing the nature and extent of his wound.

"Ha!" he exclaimed, on awaking suddenly after a slumber of an hour, "I'm the better of that nap, Ralph;

I feel twice the man I was;" and he attempted to rise, but sank back again immediately with a deep groan.

"Nay, Bill, you must not move, but lie still while I look at your wound. I'll make a comfortable bed for you here on deck, and get you some breakfast. After that you shall tell me how you got it. Cheer up, Bill," seeing that he turned his head away; "you'll be all right in a little, and I'll be a capital nurse to you, though I'm no doctor."

I then left him, and lighted a fire in the caboose. While it was kindling, I went to the steward's pantry and procured the materials for a good breakfast, with which, in little more than half-an-hour, I returned to my companion. He seemed much better, and smiled kindly on me as I set before him a cup of coffee and a tray with several eggs and some bread on it.

"Now then, Bill," said I cheerfully, sitting down beside him on the deck, "let's fall to. I'm very hungry myself, I can tell you; but—I forgot—your wound," I added, rising; "let me look at it."

I found that the wound was caused by a pistol-shot in the chest. It did not bleed much, and as it was on the right side, I was in hopes that it might not be very serious. But Bill shook his head. "However," said he, "sit down, Ralph, and I'll tell you all about it.

"You see, after we left the boat an' began to push through the bushes, we went straight for the line of my musket, as I had expected; but by some unlucky chance it didn't explode, for I saw the line torn away by the men's legs, and heard the click o' the lock; so I fancy the priming had got damp and didn't catch. I was in a great quandary now what to do, for I couldn't concoct in my mind, in the hurry, any good reason for firin' off my piece.

But they say necessity's the mother of invention; so just as I was givin' it up and clinchin' my teeth to bide the worst o't and take what should come, a sudden thought came into my head. I stepped out before the rest, seemin' to be awful anxious to be at the savages, tripped my foot on a fallen tree, plunged head foremost into a bush, an ov coorse, my carbine exploded! Then came such a screechin' from the camp as I never heard in all my life. I rose at once, and was rushing on with the rest, when the captain called a halt.

"You did that a-purpose, you villain!" he said with a tremendous oath, and drawin' a pistol from his belt, let fly right into my breast. I fell at once, and remembered no more till I was startled and brought round by the most awful yell I ever heard in my life—except, maybe, the shrieks o' them poor critters that were crushed to death under yon big canoe. Jumpin' up, I looked round, and through the trees saw a fire gleamin' not far off, the light of which showed me the captain and men tied hand and foot, each to a post, and the savages dancin' round them like demons. I had scarce looked for a second, when I saw one o' them go up to the captain flourishing a knife, and before I could wink he plunged it into his breast, while another yell, like the one that roused me, rang upon my ear. I didn't wait for more, but bounding up, went crashing through the bushes into the woods. The black fellows caught sight of me, however, but not in time to prevent me jumpin' into the boat, as you know."

Bill seemed to be much exhausted after this recital, and shuddered frequently during the narrative, so I refrained from continuing the subject at that time, and endeavoured to draw his mind to other things.

"But now, Bill," said I, "it behoves us to think about the future, and what course of action we shall pursue. Here we are, on the wide Pacific, in a well-appointed schooner, which is our own—at least no one has a better claim to it than we have—and the world lies before us. Moreover, here comes a breeze, so we must make up our minds which way to steer."

"Ralph, boy," said my companion; "it matters not to me which way we go. I fear that my time is short now. Go where you will; I'm content."

"Well then, Bill, I think we had better steer to the Coral Island, and see what has become of my dear old comrades, Jack and Peterkin. I believe the island has no name, but the captain once pointed it out to me on the chart, and I marked it afterwards; so, as we know pretty well our position just now, I think I can steer to it. Then, as to working the vessel, it is true I cannot hoist the sails single-handed, but luckily we have enough of sail set already; and if it should come on to blow a squall, I could at least drop the peaks of the main and fore sails, and clew them up partially without help, and throw her head close into the wind, so as to keep her all shaking till the violence of the squall is past. And if we have continued light breezes, I'll rig up a complication of blocks and fix them to the top-sail halyards, so that I shall be able to hoist the sails without help. 'Tis true I'll require half a day to hoist them, but we don't need to mind that. Then I'll make a sort of erection on deck to screen you from the sun, Bill; and if you can only manage to sit beside the tiller and steer for two hours every day, so as to let me get a nap, I'll engage to let you off duty all the rest of the twenty-four hours. And if you don't feel able for steering, I'll lash the helm and heave-to, while I get you your breakfasts and dinners; and so we'll manage famously, and soon reach the Coral Island."

Bill smiled faintly as I ran on in this strain.

"And what will you do," said he, "if it comes on to blow a storm?"

This question silenced me, while I considered what I should do in such a case. At length I laid my hand on his arm, and said, "Bill, when a man has done all that he *can* do, he ought to leave the rest to God."

"O Ralph," said my companion in a faint voice, looking anxiously into my face, "I wish that I had the feelin's about God that you seem to have, at this hour. I'm dyin', Ralph; yet I, who have braved death a hundred times, am afraid to die. I'm afraid to enter the next world. Something within tells me there will be a reckoning when I go there. But it's all over with me, Ralph. I feel that there's no chance o' my bein' saved."

"Don't say that, Bill," said I in deep compassion; "don't say that. I'm quite sure there's hope even for you, but I can't remember the words of the Bible that make me think so. Is there not a Bible on board, Bill?"

"No; the last that was in the ship belonged to a poor boy that was taken aboard against his will. He died, poor lad—I think through ill-treatment and fear. After he was gone the captain found his Bible and flung it overboard."

I now reflected, with great sadness and self-reproach, on the way in which I had neglected my Bible; and it flashed across me that I was actually in the sight of God a greater sinner than this blood-stained pirate; for, thought I, he tells me that he never read the Bible, and was never brought up to care for it; whereas I was carefully taught to read it by my own mother, and had read it daily as long as I possessed one, yet to so little purpose that I could not now call to mind a single text that would meet this poor man's case, and afford him the consolation he so much required. I was much distressed, and taxed my memory for a long time. At last a text did flash into my mind, and I wondered much that I had not thought of it before.

"Bill," said I in a low voice, "'Believe on the Lord Jesus Christ, and thou shalt be saved.'"

"Ay, Ralph, I've heard the missionaries say that before now, but what good can it do me? It's not for me, that; it's not for the likes o' me."

I knew not now what to say, for although I felt sure that that word was for him as well as for me, I could not remember any other word whereby I could prove it.

After a short pause, Bill raised his eyes to mine and said, "Ralph, I've led a terrible life. I've been a sailor since I was a boy, and I've gone from bad to worse ever since I left my father's roof. I've been a pirate three years now. It is true I did not choose the trade, but I was inveigled aboard this schooner and kept here by force till I became reckless and at last joined them. Since that time my hand has been steeped in human blood again and again. Your young heart would grow cold if I— But why should I go on? 'Tis of no use, Ralph; my doom is fixed."

"Bill," said I, "'Though your sins be red like crimson, they shall be white as snow.' Only believe."

"Only believe!" cried Bill, starting up on his elbow. "I've heard men talk o' believing as if it was easy. Ha! 'tis easy enough for a man to point to a rope and say, 'I believe that would bear my weight;' but 'tis another thing for a man to catch hold o' that rope and swing himself by it over the edge of a precipice!"

The energy with which he said this, and the action with which it was accompanied, were too much for Bill. He sank back with a deep groan. As if the very elements sympathised with this man's sufferings, a low moan came sweeping over the sea.

"Hist, Ralph!" said Bill, opening his eyes; "there's a squall coming, lad. Look alive, boy! Clew up the fore-sail. Drop the main-sail peak. Them squalls come quick sometimes."

I had already started to my feet, and saw that a heavy squall was indeed bearing down on us. It had hitherto escaped my notice, owing to my being so much engrossed by our conversation. I instantly did as Bill desired, for the schooner was lying motionless on the glassy sea. I observed with some satisfaction that the squall was bearing down on the larboard bow, so that it would strike the vessel in the position in which she would be best able to stand the shock. Having done my best to shorten sail, I returned aft, and took my stand at the helm.

"Now, boy," said Bill in a faint voice, "keep her close to the wind."

A few seconds afterwards he said, "Ralph, let me hear those two texts again."

I repeated them.

"Are ye sure, lad, ye saw them in the Bible?"

"Quite sure," I replied.

Almost before the words had left my lips the wind burst upon us, and the spray dashed over our decks. For a time the schooner stood it bravely, and sprang forward against the rising sea like a war-horse. Meanwhile clouds darkened the sky, and the sea began to rise in huge billows. There was still too much sail on the schooner, and as the gale increased, I feared that the masts would be torn out of her or carried away, while the wind whistled and shrieked through the strained rigging. Suddenly the wind shifted a point, a heavy sea struck us on the bow, and the schooner was almost laid on her beam ends, so that I could scarcely keep my legs. At the same moment Bill lost his hold of the belaying-pin which had served to steady him, and he slid with stunning violence against the skylight. As he lay on the deck close beside me, I could see that the shock had rendered him insensible; but I did not dare to quit the tiller for an instant, as it required all my faculties, bodily and mental, to manage the schooner. For an hour the blast drove us along, while, owing to the sharpness of the vessel's bow and the press of canvas, she dashed through the waves instead of breasting over them, thereby drenching the decks with water fore and aft. At the end of that time the squall passed away, and left us rocking on the bosom of the agitated sea.

My first care, the instant I could quit the helm, was to raise Bill from the deck and place him on the couch. I then ran below for the brandy bottle, and rubbed his face and hands with it, and endeavoured to pour a little down his throat. But my efforts, although I continued them long and assiduously, were of no avail; as I let go the hand which I had been chafing, it fell heavily on the deck. I laid my hand over his heart, and sat for some time quite motionless; but there was no flutter there— the pirate was dead!

CHAPTER XXVIII

Alone on the deep—Necessity the mother of invention—A valuable book discovered—Natural phenomenon—A bright day in my history.

IT was with feelings of awe, not unmingled with fear, that I now seated myself on the cabin skylight and gazed upon the rigid features of my late comrade, while my mind wandered over his past history and contemplated with anxiety my present position. Alone, in the midst of the wide Pacific, having a most imperfect knowledge of navigation, and in a schooner requiring at least eight men as her proper crew! But I will not tax the reader's patience with a minute detail of my feelings and doings during the first few days that followed the death of my companion. I will merely mention that I tied a cannon-ball to his feet, and, with feelings of the deepest sorrow, consigned him to the deep.

For fully a week after that a steady breeze blew from the east, and as my course lay west and by north, I made rapid progress towards my destination. I could not take an observation, which I very much regretted, as the captain's quadrant was in the cabin; but from the day of setting sail from the island of the savages I had kept a dead reckoning, and as I knew pretty well now how much leeway the schooner made, I hoped to hit the Coral Island without much difficulty. In this I was the more confident that I knew its position on the chart (which I

understood was a very good one), and so had its correct
bearings by compass.

As the weather seemed now quite settled and fine, and
as I had got into the trade-winds, I set about preparations for hoisting the top-sails. This was a most arduous
task, and my first attempts were complete failures, owing,
in a great degree, to my reprehensible ignorance of mechanical forces. The first error I made was in applying
my apparatus of blocks and pulleys to a rope which was
too weak, so that the very first heave I made broke it in
two, and sent me staggering against the after-hatch, over
which I tripped, and, striking against the main-boom,
tumbled down the companion-ladder into the cabin. I
was much bruised and somewhat stunned by this unto-
ward accident. However, I considered it fortunate that
I was not killed. In my next attempt I made sure of
not coming by a similar accident, so I unreeved the
tackling and fitted up larger blocks and ropes. But
although the principle on which I acted was quite
correct, the machinery was now so massive and heavy
that the mere friction and stiffness of the thick cordage
prevented me from moving it at all. Afterwards, however, I came to proportion things more correctly; but I
could not avoid reflecting at the time how much better it
would have been had I learned all this from observation
and study, instead of waiting till I was forced to acquire
it through the painful and tedious lessons of experience.

After the tackling was prepared and in good working
order, it took me the greater part of a day to hoist the
main top-sail. As I could not steer and work at this at
the same time, I lashed the helm in such a position that,
with a little watching now and then, it kept the schooner

in her proper course. By this means I was enabled also to go about the deck and down below for things that I wanted, as occasion required; also to cook and eat my victuals. But I did not dare to trust to this plan during the three hours of rest that I allowed myself at night, as the wind might have shifted, in which case I should have been blown far out of my course ere I awoke. I was, therefore, in the habit of *heaving-to* during those three hours—that is, fixing the rudder and the sails in such a position as that, by acting against each other, they would keep the ship stationary. After my night's rest, therefore, I had only to make allowance for the leeway she had made, and so resume my course.

Of course I was to some extent anxious lest another squall should come, but I made the best provision I could in the circumstances, and concluded that by letting go the weather-braces of the top-sails and the top-sail hal-yards at the same time, I should thereby render these sails almost powerless. Besides this, I proposed to myself to keep a sharp look-out on the barometer in the cabin, and if I observed at any time a sudden fall in it, I re-solved that I would instantly set about my multiform appliances for reducing sail, so as to avoid being taken unawares. Thus I sailed prosperously for two weeks, with a fair wind, so that I calculated I must be drawing near to the Coral Island; at the thought of which my heart bounded with joyful expectation.

The only book I found on board, after a careful search, was a volume of Captain Cook's voyages. This, I suppose, the pirate captain had brought with him in order to guide him, and to furnish him with information regarding the islands of these seas. I found this a most delightful book indeed, and I not only obtained much interesting know-

ledge about the sea in which I was sailing, but I had
many of my own opinions, derived from experience, corroborated, and not a few of them corrected. Besides the
reading of this charming book, and the daily routine of
occupations, nothing of particular note happened to me
during this voyage, except once, when on rising one night,
after my three hours' nap, while it was yet dark, I was
amazed and a little alarmed to find myself floating in
what appeared to be a sea of blue fire. I had often
noticed the beautiful appearance of phosphorescent light,
but this far exceeded anything of the sort I ever saw
before. The whole sea appeared somewhat like milk, and
was remarkably luminous.

I rose in haste, and letting down a bucket into the sea,
brought some of the water on board and took it down to
the cabin to examine it; but no sooner did I approach
the light than the strange appearance disappeared, and
when I removed the cabin lamp the luminous light appeared again. I was much puzzled with this, and took up
a little of the water in the hollow of my hand and then
let it run off, when I found that the luminous substance
was left behind on my palm. I ran with it to the lamp,
but when I got there it was gone. I found, however, that
when I went into the dark my hand shone again; so I
took the large glass of the ship's telescope and examined
my hand minutely, when I found that there were on it
one or two small patches of a clear, transparent substance
like jelly, which were so thin as to be almost invisible to
the naked eye. Thus I came to know that the beautiful
phosphoric light, which I had so often admired before,
was caused by animals, for I had no doubt that these were
of the same kind as the medusæ or jelly-fish which are
seen in all parts of the world.

On the evening of my fourteenth day I was awakened out of a nap into which I had fallen by a loud cry, and starting up I gazed around me. I was surprised and delighted to see a large albatross soaring majestically over the ship. I immediately took it into my head that this was the albatross I had seen at Penguin Island. I had, of course, no good reason for supposing this, but the idea occurred to me, I know not why, and I cherished it, and regarded the bird with as much affection as if he had been an old friend. He kept me company all that day, and left me as night fell.

Next morning, as I stood motionless and with heavy eyes at the helm—for I had not slept well—I began to weary anxiously for daylight, and peered towards the horizon, where I thought I observed something like a black cloud against the dark sky. Being always on the alert for squalls, I ran to the bow. There could be no doubt it was a squall, and as I listened I thought I heard the murmur of the coming gale. Instantly I began to work might and main at my cumbrous tackle for shortening sail, and in the course of an hour and a half had the most of it reduced—the top-sail yards down on the caps, the top-sails clewed up, the sheets hauled in, the main and fore peaks lowered, and the flying-jib down. While thus engaged the dawn advanced, and I cast an occasional furtive glance ahead in the midst of my labour. But now that things were prepared for the worst, I ran forward again and looked anxiously over the bow. I now heard the roar of the waves distinctly, and as a single ray of the rising sun gleamed over the ocean I saw—what! could it be that I was dreaming?—that magnificent breaker with its ceaseless roar!—that mountain top!—yes, once more I beheld the Coral Island!

CHAPTER XXIX

The effect of a cannon-shot—A happy reunion of a somewhat moist
nature—Retrospect and explanations—An awful dive—New
plans—The last of the Coral Island.

I ALMOST fell upon the deck with the tumult of
mingled emotions that filled my heart as I gazed
ardently towards my beautiful island. It was still many
miles away, but sufficiently near to enable me to trace distinctly the well-remembered outlines of the two mountains.
My first impulse was to utter an exclamation of gratitude
for being carried to my former happy home in safety ; my
second, to jump up, clap my hands, shout, and run up and
down the deck, with no other object in view than that of
giving vent to my excited feelings. Then I went below
for the telescope, and spent nearly ten minutes of the
utmost impatience in vainly trying to get a focus, and in
rubbing the skin nearly off my eyes, before I discovered
that having taken off the large glass to examine the phosphoric water with I had omitted to put it on again.

After that I looked up impatiently at the sails, which I
now regretted having lowered so hastily, and for a moment
thought of hoisting the main top-sail again ; but recollecting that it would take me full half a day to accomplish,
and that, at the present rate of sailing, two hours would
bring me to the island, I immediately dismissed the idea.

The remainder of the time I spent in making feverish
preparations for arriving and seeing my dear comrades.

270

I remembered that they were not in the habit of rising before six, and as it was now only three, I hoped to arrive before they were awake. Moreover, I set about making ready to let go the anchor, resolving in my own mind that, as I knew the depth of water in the passage of the reef and within the lagoon, I would run the schooner in and bring up opposite the bower. Fortunately the anchor was hanging at the cat-head, otherwise I should never have been able to use it. Now, I had only to cut the tackling, and it would drop of its own weight. After searching among the flags, I found the terrible black one, which I ran up to the peak. While I was doing this a thought struck me. I went to the powder-magazine, brought up a blank cartridge and loaded the big brass gun, which, it will be remembered, was unhoused when we set sail, and as I had no means of housing it, there it had stood, bristling alike at fair weather and foul all the voyage. I took care to grease its mouth well, and before leaving the fore part of the ship, thrust the poker into the fire.

All was now ready. A steady five-knot breeze was blowing, so that I was now not more than quarter of a mile from the reef. I was soon at the entrance, and as the schooner glided quickly through, I glanced affectionately at the huge breaker, as if it had been the same one I had seen there when I bade adieu, as I feared for ever, to the island. On coming opposite the Water Garden, I put the helm hard down. The schooner came round with a rapid, graceful bend, and lost way just opposite the bower. Running forward, I let go the anchor, caught up the red-hot poker, applied it to the brass gun, and saluted the mountains with a *bang* such as had only once before broke their slumbering echoes!

Effective although it was, however, it was scarcely equal
to the bang with which, instantly after, Peterkin bounded
from the bower, in scanty costume, his eyeballs starting
from his head with surprise and terror. One gaze he gave,
one yell, and then fled into the bushes like a wild cat.
The next moment Jack went through exactly the same
performance, the only difference being that his movements
were less like those of Jack-in-the-box, though not less
vigorous and rapid than those of Peterkin.

"Hallo!" I shouted, almost mad with joy, "what ho!
Peterkin! Jack! hallo! it's *me!*"

My shout was just in time to arrest them. They halted
and turned round, and the instant I repeated the cry I
saw that they recognised my voice, by both of them running at full speed towards the beach. I could no longer
contain myself. Throwing off my jacket, I jumped overboard at the same moment that Jack bounded into the
sea. In another moment we met in deep water, clasped
each other round the neck, and sank, as a matter of course,
to the bottom! We were well-nigh choked, and instantly
struggled to the surface, where Peterkin was sputtering
about like a wounded duck, laughing and crying by turns,
and choking himself with salt water!

It would be impossible to convey to my reader, by description, an adequate conception of the scene that followed
my landing on the beach, as we stood embracing each
other indiscriminately in our dripping garments, and giving
utterance to incoherent rhapsodies, mingled with wild
shouts. It can be more easily imagined than described,
so I will draw a curtain over this part of my history, and
carry the reader forward over an interval of three days.

During the greater part of that period Peterkin did

nothing but roast pigs, taro, and bread-fruit, and ply me
with plantains, plums, potatoes, and cocoa-nuts, while I
related to him and Jack the terrible and wonderful adventures I had gone through since we last met.   After I had
finished the account, they made me go all over it again;
and when I had concluded the second recital, I had to go
over it again, while they commented upon it piecemeal.
They were much affected by what I told them of the probable fate of Avatea, and Peterkin could by no means
brook the idea of the poor girl being converted into a *long
pig!* As for Jack, he clinched his teeth, and shook his
fist towards the sea, saying at the same time that he
was sorry he had not broken Tararo's head, and he only
hoped that one day he should be able to plant his knuckles
on the bridge of that chief's nose! After they had "pumped
me dry," as Peterkin said, I begged to be informed of what
had happened to them during my long absence, and
particularly as to how they got out of the Diamond
Cave.

"Well, you must know," began Jack, "after you had
dived out of the cave, on the day you were taken away
from us, we waited very patiently for half-an-hour, not
expecting you to return before the end of that time.
Then we began to upbraid you for staying so long, when
you knew we would be anxious; but when an hour passed,
we became alarmed, and I resolved at all hazards to dive
out, and see what had become of you, although I felt for
poor Peterkin, because, as he truly said, 'If you never
come back I'm shut up here for life.' However, I promised not to run any risk, and he let me go; which, to
say truth, I thought very courageous of him!"

"I should just think it was," interrupted Peterkin,

looking at Jack over the edge of a monstrous potato
which he happened to be devouring at the time.

"Well," continued Jack, "you may guess my consternation when you did not answer to my halloo. At first I
imagined that the pirates must have killed you, and left
you in the bush or thrown you into the sea; then it
occurred to me that this would have served no end of
theirs, so I came to the conclusion that they must have
carried you away with them. As this thought struck me,
I observed the pirate schooner standing away to the nor'ard,
almost hull down on the horizon, and I sat down on the
rocks to watch her as she slowly sank from my sight.
And I tell you, Ralph my boy, that I shed more tears
that time at losing you than I have done, I verily believe,
all my life before——"

"Pardon me, Jack, for interrupting," said Peterkin;
"surely you must be mistaken in that: you've often told
me that when you were a baby you used to howl and
roar from morning to——"

"Hold your tongue, Peterkin," cried Jack. "Well,
after the schooner had disappeared, I dived back into the
cave, much to Peterkin's relief, and told him what I had
seen. We sat down and had a long talk over this matter,
and then we agreed to make a regular, systematic search
through the woods, so as to make sure at least that you
had not been killed. But now we thought of the difficulty of getting out of the cave without your help.
Peterkin became dreadfully nervous when he thought of
this; and I must confess I felt some alarm, for, of course,
I could not hope alone to take him out so quickly as we
two together had brought him in; and he himself vowed
that, if we had been a moment longer with him that time,

he would have had to take a breath of salt water. However, there was no help for it, and I endeavoured to calm his fears as well as I could; 'For,' said I, 'you can't live here, Peterkin;' to which he replied, 'Of course not, Jack, I can only die here, and as that's not at all desirable, you had better propose something.' So I suggested that he should take a good long breath, and trust himself to me.

"'Might we not make a large bag of cocoa-nut cloth, into which I could shove my head, and tie it tight round my neck?' he asked with a haggard smile. 'It might let me get one breath under water!'

"'No use,' said I, 'it would fill in a moment and suffocate you. I see nothing for it, Peterkin, if you really can't keep your breath so long, but to let me knock you down, and carry you out while in a state of insensibility.'

"But Peterkin didn't relish this idea. He seemed to fear that I would not be able to measure the exact force of the blow, and might, on the one hand, hit him so softly as to render a second or third blow necessary, which would be very uncomfortable; or, on the other hand, give him such a smash as would entirely spoil his figure-head, or mayhap knock the life out of him altogether! At last I got him persuaded to try to hold his breath, and commit himself to me; so he agreed, and down we went. But I had not got half-way through, when he began to struggle and kick like a wild bull, burst from my grasp, and hit against the roof of the tunnel. I was therefore obliged to force him violently back into the cave again, where he rose panting to the surface. In short, he had lost his presence of mind, and——"

"Nothing of the sort," cried Peterkin indignantly, "I only lost my wind; and if I had not had presence of mind enough to kick as I did, I should have bu'st in your arms!"

"Well, well, so be it," resumed Jack with a smile; "but the upshot of it was, that we had to hold another consultation on the point, and I really believe that, had it not been for a happy thought of mine, we should have been consulting there yet."

"I wish we had," again interrupted Peterkin with a sigh.—"I'm sure, Ralph, if I had thought that you were coming back again, I would willingly have awaited your return for months rather than have endured the mental agony which I went through. But proceed."

"The thought was this," continued Jack, "that I should tie Peterkin's hands and feet with cords, and then lash him firmly to a stout pole about five feet long, in order to render him quite powerless, and keep him straight and stiff. You should have seen his face of horror, Ralph, when I suggested this; but he came to see that it was his only chance, and told me to set about it as fast as I could; 'For,' said he, 'this is no jokin', Jack, I can tell you, and the sooner it's done the better.' I soon procured the cordage and a suitable pole, with which I returned to the cave, and lashed him as stiff and straight as an Egyptian mummy; and, to say truth, he was no bad representation of what an English mummy would be, if there were such things, for he was as white as a dead man."

"'Now,' said Peterkin in a tremulous voice, 'swim with me as near to the edge of the hole as you can before you dive, then let me take a long breath, and as I shan't be able to speak after I've taken it, you'll watch my face, and the moment you see me wink—dive! And oh,' he added earnestly, 'pray don't be long!'

"I promised to pay the strictest attention to his wishes, and swam with him to the outlet of the cave. Here I paused. 'Now then,' said I, 'pull away at the wind, lad.'

"Peterkin drew in a breath so long that I could not help thinking of the frog in the fable, that wanted to swell itself as big as the ox. Then I looked into his face earnestly. Slap went the lid of his right eye; down went my head, and up went my heels. We shot through the passage like an arrow, and rose to the surface of the open sea before you could count twenty.

"Peterkin had taken in such an awful load of wind that, on reaching the free air, he let it out with a yell loud enough to have been heard a mile off, and then the change in his feelings was so sudden and great, that he did not wait till we landed, but began, tied up as he was, to shout and sing for joy as I supported him, with my left arm, to the shore. However, in the middle of a laugh that a hyena might have envied, I let him accidentally slip, which extinguished him in a moment.

"After this happy deliverance, we immediately began our search for your dead body, Ralph; and you have no idea how low our hearts sank as we set off, day after day, to examine the valleys and mountain sides with the utmost care. In about three weeks we completed the survey of the whole island, and had at least the satisfaction of knowing that you had not been killed. But it occurred to us that you might have been thrown into the sea, so we examined the sands and the lagoon carefully, and afterwards went all round the outer reef. One day, while we were upon the reef, Peterkin espied a small, dark object lying among the rocks, which seemed to be quite different from the surrounding stones. We hastened

towards the spot, and found it to be a small keg. On
knocking out the head we discovered that it was gunpowder."

"It was I who sent you that, Jack," said I with a smile.

"Fork out!" cried Peterkin energetically, starting to
his feet and extending his open hand to Jack. "Down
with the money, sir, else I'll have you shut up for life in
a debtor's prison the moment we return to England!"

"I'll give you an I O U in the meantime," returned
Jack, laughing, "so sit down and be quiet.—The fact is,
Ralph, when we discovered this keg of powder, Peterkin
immediately took me a bet of a thousand pounds that
you had something to do with it, and I took him a bet of
ten thousand that you had not."

"Peterkin was right then," said I, explaining how the
thing had occurred.

"Well, we found it very useful," continued Jack, "although some of it had got a little damp; and we furbished
up the old pistol, with which Peterkin is a crack shot now.
But to continue. We did not find any other vestige of
you on the reef, and finally gave up all hope of ever
seeing you again. After this the island became a dreary
place to us, and we began to long for a ship to heave in
sight and take us off. But now that you're back again,
my dear fellow, it looks as bright and cheerful as it used
to do, and I love it as much as ever.

"And now," continued Jack, "I have a great desire to
visit some of the other islands of the South Seas. Here
we have a first-rate schooner at our disposal, so I don't
see what should hinder us."

"Just the very thing I was going to propose," cried
Peterkin. "I vote for starting at once."

" Well, then," said Jack, "it seems to me that we could not do better than shape our course for the island on which Avatea lives, and endeavour to persuade Tararo to let her marry the black fellow to whom she is engaged, instead of making a long pig of her. If he has a spark of gratitude in him, he'll do it. Besides, having become champions for this girl once before, it behoves us, as true knights, not to rest until we set her free; at least, all the heroes in all the story-books I have ever read would count it foul disgrace to leave such a work unfinished."

"I'm sure I don't know or care what your knights in story-books would do," said Peterkin; "but I'm certain that it would be capital fun, so I'm your man whenever you want me."

This plan of Jack's was quite in accordance with his romantic, impulsive nature; and having made up his mind to save this black girl, he could not rest until the thing was commenced.

"But there may be great danger in this attempt," he said, at the end of a long consultation on the subject. "Will you, lads, go with me in spite of this?"

"Go with you!" we repeated in the same breath.

"Can you doubt it?" said I.

"For a moment," added Peterkin.

I need scarcely say that, having made up our minds to go on this enterprise, we lost no time in making preparations to quit the island; and as the schooner was well laden with stores of every kind for a long cruise, we had little to do except to add to our abundant supply a quantity of cocoa-nuts, bread-fruit, taro, yams, plums, and potatoes, chiefly with the view of carrying the fragrance of our dear island along with us as long as we could.

When all was ready, we paid a farewell visit to the different familiar spots where most of our time had been spent. We ascended the mountain top, and gazed for the last time at the rich green foliage in the valleys, the white sandy beach, the placid lagoon, and the barrier coral reef with its crested breakers. Then we descended to Spouting Cliff, and looked down at the pale-green monster which we had made such fruitless efforts to spear in days gone by. From this we hurried to the Water Garden, and took a last dive into its clear waters, and a last gambol amongst its coral groves. I hurried out before my companions, and dressed in haste, in order to have a long examination of my tank, which Peterkin, in the fulness of his heart, had tended with the utmost care, as being a vivid remembrancer of me, rather than out of love for natural history. It was in superb condition— the water as clear and pellucid as crystal; the red and green seaweed of the most brilliant hues; the red, purple, yellow, green, and striped anemones fully expanded, and stretching out their arms as if to welcome and embrace their former master; the star-fish, zoophytes, sea-pens, and other innumerable marine insects looking fresh and beautiful; and the crabs, as Peterkin said, looking as wide awake, impertinent, rampant, and pugnacious as ever. It was, indeed, so lovely and so interesting that I would scarcely allow myself to be torn away from it.

Last of all, we returned to the bower and collected the few articles we possessed, such as the axe, the pencil-case, the broken telescope, the penknife, the hook made from the brass ring, and the sail-needle, with which we had landed on the island; also the long boots and the

pistol, besides several curious articles of costume which we
had manufactured from time to time.

These we conveyed on board in our little boat, after
having carved our names on a chip of ironwood, thus :—

JACK MARTIN,

RALPH ROVER,

PETERKIN GAY,

which we fixed up inside of the bower. The boat was
then hoisted on board and the anchor weighed; which
latter operation cost us great labour and much time, as
the anchor was so heavy that we could not move it without the aid of my complex machinery of blocks and
pulleys. A steady breeze was blowing off shore when we
set sail, at a little before sunset. It swept us quickly
past the reef and out to sea. The shore grew rapidly
more indistinct as the shades of evening fell, while our
clipper bark bounded lightly over the waves. Slowly the
mountain top sank on the horizon, until it became a mere
speck. In another moment the sun and the Coral Island
sank together into the broad bosom of the Pacific.

CHAPTER XXX

The voyage—The island, and a consultation in which danger is
scouted as a thing unworthy of consideration—Rats and cats—
The native teacher—Awful revelations—Wonderful effects of
Christianity.

OUR voyage during the next two weeks was most interesting and prosperous. The breeze continued
generally fair, and at all times enabled us to lie our
course; for being, as I have said before, clipper-built,
the pirate schooner could lie very close to the wind and
make little leeway. We had no difficulty now in managing
our sails, for Jack was heavy and powerful, while Peterkin
was active as a kitten. Still, however, we were a very
insufficient crew for such a vessel, and if any one had
proposed to us to make such a voyage in it before we
had been forced to go through so many hardships from
necessity, we would have turned away with pity from the
individual making such proposal as from a madman. I
pondered this a good deal, and at last concluded that
men do not know how much they are capable of doing till
they try, and that we should never give way to despair in
any undertaking, however difficult it may seem—always
supposing, however, that our cause is a good one, and
that we can ask the Divine blessing on it.

Although, therefore, we could now manage our sails
easily, we nevertheless found that my pulleys were of
much service to us in some things; though Jack did
laugh heartily at the uncouth arrangement of ropes and

blocks, which had, to a sailor's eye, a very lumbering and clumsy appearance. But I will not drag my reader through the details of this voyage. Suffice it to say that, after an agreeable sail of about three weeks, we arrived off the island of Mango,* which I recognised at once from the description that the pirate Bill had given me of it during one of our conversations.

As soon as we came within sight of it we hove the ship to and held a council of war.

"Now, boys," said Jack, as we seated ourselves beside him on the cabin skylight, "before we go further in this business, we must go over the pros and cons of it; for although you have so generously consented to stick by me through thick and thin, it would be unfair did I not see that you thoroughly understand the danger of what we are about to attempt."

"Oh, bother the danger!" cried Peterkin. "I wonder to hear *you*, Jack, talk of danger. When a fellow begins to talk about it, he'll soon come to magnify it to such a degree that he'll not be fit to face it when it comes, no more than a suckin' baby."

"Nay, Peterkin," replied Jack gravely, "I won't be jested out of it. I grant you that when we've once resolved to act, and have made up our minds what to do, we should think no more of danger. But before we have so resolved it behoves us to look it straight in the face, and examine into it, and walk round it; for if we flinch at a distant view, we're sure to run away when the danger is near.—Now, I understand from you, Ralph, that the island is inhabited by thorough-going, out-and-out cannibals, whose principal law is, 'Might is right, and the weakest goes to the wall'?"

"Yes," said I; "so Bill gave me to understand. He told me, however, that at the southern side of it the missionaries had obtained a footing amongst an insignificant tribe. A native teacher had been sent there by the Wesleyans, who had succeeded in persuading the chief at that part to embrace Christianity. But instead of that being of any advantage to our enterprise, it seems the very reverse; for the chief Tararo is a determined heathen, and persecutes the Christians—who are far too weak in numbers to offer any resistance—and looks with dislike upon all white men, whom he regards as propagators of the new faith."

"'Tis a pity," said Jack, "that the Christian tribe is so small, for we shall scarcely be safe under their protection, I fear. If Tararo takes it into his head to wish for our vessel, or to kill ourselves, he could take us from them by force. You say that the native missionary talks English?"

"So I believe."

"Then, what I propose is this," said Jack. "We will run round to the south side of the island, and cast anchor off the Christian village. We are too far away just now to have been descried by any of the savages, so we shall get there unobserved, and have time to arrange our plans before the heathen tribes know of our presence. But in doing this we run the risk of being captured by the ill-disposed tribes, and being very ill used, if not—a——"

"Roasted alive and eaten," cried Peterkin. "Come, out with it, Jack. According to your own showing, it's well to look the danger straight in the face!"

"Well, that *is* the worst of it, certainly. Are you prepared, then, to take your chance of that?"

"I've been prepared and had my mind made up long ago," cried Peterkin, swaggering about the deck with his hands thrust into his breeches pockets. "The fact is, Jack, I don't believe that Tararo will be so ungrateful as to eat us; and I'm quite sure that he'll be too happy to grant us whatever we ask; so the sooner we go in and win the better."

Peterkin was wrong, however, in his estimate of savage gratitude, as the sequel will show.

The schooner was now put before the wind, and after making a long run to the southward, we put about and beat up for the south side of Mango, where we arrived before sunset, and hove-to off the coral reef. Here we awaited the arrival of a canoe, which immediately put off on our rounding-to. When it arrived, a mild-looking native, of apparently forty years of age, came on board, and, taking off his straw hat, made us a low bow. He was clad in a respectable suit of European clothes; and the first words he uttered, as he stepped up to Jack and shook hands with him, were—

"Good day, gentlemen. We are happy to see you at Mango; you are heartily welcome."

After returning his salutation, Jack exclaimed, "You must be the native missionary teacher of whom I have heard; are you not?"

"I am. I have the joy to be a servant of the Lord Jesus at this station."

"You're the very man I want to see, then," replied Jack; "that's lucky. Come down to the cabin, friend, and have a glass of wine. I wish particularly to speak with you. My men there," pointing to Peterkin and me, "will look after your people."

"Thank you," said the teacher, as he followed Jack to the cabin; "I do not drink wine, or any strong drink."

"Oh! then there's lots of water, and you can have biscuit."

"Now, 'pon my word, that's cool!" said Peterkin; "his *men*, forsooth! Well, since we are to be men, we may as well come it as strong over these black chaps as we can.—Hallo, there!" he cried to the half-dozen of natives who stood upon the deck, gazing in wonder at all they saw, "here's for you;" and he handed them a tray of broken biscuit and a can of water. Then, thrusting his hands into his pockets, he walked up and down the deck with an enormous swagger, whistling vociferously.

In about half-an-hour Jack and the teacher came on deck, and the latter, bidding us a cheerful good-evening, entered his canoe and paddled to the shore. When he was gone, Peterkin stepped up to Jack, and, touching his cap, said—

"Well, captain, have you any communications to make to your *men?*"

"Yes," cried Jack; "ready about, mind the helm, and clew up your tongue, while I con the schooner through the passage in the reef. The teacher, who seems a first-rate fellow, says it's quite deep, and good anchorage within the lagoon close to the shore."

While the vessel was slowly advancing to her anchorage, under a light breeze, Jack explained to us that Avatea was still on the island, living amongst the heathens; that she had expressed a strong desire to join the Christians, but Tararo would not let her, and kept her constantly in close confinement.

"Moreover," continued Jack, "I find that she belongs to

one of the Samoan Islands, where Christianity had been introduced long before her capture by the heathens of a neighbouring island; and the very day after she was taken she was to have joined the Church which had been planted there by that excellent body the London Missionary Society.* The teacher tells me, too, that the poor girl has fallen in love with a Christian chief, who lives on an island some fifty miles or so to the south of this one, and that she is meditating a desperate attempt at escape. So, you see, we have come in the nick of time. I fancy that this chief is the fellow whom you heard of, Ralph, at the Island of Emo. Besides all this, the heathen savages are at war among themselves, and there's to be a battle fought the day after to-morrow, in which the principal leader is Tararo; so that we'll not be able to commence our negotiations with the rascally chief till the day after."

The village off which we anchored was beautifully situated at the head of a small bay, from the margin of which trees of every description peculiar to the tropics rose in the richest luxuriance to the summit of a hilly ridge, which was the line of demarcation between the possessions of the Christians and those of the neighbouring heathen chief.

The site of the settlement was an extensive plot of flat land, stretching in a gentle slope from the sea to the mountain. The cottages stood several hundred yards from the beach, and were protected from the glare of the sea by the rich foliage of rows of large Barringtonia and other trees which girt the shore. The village was about a mile in length, and perfectly straight, with a wide road down the middle, on either side of which were rows of the tufted-topped ti tree,* whose delicate and beautiful blossoms, hanging beneath their plume-crested tops, added richness to the scene. The cottages of the natives were built beneath these trees, and were kept in the most excellent order, each having a little garden in front, tastefully laid out and planted, while the walks were covered with black and white pebbles.

Every house had doors and Venetian windows, painted partly with lamp-black made from the candle-nut, and partly with red ochre, which contrasted powerfully with the dazzling coral lime that covered the walls. On a prominent position stood a handsome church, which was quite a curiosity in its way. It was a hundred feet long by fifty broad, and was seated throughout to accommodate upwards of two thousand persons. It had six large folding doors, and twelve windows with Venetian blinds; and although a large and substantial edifice, it had been built, we were told by the teacher, in the space of two months! There was not a single iron nail in the fabric, and the natives had constructed it chiefly with their stone and bone axes and other tools, having only one or two axes or tools of European manufacture. Everything around this beautiful spot wore an aspect of peace and plenty; and as we dropped our anchor within a stone's cast of the substantial coral wharf, I could not avoid contrasting it with the wretched village of Emo, where I had witnessed so many frightful scenes. When the teacher afterwards told me that the people of this tribe had become converts only a year previous to our arrival, and that they had been living before that in the practice of the most bloody system of idolatry, I could not refrain from exclaiming, "What a convincing proof that Christianity is of God!"

On landing from our little boat, we were received with a warm welcome by the teacher and his wife; the latter being also a native, clothed in a simple European gown and a straw bonnet. The shore was lined with hundreds of natives, whose persons were all more or less clothed with native cloth. Some of the men had on a kind of poncho formed of this cloth, their legs being uncovered; others wore clumsily fashioned trousers, and no upper garment except hats made of straw and cloth. Many of the dresses, both of women and men, were grotesque enough, being very bad imitations of the European garb; but all wore a dress of some sort or other. They seemed very glad to see us, and crowded round us as the teacher led the way to his dwelling, where we were entertained, in the most sumptuous manner, on baked pig and all the varieties of fruits and vegetables that the island produced. We were much annoyed, however, by the rats: they seemed to run about the house like domestic animals. As we sat at table, one of them peeped up at us over the edge of the cloth, close to Peterkin's elbow, who floored it with a blow on the snout from his knife, exclaiming as he did so—

"I say, Mister Teacher, why don't you set traps for these brutes? Surely you are not fond of them!"

"No," replied the teacher with a smile; "we would be glad to get rid of them if we could; but if we were to trap all the rats on the island, it would occupy our whole time."

"Are they, then, so numerous?" inquired Jack.

"They swarm everywhere. The poor heathens on the north side eat them, and think them very sweet. So did my people formerly; but they do not eat so many now, because the missionary who was last here expressed disgust

at it. The poor people asked if it was wrong to eat rats;
and he told them that it was certainly not wrong, but
that the people of England would be much disgusted were
they asked to eat rats."

We had not been an hour in the house of this kind-
hearted man when we were convinced of the truth of his
statement as to their numbers; for the rats ran about the
floors in dozens, and during our meal two men were
stationed at the table to keep them off!

"What a pity you have no cats!" said Peterkin,
and he aimed a blow at another reckless intruder, and
missed it.

"We would indeed be glad to have a few," rejoined the
teacher, "but they are difficult to be got. The hogs, we
find, are very good rat-killers, but they do not seem to be
able to keep the numbers down. I have heard that they
are better than cats."

As the teacher said this, his good-natured black face
was wrinkled with a smile of merriment. Observing that
I had noticed it, he said—

"I smiled just now when I remembered the fate of the
first cat that was taken to Rarotonga. This is one of
the stations of the London Missionary Society. It, like
our own, is infested with rats, and a cat was brought at
last to the island. It was a large black one. On being
turned loose, instead of being content to stay among men,
the cat took to the mountains, and lived in a wild state,
sometimes paying visits during the night to the houses of
the natives; some of whom, living at a distance from the
settlement, had not heard of the cat's arrival, and were
dreadfully frightened in consequence, calling it a 'monster
of the deep,' and flying in terror away from it. One night

the cat—feeling a desire for company, I suppose—took its way to the house of a chief who had recently been converted to Christianity, and had begun to learn to read and pray. The chief's wife, who was sitting awake at his side while he slept, beheld with horror two fires glistening in the doorway, and heard with surprise a mysterious voice. Almost petrified with fear, she awoke her husband, and began to upbraid him for forsaking his old religion and burning his god, who, she declared, was now come to be avenged of them. 'Get up and pray! get up and pray!' she cried. The chief arose, and on opening his eyes beheld the same glaring lights and heard the same ominous sound. Impelled by the extreme urgency of the case, he commenced, with all possible vehemence, to vociferate the alphabet, as a prayer to God to deliver them from the vengeance of Satan! On hearing this, the cat, as much alarmed as themselves, fled precipitately away, leaving the chief and his wife congratulating themselves on the efficacy of their prayer."

We were much diverted with this anecdote, which the teacher related in English so good that we certainly could not have supposed him a native but for the colour of his face and the foreign accent in his tone. Next day we walked out with this interesting man, and were much entertained and instructed by his conversation, as we rambled through the cool, shady groves of bananas, citrons, limes, and other trees, or sauntered among the cottages of the natives, and watched them while they laboured diligently in the taro beds or manufactured the tapa or native cloth. To some of these Jack put questions through the medium of the missionary; and the replies were such as to surprise us at the extent of their knowledge. In-

deed, Peterkin very truly remarked that "they seemed to
know a considerable deal more than Jack himself!"

Among other pieces of interesting information that
we obtained was the following, in regard to coral formations:—

"The islands of the Pacific,"*said our friend, "are of
three different kinds or classes. Those of the first class
are volcanic, mountainous, and wild; some shooting their
jagged peaks into the clouds at an elevation of ten and
fifteen thousand feet. Those of the second class are of
crystallised limestone, and vary in height from one hundred to five hundred feet. The hills on these are not so
wild or broken as those of the first class, but are richly
clothed with vegetation, and very beautiful. I have no
doubt that the Coral Island on which you were wrecked
was one of this class. They are supposed to have been
upheaved from the bottom of the sea by volcanic agency,
but they are not themselves volcanic in their nature,
neither are they of coral formation. Those of the third
class are the low coralline islands, usually having lagoons
of water in their midst; they are very numerous.

"As to the manner in which coral islands and reefs are
formed, there are various opinions on this point. I will
give you what seems to me the most probable theory—a
theory, I may add, which is held by some of the good and
scientific missionaries. It is well known that there is
much lime in salt water; it is also known that coral is
composed of lime. It is supposed that the polypes, or
coral insects, have the power of attracting this lime to
their bodies; and with this material they build their little
cells or habitations. They choose the summit of a volcano, or the top of a submarine mountain, as a foundation

on which to build; for it is found that they never work at any great depth below the surface. On this they work; the polypes on the mountain top, of course, reach the surface first, then those at the outer edges reach the top sooner than the others between them and the centre, thus forming the coral reef surrounding the lagoon of water and the central island; after that the insects within the lagoon cease working. When the surface of the water is reached, these myriads of wonderful creatures die. Then birds visit the spot, and seeds are thus conveyed thither, which take root, and spring up, and flourish. Thus are commenced those coralline islets of which you have seen so many in these seas. The reefs round the large islands are formed in a similar manner. When we consider," added the missionary, "the smallness of the architects used by our heavenly Father in order to form those lovely and innumerable islands, we are filled with much of that feeling which induced the ancient king to exclaim, 'How manifold, O Lord, are Thy works! in wisdom hast Thou made them all.'"

We all heartily agreed with the missionary in this sentiment, and felt not a little gratified to find that the opinions which Jack and I had been led to form from personal observation on our Coral Island were thus to a great extent corroborated.

The missionary also gave us an account of the manner in which Christianity had been introduced among them. He said: "When missionaries were first sent here, three years ago, a small vessel brought them; and the chief, who is now dead, promised to treat well the two native teachers who were left with their wives on the island. But scarcely had the boat which landed them returned to the ship,

than the natives began to maltreat their guests, taking
away all they possessed, and offering them further violence,
so that, when the boat was sent in haste to fetch them
away, the clothes of both men and women were torn
nearly off their backs.

"Two years after this the vessel visited them again, and
I, being in her, volunteered to land alone, without any
goods whatever, begging that my wife might be brought
to me the following year—that is, *this* year; and, as you
see, she is with me. But the surf was so high that the
boat could not land me; so with nothing on but my
trousers and shirt, and with a few catechisms and a Bible,
besides some portions of the Scripture translated into the
Mango tongue, I sprang into the sea, and swam ashore on
the crest of a breaker. I was instantly dragged up the
beach by the natives; who, on finding I had nothing
worth having upon me, let me alone. I then made signs
to my friends in the ship to leave me; which they did.
At first the natives listened to me in silence, but laughed
at what I said while I preached the Gospel of our blessed
Saviour Jesus Christ to them. Afterwards they treated
me ill sometimes; but I persevered, and continued to
dwell among them, and dispute, and exhort them to give
up their sinful ways of life, burn their idols, and come to
Jesus.

"About a month after I landed, I heard that the chief
was dead. He was the father of the present chief, who is
now a most consistent member of the Church. It is a
custom here that when a chief dies his wives are strangled
and buried with him.* Knowing this, I hastened to his
house to endeavour to prevent such cruelty if possible.
When I arrived, I found two of the wives had already

been killed, while another was in the act of being strangled. I pleaded hard for her, but it was too late; she was already dead. I then entreated the son to spare the fourth wife, and after much hesitation my prayer was granted; but in half-an-hour afterwards this poor woman repented of being unfaithful, as she termed it, to her husband, and insisted on being strangled; which was accordingly done.

"All this time the chief's son was walking up and down before his father's house with a brow black as thunder. When he entered I went in with him, and found, to my surprise, that his father was *not* dead! The old man was sitting on a mat in a corner, with an expression of placid resignation on his face.

"'Why,' said I, 'have you strangled your father's wives before he is dead?'

"To this the son replied, 'He is dead. That is no longer my father. He is as good as dead now. He is to be *buried alive.*'

"I now remembered having heard that it is a custom among the Feejee Islanders, that when the reigning chief grows old or infirm, the heir to the chieftainship has a right to depose his father; in which case he is considered as dead, and is buried alive. The young chief was now about to follow this custom, and despite my earnest entreaties and pleadings, the old chief was buried that day before my eyes in the same grave with his four strangled wives! Oh, my heart groaned when I saw this! and I prayed to God to open the hearts of these poor creatures, as He had already opened mine, and pour into them the light and the love of the Gospel of Jesus. My prayer was answered very soon. A week afterwards, the son, who was now chief of the tribe, came to me, bearing his god on his shoulders, and groaning beneath its weight. Flinging it down at my feet, he desired me to burn it!

"You may conceive how overjoyed I was at this. I sprang up and embraced him, while I shed tears of joy. Then we made a fire, and burned the god to ashes, amid an immense concourse of the people, who seemed terrified at what was being done, and shrank back when we burned the god, expecting some signal vengeance to be taken upon us; but seeing that nothing happened, they changed their minds, and thought that our God must be the true one after all. From that time the mission prospered steadily; and now, while there is not a single man in the tribe who has not burned his household gods and become a convert to Christianity, there are not a few, I hope, who are true followers of the Lamb, having been plucked as brands from the burning by Him who can save unto the uttermost. I will not tell you more of our progress at this time; but you see," he said, waving his hand around him, "the village and the church did not exist a year ago!"

We were indeed much interested in this account, and I could not help again in my heart praying to God to prosper those missionary societies that send such inestimable blessings to these islands of dark and bloody idolatry. The teacher also added that the other tribes were very indignant at this one for having burned its gods, and threatened to destroy it altogether, but they had done nothing yet. "And if they should," said the teacher, "the Lord is on our side; of whom shall we be afraid?"

"Have the missionaries many stations in these seas?" inquired Jack.

"Oh yes. The London Missionary Society have a great

many in the Tahiti group, and other islands in that quarter. Then the Wesleyans have the Feejee Islands all to themselves, and the Americans have many stations in other groups. But still, my friend, there are hundreds of islands here the natives of which have never heard of Jesus, or the good word of God, or the Holy Spirit; and thousands are living and dying in the practice of those terrible sins and bloody murders of which you have already heard. I trust, my friends," he added, looking earnestly into our faces—"I trust that if you ever return to England, you will tell your Christian friends that the horrors which they hear of in regard to these islands are *literally true*, and that when they have heard the worst, the '*half has not been told them*;' for there are perpetrated here foul deeds of darkness of which man may not speak. You may also tell them," he said, looking around with a smile, while a tear of gratitude trembled in his eye and rolled down his coal-black cheek—"tell them of the blessings that the Gospel has wrought *here!*"

We assured our friend that we would certainly not forget his request. On returning towards the village, about noon, we remarked on the beautiful whiteness of the cottages.

"That is owing to the lime with which they are plastered," said the teacher. "When the natives were converted, as I have described, I set them to work to build cottages for themselves, and also this handsome church which you see. When the framework and other parts of the house were up, I sent the people to fetch coral from the sea. They brought immense quantities. Then I made them cut wood, and piling the coral above it, set it on fire

"'Look! look!' cried the poor people in amazement, 'what wonderful people the Christians are! He is roasting stones. We shall not need taro or bread-fruit any more; we may eat stones!'

"But their surprise was still greater when the coral was reduced to a fine, soft white powder. They immediately set up a great shout, and mingling the lime with water, rubbed their faces and their bodies all over with it, and ran through the village screaming with delight. They were also much surprised at another thing they saw me do. I wished to make some household furniture, and constructed a turning-lathe to assist me. The first thing that I turned was the leg of a sofa; which was no sooner finished than the chief seized it with wonder and delight, and ran through the village exhibiting it to the people, who looked upon it with great admiration. The chief then, tying a string to it, hung it round his neck as an ornament! He afterwards told me that if he had seen it before he became a Christian, he would have made it his god!"

As the teacher concluded this anecdote we reached his door. Saying that he had business to attend to, he left us to amuse ourselves as we best could.

"Now, lads," said Jack, turning abruptly towards us, and buttoning up his jacket as he spoke, "I'm off to see the battle. I've no particular fondness for seein' bloodshed, but I must find out the nature o' these fellows and see their customs with my own eyes, so that I may be able to speak of it again, if need be, authoritatively. It's only six miles off, and we don't run much more risk than that of getting a rap with a stray stone or an overshot arrow. Will you go?"

"To be sure we will," said Peterkin.

"If they chance to see us we'll cut and run for it," added Jack.

"Dear me!" cried Peterkin—"*you* run! I thought you would scorn to run from any one."

"So I would, if it were my duty to fight," returned Jack coolly; "but as I don't want to fight, and don't intend to fight, if they offer to attack us I'll run away like the veriest coward that ever went by the name of Peterkin. So come along."

CHAPTER XXXI

A strange and bloody battle—The lion bearded in his den—Frightful scenes of cruelty, and fears for the future.

WE had ascertained from the teacher the direction to the spot on which the battle was to be fought, and after a walk of two hours, reached it. The summit of a bare hill was the place chosen; for, unlike most of the other islanders who are addicted to bush fighting, those of Mango are in the habit of meeting on open ground. We arrived before the two parties had commenced the deadly struggle, and, creeping as close up as we dared among the rocks, we lay and watched them.

The combatants were drawn up face to face, each side ranged in rank four deep. Those in the first row were armed with long spears; the second with clubs to defend the spearmen; the third row was composed of young men with slings; and the fourth consisted of women, who carried baskets of stones for the slingers, and clubs and spears with which to supply the warriors. Soon after we arrived the attack was made with great fury. There was no science displayed. The two bodies of savages rushed headlong upon each other and engaged in a general *mêlée*, and a more dreadful set of men I have never seen. They wore grotesque war-caps made of various substances and decorated with feathers. Their faces and bodies were painted so as to make them look as frightful as possible; and as they brandished their massive clubs, leaped, shouted, yelled, and dashed each other to the ground, I thought I had never seen men look so like demons before.

We were much surprised at the conduct of the women, who seemed to be perfect furies, and hung about the heels of their husbands in order to defend them. One stout young woman we saw whose husband was hard pressed and about to be overcome she lifted a large stone, and throwing it at his opponent's head, felled him to the earth. But the battle did not last long. The band most distant from us gave way and were routed, leaving eighteen of their comrades dead upon the field. These the victors brained as they lay; and, putting some of their brains on leaves, went off with them, we were afterwards informed, to their temples to present them to their gods as an earnest of the human victims who were soon to be brought there.

We hastened back to the Christian village with feelings of the deepest sadness at the sanguinary conflict which we had just witnessed.

Next day, after breakfasting with our friend the teacher, we made preparations for carrying out our plan. At first the teacher endeavoured to dissuade us.

"You do not know," said he, turning to Jack, "the danger you run in venturing amongst these ferocious savages. I feel much pity for poor Avatea; but you are not likely to succeed in saving her, and you may die in the attempt."

"Well," said Jack quietly, "I am not afraid to die in a good cause."

The teacher smiled approvingly at him as he said this, and, after a little further conversation, agreed to accompany us as interpreter; saying that, although Tararo was unfriendly to him, he had hitherto treated him with respect.

We now went on board the schooner, having resolved to sail round the island and drop anchor opposite the heathen village. We manned her with natives, and hoped to overawe the savages by displaying our brass gun to advantage. The teacher soon after came on board, and, setting our sails, we put to sea. In two hours more we made the cliffs reverberate with the crash of the big gun, which we fired by way of salute, while we ran the British ensign up to the peak and cast anchor. The commotion on shore showed us that we had struck terror into the hearts of the natives; but, seeing that we did not offer to molest them, a canoe at length put off and paddled cautiously towards us. The teacher showed himself, and, explaining that we were friends and wished to palaver with the chief, desired the native to go and tell him to come on board.

We waited long and with much impatience for an answer. During this time the native teacher conversed with us again, and told us many things concerning the success of the Gospel among those islands; and, perceiving that we were by no means so much gratified as we ought to have been at the hearing of such good news, he pressed us more closely in regard to our personal interest in religion, and exhorted us to consider that our souls were certainly in as great danger as those of the wretched heathen whom we pitied so much, if we had not already found salvation in Jesus Christ. "Nay, further," he added, "if such be your unhappy case, you are, in the sight of God, much worse than these savages (forgive me, my young friends, for saying so): for they have no knowledge, no light, and do not profess to believe; while you, on the contrary, have been brought up in the light of the blessed Gospel, and call yourselves Christians. These poor savages are indeed the enemies of our Lord; but you, if ye be not true believers, are traitors!"

I must confess that my heart condemned me while the teacher spoke in this earnest manner, and I knew not what to reply. Peterkin, too, did not seem to like it, and I thought would willingly have escaped. But Jack seemed deeply impressed, and wore an anxious expression on his naturally grave countenance; while he assented to the teacher's remarks, and put to him many earnest questions. Meanwhile, the natives who composed our crew, having nothing particular to do, had squatted down on the deck and taken out their little books containing the translated portions of the New Testament, along with hymns and spelling-books, and were now busily engaged, some vociferating the alphabet, others learning prayers off by heart, while a few sang hymns—all of them being utterly unmindful of our presence. The teacher soon joined them, and soon afterwards they all engaged in a prayer, which was afterwards translated to us, and proved to be a petition for the success of our undertaking, and for the conversion of the heathen.

While we were thus engaged, a canoe put off from shore and several savages leaped on deck, one of whom advanced to the teacher and informed him that Tararo could not come on board that day, being busy with some religious ceremonies before the gods, which could on no account be postponed. He was also engaged with a friendly chief who was about to take his departure from the island, and therefore begged that the teacher and his friends would land and pay a visit to him. To this the teacher returned answer that we would land immediately.

"Now, lads," said Jack, as we were about to step into our little boat, "I'm not going to take any weapons with me, and I recommend you to take none either. We are altogether in the power of these savages, and the utmost we could do, if they were to attack us, would be to kill a few of them before we were ourselves overpowered. I think that our only chance of success lies in mild measures; don't you think so?"

To this I assented gladly, and Peterkin replied by laying down a huge bell-mouthed blunderbuss, and divesting himself of a pair of enormous horse-pistols with which he had purposed to overawe the natives! We then jumped into our boat and rowed ashore.

On reaching the beach we were received by a crowd of naked savages, who shouted a rude welcome, and conducted us to a house or shed where a baked pig and a variety of vegetables were prepared for us. Having partaken of these, the teacher begged to be conducted to the chief; but there seemed some hesitation, and after some consultation among themselves one of the men stood forward and spoke to the teacher.

"What says he?" inquired Jack when the savage had concluded.

"He says that the chief is just going to the temple of his god and cannot see us yet; so we must be patient, my friend."

"Well," cried Jack, rising, "if he won't come to see me, I'll e'en go and see him. Besides, I have a great desire to witness their proceedings at this temple of theirs. Will you go with me, friend?"

"I cannot," said the teacher, shaking his head; "I must not go to the heathen temples and witness their inhuman rites, except for the purpose of condemning their wickedness and folly."

"Very good," returned Jack; "then I'll go alone, for I cannot condemn their doings till I have seen them."

Jack arose, and we, having determined to go also, followed him through the banana groves to a rising ground immediately behind the village, on the top of which stood the Buré, or temple, under the dark shade of a group of iron-wood trees. As we went through the village, I was again led to contrast the rude huts and sheds and their almost naked, savage-looking inhabitants with the natives of the Christian village, who, to use the teacher's scriptural expression, were now "clothed and in their right mind."

As we turned into a broad path leading towards the hill, we were arrested by the shouts of an approaching multitude in the rear. Drawing aside into the bushes, we awaited their coming up, and as they drew near we observed that it was a procession of the natives, many of whom were dancing and gesticulating in the most frantic manner. They had an exceedingly hideous aspect, owing to the black, red, and yellow paints with which their faces and naked bodies were bedaubed. In the midst of these came a band of men carrying three or four planks, on which were seated in rows upwards of a dozen men. I shuddered involuntarily as I recollected the sacrifice of human victims at the island of Emo, and turned with a look of fear to Jack as I said—

"O Jack! I have a terrible dread that they are going to commit some of their cruel practices on these wretched men. We had better not go to the temple. We shall

only be horrified without being able to do any good, for I
fear they are going to kill them."

Jack's face wore an expression of deep compassion as he
said in a low voice, "No fear, Ralph; the sufferings of
these poor fellows are over long ago."

I turned with a start as he spoke, and glancing at the
men, who were now quite near to the spot where we stood,
saw that they were all dead. They were tied firmly with
ropes in a sitting posture on the planks, and seemed, as
they bent their sightless eyeballs and grinning mouths
over the dancing crew below, as if they were laughing in
ghastly mockery at the utter inability of their enemies to
hurt them now. These, we discovered afterwards, were
the men who had been slain in the battle of the previous
day, and were now on their way to be first presented to the
gods and then eaten. Behind these came two men leading
between them a third, whose hands were pinioned behind
his back. He walked with a firm step, and wore a look
of utter indifference on his face as they led him along; so
that we concluded he must be a criminal who was about
to receive some slight punishment for his faults. The
rear of the procession was brought up by a shouting
crowd of women and children, with whom we mingled
and followed to the temple.

Here we arrived in a few minutes. The temple was a
tall circular building, open at one side. Around it were
strewn heaps of human bones and skulls. At a table
inside sat the priest, an elderly man with a long grey
beard. He was seated on a stool, and before him lay
several knives, made of wood, bone, and splinters of
bamboo, with which he performed his office of dissecting
dead bodies. Farther in lay a variety of articles that had

been dedicated to the god, and among them were many spears and clubs. I observed among the latter some with human teeth sticking in them, where the victims had been clubbed in their mouths.

Before this temple the bodies, which were painted with vermilion and soot, were arranged in a sitting posture; and a man called a "dan-vosa" (orator), advanced, and laying his hands on their heads, began to chide them, apparently in a low, bantering tone. What he said we knew not, but as he went on he waxed warm, and at last shouted to them at the top of his lungs, and finally finished by kicking the bodies over and running away, amid the shouts and laughter of the people, who now rushed forward. Seizing the bodies by a leg or an arm, or by the hair of the head, they dragged them over stumps and stones and through sloughs until they were exhausted The bodies were then brought back to the temple and dissected by the priest, after which they were taken out to be baked.

Close to the temple a large fire was kindled, in which stones were heated red hot. When ready these were spread out on the ground, and a thick coating of leaves strewn over them to slack the heat. On this "lovo," or oven, the bodies were then placed, covered over, and left to bake.

The crowd now ran with terrible yells towards a neighbouring hill or mound, on which we observed the framework of a house lying ready to be erected. Sick with horror, yet fascinated by curiosity, we staggered after them mechanically, scarce knowing where we were going or what we did, and feeling a sort of impression that all we saw was a dreadful dream.

Arrived at the place, we saw the multitude crowding

round a certain spot. We pressed forward and obtained
a sight of what they were doing. A large wooden beam
or post lay on the ground, beside the other parts of the
frame-work of the house, and close to the end of it was a
hole about seven feet deep and upwards of two feet wide.
While we looked, the man whom we had before observed
with his hands pinioned was carried into the circle. His
hands were now free, but his legs were tightly strapped
together. The post of the house was then placed in the
hole, and the man put in beside it. His head was a good
way below the surface of the hole, and his arms were
clasped round the post. Earth was now thrown in until
all was covered over and stamped down; and this, we
were afterwards told, was a *ceremony* usually performed at
the dedication of a new temple or the erection of a chief's
house!

"Come, come," cried Jack, on beholding this horrible
tragedy; "we have seen enough, enough—far more than
enough! Let us go."

Jack's face looked ghastly pale and haggard as we
hurried back to rejoin the teacher, and I have no doubt
that he felt terrible anxiety when he considered the
number and ferocity of the savages, and the weakness of
the few arms which were ready indeed to essay, but im-
potent to effect, Avatea's deliverance from these ruthless
men.

CHAPTER XXXII

An unexpected discovery, and a bold, reckless defiance, with its
consequences—Plans of escape, and heroic resolves.

WHEN we returned to the shore and related to our
friend what had passed, he was greatly distressed,
and groaned in spirit; but we had not sat long in conversation, when we were interrupted by the arrival of
Tararo on the beach, accompanied by a number of followers bearing baskets of vegetables and fruits on their
heads.

We advanced to meet him, and he expressed, through
our interpreter, much pleasure in seeing us.

"And what is it that my friends wish to say to me?"
he inquired.

The teacher explained that we came to beg that Avatea
might be spared.

"Tell him," said Jack, "that I consider that I have a
right to ask this of him, having not only saved the girl's
life, but the lives of his own people also; and say that I
wish her to be allowed to follow her own wishes, and join
the Christians."

While this was being translated, the chief's brow
lowered, and we could see plainly that our request met
with no favourable reception. He replied with considerable energy, and at some length.

"What says he?" inquired Jack.

"I regret to say that he will not listen to the proposal. He says he has pledged his word to his friend that the girl shall be sent to him, and a deputy is even now on this island awaiting the fulfilment of the pledge."

Jack bit his lip in suppressed anger. "Tell Tararo," he exclaimed with a flashing eye, "that if he does not grant my demand it will be worse for him. Say I have a big gun on board my schooner that will blow his village into the sea, if he does not give up the girl."

"Nay, my friend," said the teacher gently, "I will not tell him that; we must 'overcome evil with good.'"

"What does my friend say?" inquired the chief, who seemed nettled by Jack's looks of defiance.

"He is displeased," replied the teacher.

Tararo turned away with a smile of contempt, and walked towards the men who carried the baskets of vegetables, and who had now emptied the whole on the beach in an enormous pile.

"What are they doing there?" I inquired.

"I think that they are laying out a gift which they intend to present to some one," said the teacher.

At this moment a couple of men appeared, leading a young girl between them, and, going towards the heap of fruits and vegetables, placed her on top of it. We started with surprise and fear, for in the young female before us we recognised the Samoan girl Avatea.

We stood rooted to the earth with surprise and thick-coming fears.

"Oh my dear young friend," whispered the teacher in a voice of deep emotion, while he seized Jack by the arm, "she is to be made a sacrifice even now!"

"Is she?" cried Jack with a vehement shout, spurning

the teacher aside, and dashing over two natives who stood in his way, while he rushed towards the heap, sprang up its side, and seized Avatea by the arm. In another moment he dragged her down, placed her back to a large tree, and, wrenching a war-club from the hand of a native who seemed powerless and petrified with surprise, whirled it above his head, and yelled, rather than shouted, while his face blazed with fury, " Come on, the whole nation of you, an ye like it, and do your worst ! "

It seemed as though the challenge had been literally accepted ; for every savage on the ground ran precipitately at Jack with club and spear, and doubtless would speedily have poured out his brave blood on the sod, had not the teacher rushed in between them, and, raising his voice to its utmost, cried—

"Stay your hands, warriors ! It is not your part to judge in this matter. It is for Tararo, the chief, to say whether or not the young man shall live or die."

The natives were arrested ; and I know not whether it was the gratifying acknowledgment of his superiority thus made by the teacher, or some lingering feeling of gratitude for Jack's former aid in time of need, that influenced Tararo, but he stepped forward, and, waving his hand, said to his people, " Desist. The young man's life is mine." Then, turning to Jack, he said, " You have forfeited your liberty and life to me. Submit yourself, for we are more numerous than the sand upon the shore. You are but one ; why should you die ? "

" Villain ! " exclaimed Jack passionately, " I may die, but assuredly I shall not perish alone. I will not submit until you promise that this girl shall not be injured."

" You are very bold," replied the chief haughtily, " but

very foolish. Yet I will say that Avatea shall not be sent away—at least, for three days."

"You had better accept these terms," whispered the teacher entreatingly. "If you persist in this mad defiance, you will be slain, and Avatea will be lost. Three days are worth having."

Jack hesitated a moment, then lowered his club, and throwing it moodily to the ground, crossed his arms on his breast and hung down his head in silence.

Tararo seemed pleased by his submission, and told the teacher to say that he did not forget his former services, and therefore would leave him free as to his person, but that the schooner would be detained till he had further considered the matter.

While the teacher translated this, he approached as near to where Avatea was standing as possible, without creating suspicion, and whispered to her a few words in the native language. Avatea, who during the whole of the foregoing scene had stood leaning against the tree perfectly passive, and seemingly quite uninterested in all that was going on, replied by a single rapid glance of her dark eye, which was instantly cast down again on the ground at her feet.

Tararo now advanced, and taking the girl by the hand, led her unresistingly away; while Jack, Peterkin, and I returned with the teacher on board the schooner.

On reaching the deck, we went down to the cabin, where Jack threw himself, in a state of great dejection, on a couch; but the teacher seated himself by his side, and laying his hand upon his shoulder, said—

"Do not give way to anger, my young friend. God has given us three days, and we must use the means that are in our power to free this poor girl from slavery. We must not sit in idle disappointment, we must act——"

"Act!" cried Jack, raising himself and tossing back his hair wildly; "it is mockery to talk of acting when one is bound hand and foot. How can I act? I cannot fight a whole nation of savages single-handed. Yes," he said with a bitter smile, "I *can* fight them, but I cannot conquer them, or save Avatea."

"Patience, my friend; your spirit is not a good one just now. You cannot expect that blessing which alone can ensure success unless you are more submissive. I will tell you my plans if you will listen."

"Listen!" cried Jack eagerly: "of course I will, my good fellow; I did not know you had any plans. Out with them. I only hope you will show me how I can get the girl on board of this schooner, and I'd up anchor and away in no time. But proceed with your plans."

The teacher smiled sadly. "Ah, my friend! if one fathom of your anchor chain were to rattle as you drew it in, a thousand warriors would be standing on your deck. No, no, that could not be done. Even now your ship would be taken from you were it not that Tararo has some feeling of gratitude towards you. But I know Tararo well. He is a man of falsehood, as all the unconverted savages are. The chief to whom he has promised this girl is very powerful, and Tararo *must* fulfil his promise. He has told you that he would do nothing to the girl for three days, but that is because the party who are to take her away will not be ready to start for three days. Still, as he might have made you a prisoner during those three days, I say that God has given them to us."

" Well, but what do you propose to do ? " said Jack impatiently.

" My plan involves much danger, but I see no other, and I think you have courage to brave it. It is this. There is an island about fifty miles to the south of this, the natives of which are Christians, and have been so for two years or more, and the principal chief is Avatea's lover. Once there, Avatea would be safe. Now, I suggest that you should abandon your schooner. Do you think that you can make so great a sacrifice ? "

" Friend," replied Jack, " when I make up my mind to go through with a thing of importance, I can make any sacrifice."

The teacher smiled. " Well, then, the savages could not conceive it possible that for the sake of a girl you would voluntarily lose your fine vessel ; therefore as long as she lies here they think they have you all safe : so I suggest that we get a quantity of stores conveyed to a sequestered part of the shore, provide a small canoe, put Avatea on board, and you three would paddle to the Christian island."

" Bravo ! " cried Peterkin, springing up and seizing the teacher's hand. " Missionary, you're a regular brick. I didn't think you had so much in you."

" As for me," continued the teacher, " I will remain on board till they discover that you are gone. Then they will ask me where you are gone to, and I will refuse to tell."

" And what'll be the result of that ? " inquired Jack.

" I know not. Perhaps they will kill me ; but," he added, looking at Jack with a peculiar smile, " I, too, am not afraid to die in a good cause ! "

" But how are we to get hold of Avatea ? " inquired Jack.

"I have arranged with her to meet us at a particular spot, to which I will guide you to-night. We shall then arrange about it. She will easily manage to elude her keepers, who are not very strict in watching her, thinking it impossible that she could escape from the island. Indeed, I am sure that such an idea will never enter their heads. But, as I have said, you run great danger. Fifty miles in a small canoe, on the open sea, is a great voyage to make. You may miss the island, too, in which case there is no other in that direction for a hundred miles or more; and if you lose your way and fall among other heathens, you know the law of Feejee—a castaway who gains the shore is doomed to die. You must count the cost, my young friend."

"I have counted it," replied Jack. "If Avatea consents to run the risk, most certainly I will; and so will my comrades also. Besides," added Jack, looking seriously into the teacher's face, "your Bible—*our* Bible—tells of ONE who delivers those who call on Him in the time of trouble; who holds the winds in His fists, and the waters in the hollow of His hand."

We now set about active preparations for the intended voyage; collected together such things as we should require, and laid out on the deck provisions sufficient to maintain us for several weeks, purposing to load the canoe with as much as she could hold consistently with speed and safety. These we covered with a tarpaulin, intending to convey them to the canoe only a few hours before starting. When night spread her sable curtain over the scene, we prepared to land; but first kneeling along with the natives and the teacher, the latter implored a blessing on our enterprise. Then we rowed quietly to the shore and followed our sable guide, who led us by a long detour, in order to avoid the village, to the place of rendezvous. We had not stood more than five minutes under the gloomy shade of the thick foliage when a dark figure glided noiselessly up to us.

" Ah! here you are," said Jack, as Avatea approached. —" Now, then, tell her what we've come about, and don't waste time."

" I understan' leetl English," said Avatea in a low voice.

" Why, where did you pick up English?" exclaimed Jack in amazement; " you were dumb as a stone when I saw you last."

" She has learned all she knows of it from me," said the teacher, " since she came to the island."

We now gave Avatea a full explanation of our plans, entering into all the details, and concealing none of the danger, so that she might be fully aware of the risk she ran. As we had anticipated, she was too glad of the opportunity thus afforded her to escape from her perse-cutors to think of the danger or risk.

" Then you're willing to go with us, are you?" said Jack.

" Yis, I willing to go."

" And you're not afraid to trust yourself out on the deep sea so far?"

" No, I not 'fraid to go. Safe with Christian."

After some further consultation, the teacher suggested that it was time to return, so we bade Avatea good-night, and having appointed to meet at the cliff where the canoe lay on the following night, just after dark, we hastened away—we to row on board the schooner with muffled oars, Avatea to glide back to her prison-hut among the Mango savages.

CHAPTER XXXIII

The flight—The pursuit—Despair and its results—The lion bearded in his den again—Awful danger threatened and wonderfully averted—A terrific storm.

A S the time for our meditated flight drew near, we became naturally very fearful lest our purpose should be discovered, and we spent the whole of the following day in a state of nervous anxiety. We resolved to go ashore and ramble about the village, as if to observe the habits and dwellings of the people, as we thought that an air of affected indifference to the events of the previous day would be more likely than any other course of conduct to avert suspicion as to our intentions. While we were thus occupied, the teacher remained on board with the Christian natives, whose powerful voices reached us ever and anon as they engaged in singing hymns or in prayer.

At last the long and tedious day came to a close, the sun sank into the sea, and the short-lived twilight of those regions, to which I have already referred, ended abruptly in a dark night. Hastily throwing a few blankets into our little boat, we stepped into it, and whispering fare-well to the natives in the schooner, rowed gently over the lagoon, taking care to keep as near to the beach as possible. We rowed in the utmost silence, and with muffled oars, so that had any one observed us at the distance of a few yards, he might have almost taken us for a phantom-boat, or a shadow on the dark water. Not a breath of air was stirring ; but, fortunately, the gentle ripple of the sea upon the shore, mingled with the soft roar of the breaker on the distant reef, effectually drowned the slight plash that we unavoidably made in the water by the dipping of our oars.

A quarter of an hour sufficed to bring us to the overhanging cliff under whose black shadow our little canoe lay, with her bow in the water ready to be launched, and most of her cargo already stowed away. As the keel of our little boat grated on the sand, a hand was laid upon the bow, and a dim form was seen.

"Ha!" said Peterkin in a whisper, as he stepped upon the beach, "is that you, Avatea?"

"Yis, it am me," was the reply.

"All right! Now, then, gently. Help me to shove off the canoe," whispered Jack to the teacher; "and, Peterkin, do you shove these blankets aboard—we may want them before long. Avatea, step into the middle—that's right."

"Is all ready?" whispered the teacher.

"Not quite," replied Peterkin.—"Here, Ralph, lay hold o' this pair of oars, and stow them away if you can. I don't like paddles. After we're safe away I'll try to rig up rollicks for them."

"Now, then, in with you and shove off."

One more earnest squeeze of the kind teacher's hand, and with his whispered blessing yet sounding in our ears, we shot like an arrow from the shore, sped over the still waters of the lagoon, and paddled as swiftly as strong arms and willing hearts could urge us over the long swell of the open sea.

All that night and the whole of the following day we plied our paddles in almost total silence and without a halt,

save twice to recruit our failing energies with a mouthful
of food and a draught of water. Jack had taken the bearing of the island just after starting, and, laying a small
pocket-compass before him, kept the head of the canoe
due south, for our chance of hitting the island depended
very much on the faithfulness of our steersman in keeping
our tiny bark exactly and constantly on its proper course.
Peterkin and I paddled in the bow, and Avatea worked
untiringly in the middle.

As the sun's lower limb dipped on the gilded edge of
the sea, Jack ceased working, threw down his paddle, and
called a halt.

" There ! " he cried, heaving a deep, long-drawn sigh,
" we've put a considerable breadth of water between us and
these black rascals, so now we'll have a hearty supper and
a sound sleep."

" Hear, hear ! " cried Peterkin. "Nobly spoken, Jack.—
Hand me a drop of water, Ralph.—Why, girl, what's
wrong with you ?   You look just like a black owl blinking
in the sunshine."

Avatea smiled. " I sleepy," she said ; and as if to prove
the truth of this, she laid her head on the edge of the
canoe and fell fast asleep.

"That's uncommon sharp practice," said Peterkin with
a broad grin. " Don't you think we should awake her to
make her eat something first ? Or perhaps," he added,
with a grave, meditative look—" perhaps we might put
some food in her mouth, which is so elegantly open at the
present moment, and see if she'd swallow it while asleep.
If so, Ralph, you might come round to the front here and
feed her quietly, while Jack and I are tucking into the
victuals.   It would be a monstrous economy of time."

I could not help smiling at Peterkin's idea, which indeed, when I pondered it, seemed remarkably good in theory; nevertheless I declined to put it in practice, being fearful of the result should the victual chance to go down the wrong throat. But on suggesting this to Peterkin, he exclaimed—

"Down the wrong throat, man! why, a fellow with half an eye might see that if it went down Avatea's throat it could not go down the wrong throat!—unless, indeed, you have all of a sudden become inordinately selfish, and think that all the throats in the world are wrong ones except your own. However, don't talk so much, and hand me the pork before Jack finishes it. I feel myself entitled to at least one minute morsel."

"Peterkin, you're a villain—a paltry little villain," said Jack quietly, as he tossed the hind-legs (including the tail) of a cold roast pig to his comrade; "and I must again express my regret that unavoidable circumstances have thrust your society upon me, and that necessity has compelled me to cultivate your acquaintance. Were it not that you are incapable of walking upon the water, I would order you, sir, out of the canoe."

"There! you've awakened Avatea with your long tongue," retorted Peterkin with a frown, as the girl gave vent to a deep sigh. "No," he continued, "it was only a snore. Perchance she dreameth of her black Apollo.—I say, Ralph, do leave just one little slice of that yam. Between you and Jack I run a chance of being put on short allowance, if not—yei—a—a—ow!"

Peterkin's concluding remark was a yawn of so great energy that Jack recommended him to postpone the conclusion of his meal till next morning—a piece of advice which he followed so quickly that I was forcibly reminded of his remark, a few minutes before, in regard to the sharp practice of Avatea.

My readers will have observed, probably, by this time that I am much given to meditation; they will not, therefore, be surprised to learn that I fell into a deep reverie on the subject of sleep, which was continued without intermission into the night, and prolonged without interruption into the following morning. But I cannot feel assured that I actually slept during that time, although I am tolerably certain that I was not awake.

Thus we lay like a shadow on the still bosom of the ocean, while the night closed in, and all around was calm, dark, and silent.

A thrilling cry of alarm from Peterkin startled us in the morning, just as the grey dawn began to glimmer in the east.

" What's wrong ? " cried Jack, starting up.

Peterkin replied by pointing with a look of anxious dread towards the horizon; and a glance sufficed to show us that one of the largest-sized war-canoes was approaching us !

With a groan of mingled despair and anger Jack seized his paddle, glanced at the compass, and in a suppressed voice commanded us to "give way." But we did not require to be urged. Already our four paddles were glancing in the water, and the canoe bounded over the glassy sea like a dolphin, while a shout from our pursuers told that they had observed our motions.

"I see something like land ahead," said Jack in a hopeful tone. "It seems impossible that we could have made the island yet; still, if it is so, we may reach it before these fellows can catch us, for our canoe is light and our muscles are fresh."

No one replied; for, to say truth, we felt that in a long chase we had no chance whatever with a canoe which held nearly a hundred warriors. Nevertheless, we resolved to do our utmost to escape, and paddled with a degree of vigour that kept us well in advance of our pursuers. The war-canoe was so far behind us that it seemed but a little speck on the sea, and the shouts, to which the crew occasionally gave vent, came faintly towards us on the morning breeze. We therefore hoped that we should be able to keep in advance for an hour or two, when we might perhaps reach the land ahead. But this hope was suddenly crushed by the supposed land not long after rising up into the sky, thus proving itself to be a fog-bank!

A bitter feeling of disappointment filled each heart, and was expressed on each countenance, as we beheld this termination to our hopes. But we had little time to think of regret. Our danger was too great and imminent to permit of a moment's relaxation from our exertions. No hope now animated our bosoms; but a feeling of despair, strange to say, lent us power to work, and nerved our arms with such energy that it was several hours ere the savages overtook us. When we saw that there was indeed no chance of escape, and that paddling any longer would only serve to exhaust our strength, without doing any good, we turned the side of our canoe towards the approaching enemy, and laid down our paddles.

Silently, and with a look of bitter determination on his face, Jack lifted one of the light boat-oars that we had brought with us, and resting it on his shoulder, stood up in an attitude of bold defiance. Peterkin took the other oar and also stood up, but there was no anger visible on his countenance. When not sparkling with fun, it usually wore a mild, sad expression, which was deepened on the present occasion, as he glanced at Avatea, who sat with her face resting in her hands upon her knees. Without knowing very well what I intended to do, I also arose and grasped my paddle with both hands.

On came the large canoe like a war-horse of the deep, with the foam curling from its sharp bow, and the spear-heads of the savages glancing in the beams of the rising sun. Perfect silence was maintained on both sides, and we could hear the hissing water, and see the frowning eyes of the warriors, as they came rushing on. When about twenty yards distant, five or six of the savages in the bow rose, and, laying aside their paddles, took up their spears. Jack and Peterkin raised their oars, while, with a feeling of madness whirling in my brain, I grasped my paddle and prepared for the onset. But before any of us could strike a blow, the sharp prow of the war-canoe struck us like a thunderbolt on the side, and hurled us into the sea!

What occurred after this I cannot tell, for I was nearly drowned; but when I recovered from the state of insensibility into which I had been thrown, I found myself stretched on my back, bound hand and foot between Jack and Peterkin, in the bottom of the large canoe.

In this condition we lay the whole day, during which time the savages only rested one hour. When night came, they rested again for another hour, and appeared to sleep just as they sat. But we were neither unbound nor allowed to speak to each other during the voyage, nor was a morsel of food or a draught of water given to us. For food, however, we cared little; but we would have given much for a drop of water to cool our parched lips, and we would have been glad, too, had they loosened the cords that bound us, for they were tightly fastened and occasioned us much pain. The air, also, was unusually hot, so much so that I felt convinced that a storm was brewing. This also added to our sufferings. However, these were at length relieved by our arrival at the island from which we had fled.

While we were being led ashore, we caught a glimpse of Avatea, who was seated in the hinder part of the canoe. She was not fettered in any way. Our captors now drove us before them towards the hut of Tararo, at which we speedily arrived, and found the chief seated with an expression on his face that boded us no good. Our friend the teacher stood beside him, with a look of anxiety on his mild features.

"How comes it," said Tararo, turning to the teacher, "that these youths have abused our hospitality?"

"Tell him," replied Jack, "that we have not abused his hospitality, for his hospitality has not been extended to us. I came to the island to deliver Avatea, and my only regret is that I have failed to do so. If I get another chance, I will try to save her yet."

The teacher shook his head. "Nay, my young friend, I had better not tell him that; it will only incense him."

"I care not," replied Jack. "If you don't tell him that, you'll tell him nothing, for I won't say anything softer."

On hearing Jack's speech, Tararo frowned and his eye flashed with anger.

"Go," he said, "presumptuous boy. My debt to you is cancelled. You and your companions shall die."

As he spoke he rose and signed to several of his attendants, who seized Jack and Peterkin and me violently by the collars, and dragging us from the hut of the chief, led us through the wood to the outskirts of the village. Here they thrust us into a species of natural cave in a cliff, and having barricaded the entrance, left us in total darkness.

After feeling about for some time—for our legs were unshackled, although our wrists were still bound with thongs—we found a low ledge of rock running along one side of the cavern. On this we seated ourselves, and for a long time maintained unbroken silence.

At last I could restrain my feelings no longer. "Alas! dear Jack and Peterkin," said I, "what is to become of us? I fear that we are doomed to die."

"I know not," replied Jack in a tremulous voice, "I know not. Ralph, I regret deeply the hastiness of my violent temper, which, I must confess, has been the chief cause of our being brought to this sad condition. Perhaps the teacher may do something for us. But I have little hope."

"Ah no!" said Peterkin with a heavy sigh, "I am sure he can't help us. Tararo doesn't care more for him than for one of his dogs."

"Truly," said I, "there seems no chance of deliverance, unless the Almighty puts forth His arm to save us. Yet I must say that I have great hope, my comrades; for we have come to this dark place by no fault of ours—unless it be a fault to try to succour a woman in distress."

I was interrupted in my remarks by a noise at the entrance to the cavern, which was caused by the removal of the barricade. Immediately after, three men entered, and taking us by the collars of our coats, led us away through the forest. As we advanced, we heard much shouting and beating of native drums in the village, and

at first we thought that our guards were conducting us
to the hut of Tararo again. But in this we were mistaken. The beating of drums gradually increased, and
soon after we observed a procession of the natives coming
towards us. At the head of this procession we were
placed, and then we all advanced together towards the
temple where human victims were wont to be sacrificed!

A thrill of horror ran through my heart as I recalled
to mind the awful scenes that I had before witnessed at
that dreadful spot. But deliverance came suddenly from
a quarter whence we little expected it. During the whole
of that day there had been an unusual degree of heat in
the atmosphere, and the sky assumed that lurid aspect
which portends a thunder-storm. Just as we were approaching the horrid temple, a growl of thunder burst
overhead and heavy drops of rain began to fall.

Those who have not witnessed gales and storms in
tropical regions can form but a faint conception of the
fearful hurricane that burst upon the island of Mango at
this time. Before we reached the temple, the storm burst
upon us with a deafening roar, and the natives, who knew
too well the devastation that was to follow, fled right and
left through the woods in order to save their property,
leaving us alone in the midst of the howling storm. The
trees around us bent before the blast like willows, and
we were about to flee in order to seek shelter, when the
teacher ran towards us with a knife in his hand.

"Thank the Lord," he said, cutting our bonds, "I am
in time! Now, seek the shelter of the nearest rock."

This we did without a moment's hesitation, for the
whistling wind burst, ever and anon, like thunder-claps
among the trees, and tearing them from their roots,

hurled them with violence to the ground. Rain cut across the land in sheets, and lightning played like forked serpents in the air, while high above the roar of the hissing tempest the thunder crashed and burst and rolled in awful majesty.

In the village the scene was absolutely appalling. Roofs were blown completely off the houses in many cases, and in others the houses themselves were levelled with the ground. In the midst of this the natives were darting to and fro, in some instances saving their goods, but in many others seeking to save themselves from the storm of destruction that whirled around them. But terrific although the tempest was on land, it was still more tremendous on the mighty ocean. Billows sprang, as it were, from the great deep, and while their crests were absolutely scattered into white mist, they fell upon the beach with a crash that seemed to shake the solid land. But they did not end there. Each successive wave swept higher and higher on the beach, until the ocean lashed its angry waters among the trees and bushes, and at length, in a sheet of white curdled foam, swept into the village and upset and carried off, or dashed into wreck, whole rows of the native dwellings! It was a sublime, an awful scene, calculated, in some degree at least, to impress the mind of beholders with the might and majesty of God.

We found shelter in a cave that night and all the next day, during which time the storm raged in fury; but on the night following it abated somewhat, and in the morning we went to the village to seek for food, being so famished with hunger that we lost all feeling of danger and all wish to escape in our desire to satisfy the cravings of nature. But no sooner had we obtained food than we began to wish that we had rather endeavoured to make our escape into the mountains. This we attempted to do soon afterwards; but the natives were now able to look after us, and on our showing a disposition to avoid observation and make towards the mountains, we were seized by three warriors, who once more bound our wrists and thrust us into our former prison.

It is true Jack made a vigorous resistance, and knocked down the first savage who seized him with a well-directed blow of his fist, but he was speedily overpowered by others. Thus we were again prisoners, with the prospect of torture and a violent death before us.

CHAPTER XXXIV

Imprisonment—Sinking hopes—Unexpected freedom to more than one, and in more senses than one.

FOR a long, long month we remained in our dark and dreary prison, during which dismal time we did not see the face of a human being, except that of the silent savage who brought us our daily food.

There have been one or two seasons in my life during which I have felt as if the darkness of sorrow and desolation that crushed my inmost heart could never pass away until death should make me cease to feel. The present was such a season.

During the first part of our confinement we felt a cold chill at our hearts every time we heard a footfall near the cave—dreading lest it should prove to be that of our executioner. But as time dragged heavily on, we ceased to feel this alarm, and began to experience such a deep, irrepressible longing for freedom, that we chafed and fretted in our confinement like tigers. Then a feeling of despair came over us, and we actually longed for the time when the savages would take us forth to die! But these changes took place very gradually, and were mingled sometimes with brighter thoughts; for there were times when we sat in that dark cavern on our ledge of rock and conversed almost pleasantly about the past, until we well-nigh forgot the dreary present. But we seldom ventured to touch upon the future.

A few decayed leaves and boughs formed our bed, and a scanty supply of yams and taro, brought to us once a day, constituted our food.

"Well, Ralph, how have you slept?" said Jack in a listless tone, on rising one morning from his humble couch. "Were you much disturbed by the wind last night?"

"No," said I; "I dreamed of home all night, and I thought that my mother smiled upon me, and beckoned me to go to her; but I could not, for I was chained."

"And I dreamed, too," said Peterkin; "but it was of our happy home on the Coral Island. I thought we were swimming in the Water Garden; then the savages gave a yell, and we were immediately in the cave at Spouting Cliff, which, somehow or other, changed into this gloomy cavern; and I awoke to find it true."

Peterkin's tone was so much altered by the depressing influence of his long imprisonment that, had I not known it was he who spoke, I should scarcely have recognised it, so sad was it, and so unlike to the merry, cheerful voice we had been accustomed to hear. I pondered this much, and thought of the terrible decline of happiness that may come on human beings in so short a time; how bright the sunshine in the sky at one time, and in a short space how dark the overshadowing cloud! I had no doubt that the Bible would have given me much light and comfort on this subject, if I had possessed one, and I once more had occasion to regret deeply having neglected to store my memory with its consoling truths.

While I meditated thus, Peterkin again broke the silence of the cave by saying, in a melancholy tone, "Oh, I wonder if we shall ever see our dear island more!"

His voice trembled, and covering his face with both

hands, he bent down his head and wept. It was an unusual sight for me to see our once joyous companion in tears, and I felt a burning desire to comfort him; but alas! what could I say? I could hold out no hope; and although I essayed twice to speak, the words refused to pass my lips. While I hesitated, Jack sat down beside him, and whispered a few words in his ear; while Peterkin threw himself on his friend's breast, and rested his head on his shoulder.

Thus we sat for some time in deep silence. Soon after we heard footsteps at the entrance of the cave, and immediately our jailer entered. We were so much accustomed to his regular visits, however, that we paid little attention to him, expecting that he would set down our meagre fare, as usual, and depart. But to our surprise, instead of doing so, he advanced towards us with a knife in his hand, and, going up to Jack, he cut the thongs that bound his wrists, then he did the same to Peterkin and me! For fully five minutes we stood in speechless amazement, with our freed hands hanging idly by our sides. The first thought that rushed into my mind was that the time had come to put us to death; and although, as I have said before, we actually wished for death in the strength of our despair, now that we thought it drew really near, I felt all the natural love of life revive in my heart, mingled with a chill of horror at the suddenness of our call.

But I was mistaken. After cutting our bonds, the savage pointed to the cave's mouth, and we marched, almost mechanically, into the open air. Here, to our surprise, we found the teacher standing under a tree, with his hands clasped before him, and the tears trickling down his dark cheeks. On seeing Jack, who came out first, he sprang towards him, and, clasping him in his arms, exclaimed—

"Oh, my dear young friend, through the great goodness of God you are free!"

"Free?" cried Jack.

"Ay, free," repeated the teacher, shaking us warmly by the hands again and again—"free to go and come as you will. The Lord has unloosed the bonds of the captive, and set the prisoners free. A missionary has been sent to us, and Tararo has embraced the Christian religion! The people are even now burning their gods of wood! Come, my dear friends, and see the glorious sight."

We could scarcely credit our senses. So long had we been accustomed in our cavern to dream of deliverance, that we imagined for a moment this must surely be nothing more than another vivid dream. Our eyes and minds were dazzled, too, by the brilliant sunshine, which almost blinded us after our long confinement to the gloom of our prison, so that we felt giddy with the variety of conflicting emotions that filled our throbbing bosoms; but as we followed the footsteps of our sable friend, and beheld the bright foliage of the trees, and heard the cries of the paroquets, and smelt the rich perfume of the flowering shrubs, the truth, that we were really delivered from prison and from death, rushed with overwhelming power into our souls, and with one accord, while tears sprang to our eyes, we uttered a loud, long cheer of joy.

It was replied to by a shout from a number of the natives who chanced to be near. Running towards us, they shook us by the hand with every demonstration of kindly feeling. They then fell behind, and forming a sort of procession, conducted us to the dwelling of Tararo.

The scene that met our eyes here was one that I shall never forget. On a rude bench in front of his house sat the chief. A native stood on his left hand, who from his dress seemed to be a teacher. On his right stood an English gentleman, who I at once and rightly concluded was a missionary. He was tall, thin, and apparently past forty, with a bald forehead and thin grey hair. The expression of his countenance was the most winning I ever saw, and his clear grey eye beamed with a look that was frank, fearless, loving, and truthful. In front of the chief was an open space, in the centre of which lay a pile of wooden idols, ready to be set on fire; and around these were assembled thousands of natives, who had come to join in or to witness the unusual sight. A bright smile overspread the missionary's face as he advanced quickly to meet us, and he shook us warmly by the hands.

"I am overjoyed to meet you, my dear young friends," he said. "My friend and *your* friend, the teacher, has told me your history; and I thank our Father in heaven, with all my heart, that He has guided me to this island, and made me the instrument of saving you."

We thanked the missionary most heartily, and asked him in some surprise how he had succeeded in turning the heart of Tararo in our favour.

"I will tell you that at a more convenient time," he answered; "meanwhile we must not forget the respect due to the chief. He waits to receive you."

In the conversation that immediately followed between us and Tararo, the latter said that the light of the Gospel of Jesus Christ had been sent to the island, and that to it we were indebted for our freedom. Moreover, he told us that we were at liberty to depart in our schooner whenever we pleased, and that we should be supplied with as much provision as we required. He concluded by shaking hands with us warmly, and performing the ceremony of rubbing noses.

This was indeed good news to us, and we could hardly find words to express our gratitude to the chief and to the missionary.

"And what of Avatea?" inquired Jack.

The missionary replied by pointing to a group of natives in the midst of whom the girl stood. Beside her was a tall, strapping fellow, whose noble mien and air of superiority bespoke him a chief of no ordinary kind.

"That youth is her lover. He came this very morning in his war-canoe to treat with Tararo for Avatea. He is to be married in a few days, and afterwards returns to his island home with his bride!"

"That's capital," said Jack, as he stepped up to the savage and gave him a hearty shake of the hand. "I wish you joy, my lad; and you too, Avatea."

As Jack spoke, Avatea's lover took him by the hand and led him to the spot where Tararo and the missionary stood, surrounded by most of the chief men of the tribe. The girl herself followed, and stood on his left hand while her lover stood on his right, and, commanding silence, made the following speech, which was translated by the missionary:—

"Young friend, you have seen few years, but your head is old. Your heart also is large and very brave. I and Avatea are your debtors, and we wish, in the midst of this assembly, to acknowledge our debt, and to say that it is one which we can never repay. You have risked your life for one who was known to you only for a few days. But she was a woman in distress, and that was enough to secure to her the aid of a Christian man. We, who live in these islands of the sea, know that the true Christians always act thus. Their religion is one of love and kindness. We thank God that so many Christians have been sent here; we hope many more will come. Remember that I and Avatea will think of you and pray for you and your brave comrades when you are far away."

To this kind speech Jack returned a short, sailor-like reply, in which he insisted that he had only done for Avatea what he would have done for any woman under the sun. But Jack's forte did not lie in speech-making, so he terminated rather abruptly by seizing the chief's hand and shaking it violently, after which he made a hasty retreat.

"Now then, Ralph and Peterkin," said Jack, as we mingled with the crowd, "it seems to me that the object we came here for having been satisfactorily accomplished, we have nothing more to do but get ready for sea as fast as we can, and hurrah for dear old England!"

"That's my idea precisely," said Peterkin, endeavouring to wink; but he had wept so much of late, poor fellow, that he found it difficult. "However, I'm not going away till I see these fellows burn their gods."

Peterkin had his wish, for in a few minutes afterwards fire was put to the pile, the roaring flames ascended, and amid the acclamations of the assembled thousands the false gods of Mango were reduced to ashes!

CHAPTER XXXV

Conclusion

TO part is the lot of all mankind. The world is a scene of constant leave-taking, and the hands that grasp in cordial greeting to-day are doomed ere long to unite for the last time, when the quivering lips pronounce the word—"Farewell." It is a sad thought, but should we on that account exclude it from our minds? May not a lesson worth learning be gathered in the contemplation of it? May it not, perchance, teach us to devote our thoughts more frequently and attentively to that land where we meet, but part no more?

How many do we part from in this world with a light good-bye whom we never see again! Often do I think, in my meditations on this subject, that if we realised more fully the shortness of the fleeting intercourse that we have in this world with many of our fellow-men, we would try more earnestly to do them good, to give them a friendly smile, as it were, in passing (for the longest intercourse on earth is little more than a passing word and glance), and show that we have sympathy with them in the short, quick struggle of life, by our kindly words and looks and actions.

The time soon drew near when we were to quit the islands of the South Seas; and strange though it may appear, we felt deep regret at parting with the natives of the island of Mango: for after they embraced the Christian faith, they sought, by showing us the utmost kindness, to compensate for the harsh treatment we had experienced at their hands; and we felt a growing affection for the native teachers and the missionary, and especially for Avatea and her husband.

Before leaving we had many long and interesting conversations with the missionary, in one of which he told us that he had been making for the island of Rarotonga, when his native-built sloop was blown out of its course, during a violent gale, and driven to this island. At first the natives refused to listen to what he had to say; but after a week's residence among them, Tararo came to him and said that he wished to become a Christian, and would burn his idols. He proved himself to be sincere, for, as we have seen, he persuaded all his people to do likewise. I use the word "persuaded" advisedly; for, like all the other Feejee chiefs, Tararo was a despot, and might have commanded obedience to his wishes; but he entered so readily into the spirit of the new faith, that he perceived at once the impropriety of using constraint in the propagation of it. He set the example, therefore; and that example was followed by almost every man of the tribe.

During the short time that we remained at the island, repairing our vessel and getting her ready for sea, the natives had commenced building a large and commodious church, under the superintendence of the missionary, and several rows of new cottages were marked out; so that the place bid fair to become, in a few months, as prosperous and beautiful as the Christian village at the other end of the island.

After Avatea was married, she and her husband were sent away loaded with presents, chiefly of an edible nature. One of the native teachers went with them, for the purpose of visiting still more distant islands of the sea, and spreading, if possible, the light of the glorious Gospel there.

As the missionary intended to remain for several weeks longer, in order to encourage and confirm his new converts, Jack and Peterkin and I held a consultation in the cabin of our schooner—which we found just as we had left her, for everything that had been taken out of her was restored. We now resolved to delay our departure no longer. The desire to see our beloved native land was strong upon us, and we could not wait.

Three natives volunteered to go with us to Tahiti, where we thought it likely that we should be able to procure a sufficient crew of sailors to man our vessel, so we accepted their offer gladly.

It was a bright, clear morning when we hoisted the snow-white sails of the pirate schooner and left the shores of Mango. The missionary and thousands of the natives came down to bid us God-speed, and to see us sail away. As the vessel bent before a light, fair wind, we glided quickly over the lagoon under a cloud of canvas.

Just as we passed through the channel in the reef the natives gave us a loud cheer; and as the missionary waved his hat, while he stood on a coral rock with his grey hairs floating in the wind, we heard the single word "Farewell" borne faintly over the sea.

That night, as we sat on the taffrail gazing out upon the wide sea and up into the starry firmament, a thrill of joy, strangely mixed with sadness, passed through our hearts; for we were at length "homeward bound," and were gradually leaving far behind us the beautiful, bright green coral islands of the Pacific Ocean.

THE END

EXPLANATORY NOTES

6 *jack-tar*: sailor.

18 *German-silver*: white alloy of nickel, zinc, and copper.

19 *sixteen portraits of Lord Nelson*: the hero-worship of Nelson after his victories over the French in the first decade of the century had a large dimension of what would now be called merchandizing; his portrait was used to sell all sorts of souvenirs and gifts. Ballantyne uses the handkerchief as a bit of period colour which is also good for Peterkin's running joke; his readers would be familiar with souvenirs still printed in this way to exploit all sorts of current crazes.

22 *"the very ticket"*: Ballantyne's use of fragments of schoolboy slang in Peterkin's conversation is carefully calculated—too much of it would have put off adult purchasers of his books, who were consciously seeking reading matter free of the objectionable language they feared boys found in cheap periodicals; but he also wished to attract the boys themselves. He uses Ralph, his narrator, to draw attention to the slang and at the same time to bracket it off in mock disapproval; for the boy reader the mockery is at the expense of 'old-fashioned' Ralph.

25 *three nuts, each as large as a man's fist*: this is the famous botanical mistake which Ballantyne noted in his autobiography, *Personal Reminiscences in Bookmaking* (1893); it was pointed out to him in readers' letters that coconuts do not grow in the form they appear in greengrocers' shops but have a thick outer husk, making them as large as a head rather than a fist. He made this slip his excuse in later years for embarking upon elaborate personal adventures, riding with the Fire Brigade or trying out diving suits, as 'research' for his books. James Bowman's *The Island Home*, one of Ballantyne's sources for this book, begins with a description of boys climbing a tree for coconuts and eating them, with no mention of difficulties over an outer husk. *Recent Exploring Expeditions to the Pacific, and the South Seas*, by J. S. Jenkins, another important

source for *The Coral Island*, mentions the making of twine from the fibres of the husk, and Ballantyne makes use of this information on p. 131 without thinking of its incongruity with the description of the nut here.

43 *bread-fruit tree*: *Artocarpus incisa* L.; Jenkins stresses its centrality in Tahitian domestic economy.

59 *paddock-stool*: toadstool; 'paddock' is a Scots word for toad, and so presumably a term from Ballantyne's boyhood.

67 *candle-nut tree*: *Aleurites triloba*; Ballantyne makes the same mistake over these nuts as over the coconuts, since they are much larger than walnuts, up to 2.5 inches across, before they are husked. Only the kernels are burned for light; this again is a detail Ballantyne may have taken over directly from Bowman, who also has his castaways string the nuts on a coconut stalk (chap. XXII); he mentions the striking white foliage of the tree in chap. XIV.

70 *David slaying Goliath the Philistine*: I Sam. 17; the biblical story of the Philistine giant whom the boy David defeated with a slingshot in the eye is a favourite reference for Victorian children's writers, who normally, however, make it a figurative illustration of the power of the weak to overcome giant temptations or the threats of the ungodly. In turning it into a literal commendation of an easily made boyish weapon, Ballantyne is again showing his genius for making himself popular with young readers under cover of an unexceptionable respectability.

75 *picture-books of Jack the Giant Killer*: the chap-books telling fairy-tales and wonders which were the only children's reading half a century before, had Jack and his expedition to kill the giant as a favourite subject.

82 *taro*: *Arum esculentium*, mentioned by Jenkins, who also says that its root is baked before being eaten; indeed, it is toxic until cooked, a fact Ballantyne does not seem to have noted in his description of the boys' supper preparations, p. 90.

83 *banyan tree*: *Ficus benghalensis* L., the Indian fig. In *The Island Home* a banyan tree forms the fortress defended by the boys at the climax of the tale.

84 *chestnut*: Jenkins mentions 'a native chestnut, the rata (*Tuscarpus edulis*)' as 'an agreeable substitute for bread-fruit' (p. 168), and

Bowman mentions 'the inocarpus, a kind of tropical chestnut' (chap. XIV).

87   *magnum-bonum plum*: there were both red and white plums known as magnum bonum, old varieties widely grown in Victorian gardens; the white was very like the egg plum. Jenkins mentions 'the vi-apple' which 'resembles the egg plum, and is the product of a rough tree like the oak' (p. 169). In the next paragraph he describes pigs being allowed to feed on the abundance of fallen fruit under guava trees.

88   *When Greek meets Greek ... then comes the tug of* [war]: a proverbial misquotation of a line from Nathaniel Lee's Restoration tragedy *The Rival Queens*, 'When Greeks joined Greeks, then was the tug of war!' (IV. ii).

202 *rare cove*: 'cove' was a piece of the London underworld slang which popular writers had taken up to decorate their narratives of low life; it simply means 'man', but its use here implies confederate, fellow criminal. The use of slang terms throughout this conversation is another instance of Ballantyne's ability to indulge his boy readers with excitingly illicit language under cover of pretences to verisimilitude.

212 *beaver hat*: European man's hat, with a straight-sided crown and brim all round, made of beaver skin, black and shiny if well brushed.

       Aitutaki ... Rarotonga: islands in the Cook Islands group, Christianized by native missionaries in the early 1820s, and described at length in the Rt. Revd Michael Russell's *Polynesia*, a third source for Ballantyne. This is the only precise geographical fix in the book, but see below, Emo (p. 224) and Mango (p. 283).

224 *Emo*: appears to be a fictional island; the nearest South Sea Island name would perhaps be Eimeo, cited by Jenkins as the centre of missionary work in the Society Islands, and described at length by Russell. The chapter heading on p. 218 describes Romata as 'a Feejee chief'; perhaps Ballantyne places Emo in this island group because its inhabitants had a reputation for extreme ferocity.

225 *maro*: the maro is the garment itself, the loincloth, rather than the fabric of which it is made; it is frequently mentioned by Jenkins, often with some disdain. In describing the Samoans, he goes

into detail about their maro, 'constructed of leaves of the Ti (Dracaena) . . . worn wrapped about the loins and disposed between the legs' and requiring 'frequent changing, as the leaves soon wilt and decay' (p. 192). He is rather more complimentary than Ballantyne about the ceremonial dress of chiefs, but he also mentions the wooden comb when talking about the Feejeean Islands, where the king wears one 'on the front of his mop of hair' (p. 348).

Chinese paper-mulberry: this is a detail taken from *The Island Home*, where one of the boys speaks of 'the whole process of making tappa, or native cloth, from the bark of the paper mulberry' (chap. XVI). Jenkins only speaks of tapa made of fibres from the branches of the bread-fruit tree, and notes that it was already being displaced by imported calico.

228 *pandanus*: Jenkins mentions *Pandanus odoratissimus* as a valued product of the Pacific islands (p. 147) and repeatedly describes its uses.

231 *Areoi*: Jenkins (p. 161), describing the benighted state of the islanders of the Society Islands in times gone by, has a footnote about this society, whose members, he avers, were obliged to put their children to death; he thought that such practices had been instrumental in reducing the population of the islands. He gives none of Ballantyne's lurid detail, nor does Russell, who likens them to Freemasons in their hierarchical organization but also to 'the priests of Cybele and Bacchus' who 'while they freely indulged their immoderate desires, were not allowed to encumber themselves with the inconvenience of progeny' (pp. 84–8). Bowman also likened them to Freemasons, holding 'great celebrations, like the pow-wows and war dances of our American Indians' (chap. VIII). Twentieth-century Christian writing describes the Society of the Arioi as troupes of dedicated players, serving the fertility god Oro of Raiatea in a phallic dance-drama, which they took from community to community; children they fathered, as part of their sacred role, were killed by the mothers. Theirs was the most active cult superseded by the first Christian missionaries in the South Seas, a rivalry which presumably accounts for the hostile tone of nineteenth-century accounts (see John Garrett, *To Live Among the Stars*, World Council of Churches; Geneva, 1982, p. 7).

236 *surf-swimming*: Jenkins describes the use of surf-boards by the Sandwich (Hawaiian) islanders, p. 373; Ballantyne has transcribed his careful account rather inaccurately, greatly exaggerating the distance the surfer goes out to sea, and describing the board as 'short and flat', where Jenkins gives it credible dimensions and profile. The description of Tararo's panting arrival on the beach is directly from Jenkins's description; the idea of the face-paint transferred by the greeting occurs at a much earlier point in the source, when Jenkins first describes rubbing noses (p. 150) as a Tahitian habit.

283 *Mango*: like Emo, this seems to be an invented island name; Russell describes Mangaia (pp. 221–2), one of the Hervey or Cook Islands.

287 *London Missionary Society*: founded in 1795 by a group of Calvinist Methodists and Anglicans inspired by accounts of voyages to Tahiti published by Cook and Bligh, it became known as the London Missionary Society in 1818. The excited millennial enthusiasm of the first ventures gave way to expeditions that were better equipped and informed, increasingly dominated by Congregationalists, and therefore increasingly involving local initiatives and native Christians. See the Introduction for a discussion of British attitudes to South Sea missionary work at the time Ballantyne was writing.

ti tree: Jenkins mentions the ti root, *Dracaena terminalis*, as an ingredient of native spirits, and the ti leaf as material for the maro in Samoa; he also says it makes a good hedging plant.

292 *The islands of the Pacific*: this passage, a deliberately and rather heavily didactic insertion in the story, seems to be taken from Russell, pp. 24–7, and includes several direct quotations.

294 *buried with him*: Russell (p. 72) describes the 'horrible obsequies of the Feejeeans' and the strangling of wives. Atrocity stories of this kind were unscrupulously used in fund-raising for missionary ventures in the first part of the nineteenth century.

GLOSSARY OF
NAUTICAL TERMS

after-hatch, the entrance to the lower deck nearest to the stern

beam ends, the beams were the horizontal cross-timbers of the ship, supporting the deck and joining the sides; so 'laid on her beam ends' means capsizing sideways, with the beam ends in the water

belaying pin, wooden or metal pin to which ropes were tied

binnacle, fixed case or box on deck which held the compass

block, the shaped and pierced piece of wood through which a rope for lashing spars, managing the sails, or as part of a pulley, was led or strained

bulwark, ship's side above deck level

caboose, hut on the deck, for cooking

cap, doubly pierced block fixed at the top of a mast for reeving an extra spar in place, to extend it upwards

carronade, short, large-calibre ship's gun

cat-head, horizontal beam across the ship's bow, for raising and carrying the anchor; it would otherwise be hauled inboard, as was the anchor of *The Arrow* on Ralph's first voyage (see p. 6).

clew up, draw the lower ends of sails (the clews) up to the yard for furling

clipper-built, with forward-raking bows and aft-raking masts, designed for speed

coasting vessel, small ship trading and carrying goods between British ports

cross-trees, two horizontal cross-timbers bolted to the head of a lower mast to support another mast above

dead reckoning, rough calculation of the ship's position by means of the distance covered, and compass bearing, when accurate instrumental observation is not possible

fluke (of anchor), broad triangular plate on the arm of the anchor

flying-jib, the jib-boom was a spar running out from the bowsprit, at the very front of the vessel; on it a triangular sail was set called the jib, and the flying jib was a smaller sail set further forward still

give way, begin to row, pull on the oars

halyards, ropes for working sails, yards etc.

hull down, so far off that the hull is invisible below the horizon

kedge anchor, small anchor, for use when moving the ship by winding in a hawser anchored at a distance

leeway, lateral drift away from the wind

mainboom, the spar, fastened to the mast at one end, to which the lower edge of the mainsail was attached; the pirate ship is a schooner, rigged fore and aft, its sails stretched parallel to its hull

messmates, members of the same mess, a division of a ship's crew (normally four or eight men) who ate together

paid, to pay was to coat with pitch or tar, a necessary, repetitive job on a wooden vessel

peak, upper outer corner of a sail, held extended by a gaff or small spar

quadrant, navigational instrument used for measuring the height of the sun above the horizon at midday, to calculate the ship's position

reef, reeve, to thread rope through a block or other aperture and tie it, to fasten the rope off; or to reduce the area of a sail by rolling or taking it up in a tuck along its top or bottom

reef points, short pieces of rope attached to the sail for reeving (see above), left flapping against the canvas when undone

tafferel, taffrail, rail round the stern of a vessel

sheets, ropes attached to lower corners of sails for adjusting and working them

standing and running rigging, the standing rigging was the fixed network of ropes and gear which held the masts and so on in place; running rigging indicates the ropes handled by the crew to work the sails

supercargo, the person whose job was to manage the cargo on a merchant vessel tiller, lever fitted to the head of the rudder, for steering

truck, wooden disc at the top of the mast, with holes for ropes to pass through or be attached

weather-braces, the ropes attached to the yards on the windward side. (The schooner had its mainsails fore and aft, but its topsails were square-rigged, and so these were the yards Ralph planned to let go in an emergency.)

yards, spars slung horizontally on the masts from the mid-point to support square-rigged sails

